1 3 2016

"*Power Pl[...]* [...]ory; snappy dialogue; and characters, uncluttered by backstory drama, whose personalities still leap off the page."

—*Library Journal*

"Sexy, intriguing, and timely."

—*Booklist* on *Power Play*

"Bova proves himself equal to the task of showing how adversity can temper character in unforeseen ways."

—*The New York Times*

"Bova's latest novel is one of his best and a classic use of the old SF theme of humanity reaching out for immortality among the stars."

—*Booklist* (starred review) on *Farside*

"The sort of gritty, hands-on, you-are-there yarn at which Bova has long excelled."

—*Kirkus Reviews* on *Farside*

"[Bova's] excellence at combining hard science with believable characters and an attention-grabbing plot makes him one of the genre's most accessible and entertaining storytellers."

—*Library Journal*

"Bova gets better and better, combining plausible science with increasingly complex fiction."

—*Los Angeles Daily News*

# POWER SURGE

## BEN BOVA

A TOM DOHERTY ASSOCIATES BOOK | NEW YORK

POWER SURGE

A Tor Book
Published by Tom Doherty Associates, LLC
175 Fifth Avenue
New York, NY 10010

www.tor-forge.com

Tor® is a registered trademark of Tom Doherty Associates, LLC.

ISBN 978-0-7653-7021-1

Our books may be purchased in bulk for promotional, educational, or business use. Please contact your local bookseller or the Macmillan Corporate and Premium Sales Department at 1-800-221-7945, extension 5442, or by e-mail at MacmillanSpecialMarkets@macmillan.com.

First Edition: August 2015
First Mass Market Edition: May 2016

Printed in the United States of America

0  9  8  7  6  5  4  3  2  1

*To the ravishing Rashida and to Neville Williams,
both of whom light up the world—in different ways*

Politics, *n*. A strife of interests masquerading as a contest of principles.

AMBROSE BIERCE
*The Devil's Dictionary*

It has been said that politics is the second oldest profession. I have learned that it bears a striking resemblance to the first.

RONALD REAGAN

# POWER SURGE

# Senator Tomlinson's Office

The room smelled new. Jacob Ross hesitated at the door to the senator's inner office and looked around at the light walnut paneling, the wall-to-wall carpeting, the pearl gray drapes on the long windows. Not standard government issue, he realized. The senator had spent his own money on his office's décor.

Why not? Jake thought. He's got plenty to spend.

Outside the private office, the senator's suite was almost empty; hardly anyone had shown up yet. And Jake was almost an hour late for this meeting. Washington was blanketed with three inches of snow from the first storm of the new year. In his home state of Montana, nobody would even notice a paltry three inches, but here in DC the city was practically paralyzed. It had taken Jake more than an hour to drive from his newfound apartment to the Hart Senate Office Building, crawling through skidding, slow-moving traffic and stalled cars. He had narrowly missed being sideswiped by a city bus.

"You made it, Jake!" called the senator, from behind his impressive wide desk. "We were beginning to worry about you."

Another man was sitting in one of the bottle green leather chairs in front of the desk. Jake stepped across the office and took the empty chair. He saw a gleaming new nameplate on the desk: SEN. B. FRANKLIN TOMLINSON, in gold letters, no less.

Tomlinson glowed with the kind of youthful vigor that comes with family money. In his shirtsleeves and fire-engine red suspenders, he was smiling handsomely.

"Jake, I want you to meet my chief of staff, Kevin O'Donnell. Kevin, this is Dr. Jacob Ross, my science advisor."

Jake was one of the few people that Tomlinson had brought to Washington with him from Montana. Most of the office staff were local talent, knowledgeable Beltway insiders who had stayed home because of the snow.

The senator's chief of staff was thin, edgy-looking. Suspicious dark eyes peering out of a pinched face. His light brown hair was thinning badly, and he had it combed in an obvious flop-over that accentuated his incipient baldness more than hid it.

O'Donnell put out his hand. "Hello, Dr. Ross," he said, in a reedy, sharp voice.

"Jake," said Jake as he took the proffered hand. O'Donnell's grip was surprisingly strong.

Beaming and relaxed, Senator Tomlinson leaned back in his swivel chair and said, "Jake is putting together the energy plan I told you about, Kevin."

O'Donnell muttered, "Energy plan."

"I've gotten onto the energy committee," Tomlinson said, "and I want to make an impression."

Smiling knowingly, O'Donnell warned, "New senators usually keep pretty quiet until they learn the procedures, make a few friends, get accustomed to the Senate."

Brushing that aside with a wave of his hand, Tomlinson repeated, "I want to make an impression. I got elected to help make new energy technology boost my state's economy. I don't want to waste any time."

The staff chief's smile turned wary. "You want to make a name for yourself."

"Damned right."

"That could be dangerous, Senator. You don't want to be too pushy right off the bat. You don't want to get known as a glory hog."

"Me?" Tomlinson looked surprised, almost hurt.

O'Donnell fell silent, but the expression on his face was cautious, guarded.

Jake took up the slack. "Energy is a key issue, Mr. O'Donnell."

"Kevin."

"Okay, Kevin. Energy is important to everything we do. It affects our economy, our balance of payments overseas, it impacts the global climate—"

"Hold it right there," O'Donnell said, raising a hand in a stop signal. "You're one of these guys who thinks he's going to change the world, make everything better. Well, it just doesn't work that way."

"But it should," Jake snapped.

Turning back to the senator again, O'Donnell explained, "A brand-new senator can't go barging into this town trying to change everything. It's political suicide."

"We're not trying to change everything," Jake countered. "We just want to put the nation's energy policy on a solid, sustainable, comprehensive basis."

"Why do we need a comprehensive energy plan? We don't have an energy crisis anymore. We're doing pretty well these days."

Softly, Tomlinson asked, "For how long, Kevin? How long will it be before we fall into another disaster?"

Shaking his head, O'Donnell said, "Look, Senator, I can understand that you want to push the energy issue for your constituents back home. What's your new technology called? MHD, isn't it?"

"Magnetohydrodynamic power generation," Jake said, feeling some resentment at the chief of staff's obtuseness. "MHD power generators can burn the coal we can't use now because of its high sulfur content, without polluting the atmosphere."

"Fine."

"And MHD generators are more than twice as efficient as today's power generators. We can lower people's electricity bills."

"That's wonderful," said O'Donnell, without a trace of enthusiasm. "Stick to that and you might be able to get it through."

Senator Tomlinson shook his head. "No, Kevin. I'm not going to allow myself to appear as a man who's only pushing for some pork-barrel legislation for his home state. I want to push for a comprehensive energy plan that can make the United States the world's leader in energy production and in new energy technology, as well."

Frowning, O'Donnell asked, "That's what you want?"

"That's what I want," Tomlinson replied.

With a reluctant sigh, the staff chief said, "Okay, you're the boss. But take it slow. And don't go making any public pronouncements until you've talked to me about it. I'm here to protect you, you know."

Tomlinson broke into a bright, easy smile. "Fine. No problem. Jake, you coordinate everything you do with Kevin."

"Okay," said Jake, warily.

"Okay," said Kevin O'Donnell, equally unenthusiastic.

They chatted on for more than half an hour. Then, when Jake left the senator's office and headed for his own, his cell phone buzzed.

Pulling it out of his pocket, he saw that the caller was from back home in Montana. But he didn't recognize the name.

"Dr. Ross?" a woman's strained voice asked.

"Yes," said Jake.

"This is Amanda Yañez, at Mercy Hospital. Dr. Leverett Caldwell has been admitted here, with a cerebral ischemia."

"A what?"

"A stroke. We found your name—"

"A stroke? How bad is it?"

A hesitation. Then, "He probably won't last the night."

# Unitarian Universalist Congregational Church

Jake flew back to Helena for the funeral. The service was quiet, subdued. Sitting in the front pew, it was hard for Jake to count the actual number of mourners, but he knew it couldn't be more than forty.

A lousy forty people, he said to himself as the minister stumbled through a thoroughly lackluster service.

"Leverett Caldwell was a pillar of his community," the minister intoned, "a man dedicated to education and science. As director of the Van Allen Museum of Science's planetarium for many years . . ."

It's the Bart J. Bok Planetarium, Jake grumbled inwardly. And he was director for thirty-eight goddamn years.

Caldwell's death was a shock to Jake. Lev wasn't even seventy, he knew. But when his wife died, Lev just seemed to shrivel up and fade away.

Jake shook his head. Leverett Caldwell had been more than a mentor to him; he'd been almost like a father. If it weren't for Lev I'd still be back in the old neighborhood, a nobody going no place. Instead, I've moved all the way to Washington, DC, the science advisor to Senator B. Franklin Tomlinson.

And when Lev got sick, when he needed me, I was in Washington instead of here at home where I might have helped him. I should have come to him, I should have been with him. But by the time I got here it was too late. I should have done better for Lev.

"Let us pray," said the minister.

Jake bowed his head to mutter supplications to a god he didn't believe existed. Out of the corner of his eye he saw Alexander Tomlinson, the newly elected senator's father, sitting rigid and stern a few places along the pew. His son had stayed in Washington. Caldwell meant nothing to Franklin, but his father had known Lev and had helped him get the planetarium job, thirty-eight years earlier.

Thirty-eight years, Jake mused. How many people had come to the planetarium over those years to watch Lev unfold the universe before their eyes?

The planetarium held 422 seats, Jake knew. As a youngster he had counted them many times while waiting for Lev's lecture to begin. Four hundred and twenty-two times twelve shows a week for thirty-eight years. He did the math in his head. That's more than ten million people! Ten million people took in Lev's lectures. And not even fifty of them showed up for his funeral.

The service droned to an end at last. One by one the people in the church filed by the casket to pay their last respects. Lev lay there, so tiny and frail, in his usual light gray suit and jaunty little bow tie. But the undertakers had erased the quizzical little smile that had always lit his face.

So long, Lev, Jake said silently as he looked down at the body. Thanks for everything. I'm sorry I didn't do better by you. He felt tears welling and turned away.

• • •

Outside, it was a chilly winter afternoon. Mounds of snow were heaped along the curbside. Buttoning his overcoat, Jake stood at the top of the church steps as the handful of mourners filed out.

"Jacob Ross."

No mistaking that imperious voice. Jake turned and saw Alexander Tomlinson advancing toward him: tall and slim, his short-cropped hair iron gray, his black suit impeccably tailored. No topcoat; the old man would not admit that something as commonplace as the weather could bother him. Even at eighty-some years, Tomlinson radiated vigor and purposefulness.

"I won't be able to go to the cemetery," Tomlinson said brusquely. "But I want to extend my sympathy to you. I know you and Lev were close."

Jake accepted the old man's extended hand. *Close* doesn't even begin to tell it, he thought. But he said nothing, merely nodded.

"I presume you'll be heading back to DC?" It sounded more like a command than a guess.

"Yessir," Jake said. "Tomorrow morning."

It was Tomlinson's turn to nod. "I'll be flying out there tomorrow myself. You'll be at the wedding, of course."

"Of course," said Jake.

"Good. See you then."

With that, Alexander Tomlinson turned and started down the stone steps, heading for his waiting black BMW sedan and its black-liveried chauffeur.

Jake watched him duck into the car. The old man's flying to Washington in his private jet, he knew. Wouldn't cost him a nickel to take me with him. But the thought never occurred to him. I'm one of the hired help, far as he's concerned. He doesn't invite the hired help to fly in his plane.

With a sigh that was almost a snort, Jake squared his shoulders and started down the steps. Toward the cemetery. And then, tomorrow, back to Washington, DC.

# Jacob Ross

He was born during the coldest winter on record, to a workingman's family in a run-down neighborhood of narrow streets and row houses. Lack of sunshine and fresh fruits and vegetables led to rickets when he was an infant, which he overcame, thanks to the free clinic and a daily regimen of vitamins and all the fresh fruits and vegetables his mother could stuff into him. Young Jake enjoyed the fruit, especially peaches and the occasional watermelon. He learned to tolerate the vegetables, all except broccoli.

In school the bullies picked on him, on suspicion of his being a Jew, if for no other reason. Jake tried to explain that he was of Italian descent, his family name was originally Rossetti. Made no difference, the bullies kept beating him up—until Jake learned that by doing homework for a few of them, he could earn their protection from the others.

He grew into a reasonably healthy young man, a shade under six feet tall, with dark hair and a wary, solemn face. He was wiry and fairly strong, thanks to regular exercise. The neighborhood Boys and Girls Club was his refuge and his joy, where he learned to shoot pool and play a passable game of basketball without being hassled by the neighborhood wiseguys.

He was eleven when, as part of a mandatory class trip, he went to the Bok Planetarium for the first time. When they turned on the stars across the domed ceiling,

Jake got turned on, too. He got hooked on astronomy. Leverett Caldwell took young Jacob Ross under his wing and encouraged the preteen's budding intellect. Thanks to Lev, Jake eventually became an assistant professor of astronomy at the state university.

Jake married his high school sweetheart, but when she was killed in an automobile accident it nearly destroyed him.

It was Caldwell who prodded Jake out of his mourning funk and talked him into volunteering for B. Franklin Tomlinson's campaign for the US Senate. As Tomlinson's science advisor, Jake helped the handsome, wealthy scion of the powerful Tomlinson family win the election.

So Jake moved to Washington with B. Franklin Tomlinson and his entourage. Which included Amy Wexler, an aide to young Tomlinson. Amy and Jake had conducted an on-again, off-again affair through the months of the political campaign.

Then Amy told Jake she was going to marry Tomlinson. Jake had merely been a means to that end.

Jake had enjoyed the means. Amy had brought him back to life after the shock of his wife's sudden death.

But he had not anticipated the end. And now he was to attend the wedding in Washington of his boss, the newly elected Senator Tomlinson, and his former bed partner, Amy Wexler.

# Washington, DC

The bride wore white. The entire cathedral seemed to vibrate to the deep tones of the pipe organ as Amy started down the aisle in her long-skirted gown, radiant and beaming, her bright eyes sparkling. Jake kept his expression as blank as he could, fighting down the urge to scowl at her. You didn't love her any more than she loved you, he insisted to himself. She was using you, yeah, but you were using her, too.

Still, he seethed inwardly.

Amy looked slim and energetic, her honey-blond hair touching her bare shoulders. That gown must have cost a fortune, Jake thought. What the hell, Tomlinson can afford it. He can afford anything he wants.

Up at the altar, Senator B. Franklin Tomlinson looked resplendent in morning coat and striped trousers, flanked by three similarly clad family friends, his patented dazzling smile aimed at his approaching bride. Tomlinson was not quite as tall as his father, but like the old man he was trim and lean as a saber blade. A brand-new senator, he was determined to make a mark for himself. He was already thinking about the White House, Jake knew.

The cathedral was jammed with people. Friends of the Tomlinson family, relatives, hangers-on and photographers, plenty of photographers. Flashbulbs popped like an artillery barrage as Amy proceeded to the altar.

The music ended and Amy and Tomlinson knelt at

the altar for the beginning of the wedding mass. Jake let his attention drift to the architecture of the sumptuous cathedral. He'd never seen so many different shades of marble: green, pink, red as dark as blood. Pillars, altar rail, vaulted ceiling, huge frescoes of saints and martyrs. The crucifix above the altar was almost two stories tall. Impressive, he thought. The main altar glittered with gold and silver; so did the smaller altars tucked into the apses that lined both sides of the huge church.

He listened to the matrimonial mass with only half an ear, but a line that the bishop spoke to the kneeling couple caught his attention. Something about "only love can make marriage endurable."

Love. Big word, Jake thought. Does Amy really love him? She said she does. She told me while we were in bed together. True love, for sure.

• • •

The reception was held in the ballroom of the old Hilton Hotel, just a few hundred close friends and political associates. Jake decided to take a glass of champagne, wish the newlyweds a lifetime of happiness, and then get back to his desk in the Hart Senate Office Building. He had plenty of work to do.

There was a mob swarming each of the bars that had been set up in the corners of the ballroom, but a pert waitress smiled through the crowd, carrying a tray of champagne flutes. Jake took one from her and started shouldering his way toward the happy couple.

"Jake! Hey!"

Turning at the sound of his name, Jake saw Bob Rogers grinning at him.

"Bob!" he said, genuinely pleased. "I didn't expect to see you here."

Rogers was the head of the MHD power generator program at the university back home, in Montana. He looked distinctly out of place among this Washington crowd in his western-cut tan jacket and bolo neckpiece: a working physicist in the midst of politicians and appointees.

Rogers was nearly ten years older than Jake. He had the seamed, leathery face of an outdoorsman, crinkly pale blue eyes, and wispy sandy hair.

"I got an invitation from the senator," Rogers explained, smiling boyishly, "and I wanted to touch base with you anyway, so here I am."

"Good to see you," Jake said, really meaning it.

"Keeping busy?"

"You don't know the half of it," Jake replied fervently. "I'm just the science advisor to a junior senator, but everybody from fracking experts to astronauts wants to sell me his favorite scheme. Stem cell researchers, fundamentalists who're against stem cell research, oilmen, environmentalists, biofuels people, NIH, NSF . . . I must be the most popular guy in town."

"So how's your social life?"

With a shrug, Jake said, "Pretty close to zero. Too much to do at the office. Too many hustlers. You have no idea how many people have barged in on me, pushing their favorite schemes."

"You won't forget about MHD, will you?" Rogers smiled as he asked, but Jake could see real concern in his eyes.

"Hell no. MHD is going to be part of our energy plan, an important part."

"Noisy, isn't it?" Rogers said, looking around at the crowd uneasily.

"Too many people," said Jake.

"All talking at once. Nobody's listening."

Jake laughed. "Come on, let's congratulate the newlyweds and then get the hell out of here."

"Good thinking."

As they pushed through the crowd, Jake asked, "How's Tim and the rest of the team?"

"Tim's as cantankerous as ever," Rogers replied, grinning, "but he's got the big rig close to seventy-five megawatts."

"For how long?"

"Sixty hours, the latest run."

Jake knew that the university and the National Association of Electric Utilities were committed to building a demonstration MHD power plant once the experimental rig in the town of Lignite reached a hundred megawatts for a thousand hours continuously. He had the feeling the NAEU felt that such a goal was unattainable and that they wouldn't ever have to put up any money for the demo plant.

"Still got a long way to go," Jake said.

With an easygoing nod, Rogers said, "We'll get there. Tim won't stop until we do."

Jake wondered if the utility people really meant to honor their commitment or whether they were simply stalling, holding off the decision as long as possible.

Then he surprised himself by asking, "And Glynis? How's she?"

"She and Tim got married last month. Didn't you know?"

Jake had expected that, but he still felt it like a punch to the solar plexus.

"No, I didn't know."

"They ran off to Las Vegas. All of a sudden, just like that." Rogers snapped his fingers.

Jake had cared for Glynis Colwyn and she knew it. But she had married rough, sour-faced, hard-driving Tim Younger. It's not my day, Jake thought.

They finally reached Tomlinson and Amy, surrounded by well-wishers. Jake mumbled his congratulations while

Rogers stood beside him and shook the senator's hand. Amy smiled her bright cheerleader's smile.

Tomlinson was grinning from ear to ear. Not his patented politician's smile, but a real beaming expression of happiness.

"Where you going on your honeymoon?" one of the others asked.

"It's a secret," said Tomlinson.

"He won't even tell me," Amy said happily. "He just told me to pack a bikini and my passport."

Jake knew Tomlinson was going to sail his yacht to Bermuda and back. Just the two of them on the boat for two weeks or so. Tomlinson might want to keep his plans secret from most people, even his bride, but he had to let his office staff know where he would be.

Jake couldn't help saying, "Well, smooth sailing, wherever you go."

Tomlinson started to frown, caught himself, and said, "You just make sure you show up at the office bright and early every day, Jake. No days off for the staff."

"Aye, aye, sir," said Jake.

# Hart Senate Office Building

I n a wryly ironic way, it amused Jake that the Senate office buildings were known throughout Washington as S.O.B.s. The Hart S.O.B. was the newest of them, modernistic in design where the older buildings were quasi-Greek temples in style. Still, the building was clad in marble, inside and out. DC formica, Jake called it.

For a new senator, Tomlinson had a respectable suite of offices, on the building's second floor. Jake could hustle up the marble stairs instead of waiting for an elevator. The rooms themselves were almost plush, with real walnut paneling for the offices of the senator and his top staff aides. Jake's office, on the other side of the suite, had plaster walls, painted eggshell white.

As soon as he stepped into the outer office, the head of the secretarial staff called to him in her toothache of a voice, "You have a visitor, Dr. Ross."

It was barely nine a.m.

Surprised, Jake asked, "A visitor?"

The woman was an old hand at running government offices. She was nearly retirement age, lean and flinty, her flaming red hair obviously dyed. She calmly picked a calling card from her desk and read in her shrill adenoidal tone, "Steven Brogan, Department of Energy."

The outer office was only half filled, Jake saw. There were more people clustered around the coffeemaker than at their desks.

Jake asked, "Where is he?"

"In your office, Dr. Ross."

"In my office?"

The secretary shrugged. "I thought he'd be more comfortable there."

"Great." Jake frowned as he turned and started down the hallway toward his office.

"Would you like some coffee?" the secretary called after him.

"Yeah. Sure," he replied over his shoulder.

Who the hell is this guy from the Department of Energy? he asked himself. Why's he here? What does he want? He doesn't have an appointment; he just barged in here first thing in the morning.

Jake had a meeting scheduled for ten thirty with a pair of NASA executives and a luncheon at noon with the head of an environmental lobbying firm. I've got to finish the outline of the energy plan before Frank gets back from his honeymoon, he reminded himself.

Jake's office was neither large nor fancy. There was room for a government-issue wooden desk, two reasonably comfortable chairs for visitors, a file cabinet, and a mostly empty bookcase. No pictures on the walls; nothing personal in sight. Not yet. The one window looked out on the north façade of the Supreme Court building.

Sitting half slumped in one of the visitors' chairs was a rumpled-looking man who had probably been a solid middleweight at one time, but now he had apparently let himself get seriously out of shape. He was balding, flabby, his suit jacket hanging unbuttoned around his spreading middle, his open-necked shirt looking wrinkled, as if he'd slept in it all night.

He pushed himself up from the chair as Jake stepped in.

"Dr. Ross, I presume." The man's voice was a low rumble. His face was sagging, his eyes pouchy.

"Mr., eh . . ." Jake struggled to remember. "Brogan, is it?"

"Yeah. Steve Brogan."

Jake went around his desk and sat down. Brogan sank back into his seat.

"Department of Energy?" Jake asked.

With a curt nod, Brogan said, "Office of Coal Utilization."

Trying to be polite, Jake said, "I can only give you a few minutes, Mr. Brogan. I have a very busy schedule."

"Uh-huh."

"What do you want?"

Brogan almost smiled. "No, that's not the way you do it. You ask your visitor, 'What can I do for you?'"

Puzzled and more than a little annoyed, Jake replied, "Okay, what can I do for you?"

Brogan pulled a single sheet of paper from his jacket pocket. As he unfolded it, he explained, "It's about this request for a report on my office's program plans for the coming five years."

"I sent that request to every division of the Energy Department."

The door swung open and another of the staff secretaries—much younger, attractive in a nubby light blue sweater—carried in a tray with two steaming mugs on it.

Neither Jake nor Brogan said a word as she placed the mugs on Jake's desk and left, closing the door softly behind her.

Jake ignored his coffee. Brogan placed his sheet of paper on Jake's desk and reached for his mug with both hands, as if his life depended on it.

"I'm drafting a comprehensive national energy plan

for Senator Tomlinson," Jake explained while Brogan gulped away. "It's time that this nation had a plan—"

"Yeah, yeah," Brogan said impatiently, still clutching the mug with both hands. "Your senator wants to produce a national energy strategy. Big deal."

"It's important."

"Sure it is. The US is becoming the biggest producer of petroleum and natural gas in the world, thanks to fracking and shale oil, and you want to write a national energy plan."

Jake felt himself frowning. Jabbing a finger at Brogan, he argued, "Now's the time to work out a rational plan that will secure our energy future. We can't just go on lurching from one crisis to another."

"There isn't any crisis," Brogan countered. "We're doing damned well now. Christ, we're even starting to export oil again."

"But it won't always be that way."

Brogan shrugged and conceded, "Maybe not."

"So where's your report?"

"Right here." Brogan pushed the single sheet across Jake's desk.

Frowning at the paper, Jake said, "This is my request for your report. Where's the report?"

"Right there." Brogan pointed. "At the bottom of the page."

Jake stared at the paper. At the bottom of his neatly typed letter was scrawled, *If it runs against the coal and oil lobbies, forget it.*

Looking up at Brogan, Jake said, "What is this, some kind of a joke?"

"No joke." Brogan drained his coffee mug and put it back on the desk.

"I want a comprehensive—"

Shaking his head, Brogan interrupted, "You can put

together all the effing comprehensive plans you want. If the coal and oil people don't want it to happen, it won't happen. Period."

"But—"

"I'm saving us both a lot of busywork. If you really want to know what the Office of Coal Utilization's projected five-year program is, you can look it up on our Web site. But I'm telling you this: anything you put in your big, fancy five-year projection that the coal and oil guys don't like is never going to see the light of day. Never."

Jake felt anger stirring inside him. "You mean solar, wind energy, synfuels, the government won't support them?"

"Not in any meaningful way. Lip service, that's all."

"What about electric cars? The government gives buyers a subsidy."

"A seventy-five-hundred-dollar tax break if you buy a ninety-thousand-dollar car," Brogan scoffed. "Big effing subsidy."

Frowning, Jake said, "Part of my plan includes MHD power generation. Based on western coal."

"That might get through. But the electric utilities are switching away from coal, to natural gas. It's cheaper and cleaner. They've already cut the nation's carbon dioxide emissions by more than ten percent."

"With MHD we can make coal competitive again," Jake insisted.

Looking almost exasperated, Brogan explained, "Yeah, maybe. But why should the utilities build new power plants? They like the ones they've got just fine. They're a regulated industry, there's no incentive for them to sink a lot of money into new plants."

"You make it sound like a big conspiracy."

"It's not a conspiracy. It's politics." Brogan shifted his weight in the chair. "Newcomers like you, you think you're going to change everything. Solar power. Windmills. Electric cars. Hydrogen fuels to replace gasoline. Forget it! Nobody has more muscle in this town than the fossil fuel industry. You can write all the fancy plans you want to, and it won't get you anything but writer's cramp."

"I can't believe that," Jake said.

With an impatient shake of his head, Brogan said, "Look, pal, it's a different world inside the Beltway. Different set of rules, different priorities."

"Not really."

Brogan scoffed, "Oh no? Remember the Keystone pipeline? The environmentalists said it would be a disaster. The president of the United States said he was against it, sort of. What happened?"

"They built the pipeline," Jake admitted grudgingly.

"They sure as hell did. So now they're strip-mining Manitoba for the oil sands and piping the slurry down to our refineries on the Gulf of Mexico. Big Oil, one; the environment, zero."

"Well," said Jake, "that's the kind of thing my boss wants to stop. That's why he got himself put on the Senate's energy committee."

"The energy committee." Brogan actually smirked. "Somebody ought to introduce you to Senator Santino."

"Mario Santino, he's the chairman of the Senate energy committee."

"Yeah, the Little Saint. That's him."

"I'd like to meet him."

"Have one of your girls call one of his girls. He'll be glad to see you. Specially if you bring your senator along with you."

"Senator Tomlinson's on his honeymoon."

"So are you, kid."

"I'm not a kid," Jake snapped.

"Yeah, right. Sorry. It's just that . . . you're new to this town, you don't know the ropes yet."

"And you do."

With an unhappy nod Brogan said, "Yeah, I do. I've put in more than twenty years on this merry-go-round. I know the ropes, all right."

"Do you know Senator Santino?"

"I've seen him often enough, in committee hearings, cocktail parties. Can't say we're friends, though."

"What's he like?"

Brogan hesitated. Peering at Jake as if he were some rare specimen of an endangered species, he finally answered, "He's the kind of guy who can smile at you while he's knifing you in the back."

Despite himself, Jake chuckled. "You make him sound like a contortionist."

"That he is, pal. That he is."

"Well, we'll see."

"You sure as hell will. When you shake hands with the Little Saint, be sure to count your fingers afterward."

Jake scowled at him.

Brogan pushed himself out of the chair.

"Wait a minute," Jake said. Tapping the sheet of paper on his desk, he asked, "You came over here just to drop this in my lap?"

"Oh, I was curious to see what you're like. Word around my office is that you and your senator genuinely want to do some good. I was wondering how long that would last."

"As long as it takes to get the job done."

Shaking his head, Brogan said, "Or until you come down with Potomac fever."

"What do you mean by that?"

"Look, I've taken up enough of your time. You've got better things to do and so do I."

"I've got until ten o'clock."

"I don't." Brogan started for the door, but turned

back to Jake. "Tell you what. Meet me for a drink, six o'clock, Ebbitt Grill. Know where that is?"

"I can find it."

"Good. I'll explain what Potomac fever is to you. And a few other things."

# Old Ebbitt Grill

The place was a mob scene. People lined up four and five deep along the bar; all the tables and booths were filled. Mostly men, Jake saw, although there were plenty of women in the crowd. Everybody talking at once.

Jake hated crowds. He hated having to strain to hear what the person next to him was saying, hated having to shout to make himself heard. Hated the senseless chatter and the game-playing that went on. The bigger the crowd, the worse everything was.

Then he spotted Brogan sitting alone in a booth at the far end of the bar. The man looked even more tired and rumpled than he had that morning.

Jake elbowed his way through the throng and slid into the booth, opposite Brogan.

"I was starting to wonder if you'd show up," Brogan said. He had a half-empty pilsner glass of beer in front of him. It looked flat, as if it had been poured some time ago.

Leaning across the table to make himself heard, Jake answered, "I had some work to finish up."

Brogan waved toward the bar and an Asian-looking waitress in a black cocktail dress appeared at the booth, as if by magic.

"Ready for another?" she asked Brogan, in a cheerful, chirpy voice.

"Yeah, why not?"

"And you?"

"White wine," said Jake. "Soave, please."

"We got pinot grigio, is that okay?"

"Okay."

The waitress flounced back into the mob. Loosening his necktie, Jake leaned across the table again and asked Brogan, "So what was that this morning about Potomac fever?"

Brogan's deep, rumbling voice penetrated the background noise. "It's what happens to you after you've been in this town a while. You never leave."

Shaking his head, Jake said, "I'm not going to spend the rest of my life in this nuthouse."

Nodding toward a gray-haired man in a checkered sports jacket standing at the crowded bar, Brogan said, "Neither was he, when he first got here, twelve years ago. Came in as a new member of the House of Representatives. Lost his reelection two years later, got himself a job with a lobbying firm. Now he's one of those talking heads on a TV news show. An expert," Brogan scoffed.

"That's him, not me."

"Not yet." Pointing, Brogan said, "Look at the fat guy with the loud tie. He came to this town to work at the Environmental Protection Agency. He was going to save the environment from the polluters. Now he works for the oil industry, at three times his EPA salary."

"You mean he works *against* the EPA?"

"Sure as hell does. It's a disease, pal. Potomac fever. This town is like a Roach Motel: they come in, but they never leave."

Before Jake could say anything Brogan continued, "Look at them, kid. Every one of these people came to Washington to do good. Every one of them is still here, in one job or another, sucking off the government tit in one way or another. A lot of 'em get into the news media: expert commentators. They all come down with Potomac fever, sooner or later. They never leave DC. Never."

"You, too?"

The waitress reappeared, with another tall glass of beer for Brogan and a stemmed wineglass for Jake.

Once she left, Jake repeated, "What about you?"

Brogan made a sad little smile. "I was born in this town. I'm a career bureaucrat, one of the guys that makes the system work, no matter what the politicians do."

Jake reached for his wineglass.

"I've got a wife with early-onset Alzheimer's and a kid who hasn't held a job for more than six months at a time since he was a teenager. I watch these guys—and plenty of the women, too—come in here and clean up big bucks. It's easy. All you have to do is suck up to the money people."

"Sell your soul, you mean."

"I don't believe in souls. Or maybe I don't believe most of these jerks ever had souls to begin with."

"That's pretty damned bitter."

"Yeah, I guess it is."

"But we've got to do something about energy!" Jake insisted. "We can't just go on burning fossil fuels and ruining the climate."

"Tell that to the Little Saint."

"And there's biomedical research: stem cell therapy, artificial organs and limbs, new vaccines . . ."

Brogan smiled tiredly. "And the pharmaceutical industry. And the pro-lifers."

"And the space program. There are private companies that want to build tourist hotels in orbit. And other facilities."

"Yeah, sure."

"You make it sound impossible to get anything done."

Brogan said nothing for several heartbeats, peering at Jake as if studying him, measuring him.

At last he replied, "You can get some things done, but you've got to be damned careful how you go about it."

"What do you mean?"

"You can't work your way around the Little Saint. He's in the pocket of the fossil fuel guys. But maybe, with a little smarts, you might be able to get your MHD program through."

"That's what Frank Tomlinson campaigned on. That's what won him the election."

"I know. You might get that through. The coal lobby might support it. Make them look good, progressive."

"But not solar energy? Not electric cars?"

Brogan's cynical smile returned. "Solar energy cuts into the existing power companies' turf. No go. Electric cars?" His expression turned thoughtful. "Maybe, if you played your cards right. You have to be very careful, of course, but you just might be able to pull something off there."

"Really?" Jake started to feel enthused.

With a shrug, Brogan said, "Where do you think the electricity for those cars comes from? You'd be pitting the coal guys against the gasoline guys, but it just might work."

Jake looked at the older man's dead, sagging face. "Would you help me?" he asked.

"Me? No way. I can't afford to get mixed up with a do-gooder."

"But it's the right thing to do!" Jake insisted.

"So was biofuels, once upon a time. Now it's just another big boondoggle."

"Come on," Jake pleaded, surprised at his feeling of need. "We can change things. I know we can. Show me the ropes. Help me."

Brogan took a long swill of his beer. Then, "I can't do

it officially. I can't be seen helping a young squirt who wants to take on the fossil fuel industry."

"But unofficially?"

Brogan hesitated again. But at last he said, "Yeah, why the hell not? Might even be fun—as long as I don't get caught."

"What do we do?" Jake asked. "How do we start?"

"You start by getting an appointment with Senator Santino. He's the chairman of the energy committee. Nothing happens without him supporting it."

"Okay, just as soon as I finish the outline of my program plan and Senator Tomlinson okays it."

Brogan nodded. "Okay. I'd like to see your plan, too."

"Sure!"

It wasn't until he returned to the basement apartment he was renting, out in the American University neighborhood, that Jake realized he had found a new mentor.

He's not Lev, Jake reminded himself. But he could help me, just the way Lev did.

Maybe.

# Senator Mario Santino

The Little Saint sat behind his broad, gleamingly polished desk and smiled at his two visitors.

"And what can I do for you?" he asked, in a pleasant soft voice.

Senator Santino was nearing seventy-five, Jake knew from studying the man's biography. He'd been in the US Senate for more than a quarter of a century, elected and reelected by the people of Rhode Island—and by the political machine that ran the tiny state.

Chairman of the Senate Committee on Energy and Natural Resources, Santino was a tiny man, lean and spare, with thinning gray hair and a little half smile on his thin lips. He wore a light gray suit with a carefully knotted cobalt blue tie. His skin was wrinkled and lined, his cheeks hollow, his nose little more than a wart in the center of his face. But his eyes were a cold, icy gray, despite his smile.

Senator B. Franklin Tomlinson, newly returned from his honeymoon cruise, seemed slightly ill at ease in front of the Little Saint. Politely deferential, of course, but Jake felt that Tomlinson was somewhat in awe of the older man. Something like the way Frank acts around his father, Jake thought.

Tomlinson was bright and young and handsome as ever. He had returned from his honeymoon cruise tanned and smiling. When Jake showed him his outline of a master plan for a national energy program, the senator had barely glanced at it. He merely asked, "Is MHD central to your program?"

"Yes, it is," Jake had replied.

"Good. Now we've got to show it to Santino."

"I've already arranged a meeting with him," said Jake.

Tomlinson beamed. "Great. Wonderful. Good work, Jake."

Despite himself, Jake felt thrilled.

• • •

Capitol Hill is honeycombed by a network of tunnels that connect the various Senate and House Office Buildings with each other and the Capitol itself. But the morning of their scheduled meeting with the Little Saint, Tomlinson decided to walk out in the open along the block and a half from their offices to the Russell S.O.B., where Santino was ensconced.

It was a pleasant spring morning, bright with sunshine and a clear blue sky. Even though C Street was off the usual tourist area, there were plenty of pedestrians on the sidewalk, and the street was crowded with cars and taxis and the occasional limousine.

"It's a great day to be alive," Tomlinson said, smiling at the young women passing by.

"Going to get hot this afternoon," said Jake. "They're predicting a high near ninety."

"This early in the spring?"

"Global warming."

"Really?"

"Really. It's happening, Frank, no matter how much some people deny it."

Tomlinson's smile faded only a little. "Well, don't mention it in front of Santino. He doesn't believe in it."

"He wants to keep the world safe for the fossil fuel industry, I know."

"Don't worry about it, Jake. Santino won't be there forever. I just might have his job some day."

Jake blinked with surprise.

"It'd be a good step on the way to the White House," Tomlinson said. And Jake saw that his boss was completely serious.

Now the two of them sat before Senator Santino's desk, with the old man smiling benignly at them.

"And what can I do for you?" Senator Santino asked. No offer of coffee or any refreshments. Strictly business.

Tomlinson glanced at Jake, then replied, "My science advisor, here, is working on a blueprint for a national energy policy," he began.

"So I've heard," Santino said, his benign smile stretching slightly.

Tomlinson went on, "I've felt for a long time that the nation needs a comprehensive plan, a program that balances our energy needs for the future and our natural resources, plus our scientific and technological capabilities."

"I couldn't agree more," said Santino. Turning to focus his ice gray eyes on Jake, he added, "I presume your plan features magnetohydrodynamic power generation."

Impressed by Santino's knowledge and his correct pronunciation of the jawbreaker, Jake replied, "MHD is part of the plan, yessir."

"A very wise move," said Santino. "MHD will allow us to make use of high-sulfur coal from our western states, won't it." It was not a question.

Jake replied, "Of course, MHD is only one part of a comprehensive energy program."

"But a key part, I should think."

Tomlinson answered, "Yes, it is."

Almost sheepishly, Jake said, "What we've done so far is merely an outline. But I think we've covered most of the important aspects of the energy picture."

"That's fine," said Senator Santino.

Jake went on, "I mean, there are other aspects to consider as well: solar, wind energy, hydroelectric power—"

"Renewable energy sources," said Santino. "Of course. Certainly."

Tomlinson said, "It's good to see that you're so knowledgeable about all this."

Santino put on an almost humble expression. "I wouldn't be much of an energy committee chairman if I didn't know at least a little about these things."

They chatted amiably for a few minutes more. Santino asked Tomlinson how he was adjusting to living in DC. Tomlinson admitted that the city was a little bewildering to him. "But I'm getting used to it," he concluded.

"That's good," said Santino, rising from his desk chair. "That's very good."

Jake realized that the man was only a few inches taller than five feet. Tomlinson towered over him.

To Jake, the Little Saint said, "Please send a copy of your outline over to me as soon as you can. I want to study it in detail before I schedule a committee hearing about it."

"Certainly," said Jake. "Right away. This afternoon!"

"Good. Good." Santino came around the desk and, with one hand on the elbow of each of his visitors, he skillfully ushered them to the door.

Once outside on the sunny, warm street again, Tomlinson said smilingly, "Well, that went very smoothly, I think."

Jake nodded, but he heard in his head Brogan's advice to count your fingers after shaking hands with the Little Saint.

# 49th Street NW

Jake's one-bedroom apartment was in the basement of a modest Federal-style brick house on a quiet, tree-shaded residential street. His landlord was a biologist at the National Institutes of Health, tall and lean, with thick dark hair and a grave expression on his face, taciturn to the point of muteness, almost. His wife was a professor of sociology at Howard University. Jake seldom saw them and rarely heard any noise from overhead.

His landlord seemed very proud of the garden he had created out of the house's backyard. Neat rows of vegetables and flowers lined the yard, beneath a pair of graceful old oak trees standing at the end of his property. A wall of bottlebrush pines ran along the property line separating the house from the one next door.

"Feel free to come out here and relax any time you like," his landlord told him. It was the longest sentence Jake had ever heard him speak. But whenever Jake did come out to sit in the shade of the trees, he noticed his landlord, or his wife, or both of them, watching him from their kitchen window. Soon enough, he stopped going out there.

Now, as he sat in the living room of his apartment, Jake heard a car pull up outside. Standing on tiptoes to look through the window, he saw an old-model gray Volvo backing into the parking space he had left at the curb. Steve Brogan climbed out, looked around as if he was afraid he'd be spotted by enemy agents, then came around to the side door that opened onto the apartment.

Jake opened the door before he could knock on it and let him in.

Brogan took in the room with a glance. "Nice location," he said. "Not far from Bethesda."

"It's convenient," Jake agreed, gesturing Brogan to the futon that served as a sofa.

Brogan looked as tired and scruffy as usual, his gray suit jacket hanging unbuttoned, his balding pate disheveled, windswept.

"So what do you think of the Little Saint?" he asked as he sank wearily onto the futon.

"He's much more knowledgeable than I expected," Jake admitted as he sat in the squeaky little plastic chair next to Brogan.

"He does his homework," Brogan said. "Or at least, he gets somebody on his staff to do it."

"He knows about MHD."

Brogan made a sound halfway between a sigh and a grunt. "He knows your boss is hot for MHD, and he wants to keep Tomlinson in his pocket."

With a shake of his head, Jake said, "Frank isn't going into anybody's pocket."

"Want to bet? We already got a memo from Santino about MHD. He wants our office's official assessment of the technology."

"Really? That's great!"

Brogan held up a warning finger. "Don't start the victory party just yet. An official assessment means a detailed study of the technology. That could take a year or more."

"But I can give you the complete record of our work. All tied up in a bow."

"Doesn't work that way, pal. Our assessment has to be

independent of your work. We can't just rubber-stamp your reports."

Disappointed, Jake said, "So you have to reinvent the wheel?"

"Maybe, maybe not. It all depends on what Santino wants to see in our assessment. My department chief is talking to the Little Saint's people about that."

Jake felt puzzled. "Wait a minute. You find out what he wants your conclusions to be, and *then* you make the assessment?"

"Now you're seeing the light."

"That's crazy!"

"No, it's politics. Santino doesn't care beans about your super-duper technology. But he does care about how it could affect him—and the people he owes."

"The coal industry."

"Right. And remember, the Little Saint has to keep his oil industry backers happy, too."

Jake sank back in the uncomfortable little chair. "This gets complicated, doesn't it?"

"And then some," said Brogan. "It would help if your MHD machines could burn petroleum products as well as coal."

"Sure they can. Diesel, natural gas . . . the fuel doesn't matter, as long as it can produce a hot-enough exhaust gas."

Brogan broke into a happy grin. "Why didn't you tell me that in the first place?"

"It's in the material I sent you." Then Jake realized, "You haven't read what I sent you, have you?"

"I read enough," Brogan said.

"So? What do you think?"

"Your plan is pretty comprehensive, I'll give you that."

"But?" Jake prompted.

"Have you bothered to do a cost analysis?"

Nodding, Jake replied, "Sure. It's in Appendix D. Or maybe it's E."

Before Jake could get up to go to his computer, Brogan said, "Your plan's going to be damned expensive, pal. Funding MHD, tax breaks for renewables, upgrading the power grid . . ."

"Not all of that comes out of tax money," Jake objected. "The private sector has to contribute—"

"In your dreams, pal."

"But the eventual payoff—"

With a weary shake of his head, Brogan explained, "Politics isn't about eventual payoffs, Jake. It's about here and now. The future goes only as far as the next election."

Jake sat there, looking into Brogan's sad eyes, trying to think of something to say.

"The way your plan stands," the older man said, "Santino and his people can reject it because it costs so damned much. No discussion of its merits. They'll kill it on fiscal grounds."

Jake muttered a heartfelt, "Shit."

"You've got to make your plan revenue neutral, pal. Rig the cost and benefit figures so they come out even."

"But they don't. We have to invest in new technology to make the nation secure, energy-wise."

Patiently, Brogan said, "Show the benefits in dollars and cents. Make the plan revenue neutral. Otherwise it doesn't have a chance."

# Coalville, Kentucky

Hunched tensely at his desk, Jake eyed the rows of figures on his computer screen. Dollars, millions of dollars, hundreds of millions. No matter how he juggled the numbers, the bottom line of his draft of the energy plan still came out deeply in the red.

"Revenue neutral," he muttered to himself. He wondered how he could make the plan revenue neutral when so much had to be spent on new technology, on building new high-capacity electrical transmission lines, on giving tax breaks for businesses that met new standards for energy efficiency.

It all looked so hopeless.

Glancing at the digital clock readout in the corner of his computer screen, Jake saw that in twenty minutes he was supposed to be having lunch with a pair of slick lawyers who represented an environmental lobbying firm. Well, he thought, maybe they can update me on how much money we can recoup from cutting down on air pollution.

But he shook his head. Damned tricky to factor in money nobody will have to spend because the incidence of lung cancer will have gone down, thanks to our cleaner energy production.

• • •

He returned from lunch feeling even more frustrated than before. One of the environmental lobbyists was a very attractive young blonde in a tight sweater whose wide blue eyes shone with fervor.

"We *can't* let them tear up the landscape and pollute the groundwater," she insisted earnestly. "We've got to stop this fracking business before it destroys everything."

Jake tried to explain that it was already too late to stop the fracking operations that were allowing natural gas to overtake coal as the nation's most important fuel. While she protested with tears in her eyes, he wondered if he dared to invite her to dinner.

As they left the posh restaurant, she handed Jake her card. "Call me," she said breathily. "Any time, day or night."

Jake saw that her partner, an older, grayer veteran in a dark three-piece suit, was smirking knowingly. Jake put her card in his pocket and all ideas of calling her out of his mind.

Once back in his office, Jake saw that he had an appointment with still another lobbyist, this one from the coal industry.

When will it end? he moaned to himself.

Paul Adrian didn't look like a lawyer, Jake thought as the man sat down in front of his desk. True, Adrian was wearing a suit, but it was light blue, and it looked in need of a pressing: not much like the typical DC uniform. His tie was a splashy conglomeration of colors. The man was lean and flinty-looking, gray of hair and pallor, noticeably older than most of the sleek well-fed lobbyists Jake had become accustomed to.

Remembering Steve Brogan's advice, Jake started their conversation with, "What can I do for you, Mr. Adrian?"

"You can come with me down to Kentucky." Adrian's voice was somewhere between a creak and a groan.

"Kentucky?"

His face was bony, almost gaunt. "You're working on an energy program that involves coal, aren't you?"

"Among many other things," said Jake.

"Then you ought to see the people that your plan will affect. You owe them that much."

I owe them? Jake thought. Looking across his desk at Adrian's utterly serious face, Jake asked himself, What's this guy after? But then he thought, Maybe it would be good to get out of town for a day or two. Maybe I ought to take him up on his offer.

• • •

That Friday morning, Jake was picked up at his apartment by a sleek black Mercedes sedan and driven to Reagan National Airport, where an even sleeker twin-jet private plane was waiting for him. Adrian was standing at the stairs leading into the plane, in the same blue suit, although this time his tie was a pattern of red and gold.

As they flew to Lexington, Kentucky, Adrian explained, "Where we're going, coal mining isn't the major industry—it's the *only* industry. I want you to see what happens to the people there when mining companies shut down."

At the airport in Lexington, Adrian led Jake to a modest Chevrolet minivan and headed out onto the freeway.

"We're going to Coalville. Local mine is going to close down, and the whole town's going to be out of work."

Jake said, "You know, the energy plan I'm working on includes MHD power generation."

"I've heard of that."

"MHD will allow power plants to burn coal without as much pollution as conventional power plants. They're more efficient, too, so you can get more kilowatts of output per ton of coal input."

Without taking his eyes off the road, Adrian said, "That's all in the sweet by-and-by, friend. We've got problems right here and now. Serious problems."

Adrian lapsed into silence, and Jake leaned back in his seat and watched the scenery roll by. It felt good to be out of the office, away from Washington, out in the lovely green rolling hills.

The greenery faded in less than an hour. As Adrian turned onto a secondary road, the trees thinned, then disappeared altogether. The land turned gray and scrubby. Little towns flashed past, looking dilapidated, seedy, desperate.

"Lots of electric utilities are switching from coal to natural gas," Adrian muttered as he drove along.

Jake said, "Gas is cheaper now, with fracking, and it's cleaner than coal. We've cut our greenhouse emissions more than twenty percent by shifting to natural gas."

"That's not all we've cut," Adrian said.

They passed a sagging roadside sign that proclaimed COALVILLE. POPULATION 11,379.

"Old sign," Adrian said. "Population's down below nine thousand now."

The town reminded Jake of Lignite, back in Montana, slowly dying because the market for its coal had disappeared. Men in faded coveralls were standing in front of the general store, another group clustered at the barber shop. The town's one hotel was boarded up. Cars and pickups parked along the main street were years old, battered, faded.

"The local coal company is going to shut down the mine altogether," Adrian said as he parked in front of a two-story wood-frame building. Its storefront window proclaimed COALVILLE MINING ASSOC. in black-bordered faded red letters.

Pulling his tie off and stuffing it into his jacket pocket,

Adrian said, "I'm supposed to assess the impact the closing will have on the local economy."

Jake blinked. "There's a local economy?"

"Not much of one," Adrian admitted, as he opened the car door.

Once Jake got out, Adrian told him, "I've got to meet with the association's board. You circulate around town, take a look at how energy decisions affect real people."

So that's why he brought me down here, Jake realized. To see how decisions in Washington play out in Coaltown and other communities across the country.

• • •

People eyed Jake with a mixture of curiosity and mistrust as he ambled up the few blocks of the main street, to the edge of town, and then back down the other side again. Feeling overdressed in his sports coat and slacks, Jake said hello to the men sitting on the wooden benches in front of the general store, the local garage, the shuttered hotel. At last he stopped in front of the corner saloon.

"Where ya from?" asked a lanky young man, wearing baggy denims and a checkered shirt. He was standing in front of the saloon with a trio of other men, mostly his own age, although one of them was gray-haired and portly.

"Washington," said Jake. Guardedly.

"I been there," said the young man. "High school graduation trip. Must be eight years ago, now."

"More like ten, Lenny," said the man beside him.

They fell into conversation. Jake asked what they did for a living. Two of the young men were miners, the third a clerk in the mining company's office. The older man owned the garage down the street.

"I hear they're going to close the mine," Jake said.

Mutterings and dark frowns.

"You here to stop 'em?" asked the garage owner.

Shaking his head, Jake said, "I'm afraid not."

"So what's Washington gonna do 'bout us?"

Before he thought about it, Jake said, "We're working on a plan to make coal more marketable."

"Yeah?"

"If the plan gets approved, there'll be new markets for coal opening up."

"That'd be good," one of the younger men said. But there was no enthusiasm in his voice. No hope.

"It might take some time before things work out," Jake warned. "It's not going to happen overnight."

"That's okay, mister. We got all the time in the world," said the young man.

"Long as the food stamps hold out," the garage owner added.

• • •

As Adrian drove back to the airport, Jake asked, "How'd your meeting go?"

Adrian grunted. "We were just rearranging the deck chairs on the *Titanic*."

"So they're going to close the mine?"

"Yep."

"What're those people going to do?"

"Same as they've been doing. Live in poverty."

"But can't something be done to help them?"

With a sardonic little laugh, Adrian said, "John F. Kennedy came down here to Appalachia when he was running for president, more than half a century ago. This is a popular spot for politicians when they're running for office."

"But nothing gets changed."

"Like the old song says, 'Another day older and deeper in debt.'"

As they headed for the highway, and the airport, and Washington, Adrian said softly, "You know, I was born here. Not in Coalville, but not that far away from it, either. I was lucky. I got away. But these people . . ." He shook his head.

And Jake suddenly understood why Adrian looked different from the other lobbyists he'd met. Take the man out of that suit and dress him in coveralls, Jake said to himself, and Paul Adrian would look just like the men hanging around the barber shop and general store. He's one of them.

Trying to sound hopeful, Jake said, "Well, we're going to change things. MHD power generation will revitalize the coal industry."

"Lots of luck, friend," said Adrian. "All the luck in the world. You're going to need it."

# Dinner Invitation

For the next several days, Jake tried to figure out not merely how to make his plan revenue neutral but also how to make it work for the benefit of the people he'd seen in Coalville—and Lignite, back in Montana—and all the conflicting interests that were involved in the nation's energy systems.

There's got to be a way, he told himself. There's got to be. But he couldn't find it.

One bright morning, one of the staff secretaries burst into his office and announced breathlessly, "You've been invited to the White House!"

"Me?"

"The senator, of course," she said, making herself comfortable on one of the visitors' chairs. "But he told me to make sure you got yourself a tuxedo and a date. It's dinner and a dance! Formal!"

Jake owned a tuxedo that he'd used exactly five times in five years. Maybe I'll get a new tie for it, he thought. Then he realized that he didn't know anyone in DC he could ask to go out with him. He realized that he hadn't had sex since Amy told him she was going to marry Tomlinson. God, that was more than a year ago!

The secretary, Penny Hanscomb, was young and bright and smiling. She looked very pretty in a buttercup yellow blouse. Complements her chestnut brown hair, he thought. But dating a coworker could be tricky,

Jake told himself. Office romances can turn into quagmires.

Penny's smile was enticing, though. And as she crossed her long legs she asked, "Do you have a tux? You can rent one at a discount through the office, you know."

"No, I . . . uh, I have my own tuxedo," Jake stammered.

"Oh. That's nice." She got to her feet.

"When is this shindig?" Jake asked.

"Sunday night. Cocktails at six, dinner at seven."

"In the White House."

"Yes! Exciting, isn't it?"

He sat behind his desk and watched her prance out of his office, wondering if asking her to go to the White House with him constituted a breach of office ethics.

• • •

Frank Tomlinson ended Jake's quandary later that afternoon. He stepped into Jake's office, leading a young woman by the wrist.

"Jake, I want you to meet my cousin, Constance Zeeman."

"Connie," she said, pulling her wrist free of Tomlinson's grasp and extending her hand to Jake.

Good looks must run in his family, Jake thought as he rose to his feet and reached for her hand. Her grip was firm, warm.

"You must be a tennis player," he heard himself say to her.

"A little," she said. "Mostly golf."

Connie Zeeman was almost Jake's height, a little fleshy but quite attractive, with a generous figure and sensuous, pouty lips painted a warm pink. Smiling sky blue eyes and short-cropped sandy hair.

Grinning, Tomlinson said, "Connie's from the Dutch side of our family. This is her first time in Washington."

"Welcome to the nation's capital," Jake said. He thought it sounded pretty lame, but Connie's smile widened and she replied, "Thank you, kind sir."

"Jake, I thought you might take Connie to the White House dinner Sunday night. If you're not already committed."

"No, that's a great idea," Jake said, genuinely pleased. Then he asked Connie, "If it's all right with you, that is."

"It's fine with me," said Connie.

"It's a date, then," Tomlinson said. "I'll have a car pick you up at five forty-five, Jake."

"Great," Jake said, feeling a little bewildered. But happy.

• • •

"How's it going?" Brogan asked.

Brogan kept their meetings short, and never at the same place twice. This evening they were sitting at the bar of a restaurant on Wisconsin Avenue, not far from Jake's apartment.

Jake took a sip of the white wine he'd been nursing before answering, "Not so good. Trying to make the plan revenue neutral isn't easy."

"You have to massage the numbers."

"You mean jigger them."

Brogan shrugged. "Make them come out the way you want. Somebody argues with 'em, you hang tough."

Jake took a bigger swallow of wine.

"I hear you're going to the White House Sunday night."

"You have big ears."

"You know Santino's going to be at the dinner," Brogan said. It sounded to Jake like a warning.

"I'm not surprised," Jake replied. "The dinner's honoring three scientists who've made major contributions to energy technology."

"Major contributions," Brogan groused. "Fracking, strip-mining, and a new way to store radioactive wastes. Some contributions."

Jake had been disappointed that Bob Rogers wasn't among the honorees, for his work on MHD power generation. Maybe next year, he thought.

Glancing around the bar and restaurant as though afraid he was being followed, Brogan said, "When you see the Little Saint, be polite and friendly. But no shop talk."

"Not even if he wants to talk shop?"

"He won't. This is a social occasion. Rub elbows with the high and mighty. Glad-handing."

"No shop talk," Jake confirmed.

"Too many people around to talk about anything serious. Just be friendly and sociable."

"And say hello to the president."

"That, too," said Brogan, scanning the place as though it was crawling with spies.

Jake nodded glumly. Brogan was taking all the excitement out of the occasion. Well, maybe not all of it, Jake thought, picturing Connie Zeeman's smiling face.

Brogan added, "Oh, if anybody mentions the civil war in Venezuela, you stay strictly noncommittal. There's no way to win an argument about that, no matter which side you pick."

"Noncommittal," Jake echoed.

"That's the ticket," said Brogan. "Speak no evil."

Jake pictured the famous image of the three monkeys, and saw himself as the one with his hands covering his mouth.

# The White House

Promptly at five forty-five Jake left his apartment, climbed up the four steps to ground level, and hurried around to the front of the house. It was drizzling rain, so he stepped onto the roofed porch, hoping his landlord wouldn't mind.

A white stretch limousine came cruising slowly down the street and stopped without even trying to pull over to the curb.

Mafia staff car, Jake said to himself, remembering the street slang of his earlier days in the old neighborhood.

A liveried chauffeur came around to open the rear door for him as Jake scurried through the spattering rain and ducked into the limo.

Tomlinson was already inside, with Amy and Connie Zeeman on either side of him, all of them holding cut-glass tumblers of whiskey. Connie was wearing a pale green gown with a plunging neckline, showing plenty of cleavage. Amy's gown was off-white, more conservative, but she glittered with sapphires.

Tomlinson grinned lazily and said, "Climb aboard, Jake."

The rear bench of the limo was filled by the three of them, so Jake crawled to the seat that ran along the side of the vehicle and sat down. He saw that the other side was a well-stocked bar.

"Help yourself," said Tomlinson grandly.

Jake poured himself a glass of club soda, careful not

to spill it as the limo accelerated down the street, toward the White House.

He glanced at Amy, then quickly looked away. Remembering their times in bed together, Jake told himself sternly, That's all over and done with now. She's Frank's wife. She's not interested in you anymore. She never really was interested in you.

• • •

"Ladies and gentlemen, the president of the United States."

Jake had counted exactly fifty guests, all jammed into the sumptuous Red Room for cocktails before dinner. Senator Santino was there, flanked by two middle-aged men who radiated wealth. One of them looked vaguely familiar to Jake, but he couldn't quite place the face. Tomlinson had the same glow of affluence to him, although he was at least fifteen or twenty years younger than the bozos with Santino, Jake thought.

Everyone turned to the door as the president and her husband entered the room, smiling graciously.

Standing between Jake and Amy, Connie whispered to Tomlinson's wife, "She looks a lot older than she does on TV."

"And dumpier," Amy whispered back.

Jake thought the president looked resplendent in a floor-length gown of pale orange. There were lines in her face that her makeup didn't cover, but what the hell, he thought, every president ages in the job. It's the toll that all the responsibility takes on you.

The civil war in Venezuela was threatening to spill into Colombia and Brazil, health care costs had hit an all-time high with no sign of coming down, Russia's struggle with Chechnya was triggering terrorism around half the world, and Pakistan had just suffered another military coup. I'd go gray under those burdens, too, Jake told himself.

With Amy and Connie whispering to each other like schoolgirls, Jake found it hard to keep from frowning. But as the president passed by him, he made a smile that he hoped didn't look too forced. The president's smile seemed genuine enough, he thought. Her husband was actually grinning slyly, as though he were in on some private joke.

Most of the guests clustered around the president, of course. Jake followed Tomlinson toward Senator Santino, the two women on their arms. Santino was a life-long bachelor, although there were rumors that he was hardly celibate.

"Ahh, Senator Tomlinson," Santino said, looking up into the younger man's face. "And Dr. Ross. So good to see you again."

Tomlinson introduced his wife and his cousin; Santino introduced the two men standing with him:

"This is Hugo Nuñez, director of the Office of Coal Utilization—"

Brogan's boss, Jake realized. Nuñez was an amiable-looking Hispanic man, round-faced and round-bellied, his skin the color of tobacco leaf, with a neatly trimmed dark mustache.

"—and this is Francis X. O'Brien," Santino went on, "chairman of the National Association of Electric Utilities."

Jake suddenly remembered where he'd seen O'Brien before. The man had come out to see their MHD generator more than a year ago. He was a tiny man, lean and narrow-jawed, with a hooked nose and a toothy smile. A rat's face, Jake thought. His hair was so luxuriantly dark and perfectly coiffed that Jake thought it had to be a toupee. It didn't match the wrinkled, faded pallor of his face or his cold hard eyes.

"Good to see you again," Tomlinson said to O'Brien.

O'Brien nodded briefly. Jake remembered that despite his avowed interest in MHD, the NAEU had consistently delayed the decision to build a demonstration MHD power plant.

Nuñez smiled toothily at Jake. "I understand that you've had some contact with my people, Dr. Ross."

Suddenly fearful that Nuñez knew of Jake's liaisons with Brogan, Jake stammered, "A little . . . part of the . . . uh, the comprehensive energy program we're trying to work out."

"Very commendable," said Santino, in a flatly dismissive tone.

Tomlinson turned on his megawatt smile. "I hope I can make a real contribution to the energy committee, Senator Santino."

"Mario," said the senator. "My friends call me Mario."

"Mario," Tomlinson echoed. "And my friends call me Frank."

Nuñez said, "Looks like we're going to have a hot summer."

"That's what the weather forecasters are saying," Tomlinson agreed.

"Weather forecasters," O'Brien scoffed in his nasal, reedy voice. "Might as well use a crystal ball."

Santino agreed with a nod. "The news media will start their global warming propaganda again."

Jake bit back the reply he wanted to make. He remembered Brogan's advice, *No shop talk*.

Just then, the doors to the State Dining Room opened and a butler announced in a deep voice that penetrated the cocktail chatter: "Dinner is served."

• • •

It was well past midnight when Tomlinson's limousine pulled up to the front entrance of the Jefferson Hotel.

"My stop," said Connie.

"Good night, kiddo," Tomlinson said.

"It was a fun evening, wasn't it?" Amy said. "It's not every night you get to gossip about the president's looks."

The chauffeur opened the door and, on an impulse, Jake ducked past Connie and stepped out onto the driveway before her. He reached back into the limo and offered her his hand.

"Why, thank you, Jake," she said as she stepped out. Standing beside him and smoothing her gown, she added, "I think I owe you a drink for being so gallant."

Happily surprised, Jake said, "That'd be great."

Tomlinson stuck his head partway out the open door and asked, "You'll be able to get home okay, Jake?"

Jake nodded. "I'll get a taxicab."

He stood there with Connie beside him while the limousine drove off. The rain had stopped, but the streets were still glistening wet.

As they went into the hotel's lobby, Jake wondered aloud, "I hope the bar's still open."

With a warm smile, Connie said, "Oh, let's not go to the bar. I've had enough of crowds. Let's go right up to my suite. We can raid the minibar and have a good time, just the two of us."

Jake couldn't think of a single objection to that idea.

As they headed for the elevators, Connie whispered, "This bra is killing me."

Jake was happy to help her out of it.

# Hart Senate Office Building

The next morning Jake was late getting to work. His evening with Connie had been joyously strenuous. She was uninhibited, and Jake was eager. They finally fell asleep as the first hint of dawn began to gray the sky.

He felt tired but cheerful as he slid into his desk chair to confront his morning's work. Activating his desktop computer, he saw he was scheduled to have another meeting with a deputy director of NASA at eleven. Plenty of time for that, he thought.

His phone buzzed. With a touch of his keyboard, Jake put Tomlinson's grinning face on his screen.

"Got a couple of minutes, Jake?"

"You have but to rub the lamp, O master."

Tomlinson's grin morphed into a wry, almost puzzled expression. "I take it that means yes?"

"I'm on my way," Jake said.

The senator was leaning back comfortably in his high-backed desk chair, in his shirtsleeves, hands clasped behind his head.

"Have a good time last night?" His grin had returned; it was almost a leer.

Trying to keep a straight face as he took one of the cushioned chairs in front of the desk, Jake responded merely, "Yep."

"Connie's quite a girl, isn't she?"

"Yep."

"You know, back when we were both kids—teens,

really—we were sort of kissing cousins. More than that, actually."

Slightly shocked, Jake could only reply, "Really?"

"I thought you two would get along well," Tomlinson went on. "You really need a social life, Jake."

That's none of your damned business, Jake said to himself. But he heard himself ask, "How long will she be in town?"

"Until the weekend. Then she flies home to California."

I've got three days, Jake thought. Better phone her as soon as I get back to the office.

• • •

The NASA deputy director was a former astronaut who seemed deeply troubled, almost desperate. But Jake found it hard to concentrate on the man's tale of woe: Connie had agreed to have dinner with him.

". . . and the entire future of human space flight is in jeopardy," the ex-astronaut was saying.

His name was Isaiah Knowles. He was an African American man with cocoa-colored skin and a tight, almost pugnacious face. Smallish, he had flown half a dozen missions to the International Space Station and had helped to construct the Big Eye telescope in orbit.

Trying to focus on his visitor's problem, Jake said, "But aren't private companies flying people to the International Space Station?"

"Yes," admitted Knowles, "but that's just a bus line that goes into orbit and back again. What about the Moon? What about Mars?"

"What about them?"

"We should be exploring them! We should be building bases on the Moon, have a permanent presence there. That's what the Chinese are doing. We shouldn't let them have the Moon to themselves. And we should be exploring Mars, reaching out to the Asteroid Belt."

"That'd be awfully expensive, wouldn't it?"

"Bullshit!" Knowles burst out. "We spend more on pizza than we do on space!"

Jake blinked at his intensity.

Visibly struggling to gather himself, Knowles leaned toward Jake's desk and said in a calmer tone, "Look, NASA gets less than one percent of the total federal budget. And look at what we've gotten back for that investment! Whole new industries are opening up in orbit. D'you realize that the cordless power tool industry began back in the Apollo days when NASA realized they couldn't run an extension cord from Cape Canaveral to Tranquility Base?"

Jake started to laugh, but Knowles plowed ahead without even taking a breath. "All the medical monitoring systems they use in hospitals are based on equipment originally developed to keep astronauts alive in space. I mean, space technology has pumped trillions of dollars into the US economy. Trillions!"

Jake stared at the man, thinking, He's like a religious zealot. Like John the Baptist: make straight the path of the Lord.

Quite gently, Jake asked, "What kind of payoffs might we get from building bases on the Moon?"

"Knowledge, man," Knowles answered without hesitation. "New knowledge always pays off in the long run."

With a sigh, Jake explained, "Congress doesn't look at the long run, I'm afraid. They want results that can help them win reelection."

Knowles glared at him for a moment, but Jake could see there were wheels turning behind his belligerent expression.

"Something practical?" Jake prompted.

His features softening, Knowles said, "Lookit, you're interested in energy problems, aren't you?"

"That's right."

"Ever hear of space solar power systems? Satellites that convert sunlight into electricity and beam the energy to Earth? Gigawatts, twenty-four hours a day, every day of the year. Clean, no pollution. And cheap, once they start running."

"But expensive to build," said Jake.

Waggling a hand, Knowles said, "No more expensive than a new nuclear plant."

"Nobody's building new nuclear plants."

"Yeah, but if we could get the raw materials from the Moon instead of lifting them up from Earth's surface, we could build solar power satellites twenty times cheaper."

"Twenty times?"

"The Moon's gravity is only one-sixth of Earth's. The Moon is airless, we could launch payloads back toward Earth's orbit with an electric catapult. Way cheaper than boosting 'em up from Earth with rockets."

Jake had familiarized himself with the concept of space solar power as part of his overall energy program but had cut the idea out of his plan because of its cost.

"You could supply the raw materials from the Moon?" he asked.

"Once we build bases there."

"I see."

"And we could build telescopes on the Moon that'd be much better than Big Eye. The astronomers would go crazy for that. And maybe even retirement habitats for people who're too old and frail to live in Earth's gravity!"

Jake put up both hands in surrender. "Okay. Okay. Could you put a plan together that puts the space solar power concept in perspective? With cost estimates—and cost benefit estimates, too."

"How soon do you want it?"

"As soon as you can produce it."

Knowles shot to his feet. "I've got all the components.

Putting them all together shouldn't take more'n a week or so."

Jake stood up and put out his hand across the desk. "Good. Keep me informed of your progress, would you?"

"Damned right I will," said Knowles, grasping Jake's proffered hand firmly. "And thanks!"

"I'm not making any promises," Jake warned.

"I know, I know." Knowles smiled brightly as he headed for the door. Once there, he turned and added, "And lunar bases would be great for training for a Mars mission."

Jake smiled politely and waved good-bye. Sitting in his desk chair again, he thought, He can have Mars. I'm having dinner tonight with Connie.

# Wilmer Nevins

Connie went back to California, and the days in Washington lengthened and grew hotter, muggier. Jake called her a few times; when she returned his calls she was polite but hardly passionate. She doesn't miss me, he realized. She's busy with other guys. I was just a one-night stand, as far as she's concerned. Well, a three-night stand.

Jake sat disconsolately at his desk, frowning at his computer screen, trying to concentrate on his job. He was working on the part of the energy plan that dealt with solar power and was highly dissatisfied with what he saw. Statistics, academic studies, graphs, lists, numbers.

It wasn't *alive*: nothing but cold facts, arguments and counterarguments.

Solar energy will be the salvation of human civilization, claimed the solar enthusiasts. No, said the coal and oil people: solar energy is for tree huggers and idealists; it will never replace conventional power systems.

Every day the sun pours a thousand times more energy onto the Earth than the entire human race uses in a hundred years. But the sun is unreliable; it doesn't shine when it's cloudy or at night.

The cost of solar panels is getting cheaper every year. The panels are only a part of the cost of solar energy.

Jake pulled up a photograph of a solar array in New Mexico that generated a megawatt of electrical power cleanly, silently—as long as the sun was shining. Works fine, he thought. But looking at the long rows of black panels, angled to catch the sunlight, he realized that it did take up a lot of acreage. They'd need to cover square miles of territory with solar panels to generate as much electricity as an average coal-fired power plant.

So what? he argued with himself. There's plenty of empty scrubland and desert out there. The Southwest could power the whole continental United States with solar electricity.

Yeah, and we'd need to build new transmission lines to carry the electricity across the country.

He shook his head, pushed his chair back from the desk, and got to his feet. His coffee mug was empty. Time for a refill.

He got as far as his door before realizing, No, it's time to get out of the office and go see a real, actual solar setup.

• • •

A quick Google scan gave Jake the name and phone number of a solar energy firm headquartered in Washington, DC. According to its Web page, Solar Solutions designed and installed solar energy systems for everything from factories to suburban shopping malls to private homes.

He called the number listed and asked for their company's CEO.

"Mr. Nevins?" answered a woman's soft, almost purring voice. "He's not in at the moment. He's on-site at an installation job."

Jake got the address of the site, in neighboring Alexandria, and decided to drive out there and see for himself a solar installation being built.

It turned out to be a private home, a gracious old Dutch Colonial with a hipped roof and dormers. Half a dozen men and women, mostly in jeans and T-shirts, were on the front lawn, sweating in the late-morning heat as they unwrapped packages of flat black solar panels. A trio of other men were up on the roof, putting together what looked to Jake like oversized picture frames, their nail guns' banging resounding through the quiet residential neighborhood.

Walking across the grass, Jake asked the nearest worker, "Mr. Nevins?"

He flicked a glance at Jake, then turned and yelled up to the roof, "Yo, Wilmer! Guy wants to see you?"

A chunky gray-haired man looked up, a power drill in one hand. "I'll be down in a minute," he hollered back.

Jake felt a little conspicuous in his sports jacket and light slacks. It was a muggy morning, getting hot despite the gray clouds covering the sky. The installation crew went back to work, ignoring him.

It took more than a minute, but eventually the man came scampering down the ladder and across the lawn to where Jake stood waiting. And perspiring.

He stuck out a meaty hand. "I'm Wilmer Nevins."

Nevins was about Jake's height, much beefier, wearing worn, stained gray shorts with a short-sleeved shirt hanging over them. His smile seemed warm and genuine.

"Jake Ross. I'm with Senator Tomlinson's office."

Nevins showed not a flicker of recognition, but his smile faded a little.

"I'm putting together a comprehensive energy plan—"

The smile disappeared altogether. "No thanks. Don't want any."

Surprised and puzzled, Jake asked, "Don't want any what?"

His brow furrowing slightly, Nevins said, "Don't want anything to do with the government."

"But solar's an important part of the energy picture."

"And you're from the government and you're here to

help me. I know. I've been there. No thanks. Just leave us alone."

"But—"

Nevins looked at his wristwatch—a Rolex, Jake noticed—then turned to his crew. "Lunch break! One hour."

The young men and women glanced at each other. "It's only eleven-thirty, Wil," one of them said.

"So lunch break comes early today. Be back on the job at twelve-thirty."

Then he grabbed Jake's arm and led him to the hybrid Toyota van parked at the curb. "Get in," he said. "You've got one hour to talk to me."

He drove to a nearby delicatessen, and once they got seated in a booth, Nevins did most of the talking. Over corned beef sandwiches and cream sodas he explained that he'd spent a good part of his life building solar lighting systems for poor villagers in Africa and southeast Asia.

"First time those people ever had electric lights," he said. His expression darkening, he added, "Government power lines went right past some of those villages, but their governments weren't interested in helping villagers. The *government's* power systems are for the city folks."

"But that's not—"

Nevins silenced Jake with an upraised hand.

"When I came back to the States I asked myself why American homes don't use solar energy. So I put together a little company and we started making and installing solar systems for individual homes."

"And shopping malls," Jake interjected. "And factories."

Nevins grinned. "You've done some homework."

"But I don't understand your attitude."

Sighing like a patient teacher, Nevins said, "Look.

Solar is inherently decentralized. One house at a time. Not big centralized power stations. Not utility companies that distribute the electricity they generate. Decentralized. Solar-powered homes generate their own electricity; they don't need anything but sunshine."

Jake started to object, but Nevins went on, "What we're doing is bringing solar energy to people from the bottom up: individual homes, individual shopping malls and other facilities. What the government does is from the top down: Washington decides who gets solar and how much solar gets installed. That's not for us," he said, shaking his head.

"But we can help you."

"Sure you can. The way you helped Solyndra. The way the Department of Energy backed half a dozen half-baked ideas that never panned out. No thanks. Just leave us alone and let us go on working from the bottom up."

Jake took a sip of cream soda. Nevins didn't seem angry or bitter, just determined to bring solar energy to the nation one home at a time.

"We're doing just fine," he went on. "Have you taken a look at the stock market? Solar firms are hot investments. People have bought more solar installations this year than they did for the past *decade*."

Almost as a challenge, Jake said, "You've benefited from tax deductions homeowners get for installing solar panels."

Conceding the point with a nod, Nevins countered, "Yeah, and when people started moving toward solar enough so that the electric utilities started to feel threatened, the tax deductions disappeared."

"We could reinstate them. Write them into the overall program."

"Try it. See how far you'll get."

Jake felt a mixture of resentment at Nevins's know-it-all attitude and admiration for his stubborn insistence on going his own way.

"All right," he said. "I'll write a tax deduction for private home solar installations into my plan."

"Fine," said Wilmer Nevins, with a knowing smile. "Look me up again when you get it through Congress."

Jake smiled back at him. "You'll be the first to know."

# Summer of Discontent

Congress adjourned for the summer. The weather became really hot. Jake had never experienced such humidity. Just walking a block or so felt as if he were swaddled in a wet towel. Back home, in the foothills of the Rockies, the summers got hot but never so blastedly, energy-sappingly sticky, clammy, muggy.

He began to understand why in the old days Washington emptied out almost completely during the summer. Built on a swamp, the city was a hotbed for yellow fever and other tropical diseases. That was before modern medicine. And air-conditioning.

Now the politicians went home, leaving the city to the bureaucrats, the workers, and the tourists.

Day by day, Jake built his comprehensive energy plan, working desperately to make it come out revenue neutral. Try as he might, though, the plan would cost billions to implement. It needed federal funding up front; the benefits would come years later. Jake saw no way around that fundamental fact. He was firmly committed to keeping the cost and benefit figures honest: no "massaging" them, in spite of Brogan's advice.

He had sent his outline to Senator Santino's office, as the old man had requested. It disappeared without a trace. Jake didn't even know if Santino had bothered to look at it. Just as well, he thought. Once I've got the cost picture under control, I'll send him a fuller draft.

Doggedly, he plowed ahead. MHD power generation

to increase the efficiency of utility power plants, while using coal or natural gas from North American resources. Solar energy, including rooftop solar panels for individual homes that could become energy-independent and disconnect themselves from the power grid. Windmills. Electric automobiles. Replacing existing nuclear power plants with new, fail-safe designs. Hydrogen fuels. New electricity transmission lines. He even added a few pages about space solar power systems, after Knowles delivered a three-volume tome on the subject.

The plan was revenue neutral—in ten years or more. Brogan insisted that no politician would look beyond the next election day.

"Look what they did to the Affordable Care Act," he warned.

Still, Jake plowed doggedly ahead.

His social life was minimal. He realized that Tomlinson had talked Connie into bedding him. Every time he met with the senator, Tomlinson grinned knowingly at him, as if Connie had provided him with video of their brief times together.

He dated a few women he'd met, mostly fellow workers at the Hart S.O.B. No one from Tomlinson's staff, though. Jake kept scrupulously free of entanglements in his workplace. But he never got past the first date with any of them. The one woman he brought back to his own apartment was pleasant enough, but Jake worried that they might disturb his landlord, overhead.

He couldn't help thinking of Louise and their years of marriage. It was all so easy—effortless, almost— being with her. He saw her smiling at him, heard her murmuring his name while they made love. Stop it! he commanded himself. She's dead, she's been dead for nearly three years now. Our marriage ended when that idiot trucker plowed into her car.

He buried himself in his work. He wanted to have a

complete, detailed, comprehensive, and revenue neutral energy plan for Tomlinson to present to the energy committee in September, when Congress reconvened. But the cost figures kept plaguing him.

He managed to take a quick trip back to Montana, to see Bob Rogers at the university and visit dour-faced Tim Younger at the big MHD experimental rig in the dusty town of Lignite. Eighty-eight megawatts for three hundred hours, Younger crowed. Jake nodded pleasantly, but he knew the utilities people weren't going to budge until they saw a hundred megawatts for a thousand hours. And maybe not even then.

He didn't even ask to see Glynis Colwyn; she was now Mrs. Tim Younger. He didn't see any of his former acquaintances from the old neighborhood, either. Thanks to Leverett Caldwell, he had left that life behind him. Lev was the only person he had been close to other than Louise, and they were both in their graves.

Driving Jake from the MHD facility back to the airport in his gas-guzzling SUV, Bob Rogers asked, "Jake, does your plan include methanol?"

"Methanol? That's wood alcohol, isn't it?"

Keeping his eyes on the road, Rogers chuckled. "It's not good to drink, but it makes a good, clean fuel. Race cars use methanol."

"Uh-huh."

"You know how we plan to capture the $CO_2$ in the generator's exhaust stream."

"And sequester it deep underground," Jake said. The costs of burying carbon dioxide, so it wouldn't add more greenhouse warming to the atmosphere, was one of the factors that were killing Jake's plan.

Rogers went on, "Yeah, well, there's some work going on out in San Diego, a group there claims they can take the $CO_2$ from a power plant and turn it into methanol, which can then be sold as fuel for cars and other vehicles."

"Really?"

"Yeah. Maybe you ought to contact them, see if what they're doing is practical."

Jake conceded, "Maybe."

• • •

Back in Washington, Jake plowed ahead with his work, trying to bring the costs under control. Until the day that Steve Brogan phoned him.

Surprised that the paranoid Brogan would call him at his office, Jake picked up the phone and asked, "Hello, Steve. How may I help you?"

"Lunch," said Brogan. "At Ebbitt Grill."

Old Ebbitt Grill was much less crowded now, in the dead of summer, but it was still a lively place. Men in the gray suits that were sort of an unofficial uniform in official Washington filled most of the places along the bar. Many of the booths were occupied by couples. Office romances? Jake wondered. A lot of the men looked faded, middle-aged. A lot of the women looked much younger and more ambitious.

Brogan was nowhere in sight, so Jake took a booth toward the back of the room and ordered a club soda. No drinking in the afternoon: that was one of his rules.

Before his club soda was served, Brogan showed up, looking as disheveled and unhappy as usual. He nodded to one of the bartenders as he shuffled toward the booth where Jake was waiting for him.

Sliding into the booth opposite Jake, Brogan announced without preliminaries, "I've been transferred."

"What?"

"To Dayton," Brogan growled. "Dayton effing Ohio."

"When did this happen? How come?"

The cocktail waitress arrived with Jake's club soda and a tall pilsner glass of beer for Brogan.

"I think Santino had a hand in it. The son of a bitch must have figured out that I was working with you."

"Can they do that? Just push you out of Washington? This is your hometown, isn't it?"

Brogan nodded morosely. "Technically, it's a promotion. I've been kicked upstairs. I'll be working at the lab that the Energy Department runs at the big Air Force base in Dayton. Better pay. The department'll pay all my moving expenses, even put me up in a hotel until I can find living quarters."

Feeling bewildered, Jake objected, "But you don't have to go, do you? I mean, they can't just push you out the window like this. Can they?"

"It's a done deal. Either I go to effing Dayton or I get riffed."

"Reduction In Force," Jake muttered. The government's version of a layoff.

"Santino found out I was helping you. That's what's behind this."

"Why would he object to you helping me?"

Brogan raised a stubby finger. "One: he doesn't want your comprehensive plan. If somehow it gets through his committee, it diminishes his power."

"Just because he didn't originate it—"

"You think he wants Tomlinson grabbing the spotlight?"

"Oh."

"Two: the coal and oil guys won't like it. Not one bit. Remember, first thing I ever told you was—"

"If it goes against the fossil fuel lobbies, it'll never get passed."

"Right."

Jake took a sip of his soda. It tasted flat. "So now what happens?"

Sighing, Brogan said, "So now I go out to effing Dayton and look for a house for my wife and kid."

"Damn."

Jabbing the same finger at him, Brogan said, "You just watch your butt, kid. Santino's out to get you. No way he's going to let your plan get through his committee."

"That means he's after Frank, too, doesn't it?"

"Tomlinson?" Brogan squeezed his eyes shut in thought for a moment, then said, "He won't have to worry about Tomlinson. Once your senator sees what happens to his plan, he'll pull in his horns and toe Santino's line."

"No," Jake snapped.

"You'll see. This is all an exercise in power, kid. Santino's showing Tomlinson who's boss."

Jake felt like throwing up.

# The Tomlinson Residence

For several days after his lunch with Brogan, Jake worked blindly, uncertain how he should proceed. What's the sense of finishing the plan if it's just going to end up in Santino's wastebasket?

Then he realized, the Little Saint is afraid of Tomlinson. He sees Frank as a threat to his own position, his own *power*, and sees the energy plan as the embodiment of Frank's challenge. How do we handle this? What should we do?

The first thing to do, he decided, is to let Frank know what I know. He punched the phone console's keyboard. The flinty red-haired chief of the secretarial staff appeared on the screen.

"The senator is at the airport," she told Jake in her nasal twang. "His father's arriving for a visit."

Jake cut the connection. He had Frank's private cell phone number, but they had agreed that Jake would use it only in an emergency. Well, Jake told himself as he tapped out the number, this is an emergency.

Tomlinson answered on the second ring.

"Jake, what's wrong?"

"I've got to talk with you, just the two of us." Jake didn't want O'Donnell or any other of the staff in on this. They're all Washington insiders, lifetime Beltway people; maybe they're in Santino's pocket. Christ, he thought, I'm getting just as paranoid as Steve. But then he remembered that even paranoids have enemies.

He could hear the frown in Tomlinson's voice. "Just the two of us? What's up?"

"It's important. I'll tell you all about it when we meet. Just the two of us."

A hesitation, then, "My father's plane is arriving in ten minutes. How about you come to my house for dinner? We can talk then."

Jake thought swiftly. His father. And Amy, of course. That should be safe enough.

"Okay. Your house."

"Six o'clock."

"Right."

• • •

Tomlinson had bought a "modest" twelve-room Georgian brick house set well back on a perfectly clipped lawn decorated with flowering bushes on a quiet, tree-shaded street not all that far from Jake's apartment. Almost within walking distance. Jake parked his battered gray two-door Mustang on the street, walked up the bricked driveway, and pressed the doorbell button.

A young man in a dark suit opened the door, with a deferential smile.

"I'm Jacob Ross, here to see the senator."

"You are expected, sir," said the butler, with just a trace of a British accent. Jake realized that Frank—or one of his staff—must have hired the young man. Local talent. All the servants at the Tomlinson mansion back home had been older, and solidly middle-American.

The butler led Jake through the modest foyer and down a corridor that appeared to run the length of the house. The furnishings were quietly luxurious, the paintings on the walls mostly reproductions of old masterpieces. *Frank hasn't been here long enough to fill the place with family stuff,* Jake thought. *Or maybe he's leaving it to Amy to decorate the house.*

Through a half-open door he could hear Alexander Tomlinson's strong, imperious voice: "You shouldn't take a stand on immigration policy. Whichever way you vote, you'll make enemies."

"But I've got to vote, Dad," Tomlinson replied.

"Abstain. Be out of town when the vote comes up. Or at least vote with your party's leadership. Don't stick your neck out. Not on that issue."

The butler pushed the door all the way open and announced, "Dr. Ross."

Jake stepped into the room. It was apparently a library, lined with books. Frank Tomlinson stood in his shirtsleeves and plaid suspenders, a cut-crystal glass of whiskey in one hand. His father, tall and stern, wore a gray checkered sports jacket over darker gray slacks, with a drink in one bony, liver-spotted hand, his other still pointing emphatically at his son.

Amy was sitting on the sofa, beneath a portrait of some Revolutionary War officer in knee breeches and powdered wig. She was wearing a sleeveless powder blue cocktail dress that set off her honey blond hair perfectly. She gave Jake her cheerful cheerleader's smile.

"What would you like to drink?" Amy asked, getting up from the sofa.

The discussion between Tomlinson *père et fils* hung suspended while Amy went to the rolling cart that held an array of bottles.

"Club soda, please," Jake said to her.

Senator Tomlinson broke into his patented smile. "Come on, Jake. The sun's over the yardarm. You can relax and have a real drink."

Jake shrugged and said, "Okay. Some white wine."

As Amy poured wine for Jake, Senator Tomlinson said, "You sounded pretty mysterious over the phone. What's this all about?"

Glancing at Tomlinson senior, Jake replied, "The energy plan. Santino's out to scrap it."

The senator's smile vanished. "Scrap it?"

Nodding, Jake accepted a stemmed wineglass from Amy and began to explain what he'd learned from Brogan.

"Some lower-level paper shuffler," the elder Tomlinson scoffed. "And paranoid, to boot."

But the senator asked, "Why would Santino want to scrap the plan? Why not take the credit for bringing it to the Senate floor?"

"Because he's afraid of you," Jake explained.

"Me? I'm just a junior member of his committee."

Amy spoke up, "But this energy plan could make you a very visible new senator. A very popular one, especially with the news media."

Tomlinson glanced at his father, who was still standing in the middle of the room, his austere face frowning.

"What is this plan you're talking about?" the old man asked.

"It's the comprehensive energy plan," said his son. "I told you about it. It could be the basis for a sound, rational energy policy for the nation."

"But isn't that the White House's job, to set policy?"

"The Senate could offer it to the administration as a guideline," said Senator Tomlinson.

"The president would see it as a Republican plan to upstage her during next year's reelection campaign," his father humphed. "Is that a smart thing to do?"

"We could present it as a nonpartisan plan," said the senator. "Beyond politics."

"Nothing is beyond politics," Tomlinson senior said sternly. "The Republicans control the Senate by just one seat."

"And the House, since last year's elections," the senator pointed out. "The president's already on very thin ice."

"Santino wouldn't mind upstaging the president," Amy said. Then she added, "Would he?"

Tomlinson put his empty glass down on the table at the end of the sofa. "The way I see it, we can present this plan as a bipartisan offer. If the president accepts it, we can take credit for it. If she fights against it, we have an issue to use against her in her reelection campaign."

Standing between Tomlinson and his father, Jake said, "There's another problem, though. The fossil fuel lobbies."

Alexander Tomlinson drained the last of his glass and said, "Jake, you'd better tell me what this plan of yours is all about."

Glancing toward the senator, Jake replied, "Okay."

"Over dinner," said Amy, and she headed for the dining room.

# The Plan

Wishing he had been prescient enough to bring his notebook, so he could show them the details of his plan, Jake spent the whole dinner explaining it from memory, point by point.

The four of them sat at one end of the long table in the elegant dining room, beneath a lavish chandelier, while the same young butler served them salad, roast beef, and a fruit cup dessert. And poured wine for them.

Sitting at Tomlinson's left, across the table from Amy, Jake ran through the energy plan, starting with MHD power generation. Tomlinson's father was seated beside Amy, eating with a determined efficiency while he listened in silence, hardly glancing at Jake all through the meal.

But when Jake began to talk about the space solar power idea, the elder Tomlinson's head snapped up.

"Satellites in orbit that beam energy from space to the ground?"

"That's the concept," Jake said.

"Drop it," the old man demanded.

"Drop it?" His son looked mildly surprised.

"But it's a valid idea," Jake protested. "A little far out, maybe, but—"

"Drop it," Tomlinson senior repeated. "Too big a giggle factor."

"Giggle factor?" Amy asked.

"You keep that in the plan and all the damned news

media will talk about is that space cadet idea. You'll be laughed out of town. Drop it."

"He's got a point, Jake," said the senator.

Thinking of Isaiah Knowles's reaction, Jake said, "But it's only a minor point in the plan, something for future consideration."

"Drop it," insisted the elder Tomlinson.

"I agree, Jake," said his son.

Jake bit his lip and nodded.

"What else?"

"I see the plan as an integrated entity," Jake said. "It's not coal versus natural gas or renewables versus fossil fuels. It includes everything, and they all mesh together. There's a place for everybody, just about."

"You want to move away from fossil fuels and toward renewables," said Tomlinson senior. "That's political suicide."

Jake defended, "It's a gradual move. And it's inevitable, in the long run."

The senator looked at his father, who was glaring at Jake.

Amy broke the silence with an impish smile as she quoted John Maynard Keynes, "In the long run, we're all dead."

"The plan helps the long-term transition away from fossil fuels, but it's very gradual," Jake explained. "We're not going to shut down the coal and oil industries."

"As if you could," the elder Tomlinson muttered.

Jake went on, "For example, if we shift to electric automobiles in a major way, we're going to have to build a lot more electricity-generating capacity. That's where MHD can be a big factor. And we need to upgrade the power grid and its transmission lines."

"That's for sure," the senator agreed.

As they talked, the butler cleared the table and brought out four bottles of various after-dinner liqueurs.

Amy reached for the cognac and poured a snifter for her father-in-law.

"So that's the whole thing?" the old man asked, as he accepted the drink from Amy's hand.

"I think it covers the waterfront," Jake said, feeling defensive. "I've been trying to make it come out revenue neutral, but there's just no way to get around the big investment the government's got to make."

"It's a good plan, Jake," said Senator Tomlinson.

"I'm glad you think so."

"But it's missing something. Something important," the senator's father said.

Feeling more than a little nettled, Jake asked, "What's that?"

Turning toward his son, Alexander Tomlinson said, "It's missing something that will make Santino fall in love with it."

"He ought to like it just as it is," Jake grumbled.

The elder Tomlinson fixed him with a stern gaze. "Young man, the best way to succeed with any plan is to make the victim a party to the crime."

His son grinned. "I get it. Make Santino an offer he can't refuse."

Jake felt his brows knitting.

"There's nothing in your plan that gives Santino something he can take home to his constituents," said Tomlinson senior.

"But it's a comprehensive national plan," Jake protested. "It'll make him a national hero."

"Bushwah," snapped the elder Tomlinson. "What's in your plan that benefits the voters in Santino's home state?"

"Rhode Island, isn't it?" asked Amy.

"You've got to give him a bone he can bring back to his people," the senator explained.

"His *people*," Jake growled, "are the coal and oil lobbies. And the plan covers the fossil fuel industries."

With a shake of his head, Senator Tomlinson said, "Jake, you're being rational. What we're talking about now is Santino's ego."

"His ego."

"We've got to give him something that will make him happy. Make him an offer he can't refuse."

"You said that before."

"What can your plan do for Rhode Island?" Tomlinson senior asked.

"Windmill farms?" Jake suggested.

"For god's sake, no," said the old man. "Don't you remember what Ted Kennedy did when somebody tried to build a windmill farm off Hyannis Port?"

"It ought to be something more specific," said the senator. "Something that would particularly benefit Rhode Island."

Jake shrugged. "It's such a little state. Most of it is coastline."

The elder Tomlinson suggested, "Didn't I read something someplace about generating electricity from the ocean?"

"Tidal power," said Jake. "You put turbines on the seabed and let the ebb and flow of the tides turn them to generate electricity."

"That's it!" said the senator. "Add that to your plan, Jake."

"But it's not a viable idea."

"I understand there's enormous energy in the tides," said Tomlinson's father.

"There's a lot of energy, yeah," Jake countered. "But it's too diffuse, too spread out to be an efficient source for generating electricity. Except in a few special places where they have tidal bores that're ten feet or more."

With a grin, the senator said, "It doesn't have to be efficient, Jake. It just has to make Santino happy."

"But it's not a good idea. It'll just be money down the drain."

Tomlinson senior waggled a hand. "So you throw a couple hundred million in Santino's direction. He'll appreciate it."

Jake held his tongue. And remembered an old-time politician's dictum: a few hundred million here, a few hundred million there, pretty soon you're talking real money.

With an inner sigh, he decided he'd have to dig up all he could find about tidal energy research and patch a few pages on the subject into his plan—near the front, where it would catch Santino's eye.

If the Little Saint deigned to read the plan at all.

# San Diego

The pressure got to him. The week after his dinner with the Tomlinsons Jake suddenly decided he had to get out of town once again. Washington's heat and humidity were draining the energy out of him. No matter that he went from air-conditioned apartment to air-conditioned automobile to air-conditioned office, the *atmosphere* of the city was squeezing the juices out of him. He had to get away.

He knew it wasn't the weather; it was his work. The energy plan loomed before him like a block of implacable granite. He had tried to put into it something to satisfy everyone, even Santino, and the effort was turning what had started as a balanced, sensible plan into a picnic basket for special interests. *This* for the coal industry, *that* for the windmill people—on and on for more than a hundred pages. Only the space solar power concept had been discarded, and Jake knew that its deletion would make an enemy of Isaiah Knowles.

Can't be helped, he told himself. The elder Tomlinson was right: keep the space power idea in the plan and you'll get laughed out of town.

That's when he realized that he *wanted* to get out of town. He had to. This week. Tomorrow. Now.

And go where? he asked himself. Not back home. He'd been there and couldn't bear to go back again, so soon, as if he were running away from Washington with his tail between his legs. Well, aren't you? he demanded of himself. Big-shot science advisor. You're in over your head. Admit it.

Thinking about his last visit to Montana, Jake remembered Bob Rogers telling him about the methanol work being done in San Diego. What the hell, he thought. I might as well go see what they're doing. Get myself out of town for a few days. He made a couple of phone calls and went home to pack a travel bag.

He slept most of the way on the flight to California, waking with a start with the noise of the plane lowering its landing gear. Houses were flashing past his window. We're going to crash! Jake screamed silently. Then he saw the concrete of the runway and heard the wheels screech, touching down. Hills dotted with houses ran along the side of the airport. One of the flight attendants announced, "Welcome to San Diego, where the local time is . . ."

Jake sucked in a deep breath. Goddamn airport's tucked in among the hills, he realized.

A young black man was waiting for him at the baggage pickup area, holding a neatly printed sign saying DR. ROSS.

Towing his rollalong bag, Jake went up to him and said, "I'm Jake Ross."

The youngster smiled, almost shyly. "I'm Vic. Your luggage is arriving on carousel—"

"No luggage," Jake said. "Just this one bag."

Vic couldn't be more than twenty-five, Jake judged. He was a short little kid, a little pudgy, the kind who must have been the butt of the bigger kids' pranks. Roundish face, dark skin, pleasant bright smile. He was wearing a white short-sleeved shirt hanging loosely over tan corduroy slacks. And tennis shoes.

As he led Jake to the parking lot, Vic said, "We're all very happy you asked to see our work. I didn't think anybody in Washington would show any interest. Not yet."

His car was a sleek-looking silver convertible. Jake couldn't recognize the manufacturer.

"Built it myself," Vic said when Jake asked. "Sort of a hobby of mine. Runs on methanol."

Of course, Jake thought, with a grin. What else?

But he asked, "Doesn't methanol burn out your engine? I read somewhere that it's very corrosive."

"Could be," Vic said easily as he slid behind the wheel. "But I sprayed the cylinders with a corrosion-resistant compound we developed. Works fine."

So far, Jake thought. Then he looked at the dashboard odometer. More than seventy thousand miles.

"How long have you had this car?"

With a laugh, Vic answered, "Hey, we run this baby night and day. To see if we've got the corrosion problem licked. We do plenty of testing in the lab, as well."

Jake was impressed.

Vic drove the convertible toward the waterfront, explaining, "Rents are cheaper down here. 'Specially when you need a lot of room. Lots of old warehouses available."

The harbor was busy, and rows of mothballed Navy ships lined the docks and stood anchored out in the deeper water, looking gray and businesslike.

They pulled up in front of a single-story structure that must have been a warehouse at one time. Now it had a spanking new coat of white paint and a sign over its main door: WAKEFIELD LABORATORY.

Vic hopped out of the car and led Jake to the door, assuring him that his travel bag would be perfectly safe, locked in the convertible's trunk. Jake worried that somebody might steal the car, but the kid seemed unbothered by that possibility.

Inside, they went down a hallway. Through the open doors on either side Jake could see men and women bent over desks and computers. Most of them were black, like Vic.

"This is the business side of the company," Vic explained. "Gotta pay the bills—and the salaries."

They went through a double door into an expanse that looked to Jake like a maze of pipes and tubes and vats holding liquids that gurgled and sloshed. Dr. Frankenstein's laboratory, Jake said to himself.

"Well, this is it," said Vic, with pride in his voice. He pointed to a row of cylinders. "Carbon dioxide feed is over there, in the next stage we introduce the hydrogen, and"—he walked Jake to the far end of the bewildering rig—"the final product is methanol."

Jake looked over the rig. "You produce methanol from carbon dioxide."

With an enthusiastic nod, Vic said, "Sure do. We could take the $CO_2$ that power plants and factories puff out their smokestacks and turn it into a clean, efficient fuel for cars, trucks, anything that moves, even planes."

"But you have to add hydrogen."

"Which we get from electrolyzing water. Split water into its components, oxygen and hydrogen. Feed the hydrogen to the $CO_2$ and you get methanol. We could sell the oxygen to Linde or some other company that deals in industrial gases."

"Electrolyzing water takes a lot of energy, though."

"Naw. We do it the way Mother Nature does, use genetically modified bacteria to do the job. They run on sunlight and chlorophyll, up on the roof."

Jake looked around at the apparatus with new respect. "You can turn waste carbon dioxide into methanol fuel by adding hydrogen that you get from water."

"Clean and efficient," said Vic, his smile gleaming. "What more could you ask for?"

Jake nodded agreement. "I'm impressed. I'd like to meet this man Wakefield."

Vic looked surprised. "That's me. I'm Victor Wakefield."

"You're . . . this is *your* operation?"

"It surely is." His smile became radiant.

Jake tied hard not to frown. But he was thinking, Jesus, this guy is younger than I am!

• • •

Vic Wakefield took Jake to his home for dinner. It was a modest clapboard house on a winding street atop a windy hill. One of the houses I saw zipping past when we landed, Jake realized.

His mother was a pleasant, roundish woman who never got farther from the kitchen than the dining room table, where she delivered platters of fried chicken with heaps of vegetables. No one else seemed to be in the house.

"My dad died from cancer when I was twelve," Vic explained. "I'm an only child."

"How did you raise the money to start your laboratory?" Jake asked.

With a shy grin and a glance at his mother, sitting at the head of the table, Vic said, "Local bank. They had faith in me. Wanted to see one of our own make good."

"They didn't loan Victor all that much money," his mother interjected. "He's been running his business on a shoestring, really."

As the evening unfolded, Jake realized that Vic's story was a lot like his own. Bright kid, picked on by the bullies in school. Smart enough to do their homework in exchange for their protection. Won a scholarship to a state university.

"I was always interested in chemistry," Vic said.

His mother added, "He damned near blew up my kitchen once."

They all laughed.

The next morning Vic showed up at Jake's hotel to drive him to the airport.

Over the noise of the wind and the other cars and trucks on the freeway, Jake asked, "Would you mind if I sent a guy to your lab to look over what you're doing? I need a second opinion, and—"

"Mind? Hell no." Vic was grinning from ear to ear. "The more people learn about what we're doing, the better off we'll be. Might even attract some of those big-time venture capitalists."

Jake nodded happily. "Yeah, you just might, at that."

# The Reaction

All through the flight back to Washington Jake bent over his notebook, folding the material on Wakefield's work into his plan.

With growing excitement, he saw that the methanol concept could make his plan revenue neutral, or close to it. Instead of the expensive chore of burying the carbon dioxide produced by burning fossil fuel, power utilities and manufacturing factories could sell their waste $CO_2$ to companies that would produce methanol from it.

The oil companies would have to switch from producing gasoline to producing methanol, but that could be phased in gradually, the way they now did with biofuels such as ethanol. And the savings from fueling transportation vehicles with methanol—which emitted half the carbon dioxide that gasoline did—would be a major factor both economically and ecologically.

By god, Jake thought, we could get the EPA backing this!

. . .

After another week of intense work, Jake set up a meeting in the conference room to show the finished project to Senator Tomlinson and his inner staff. On the day of the meeting, he was prepared with a presentation that included PowerPoint visuals and an executive summary.

Once he'd shown the last slide and turned the overhead lights on again, the staff sat uneasily around the conference table. No one said a word. Nineteen men and women, ranging from a bald corpulent veteran of Beltway insider politics to an eager twenty-something blonde in a short-skirted navy blue outfit. And not one of them had a word to say.

Just like a class of freshmen, Jake thought. Nobody wants to be the first to speak. Nobody wants to stick his neck out.

They all looked toward the senator, at the head of the table. Even Kevin O'Donnell, sitting at Tomlinson's right.

"Well," Tomlinson said, almost sternly, "what do you think?"

The blonde—a recent graduate in ecology—broke their silence. "I think it's environmentally sound, especially the part about recovering carbon dioxide from burning fossil fuels and not letting it get out into the environment."

"Seems to cover all the bases," volunteered one of the older men.

O'Donnell asked, "That bit about producing methanol fuel from carbon dioxide emissions, is that for real?"

"It is," Jake assured him solemnly. He had asked Bob Rogers, from the university back in Montana, to take a quick trip to San Diego. Rogers was a physicist and happily at home with new technology.

"Looks good to me," Rogers had told Jake once he returned from San Diego. "I think the kid really has something."

Now one of Tomlinson's staff economists was asking, "But can you scale up this methanol system to industrial proportions?"

"Yes," said Jake firmly. "No problem."

O'Donnell said, "I'm not sure you can support all those technologies and still keep the plan revenue neutral."

Jake replied, "You can if you count the savings in health care costs and the job creation that the plan will generate. And this methanol conversion will save all the money we would otherwise have to invest in burying carbon dioxide emissions."

"Do any of you see any fatal flaws in the plan?" Tomlinson asked.

They glanced around at each other. A few of them looked in Jake's direction.

"That business at the end, about tidal energy," said one of the older men. "That seems kind of iffy, don't you think?"

With a sardonic smile, Tomlinson replied, "Not to Senator Santino."

"Oh!" Nods of understanding ran up and down the conference table.

O'Donnell suggested, "Maybe you ought to put it up closer to the beginning, then."

"Good point," said the senator.

The staff made a few more desultory remarks before Tomlinson pushed his chair back and got to his feet. "Thanks, all of you. Jake, it's a good, solid plan. I'll take it to Santino as soon as I can get an appointment to see him."

That ended the meeting. Everyone got up and filed out of the conference room, leaving Jake and the senator at the table.

Scowling as he disconnected his notebook from the projector, Jake said, "It went over like a lead balloon."

But Senator Tomlinson smiled at him. "It's just fine, Jake. Don't expect them to appreciate it the way you and I do. They're not technical experts."

"I guess."

More seriously, Tomlinson said, "Now we've got to get Santino to approve it."

Jake nodded, knowing that they had an uphill battle ahead of them.

• • •

That evening, in his apartment, Jake sat down on his sagging sofa, opened his laptop, and called Steve Brogan on Skype. He probably won't want to talk to me, Jake thought. I'm the one who got him exiled to Ohio.

But on the laptop's screen Brogan looked unusually cheerful, relaxed, wearing a splashy colored T-shirt instead of his usual dark business suit.

"How do you like Dayton?"

Brogan actually smiled. "You know, it's not half bad. I drove down to Cincinnati a couple of times to see the Reds play. Never had the time for a baseball game when I was in Washington."

"Have you found a house yet?"

Gesturing, Brogan said, "That's where I am now. Nice little place. And prices here are half what they were in DC."

"And your new job?"

Some of his old cynicism returning, Brogan said, "Just busywork. A trained chimpanzee could do it."

"No strain, then."

"I never realized what a rat race I was in back in DC," Brogan went on. "Here, there's no pressure. I just show up and go through the motions, and everybody's happy."

"That's good," said Jake. "I guess."

"I'm just putting in the next three years and then retiring from the government's service. One more faceless bureaucrat heading for Florida." He seemed almost happy about the prospect.

"My tax dollars at work," Jake quipped.

"Damned right." Brogan's expression grew more serious. "So what's with you? How's the Little Saint treating you?"

"Tomlinson's got an appointment to show him the energy plan."

"Lotsa luck."

"We even stuck in some cockamamie idea about generating electricity from ocean tides. That ought to make Santino happy."

"Maybe."

"You don't think so?"

With a shrug, Brogan answered, "He's going to bury your plan. He'll smile at your boss and tell him he's going to set up hearings and bring in the nation's top experts, but all he'll really be doing is stalling for time."

"Time for what?"

"Time for your boss to get it through his head that your plan is never going to see the light of day."

"But why?" Jake asked. "Wouldn't it look good for him to bring it out? He's the chairman of the energy committee, for god's sake."

Brogan shook his head. "You still don't get it, do you?"

"Get what?"

"Why do we have a Department of Energy?"

"To solve our energy problems."

"Have our energy problems been solved?"

"Not yet. That's what I'm trying to do."

Like a patient teacher dealing with a backward student, Brogan explained, "If we solved our energy problems, what would the Department of Energy do?"

Jake blinked at the screen.

"Listen to me. You're too young to remember the space race, back in the sixties."

"I wasn't even born yet."

"Neither was I. But you ought to understand what's what. The White House created NASA and told those space geeks to get us to the Moon before the Russians got there."

"Which NASA did."

"Yeah. They solved the problem they were created to solve. So what happened? Their budget got slashed, they had to lay off a ton of people, and they've never gone farther than Earth orbit again."

"Not with people," Jake objected. "But—"

"The space geeks made a fundamental error. They solved the problem that the White House handed them. And they've been on the back burner ever since. They're not going anywhere."

The image of Isaiah Knowles's earnest, pleading face flashed into Jake's mind.

Brogan went on, "If the Energy Department really solved the nation's energy problems, it'd get downsized and forgotten, just like NASA. But that won't happen anytime soon."

"You think so?"

"I know so. The Energy Department is responsible for making hydrogen bombs, pal. As long as they have a nuclear section they'll be in business. But not to solve energy problems."

Frowning at the image on his laptop screen, Jake said, "So you're telling me that Santino doesn't want a plan that can put our energy programs on a sound, sustainable basis."

"It's not that simple, but yeah, that's what I'm saying."

"And we're all going through a pointless exercise."

"It's not pointless, pal. But the point isn't solving energy problems. The point is maintaining Santino's power. Maintaining it, or making it bigger."

"So he's going to bury my plan."

"Very nicely. Very politely. He'll bury it under hearings and studies and reports from every which kind of expert. Including me. But it'll never see the light of day."

Jake sank back on the sofa. "So this has all been an exercise in futility."

"Yeah." Brogan's brows knit slightly. "Unless . . ."

"Unless what?"

With an almost evil grin, Brogan said, "Unless you and your senator resort to an old, time-honored Washington maneuver."

"What maneuver?"

"You leak your plan to the news media."

# Leaking

eak the plan?" Senator Tomlinson looked surprised.

L Feeling slightly uneasy about the idea, Jake still nodded and replied, "We leak the plan to the news media, and the publicity will force Santino to act on it, one way or the other."

Tomlinson leaned back in his desk chair, his handsome face turning thoughtful. Beyond him, Jake saw through the office window that a few of the trees lining the avenue outside were starting to change color. It was a bright blue morning in late September.

Tomlinson sat in silence for several moments, mulling over Jake's suggestion. Jake found himself counting the seconds: one, one thousand; two, one thousand; three . . .

Between nine and ten Tomlinson stirred. Peering at his wristwatch, the senator said, "Jake, I've got to get over to the Capitol for a meeting of the agriculture committee. You handle this problem the way you think best."

Senator Tomlinson got to his feet and so did Jake.

"I'll probably be tied up all day on this or that," Tomlinson said. "I won't have time to talk to you about this matter."

Jake nodded, understanding. So I'm supposed to do the leaking, while you keep your skirts clean. If the thing blows up on us, I fall on my sword and you can claim you didn't know a thing about it.

Beaming one of his kilowatt smiles at Jake, Tomlinson said, "Amy and I would like to have you over for
dinner again sometime soon."

"Sure," said Jake. "My social calendar is pretty free."

"Good."

Jake went with the senator as far as the corridor that
led to his own office, where Kevin O'Donnell was waiting impatiently for him. Tomlinson waved a cheerful
farewell and headed out of the office suite with his staff
chief, leaving Jake standing there feeling like a man
who'd just been sent on a suicide mission.

What the hell, he thought. I can always go back to the
university.

Instead, he went back to his own office and slouched
onto his desk chair. How the hell do I go about leaking
the plan to the news media? Without dirtying Frank's
linen?

Well, he said to himself, the senator has a media relations staff. That's the place to start, I guess.

He picked up the phone and asked for the head of the
PR staff, Earl Reynolds.

"Reynolds here."

"Jake Ross. I need your advice about something," 
Jake said into the phone. "Something important."

"Sure," Reynolds replied in a strong baritone. "Come
on down to my orifice."

Jake winced at the intended pun. But he got up and
walked to Reynolds's office.

Reynolds looked like a former college jock: broad
shoulders, ruggedly handsome face, thick mop of dark
hair carefully coiffed. He wore an expensive-looking
navy blue blazer over a crisp light blue shirt and a perfectly knotted necktie of red and blue stripes. University
of Pennsylvania, Jake guessed.

Standing behind his desk, Reynolds stuck out a meaty
hand and grasped Jake's firmly.

"Dr. Ross," he said warmly.

"Jake."

With a handsome smile, Reynolds said, "Okay, Jake. And I'm Earl. Not a duke, just an earl."

Jake forced a smile.

Reynolds gestured graciously to the burgundy red leather chair in front of his desk.

"Make yourself comfortable. What can I do you for?"

"It's kind of delicate," Jake began.

"I can be the soul of discretion," said Reynolds, "when I have to be."

"You know about the energy plan I've drawn up for the senator?"

"I've heard about it," said Reynolds, his face going serious. "I couldn't get to your meeting yesterday, schedule conflict."

Jake nodded, thinking that Reynolds didn't regard the plan as important enough to take up his time.

Feeling uneasy, Jake said, "The senator's going to present the plan to Senator Santino."

"Chairman of the energy committee. Makes sense."

"And Santino's going to bury it."

"You think so?"

"It's a possibility. A strong possibility."

His forehead furrowing slightly, Reynolds said, "I suppose that it is a possibility."

"We need to get the plan out before the public," Jake said.

"Ah. You want me to set up a news conference. No sweat. The senator comes across beautifully on TV."

"No, no, no," Jake objected. "Not a news conference. The senator can't be seen talking about the plan in public. Santino wouldn't like it."

"Oh-ho," Reynolds said, his face lighting up with understanding. "You want to leak the plan to the news media."

"Without involving the senator in any way."

"A leak." Reynolds pursed his lips in thought.

"I haven't got the faintest idea of how to go about it," Jake admitted.

"Pretty delicate. A leak needs a leaker. And a leakee."

Wondering if the PR director was trying to make a pun in a ridiculous Chinese accent, Jake repeated, "The senator can't be any part of this. We've got to keep him out of it."

"Yes, sure." Jabbing a forefinger at Jake, Reynolds said, "You're going to be the leaker, but we've got to put a layer of protection between you and the person who actually leaks the story to the media."

"The leakee," Jake said.

With a lopsided grin, Reynolds said, "You catch on pretty quick, Jake."

"How do we go about doing this?"

"Let me think about it. Nobody in this office should be involved in the leak, as far as the public is concerned."

"Can you do that?"

As if he hadn't heard Jake, Reynolds mused, "Santino's a powerhouse, you know. Going up against the Little Saint won't be easy."

"So I've heard."

"Give me a little time to work this out, Jake."

"How much time?"

Reynolds brought out his lopsided smile again. "The impossible, we do right away. The miraculous takes a few days."

# Tidal Basin

Three mornings later Reynolds appeared at the door of Jake's office.

"Nice day for a picnic," he said, his bulky form filling the doorway.

Glancing out his window at the blue, cloud-flecked sky, Jake answered, "I guess."

"Why don't you go out to the Tidal Basin and rent a paddleboat." It wasn't a question.

"The Tidal Basin?"

"I can arrange for a nice young lady to meet you there. Take a boat ride around the Basin. You can talk without anybody listening in."

"Who's the nice young lady?"

"An old acquaintance of mine. She used to work for the Reuters news service downtown. Until the Little Saint got her canned."

"Santino got her fired?"

Waggling a hand, Reynolds replied, "Not directly. He's too smart for that. He never leaves fingerprints. But, yeah. She did a story about Santino holding up some environmental legislation in his committee, and a week later she's out on the street without a job."

"So she doesn't like Santino."

"Would you?"

"So what's her name? How do I recognize her?"

"Can't miss her," Reynolds said, with a leering grin.

"Her name is Tamiko Umetzu. Japanese American, from Fresno, California. Kinda small, slim. Pretty cute."

"That's not much to go on," Jake complained.

"What do you need, a photograph? How many Nips do you think'll be at the Tidal Basin precisely at high noon?"

Jake imagined a busload of Japanese tourists disgorging, but he said, "Do you have her cell phone number?"

"No. But she has yours. Have fun!" And Reynolds left Jake sitting at his desk.

It was ten forty-five. The Tidal Basin, Jake thought. At high noon.

• • •

Jake took a taxi to the paddleboat dock. Looking around the sparse crowd, he didn't see any Japanese American woman. I should have asked Reynolds how old she is, he realized.

He turned around slowly. In the distance he saw the towering obelisk of the Washington Monument and, behind a screen of trees, the square marble roof of the Lincoln Memorial. Across the basin stood the Jefferson Memorial, gleaming in the sunshine like an ancient Greek temple. But no Japanese American woman.

Feeling almost foolish, he went to the booth and rented a paddleboat. Then he lingered on the dock, waiting. The kid working on the dock asked him which boat he wanted, and Jake replied he was waiting for someone. The youngster shrugged and moved away to help an elderly couple.

It felt warm in the sunshine, despite the breeze coming across the water. Jake took off his jacket and draped it over his arm.

This is like an old-time spy movie, he thought. Waiting for your secret contact to show up.

Yeah, he said to himself. A bad movie.

Then he saw a tall, well-dressed Asian-looking woman striding along the dock toward him. Jake started to say hello to her, but she walked right past him and embraced a guy in a Navy officer's uniform. They climbed into one of the paddleboats together.

This is a fiasco, Jake complained to himself.

His cell phone buzzed. Jake fumbled it out of his jacket pocket, nearly dropped it, but at last flipped it open.

"Dr. Ross?" a woman's voice asked.

"Yes."

"I'm standing next to the ticket booth. Can you see me?"

"I'm down here on the dock," he said, waving toward the slim figure of a woman up on the concrete wall, beside the ticket booth, with a phone to her ear.

The figure began to walk onto the dock. "I see you. I'll be right there."

Tamiko Umetzu was young, in her early thirties at most, Jake guessed. Small, no taller than his shoulder, even in the heels she was wearing. Slim figure. As she approached Jake along the dock, he saw that she was quite pretty: high cheekbones, almond-shaped eyes of deep brown, dark hair falling fashionably to her shoulders. She wore a short-skirted sleeveless frock patterned in various shades of brown.

When she got close enough to extend her hand to him, she said, "Dr. Ross."

"Jake."

She smiled and her face lit up. "I'm Tami."

"Good to meet you."

Jake helped her into the paddleboat, and the young guy working the dock untied the mooring line as Jake slid into the seat and planted his feet on the pedals. He saw that Tami had slipped off her shoes and placed her feet on the pedals on her side.

The kid pushed them from the dock and they started pedaling in unison.

"Earl told me you have a problem," said Tami.

Nodding, Jake asked, "How long have you known Earl?"

"Two years . . . no, it's almost three. He helped me find the job I have now."

"Which is?"

"EarthGuard. It's an environmental lobbying firm."

Jake heard Brogan's scornful, *They never leave DC. Never.*

"You were with Reuters?"

"Yes, until they canned me over an environmental story I wanted to break."

"And the Little Saint didn't want it made public."

A suspicious, wary look flashed across her face. "Senator Santino had a hand in it, I'm pretty sure."

"He's giving me trouble, too," said Jake.

"Is he?"

As they paddled all the way across the Tidal Basin, Jake outlined his problem. Tami listened quietly until he finished.

At last she said, guardedly, "So you haven't released your plan to the news media."

"No," said Jake, equally carefully, "it's going to the energy committee."

"Santino."

With a nod, Jake said, "He'll decide when the plan should be made public."

Tami sat in silence while they paddled slowly back toward the dock. As she slipped her shoes on, Tami said, "I'd love to see your plan, if you could get a copy to me."

While the same youngster tied their boat to the dock, Jake stood up and helped her out of the paddleboat. He was thinking, She has connections back to Reuters news service. She can leak the plan to them, and then it'll spread to all the news media.

"I suppose I could get a copy to you," he said, feeling slightly ridiculous at the cloak-and-dagger aspect of their exchange.

"That would be fine," she said.

Standing on the dock beside her, Jake blurted, "Would you like to have lunch?"

She seemed to hold her breath for a moment, but then she smiled and said, "Yes. I'm starving."

They walked together up to Phillips Seafood Restaurant. A sign on the sidewalk proclaimed it served the finest Maryland blue crabs.

Tami pointed down the street. "The Cantina Marina serves Cajun food. Are you in the mood for some gumbo?"

With a grin, Jake said, "Sure, why not?"

They sat on the patio overlooking the water, and Jake found himself telling Tami all about himself, about Lev and his wife's death and his teaching at the university, his work with Senator Tomlinson. He couldn't stop talking. In the back of his mind he realized he must be boring Tami to tears with this data dump, but she seemed honestly interested. At least, that was the impression he got from her earnest, smiling expression.

At last he said, "And what about you?"

She seemed surprised. "Oh, nothing much. Born and raised in Clovis, near Fresno. Got a journalism degree at Southern Cal, moved to DC to work at Reuters. That's about it."

Jake wanted to ask her if she was involved with anyone. He could see that the ring finger of her left hand was empty, but still . . .

As they finished their desserts he asked, "Um, are you free for dinner later this week? Or next?" He mentally kicked himself for adding the "or next." Makes me sound too damned eager, too needy. Too honest.

Tami smiled a little and said, "I'm free this Friday."

"Great!" he said. "I can bring you a DVD of the plan, complete with visuals."

"That'll be fine."

As he saw her into a taxi, Jake asked himself if she was interested in having dinner with him merely because of the energy plan or because she was truly interested in him as a person.

Doesn't matter, he told himself. We're having dinner together. What happens next is in the future.

# Dinner

Tami lived near Dupont Circle, not far from the Embassy Row neighborhood. They decided to have dinner at the Ruth's Chris Steakhouse, a few blocks from her apartment. Jake walked from his place to Wisconsin Avenue and picked up a taxicab. He didn't want to drive through the city's crazy traffic circles after dark. By the time he figured in what parking would cost, he decided the taxi was almost cheaper.

She was sitting on the padded bench at the restaurant's entrance, under the eyes of a toothily smiling maître d' and two of his comely young female assistants, both long-haired blondes. Tami got to her feet as Jake came through the door, and he reached out to her with both his hands.

"Right on time," she said.

He laughed. "I'm usually early. It's a bad habit of mine."

"Nothing wrong with being early. I was."

One of the young, dark-clad assistants showed them to a table far in the rear of the restaurant. Jake asked Tami if she liked wine, and she said yes, so he asked for the wine list.

"A whole bottle?" Tami looked surprised.

"What we don't finish here, we'll take home," he said. To himself, he added, Big-time bon vivant, splurging on wine.

He ordered a modestly priced Malbec from Argentina,

mainly on the description offered in the wine list. It turned out to be dry and flavorful, as advertised.

The restaurant was noisy, but Jake didn't mind it. Makes it more difficult for eavesdroppers to overhear us, he thought. Then he realized he was getting just as paranoid as Brogan.

"Did you bring the DVD?" Tami asked, once their appetizers had been served.

Patting his jacket pocket, Jake replied, "It's right here."

"Good. I'm anxious to see it."

Suddenly Jake felt uncomfortable. Leaning slightly toward her, he said, "I want to make something clear, Tami. I'm not out to get Santino. What I'm doing isn't about that. My goal is to give this energy plan a fair hearing, that's all there is to it."

"You think that once the plan is out in the open the people will go for it," she said.

"That's what I hope. I think the plan would be very good for America. For the world, really."

"And you don't want Santino bottling it up."

"Right."

She took a sip of wine, then said, "I'm not out to get Santino, either. I'm not into revenge."

He nodded.

"Frankly," she went on, "I don't think either one of us could hurt Santino anyway. He's too entrenched, too powerful."

"I guess you're right."

With the beginnings of a crafty smile curving her lips, Tami added, "But splashing your plan in the news media would be good for your boss, wouldn't it? After all, it'd be known as Senator Tomlinson's plan, not yours."

"That's fine with me," Jake said.

"He's ambitious, isn't he?"

Jake laughed. "You show me one senator or representative that isn't."

Tami laughed with him. "You're right."

After dinner, they stepped out onto busy, bustling Connecticut Avenue. Couples were strolling by, people were jabbering into cell phones, a teenager on a skateboard maneuvered through the pedestrians. Jake started to look for a taxi.

"I live just a few blocks away," Tami said. "I can walk."

"Okay," he said, and he fell into step beside her.

After half a block, though, Tami said, "Jake, I share a tiny apartment with three other women. It's really small. I don't think it would be a good idea for them to see us together."

He felt a surge of disappointment, but said, "You're probably right."

"You can give me the DVD now. I'll look at it as soon as I get into my own room."

As he handed the slim jewel case to her, Jake muttered, "It's kind of long. And detailed. A lot to take in on one sitting."

Tami tucked the case into her purse. "I'll study it from start to finish," she promised. "Then I'll call you."

"How about dinner when you finish it?"

She smiled. "Sure. Why not?"

"Do you know any good Japanese restaurants?"

Tami broke into a delighted laughter. "A few. They're mostly dives, though. The upscale ones cater to Americans."

"Like me."

She gave him a curious look. "You might like my favorite sushi bar. If you like raw fish, that is."

"If you like it, I'm sure I'll like it."

"We'll see."

On impulse, Jake pecked at her lips, then said a swift goodnight.

It wasn't until he was in his own bed, staring at the shadowed ceiling, that he realized Tami held his future in her hands. If she lets Santino know what I've just done, I'm toast, he told himself.

But she won't do that, he thought. I can trust her.

I hope.

# Fujiyama Sushi Bar

The place didn't quite look like a dive. It was in the cellar of a house on P Street, two blocks from Tami's apartment. The decorations on the walls—mostly old landscape paintings of Japanese scenes—were faded, true enough. And Jake had to push through a wall hanging that served as a door. Otherwise the sushi bar looked clean and comfortable, although it was only half filled with customers.

"Not very crowded," he said as they passed a half dozen empty tables and found two seats together at the bar.

"Happy hour is over," said Tami.

Behind the bar two Japanese sushi chefs were chopping and dicing away with blurring speed. A tall, buxom American woman in a tight black sweater handed them menus the size of campaign posters and took their drink order. Tami asked for sake and Jake followed suit.

The sake was hot. Jake almost burned his fingers as he poured some of the wine from its ceramic mini-carafe into his thimble-sized cup. He let it sit there while he blew on his fingertips.

"You're letting it get cold," Tami said.

"A little."

She took a sip, then put her cup down. The menus were mostly incomprehensible to Jake, except for the tuna and crab rolls.

"We have a special tonight," the barmaid told them. "Hamachi kama."

Hiding behind his oversized menu, Jake whispered to Tami, "What's that?"

"The jaw of a yellowfin."

"The jaw?"

Nodding, Tami explained, "That's the sweetest part of the fish. Especially the cheeks. It's delicious."

With some trepidation, Jake ordered the special. Tami chose two different sushi rolls instead.

The TV set mounted behind the bar was tuned to the local news, but the sound was muted. Jake finally took a cautious sip of his sake and found that it was smooth and warming.

"Have you had a chance to look at the DVD?" he asked.

"I've gone through it twice," said Tami. "Jake, it's brilliant. A plan that coordinates all our energy options and reduces our carbon footprint significantly."

He felt his cheeks reddening. "Thanks. I'm glad you like it."

"I can see why Santino would want to bottle it up, though," she went on. "The fossil fuel lobbies will be dead-set against it."

"But it includes fossil fuels," Jake protested. "They're an important part of the plan."

Holding up a slim finger, Tami said, "Yes, but all the growth in energy production is in the renewables area. That, and this MHD thing."

"MHD uses fossil fuels."

"I understand, Jake. But—"

The barmaid placed their dishes in front of them. Jake asked for a fork. She gave him a slightly condescending smile, then reached under the bar and handed him a faded-looking, slightly bent aluminum fork.

Somebody stole this from an airliner, Jake thought.

"You don't know how to use chopsticks?" Tami asked.

Shaking his head, Jake said, "Not many places to learn, back home."

"Let me show you."

The barmaid saw Tami demonstrating how to wield chopsticks and came over to them with a pair held together near one end by a thick rubber band.

"That'll give you the hang of them," she said, grinning at Jake.

Tami told him, "That's how they teach children to use chopsticks." Picking up her own pair, she showed him the proper way to hold them.

As he haltingly jabbed at the jawbone on his plate, Jake returned to his subject. "The plan doesn't hurt the fossil fuel industries."

"You don't understand," Tami said. "If all the growth in your plan is in renewables, the fossil fuel lobbies will reject your plan. They've got things pretty much where they want them, and they don't want to see the competition grow."

"But if we let the fossil fuel burners grow, the carbon they'll pump into the atmosphere will heat up the global climate disastrously."

"They don't believe that. Actually, they don't care. They've convinced themselves that global warming is a problem for the next century."

"But it's what we do *now* that'll determine the how big the climate change will be."

"You know that. And I know that. And I imagine there are people within the fossil fuel industries who know it, too. But they just don't care. They're after profits, not protecting the environment. Anything more than a year or two in the future is science fiction, as far as they're concerned."

Jake jabbed at his fish and actually picked up a piece with his chopsticks. But it fell into his lap before he could get it to his mouth.

Tami did not laugh. She just said, "It takes some practice."

"I could starve to death first," Jake growled, reaching for the fork.

She said nothing, just deftly grabbed a sushi roll and popped it into her mouth.

Lowering his voice a notch, Jake asked, "So have you shown the plan to Reuters?"

"Reuters?" Tami looked alarmed. "No way. Santino would trace the leak in a hot second."

"Then . . . ?"

"I made a copy of your executive summary and passed it on to a blogger I know."

In his mind, Jake saw the image of a blogger back in Montana who called himself Freeforall. He had been useful during Tomlinson's election campaign.

"A blogger," he said.

"He's put your summary on his blog. Next, I told one of my apartment-mates to look up his blog. She works for the CBS News office here in town."

"CBS News," Jake repeated. He looked up at the TV screen behind the bar, but now it was showing some automobile race. One of the cars flipped over, smashed into the wall, and burst into flames. The info bar at the bottom of the screen read, "Two killed at speedway."

Tami put a hand on Jake's knee. "Wait for the news at eleven. It ought to be on then."

"The CBS station."

"Yes," Tami said. "My apartment-mate worships the memory of Walter Cronkite."

Jake sighed. It didn't sound like much to him.

Pointing to his plate, Tami said, "Now pick up your chopsticks and try again. Practice makes perfect."

"I'll try," said Jake. Reluctantly.

# Bacterial

Jake left Tami at Dupont Circle, not without noticing all the couples walking together or sitting on the grass by the fountain. Alone, he found a cab and returned to his dark, empty basement apartment.

By eleven he was in bed, watching the late news on the local CBS station. Suicide bomber kills fourteen people in a marketplace in Lebanon, six of them children. A tropical disturbance in the mid-Atlantic shows signs of growing into a late-season hurricane. Economists predict heating oil prices will hit an all-time high this coming winter. The Redskins squeezed out a twenty-four to twenty-one victory over the Chicago Bears.

Nothing about the energy plan, Jake realized as he sat up in his bed, disappointed, while a series of commercials pushed toothpaste, new cars (with four-hundred-horsepower engines!), a fast-food restaurant chain, and pills for low testosterone.

I've got plenty of testosterone, Jake grumbled to himself. Just no place to put it.

He was about to click the TV off when the female half of the anchor team came on with her brittle smile and said, "A new plan for developing the nation's energy systems is apparently being considered in the Senate. Joe Daley has the details."

Jake sat up straighter. The story was less than half a minute in duration. Standing in front of the Capitol, the

CBS correspondent simply said that the Senate energy committee was looking at a new comprehensive energy plan presented by the committee's newest member, Senator Tomlinson. The screen showed a still picture of Tomlinson, smiling handsomely. Jake recognized it as a photo they used during the campaign back home the previous year.

Nothing more.

But maybe, Jake thought hopefully, maybe that'll be enough. After all, it only takes a couple of pebbles to start a landslide.

• • •

In his office early the next morning, Jake surfed the Internet and found half a dozen references to the energy plan on different blog sites.

It hasn't gone viral, he had to admit to himself. But at least it's out there. With an inner laugh, he told himself the story had gone bacterial. Not viral, but maybe it will grow.

Precisely at nine a.m. his phone rang. The face on the phone screen was Isaiah Knowles, dark and decidedly unhappy.

"I didn't see any mention of space solar power in your plan," the former astronaut said, clearly irritated.

Jake nodded. "It got cut out of the plan."

"Why?"

"Giggle factor. We didn't want the whole plan to be laughed out of town because of the space element."

Knowles said nothing for several heartbeats, but his face spoke louder than words.

Finally he said in a low rumble, "You screwed me, man."

"I didn't mean to."

"Doesn't matter. I trusted you to at least include a mention of SSP. Now we've got nothing."

Jake asked, "Why doesn't NASA include space solar power in its own program plans?"

"Same reason. Giggle factor. The suits at the top of the pyramid just don't see it."

The look on the black man's face had gone from anger to despair.

"Is there any chance you could get it into your budget? Maybe as a study? Just to get a toe in the door?"

"We've done studies. I could burn down half the fuckin' city by setting a match to all the studies we've got stacked up."

Thinking furiously, Jake said, "Would it help if Senator Tomlinson met with your top people to talk about the idea?"

Knowles started to snap a reply, thought better of it, and took in a deep breath instead. Then he said, with a weary smile, "I guess it wouldn't hurt."

"I'll set it up," said Jake.

"Yeah. Okay. Um . . . thanks."

The phone screen went blank, and Jake thought that he was learning how things work in this town. Instead of doing something, you arrange a meeting.

• • •

Just before lunch Earl Reynolds popped his head through Jake's doorway. "Got a nanosecond?"

Looking up from the minutes of the latest meeting of the energy committee, Jake said, "Sure. Come on in."

Reynolds had a self-satisfied grin on his face as he settled his bulk in one of the visitors' chairs. "I have just arranged for the senator to appear on *Face the Nation* next Sunday. And I'm dickering with *Sixty Minutes* for a piece about the energy situation."

Jake's jaw dropped open. "That's terrific!"

"My phone's been jangling pretty hard. The senator's going to be a famous guy."

Before Jake could say anything, Reynolds added, "For fifteen minutes."

"More than that," Jake objected.

"We'll see," said Reynolds. "At least he's getting some attention."

"Have you looked at the blogs on the Internet?"

His expression turning scornful, Reynolds said, "There's only a couple of blogs that count in this town. He's not on either one of them."

"Political blogs," Jake guessed.

With some condescension, Reynolds said, "You can get on all the techie geek blogs you want. Doesn't make any difference. Nobody important follows them. If you want to make an impact you've got to get onto the political blogs, like *Power Talk*."

"How do we do that?"

"By going to the right parties and schmoozing with the right people."

"Do you know who they are?"

"Does the pope poop in the Vatican? Sure I know. I'm working on them even as we speak."

Jake felt his brow furrow. How can he be working on the political blogs while he's in here talking with me?

Reynolds saw his disbelief. Raising a finger, he said, "Be not afraid, O ye of little faith. The wheels are turning."

Jake managed to reply, "Good."

# Political Roundtable

Riding in the limousine with Senator Tomlinson and Earl Reynolds, Jake wondered aloud, "Where is this TV studio?"

"Out here in the boonies," Reynolds replied. "Cheaper rent."

They had left the District of Columbia and were driving past the campuslike greenery of the National Institutes of Health headquarters, in Bethesda.

"I thought WETA was located in town."

"The station is," Reynolds explained, "but the outfit that produces *Political Roundtable* is out here. They sell their shows to PBS, who broadcasts them on public TV stations all over the country."

Tomlinson, sitting between Jake and Reynolds with his long legs stretched out comfortably, said, "It's a long way to go for an hour of airtime."

"An hour on just about every PBS station in the States," Reynolds said. "Including Alaska and Hawaii."

They passed a local police car, parked beneath a NO LEFT TURN sign.

Reynolds called to the driver, "Watch your speed. They love to give tickets here."

They pulled up at last to a decrepit-looking single-story cinderblock building. The faded sign at the front door proclaimed OSTERMAN BROADCASTING COMPANY. Below that, in smaller letters, HOME OF *POLITICAL ROUNDTABLE*.

Inside, a young Levis-clad assistant producer led them into the building's one studio: fake bookcases, three aged-looking TV cameras, a long sofa, and several comfortable armchairs. Three other men and one woman were already there, the men in dark suits, the woman in a chic blouse and skirt.

Their host came smiling up to the senator. He was small, spare, dapper in a navy blue blazer and lilac necktie. His thinning hair was starting to turn silver, but his voice was deep and strong.

"Senator Tomlinson, so gracious of you to join us for today's discussion."

Tomlinson gave him a full-wattage smile. "Nice of you to invite me, Mr. Osterman."

"Call me Nate," Osterman said as he guided Tomlinson and the others onto the set.

The young assistant producer showed Jake and Reynolds to folding metal chairs off to one side of the set as teams of youthful men and women began pushing their cameras into position.

Osterman quickly introduced his five guests to each other and directed each of them to a seat. Tomlinson was assigned to one end of the sofa, next to the middle-aged woman, who looked slim and beautiful enough to have been a model.

The crew bustled around for a few minutes. The overhead lights came on, strong enough for Jake to feel their heat, and the floor director began his countdown.

"Five . . . four . . . three . . ."

The director pointed at Osterman, who smiled into the nearest camera and said, "Welcome once again to *Political Roundtable*." He drew a quick breath, then, "Fracking. What is it, and why is it important? To discuss these questions, we have with us . . ." He introduced his guests.

The woman seated next to Tomlinson turned out to

be a volunteer with an environmental group from Pennsylvania. The other three—all in three-piece suits—were from the petroleum industry, the coal industry, and the Pennsylvania Chamber of Commerce.

Osterman spent the first few minutes establishing that fracking essentially consisted of drilling deep into deposits of natural gas and pumping high-pressure water and chemicals into the rock, to fracture it and make it easier to get the gas to flow up to the surface.

"This technology is revolutionizing our energy picture," said the oil lobbyist. "Thanks to fracking, the United States is now leading the world in natural gas production."

Before Osterman could say anything, the chamber of commerce man jumped in. "Thanks to fracking, electric utilities are switching from coal to natural gas, which has reduced the nation's emissions of carbon dioxide by nearly twenty percent!"

"Doesn't this hurt the coal industry?" Osterman asked.

The coal man nodded dourly. "It's knocking the bottom out of coal prices and throwing lots of people out of work."

Osterman nodded sympathetically and turned to Tomlinson. "But I understand that Senator Tomlinson's energy plan includes new technology that can make coal competitive again."

Tomlinson took the cue. "Yes, Nate, it does. MHD power generation will allow us to burn coal cleanly and more efficiently . . ."

And on they went. The environmentalist claimed that fracking contaminates groundwater.

The oil lobbyist countered, "There's no convincing evidence of that."

"In my hometown in Pennsylvania," the environmentalist insisted, "people have gotten sick from contaminated water. And productive farmlands have been torn up and turned into wastelands! Moonscapes!"

Osterman turned to Tomlinson again. "Senator, has your plan considered the environmental damage that fracking might cause?"

Looking quite serious, Tomlinson answered, "We have. There's some fear of groundwater contamination, but studies by the Environmental Protection Agency and other groups have shown no serious problems. So far."

Obviously distressed, the environmentalist said, "Instead of tearing up the landscape and poisoning our water, we should be moving to solar energy. It's clean and abundant and—"

"Oh, come on, now!" snapped the chamber of commerce man. "Solar energy will never be more than a niche product. It's for well-to-do people who can afford to make themselves feel good."

"That's not so."

The oil man chimed in, "Germany went in for solar in a big way, until they realized how expensive it is. The European Union, too. Now they're rolling back their government subsidies for solar."

"And turning back to coal," said the coal man.

"But solar—"

Osterman cut off the environmentalist by turning to Tomlinson. "Senator, what's your take on all this?"

Smiling handsomely, Tomlinson said, "My energy plan utilizes solar, coal, fracking—every energy source we have available. I don't see our energy future as a competition among different energy sources, there's room for all of them. We need them all."

The environmentalist looked unhappy, the oil guy pleased, and the coal man just shook his head.

The chamber of commerce man said happily, "Fracking is revitalizing whole communities in Pennsylvania and other states. It's a godsend."

Jake thought that fracking was here to stay, no matter what environmental damage it might cause. It was reducing $CO_2$ emissions, was cheaper than coal, and was making the US the world leader in energy production.

The trick, Jake realized, was to set it in place alongside the other, competing energy systems. That was what his plan would do—if it got through Santino's energy committee.

# Senate Dining Room

The following morning, it was Senator Tomlinson who dropped into Jake's office. In shirtsleeves rolled up to his elbows, the senator stood before Jake's desk, between the two visitors' chairs. His suspenders were patterned like a rattlesnake's skin.

Without preamble, he announced, "Santino wants to have lunch with me."

Jake blinked with surprise. "He does?"

"Today. In the Senate dining room."

"Good . . . I guess."

"High noon."

A shootout? Jake wondered. But he said nothing.

"Wear a tie," Tomlinson said, as he turned toward the door.

"You want me to go with you?"

With a smile that looked almost grim, Tomlinson said, "He wants to talk about your plan."

Jake nodded. My plan, he thought. That's not good. If things were going well, he'd call it his plan.

• • •

The Senate dining room had barely half a dozen tables filled at high noon. It was a quiet, genteel place that spoke of understated power. Crisp white tablecloths. Gleaming silverware embossed with the seal of the United States Senate. Sparkling glassware. Waiters and busboys in spotless dark suits.

The maître d' was an elderly black gentleman who had the air of a world-weary eyewitness to history. With a discreet whisper he asked Jake and the senator to follow him to Senator Santino's table. It was in a quiet corner of the handsomely decorated room. And empty.

As they approached the table, the maître d' said softly, "Senator Santino sent word that he's been unavoidably detained. He said that I should seat you, and that he'll be here shortly."

Jake sat to Tomlinson's left. As the maître d' left their table, the senator muttered, "Santino's playing power games."

"He wants us to stew in our own juices for a while," Jake said.

Smiling sardonically, Tomlinson said, "Well, we can find better juices than that." And he beckoned to a waiter standing at attention a few feet from their table, by the window. "Let's see the wine list, please."

Santino showed up as the wine steward was pouring chardonnay for the two of them. Tomlinson and Jake both got to their feet. The Little Saint was accompanied by a short, blocky-looking dark-haired man in an ill-fitting dark blue suit. His round face looked misaligned, as if the two halves of it had been pounded out of kilter. He can't be one of Santino's staff people, Jake thought.

"I'd like you to meet Mr. Jacobi," said Santino, in his soft voice. To Jacobi, he said, "This is Senator Tomlinson and Mr.—no, it's Doctor, isn't it? Dr. Ross."

"Pleased to meetchya," said Jacobi.

They all shook hands, then sat down. Jacobi looked out of place, uncomfortable. When Tomlinson offered them some wine, Santino demurred and Jacobi said, "I'd rather have a beer."

"Mr. Jacobi grew up in my old neighborhood," Santino

said, as their waiter went for the beer, "back in Providence's Little Italy. I knew his father quite well. He was a good friend for many years. As is his son."

Jacobi actually bowed his head, as if embarrassed.

Jake thought of Monster, his friend since grammar school, who was no stranger to violence. Monster was serving time for attempted murder, among other crimes. Jacobi was much smaller, but his arms and torso seemed too thick for the suit jacket he was wearing.

The waiter brought them the beer and menus. The Little Saint said to Tomlinson, "Order the bean soup. This is the only place you can get it."

Tomlinson rarely ate anything heavier than a salad at lunch, but he dutifully ordered the bean soup. Jake asked for the roast beef sandwich, knowing he was going to eat dinner at home, by himself.

Santino kept talking amiably about committee business, and even volunteered that the full Senate would soon be facing a vote on the president's nominee for the Supreme Court.

"I believe the president should be able to have the people she wants in her Cabinet," said the Little Saint, "but a Supreme Court Justice serves for life, far beyond a president's term. We have to be very careful with this nomination."

Tomlinson nodded as he ladled up some soup.

Jake kept silent, and he noticed that Jacobi did the same. But every time he glanced up at Jacobi, the man's narrow dark eyes were on him. Jake found it unnerving.

At last, Santino said, in his mild, almost bland voice, "Your energy plan seems to have leaked to the news media, Frank."

Keeping a perfectly blank face, Tomlinson replied, "Yes, it has. We're trying to track down whoever leaked it."

"Of course you are." Turning to Jacobi, the Little

Saint suggested, "Mr. Jacobi, here, could be very helpful to you. He knows how to plug leaks."

Tomlinson made an accommodating smile, but said, "Thanks very much, but I'd prefer to keep this within my own office. If you don't mind."

"Oh, I don't mind at all," said Santino. Then he added, "As long as you find who did the leaking and take appropriate steps about it."

"I appreciate that," Tomlinson said.

Jacobi maintained his silence, but Jake couldn't help feeling that the man was glaring at him accusingly.

With a gentle smile, Santino said to Tomlinson, "I understand you'll be on *Face the Nation* next Sunday."

"Yes, they called right after the plan was leaked."

"I see."

"I couldn't refuse them," Tomlinson explained. "That might look like a cover-up."

"Of course."

After a moment's hesitation, Tomlinson admitted, "*Sixty Minutes* seems interested, too."

"Do they?" Santino glanced at Jacobi. "I didn't know that."

With an earnest expression, Tomlinson said, "I know the plan hasn't even been seen by the rest of the committee yet. If you think it's inappropriate for me to do *Sixty Minutes*, I'll turn them down."

"Oh no, no, not at all," Santino said. "As you said, the last thing we want to do is give the impression we're trying to cover up something."

"I agree," said Tomlinson. And he returned his attention to his bowl of soup.

Santino, though, turned his eyes toward Jake. "It must be gratifying to have your plan receive so much publicity, even before the energy committee has had a chance to review it."

Swallowing hard on a bite of roast beef, Jake managed to choke out, "It's all very strange to me."

"Very strange," said the Little Saint. "Yes."

Jacobi echoed, "Yeah. Real strange."

# Face the Nation

Walking back to the Hart Building, Tomlinson told Jake, "We've got to track down this man Jacobi, find out who he is."

Jake agreed. "Looks like a hood to me."

"Maybe."

They walked slowly through the muggy September afternoon, peeling off their jackets and loosening their neckties. Autumn had begun a week ago, schools were back in session, but the weather was still as hot and sultry as midsummer. The avenue was not crowded, only a few other people strolling along.

Jake said, "He knows we leaked the plan."

"Well, of course," said the senator. "It had to be someone in my office, wouldn't it?"

"No. I mean he knows it was you and me."

"I didn't leak anything," Tomlinson said.

Jake nodded, but he thought, You didn't leak it. You didn't even expressly tell me to leak it. But you didn't tell me *not* to leak it, either.

As they entered the blessedly air-conditioned Hart Building's lobby, the senator said, "Don't lose your cool, Jake. This is all going to work out well, you'll see."

"Sure," said Jake. Then he added, "We ought to prep you for your *Face the Nation* appearance."

Shaking his head, Tomlinson said, "Don't try to stuff me full of details, Jake. All I have to tell them is that my plan will make us energy-independent, create thousands of new jobs, and even balance our international trade."

So now it's your plan, Jake said to himself.

"But find out who this Jacobi guy is, will you? I don't like the looks of him."

Jake nodded obediently. Now I'm supposed to be a private investigator.

• • •

Finding who Jacobi was turned out to be far easier than Jake had feared. A bit of surfing through the Internet and Umberto Jacobi's name popped up on the Rhode Island Better Business Bureau's Web site. The man ran the biggest coal distribution firm in New England, a business that his great-grandfather had started during the depth of the Great Depression, selling five-pound bags of coal to his neighbors for a dollar a bag.

There was Jacobi's picture, looking uncomfortable in a tuxedo, standing next to Santino at some political dinner in Providence.

Probing deeper, Jake found that Jacobi was a major financial backer of Santino's, and had been since the Little Saint had first run for the state legislature, nearly half a century earlier.

Studying all the information he could pull up on Jacobi, Jake wondered why Santino had suggested the man was good at plugging leaks. As far as the Internet was concerned, Bert Jacobi was a successful businessman, a philanthropist who donated generously to many Catholic charities, and a political ally of Senator Mario Santino. Nothing more. Nothing sinister.

Leaning back in his desk chair, Jake mused, The political machine in Rhode Island has always had shadowy connections with organized crime. Is Jacobi

Mob-related? There's no mention of a police record, but that doesn't mean much. Remembering his own childhood neighborhood, Jake knew that the top Mob people were seldom connected to anything that could be proven in court. Witnesses had a way of recanting, or disappearing, or being found dead on lonely highways.

Good at plugging leaks. Jake suppressed an uneasy shudder of fear. Jacobi had to be poking into who leaked the energy plan. Either he himself or somebody he had hired.

Damn!

• • •

Over the next several days Tomlinson became strangely evasive, hard to see or talk to in private. His personal secretary guarded access to the senator with a fierce loyalty. It's as if I've come down with some disease and he doesn't want to catch it, Jake thought. The prep sessions for his television appearance were run by Kevin O'Donnell and Earl Reynolds, the PR guy. Jake attended them, but every time he tried to add something to the briefing Reynolds would sing out, "Technobabble! Technobabble!"

"But that's what the plan's about," Jake objected. "New technology."

"No," said O'Donnell firmly. "It's about jobs and the economy."

The senator sat through it all, relaxed in his shirt-sleeves, smiling genially.

It wasn't until the Sunday he was scheduled to appear on *Face the Nation* that Jake finally got to talk to Tomlinson one-on-one.

Jake got up early that morning and drove through the quiet streets downtown to the CBS News building. He was shown to the green room, which was empty.

"You're the first one here," said the young man who

escorted him. Pointing to the coffee urn and tray of pastries, he added, "Make yourself comfortable."

As Jake was pouring himself a mug of coffee, Tomlinson breezed in, accompanied by Amy and Earl Reynolds.

"Jake!" Tomlinson said heartily. "Early, as usual."

Amy looked perky and smiling, as usual. She wore a light-blue skirted suit with a single yellow rose pinned to its lapel. When she extended her hand to Jake, he took it and mumbled hello to her.

Reynolds went straight to the coffee urn, asking over his shoulder, "Anybody for java?"

"I'd like a cup, please," said Amy. "With cream, no sweetener."

Standing next to Tomlinson and his wife as Reynolds worked the urn, Jake said, "I found out who Jacobi is."

The senator's brows rose. "Oh? Who is he?"

"Businessman. Coal business. Big political contributor to Santino for years."

"The money behind Santino?"

Jake nodded. "He might be a pipeline for Mob money going to Santino."

Tomlinson pursed his lips. "That's a big jump, Jake. Do you have anything to back it up?"

"Just a gut feeling."

With a grin, the senator said, "Not every Italian is in the Mafia, Jake."

"Yeah, I know. The Mafia's all a myth anyway, right?"

Looking doubtful, Tomlinson said, "Maybe."

•  •  •

The senator came across beautifully during his interview. Looking young, handsome, vigorous, he beamed his best smile at the smoothly coiffed blond woman interviewing him and painted an enchanting picture of an energy-independent America, where new technologies brought new wealth and power to the nation, while reversing the environmental damage caused by earlier energy systems.

"You make it sound wonderful," said the interviewer, with a plastic smile.

"It can be wonderful," Tomlinson enthused. "If we use our technical knowledge and our political wisdom, we can make America clean and green, and still generate more energy than we do today. We can become an exporter of new energy technologies and help to make the whole world cleaner and greener."

Nodding thoughtfully, the woman asked, "So where does your plan stand at present?"

"I've just presented it to Senator Santino—"

"He's the chairman of the Senate Energy Committee, isn't he?"

"That's right, Adrienne. Senator Santino is the key man in this. He's the one who will arrange the hearings and studies we need to get this plan onto the floor of the Senate and eventually to the president's desk."

Her brows knitting slightly, the interviewer said, "It all sounds almost too good to be true."

Tomlinson gave her his brightest smile. "So did automobiles, at one time. And airplanes. And space travel. And the medical advances we've seen over the past few generations. New ideas, new capabilities always sound too good to be true, at first. But once we give them a chance to work, they make our lives better, richer, healthier."

She puffed out a little sigh. "I hope you're right, Senator."

Looking straight into the camera, Tomlinson grinned boyishly and said, "Trust the future. We have a great future ahead of us."

The director ran a finger across his throat and said, "Okay, we're out."

Tomlinson got to his feet as one of the camera crew, a teenaged woman with an awed expression on her face, came over to unclip the microphone from the senator's lapel.

The interviewer rose and stretched, catlike. With a cynical smile she asked Tomlinson, "Is any of that true?"

"Every blessed word," he replied. But Jake saw that, behind his back, the senator had crossed his fingers.

# Viral

The plan went viral. Or rather, Tomlinson's telegenic appearance went viral. Every TV station in town wanted to interview him. So did all the major news networks.

Reynolds began asking Jake to take some of the requests. "Our boy's more popular than Elvis," he gushed excitedly.

With some reluctance, Jake agreed to let himself be interviewed on local stations. And immediately called Tami Umetzu, happy for the excuse.

Over dinner at a Vietnamese restaurant in her Dupont Circle neighborhood, Tami told him, "On TV, what you say isn't as important as the way you say it. You've got to smile and come across as sincere and likeable."

"Sincere and likeable," Jake echoed.

"That's right," she said, nodding enthusiastically. "Just be yourself."

She thinks I'm sincere and likeable! Jake realized.

"And smile just the way you're smiling now," she said, with a warm smile of her own.

Reaching across the table to clasp her hand, Jake said, "I'll try." When she didn't pull her hand away, he added, "It'd be a big help if you came to the studio with me. Then I'd have somebody to smile at."

"Okay," Tami replied. "I'll be your audience."

• • •

For the first time in his life, Jake became something of a celebrity. Not a very big celebrity, just a local guy appearing on a couple of local TV news shows. He found he enjoyed it.

I'm more than thirty-five years old, he said to himself, and I find out I'm a ham! He marveled at it. He told himself he was doing something important, spreading the word that American technological know-how could bring new prosperity to the nation while helping to clean up the environment.

Sure, he thought. But the kick is sitting there in front of the cameras while the interviewer asks you questions and you tell them what you think, tell them about *your* plan, *your* ideas, *your* hopes.

After the third interview wrapped up, Jake and Tami went out onto the street and looked for a taxi. It was nearly midnight, cool and cloudy, threatening rain. Jake was glad he'd worn a sweater under his sports coat; Tami was in a red leather hip-length coat, with a heavy-looking tote bag slung over one shoulder.

The traffic on the street was desultory; the TV studio was not located in the best part of town.

"Let's walk up the avenue," Jake suggested. "Better chance to flag a taxi there."

"You were great, Jake," she said, as they started walking.

"Thanks to you," Jake replied, as he kept his eyes peeled for potential muggers. "I couldn't have done it without you, Tami."

"Sure you could have."

He spotted a taxi cruising in their direction and waved it down. Once they were settled inside, the driver asked, "Where to, kids?"

Jake glanced at Tami, her face in the shadows, and heard himself give the driver his own address.

Then he turned to Tami and kissed her. She kissed him back, quite tenderly.

Once they reached Jake's apartment, it turned out that Tami's capacious tote bag was carrying a nightgown, a pair of slippers, a battery-operated toothbrush, and a package of condoms.

# Christmas Eve

Halloween, Thanksgiving . . . now Christmas was approaching. The flurry of publicity about the energy plan died down, although Senator Tomlinson became a frequent guest on television news shows and—more important—in the Beltway insiders' social whirl. He smiled his way through cocktail parties and elaborate dinners, always with his wife at his side. He participated in TV panel discussions about energy and the environment. He was making a name for himself as an expert on energy policy—among the local news media, if not in the Senate.

The energy plan remained stalled in the Senate energy committee. As Steve Brogan had warned Jake at the outset, Senator Santino was quietly smothering the plan, waiting for the publicity to fade away before pigeonholing it forever.

"There must be some way to break the plan loose," Jake said, at the regular Monday morning meeting of the senator's senior staff.

Tomlinson sat at the head of the table, as usual, looking unhappy, troubled—an expression he never showed in public.

Jake realized that, of the eight people around the conference room table, he was the only one from back in Montana. The rest were all Washingtonians, either by birth or by career choice.

Kevin O'Donnell, sitting at the senator's right, shook

his head slowly. The expression on the staff chief's narrow, bony face was almost sorrowful.

"The plan is in Santino's hands. He can sit on it, he can crap on it if he wants to. There's nothing we can do about it."

"You mean he can kill it," Jake said.

"If he wants to." Turning to the senator, O'Donnell advised, "And no matter what he does, your best course of action is to smile and take it. Show the Little Saint that you're a good soldier and you can follow orders."

Tomlinson sat stonily silent.

"Listen, Senator," said the chief, "if you want to get along in this town, you've got to go along with the power flow. You can't force Santino to push your plan. If you try to, he'll freeze you out completely. You'll be a one-term senator."

Jake wanted to object, he wanted to yell, but one look at Tomlinson's face made him clamp his mouth shut. It was clear that the senator didn't like what he was hearing, but he was swallowing it.

Reynolds tried to lighten the mood. "You're a big hit on the news shows. If you leave the Senate you could find a spot as a TV news analyst."

Jake wanted to puke.

The next day was Christmas Eve. In the middle of the afternoon, while most of the staff were pulling on winter coats and heading for home or last-minute shopping, Jake got up from his desk and strolled through the suite, toward Tomlinson's private office. He saw that O'Donnell's office was empty. Good, he thought. Now, if the chief's really gone and not in with the senator, maybe I can talk honestly with Frank.

The secretary's desk in front of Tomlinson's door was vacant, as well. The office door was slightly ajar, but Jake could not hear any voices coming through.

He's alone, Jake thought. Good.

He rapped on the door once, then stuck his head through. "Got a minute?"

Tomlinson was sitting behind his desk, a tumbler of whiskey in one hand, his face somber.

He smiled wearily. "Hi, Jake. Come on in. I was just going to phone Amy, tell her I'd be home in a few minutes. We're going to a big dinner that the senior senator from Virginia is throwing."

Jake sat tensely on one of the trio of comfortable leather chairs in front of the desk.

"We've got to do something about the energy plan," he said earnestly. "We can't let Santino kill it."

Tomlinson shrugged carelessly. "Jake, the energy plan isn't the only thing I'm trying to do here."

"I know. But it's the most important thing."

"Santino doesn't think so."

"And you have to follow his lead, like a good junior senator."

"Looks that way."

Jake puffed out a breath. "It just isn't right."

"Maybe next year."

"No, not next year. Or the year after that. Santino's in the fossil fuel lobby's pocket. He'll never let the plan see the light of day."

Tomlinson took a gulp of his whiskey, then put the glass down on his desk. "Jake, do you know the Chinese advice to a woman who's about to be raped?"

Jake felt his face twist into a frown. "Relax and enjoy it," he answered. "Don't let any women hear you tell that one."

"Yeah, well, I'm getting screwed by Santino and there's nothing I can do about it. So I might as well relax and enjoy it."

"I thought leaking the plan would help," Jake muttered.

"It didn't. It just made Santino sore at me. He won't

even let me onto the coal subcommittee. I'm on his shit list."

Jake realized he was gnawing on a fingernail. Snatching his hand away, he repeated, "There ought to be something we can do about it."

"Like what?" Tomlinson challenged.

"There's got to be some chink in Santino's armor, some flaw . . ."

Tomlinson smiled sardonically. "Jake, the Little Saint's been in this town for more than a quarter century. If there was a flaw in his background, don't you think somebody would have found it by now?"

"Maybe somebody has," Jake said.

"Huh?"

Jake asked, "Why is Santino in the fossil fuel lobby's pocket?"

"Because that's where the power is," Tomlinson replied.

"Maybe. Or maybe they know something about him that nobody else knows. Something from far back in his past, maybe."

The senator got up from his desk and reached for his suit jacket, draped on the back of his chair. "Jake, you're grasping at straws."

"Maybe," Jake said. "But if anybody knows the dirt under Santino's fingernails, it'd be Jacobi."

Tomlinson's eyes widened. "Jacobi? You stay away from him. He could be big trouble."

"Yeah. Guess so," Jake said.

"I've got to go," said the senator.

Nodding, Jake said, "Have a good time."

Then he remembered he had a party to go to as well. With Tami. Just the two of them.

# The Lion's Den

Jake spent Christmas with Tami, who seemed thrilled with the opal pinkie ring he had bought her, and even more delighted that Jake was surprised by her gift to him: a DVD package of the entire set of PBS's *Nova* series on cosmology.

She had insisted on making Christmas dinner for him, and Jake had dutifully gone out and bought a small turkey and a pumpkin pie. Tami took care of everything else, and their quiet dinner together was the happiest Christmas Jake had enjoyed since his wife had died.

• • •

That night, though, as they lay together in bed, Jake's mind turned once again to Jacobi.

"He's the key to it all," Jake said. He knew he was trying to convince himself, and he knew it was working.

Lying beside him in Jake's folded-out futon, Tami asked drowsily, "He? Who?"

Jake turned to her. In the darkened room he could barely make out the profile of her face against the pale glow of the nightlight by the bedroom doorway.

"Jacobi," Jake said.

Tami asked, "Bert Jacobi?"

"You know him?"

"I've heard of him. Back when I was working for Reuter's."

"He's an old friend of Senator Santino's," Jake said.

"Childhood pals. If anybody knows some dirt about Santino, Jacobi's the one."

"You think so?"

"Yes. But how do I get him to tell me anything useful?"

Tami was wide-awake now. With a giggle, she said, "I could try my womanly wiles on him."

Jake reached across and pulled her to him. "Oh no you don't. Your womanly wiles belong to me."

"Belong?"

"Well . . . sort of."

She did not reply.

"Tami, this is serious. I've got to figure out how I can get Jacobi to talk to me."

"Why don't you tell him that you need some leverage with Santino, so would he please tell you something about the senator's sordid past."

Jake frowned. "Very funny."

"Go to sleep," she said, starting to turn over.

But Jake grabbed her bare hip, beneath the covers. "Not yet," he said.

Even in the shadows of the night he saw her smile. "It's womanly wiles time, isn't it?"

"Uh-huh."

Nearly an hour later, Tami had slipped into sleep, but Jake lay on his back, staring at the darkened ceiling. And he knew what he was going to do. It was all there, in his mind.

Funny how sexual intercourse clears away all the barriers in your brain, he thought. Lovemaking is good for your intelligence.

• • •

The next morning Jake looked up local electronics shops on his notebook computer while Tami fried eggs and perked coffee. On his way to the office, he detoured to a shop that advertised on the Internet that it specialized in state-of-the-art digital equipment.

"Audio recorder?" asked the clerk at Bits and Bytes Electronics. He was young enough to still have traces of acne marring his otherwise cheerful face.

He showed Jake an assortment of miniaturized recording devices.

"Completely digital," he said, holding up one that was no bigger than a cuff link. "Not like the old days, when you needed a separate battery pack and you had to run a wire under your shirt. You can carry this baby in your pocket, no sweat."

Jake picked the one that looked like a ballpoint pen.

"Neat choice," said the kid. "The DC narco squad uses these. All complete in this one unit. You can even write with it, if you have to."

"Great," said Jake.

"You've got to be close to the person you want to record, though; no more than five, six feet away."

"That'll be fine," Jake said, reaching into his back pocket for his wallet full of credit cards.

By the time Jake arrived at his office, he had clipped the recorder in his shirt pocket. He tried it on several of the staff secretaries, clicking the tiny device on as he engaged them in conversation. When he listened to the digital recording, behind the closed door of his office, their voices came through quite clearly.

Satisfied, Jake said to himself, Now to get into a one-on-one with Jacobi.

• • •

Once he got to his office Jake put in a phone call to Bert Jacobi, at the headquarters of Jacobi & Sons Coal Co. in Providence, Rhode Island. A woman who sounded middle-aged told him that Mr. Jacobi was out of the office, but she would pass on his message as soon as he showed up.

Jacobi called late in the afternoon. "You wanna talk to me?" He sounded curious, almost suspicious.

"Yes," said Jake.

"What about?"

"I'm going to be in Boston for a few days," Jake lied, "and I thought I'd drop in on you. Senator Santino said you were good at plugging leaks. I'd like to talk to you about that."

"I'm goin' out to Cleveland tamorra. Be back Thursday."

"Okay," said Jake. "Thursday would be good."

"See ya then, in my office."

"Fine. Thank you."

"Eleven a.m."

"Eleven. I'll be there."

Feeling that he was heading into the lion's den, Jake flew to Boston early Thursday morning, then drove a rented Kia Optima to Providence.

The car's GPS led him to a seedy part of town filled with warehouses and automobile dealerships. Bars on just about every street corner. The streets looked as though they hadn't been swept in months; trash blew along on the wind coming in from the nearby sea.

Jake remembered the run-down neighborhood where he'd grown up. It wasn't as bad as this, he thought. But then his neighborhood was mostly row houses, blue collar residential. Not this industrial slum.

Jacobi & Sons Coal Co. looked better than most of the buildings in the area. Its front appeared to have been recently painted; the big plate-glass windows were clean, the parking lot nearly filled with decent-looking cars. Jake parked in the visitors' area and pushed through the glass doors into a modern reception lobby.

The receptionist called Jacobi, and within a few seconds a dowdy gray-haired woman came through the door that led deeper into the building.

"Dr. Ross? Follow me, please." Jake recognized the voice as the woman he had spoken to on the phone a few days earlier. He clicked on the power switch of the recorder he wore clipped into his shirt pocket as he followed the woman down a quiet corridor toward the rear of the building.

Jacobi's office was on the small side, furnished with old-fashioned bookcases and photos on the walls of big sturdy coal trucks and family elders smiling stiffly into the camera.

Without getting up from his high-backed desk chair, Jacobi said, "Come on in. Siddown."

# Umberto Jacobi

oping his digital recorder was working properly, Jake went to one of the wooden chairs in front of Jacobi's heavy dark desk and sat down.

"What's this all about, kid?"

Jake felt a tic of anger at being called "kid," but he replied evenly, "As I told you on the phone, I want to talk to you about plugging the leak in Senator Tomlinson's office."

Jacobi's oddly mismatched face twisted into a cynical smile.

"Come on," he said, "we both know you did the leakin'. What're you really here for?"

Without bothering to deny the accusation Jake said, "I want to understand why Senator Santino is holding up our energy plan."

"Whyn'tcha ask him?"

"Because he wouldn't give me a straight answer."

"And you think I will?"

Leaning forward, doing his best to appear earnest, Jake said, "You're not a politician, you're a businessman. I thought we could talk honestly to each other."

"Yeah?"

"Yeah."

"Why should I?"

"Because I want to work with Santino, not against him. I don't know why he's bottling up our energy plan."

Jacobi leaned back in his chair, which creaked slightly,

and said nothing. His hands gripping the arms of his chair, he stared at Jake, as if trying to size him up.

Breaking the silence, Jake said, "This energy plan could be a big feather in Santino's cap. He could be seen as a leader of the Senate, of his whole party."

"Elections comin' up next November," Jacobi muttered.

"The energy plan could be a major campaign issue."

As if he hadn't heard that, Jacobi went on, "They already put out feelers about Mario bein' on the ticket."

"Really?"

"Vice president. I told him to turn 'em down. He's got more power as a senator."

"But it's quite an honor," Jake said.

With a disgusted sneer, Jacobi said, "Honor ain't where it's at, kid. Power. That's what it's all about."

Eagerly, Jake said, "The energy plan could make the senator a powerful figure."

"*Your* senator, maybe. Not mine."

"But if he gets behind the plan, if he moves it through the energy committee and out onto the floor of the Senate, Santino will become a real leader."

Shaking his head, Jacobi said, "Forget it, kid. It ain't gonna happen."

"But why?"

Looking mildly disgusted, Jacobi ticked off on his stubby fingers, "One: Mario's already a powerful guy in the Senate. He don't need your plan."

"But—"

"Two: Nobody wants your goddamn energy plan. We like things the way they are."

"Who's 'we'?"

A crooked grin broke across Jacobi's face. "Me, that's who. And AEP, out in Ohio. And the whole fuckin' automobile industry. And the petroleum industry. Ya need any more?"

"They'd be against a rational energy plan for the nation?" Jake prompted.

"We got a rational energy plan," Jacobi snapped. "It works fine. We don't need no do-gooders pumping money into solar and wind power and electric cars and all that crap."

"But the environment, what about that?"

Waving a meaty hand, Jacobi said, "Aah, you greenies give me a pain in the butt. What's wrong with the environment?"

"All the carbon dioxide we pump into the atmosphere from burning fossil fuels," Jake said. "It's heating up the world's climate."

"So you wanna saddle us with building equipment that'll take our smokestack gases and stick 'em in the ground someplace? Get real!"

"But the government will help pay for that."

"Yeah, sure. And you expect us to foot the rest of the bill. Bullshit! Bad enough they're tryin' to tighten up the rules on carbon emissions from coal-fired power plants."

Jake sagged back in his chair. Jacobi glared at him, like a bulldog growling, snarling.

At last Jake said, "At least the MHD power generation technology uses coal. You don't have any objection to that, do you?"

"Who's gonna foot the bill for building your fancy new electric power plants?"

"There'll be federal subsidies."

"Yah. Sure." Jacobi shook his head impatiently. "You just don't get it, do you, kid? Your fancy pie-in-the-sky energy plan ain't goin' noplace."

Before Jake could think of anything more to say,

Jacobi raised three stubby fingers. "An' I'll give you the third reason why it ain't. Because it'd make your guy Tomlinson a hero, that's why. Santino don't want that. Not for a minute. *Capisce?*"

I understand, Jake replied silently.

"Mario's worked too hard for too long to let some good-lookin' young twerp from out west take the spotlight off him. Tomlinson's goin' nowhere until he learns to behave himself."

"You mean that Santino wants to stifle the energy plan because he sees it as a threat to his position in the Senate."

"Somethin' like that, yeah."

Trying to make himself sound properly humbled, Jake asked, "So what should I tell Tomlinson when I get back to Washington?"

"You tell him to follow his leader. Tell him that Santino is the chairman of the energy committee, and he ain't gonna let any wet-behind-the-ears newcomer steal the power from him."

Jake said nothing.

Jacobi added, "And he better cancel that thing he's supposed to be doin' on *Sixty Minutes*."

"He can't cancel that! They're due to start filming it next week."

"Scrub it."

"But that would make the CBS people suspicious, they'd think he's trying to hide something from them."

Jacobi frowned with thought for a moment, then said, "Yeah, maybe. Okay, tell him to go easy about his fuckin' energy plan. Tell him to tell them it still needs a lotta work and the energy committee's gonna be workin' on it real hard."

Jake sat in silence for several moments, thinking, I didn't get what I came for, but maybe this is better. Hope the recorder got it all.

Slowly, he got up from his chair.

"I guess I've taken up enough of your time," he said.

As he turned to leave, Jacobi said, "Oh yeah, one more thing. You tell Tomlinson to fire whoever leaked your energy plan to the news media."

"Fire him?" Jake gulped.

"Yeah. As a peace offering to Santino."

"Fire him," Jake repeated.

"That's right. Good luck findin' another job, kid."

Jacobi broke into peals of laughter as Jake made his way out of the office.

# Strategy

Tomlinson and Kevin O'Donnell sat in rapt silence in the senator's office as Jake played back Jacobi's blustering voice.

The audio volume from the pen recorder was weak, but they heard Jacobi's voice easily enough. At last his hearty laughter abruptly cut off and Jake picked up the recorder from the senator's desktop and slipped it back into his shirt pocket.

"Jake, this is dynamite," Tomlinson said.

O'Donnell was less enthusiastic. "It's dynamite, all right. But it could blow up in your face, Franklin."

"I don't see how. I mean, Jacobi actually came out and said that Santino's deliberately scuttling my energy plan."

Jake suppressed a smile. Now it's *your* energy plan, he said mentally to Senator Tomlinson.

"We've got to be very careful about this," O'Donnell warned, his lean face dead serious. "A junior senator can't afford to get into a public squabble with his committee chairman."

"Even when the chairman's deliberately sitting on legislation that would benefit the nation?" Tomlinson challenged.

"Franklin, don't get emotional. This isn't about your energy plan. It's about your relationship with one of the most powerful men in the Senate."

Jake asked, "What do you think Frank should do?"

O'Donnell pressed his hands together and bowed his

head, thinking. He looked almost as if he were praying. Seeking divine guidance, Jake thought.

Finally, O'Donnell lifted his head and asked, "The crew from *Sixty Minutes* will be here Monday, right?"

"Right," said Jake and Tomlinson, in unison.

"You've got to soft-pedal the energy plan."

"But that's what they're coming to hear about," Tomlinson objected.

"I know. But you speak to them in generalities. Tell them the nation needs a comprehensive energy policy, and what you've handed to the energy committee is just the beginning of a long process. The committee has to study it, polish it, refine it . . ."

"Bury it," Jake quipped.

O'Donnell shot him an angry glance. Turning back to the senator, he said, "Listen to me, Franklin. You don't want to make an enemy of Santino."

"But he's already an enemy of ours," Tomlinson said.

"That's right. But you can't fight him in public. You have to go along with him, make him understand that you're not trying to upset anybody's apple cart."

"Buckle under," Jake groused.

"For now," said O'Donnell. "You have to use your appearance on *Sixty Minutes* as a clear signal to Santino that you're willing to go along with him."

Tomlinson frowned, but asked, "And then what?"

"You get Santino to shake loose the one part of the energy plan that you need to bring back to your constituents."

"MHD power generation."

"That's right," said O'Donnell. "You let Santino have his way with the rest of the plan and he lets you have your MHD program. Quid pro quo."

Feeling exasperated, Jake protested, "While the fossil fuel industry keeps its stranglehold on the nation's energy policy."

O'Donnell turned to Jake. "That's right. We don't have the power to change that. Not yet."

A line from Patrick Henry's "Liberty or Death" speech leaped into Jake's mind: *But when shall we be stronger? Will it be the next week, or the next year?*

Seeing the expression on Jake's face, Tomlinson said as soothingly as he could, "I'm afraid Kevin is right, Jake. We can't stand up to Santino in a straight-up fight. Not yet. We have to bide our time."

Raising a finger, O'Donnell pointed out, "But you get your MHD program. You have to get something out of this. Santino will understand and go along with you."

Tomlinson nodded.

"And," the chief of staff added, "you'll have to get rid of Jake. He'll be the sacrificial lamb."

A look of alarm flashed across Tomlinson's face. Jake had been expecting that, but he'd kept telling himself that Tomlinson would protect him.

Instead, the senator turned to Jake and said softly, "I'm sorry. I didn't want it to come to this."

Jake pushed himself up from his chair. "That's okay. The energy plan is what I came to Washington to do. If you're throwing it away, I don't have any reason to stay here."

# Sixty Minutes

It was nearly Easter by the time *Sixty Minutes* aired the segment in which Senator Tomlinson appeared.

Jake had not returned to Montana. He stayed in Washington and, with Tomlinson's help, got a job as a researcher at Washington's Public Broadcasting System station, WETA-TV.

*They never leave DC*, he heard Steve Brogan's scornful voice in his mind. Jake told himself that he needed to stay close to Tomlinson, to help him when and if the senator needed him. Besides, what was there back home? Teaching at the university? Watching Rogers and Younger pushing the MHD rig in Lignite toward higher power output, longer running times?

No, he stayed in Washington, and even picked up a guest lecturer's nighttime job at Georgetown University. Moonlighting, Jake told himself. Telling working-class undergrads about the wonders of modern technology. Big thrill.

But Tami was in Washington, and Jake did not want to end their relationship. She was easy to be with, warm and pleasant and bright and happy.

Isaiah Knowles was also still in Washington, and the NASA deputy administrator scowled at Jake whenever their paths crossed. The meeting between Senator Tomlinson and NASA's top brass never happened, and Knowles was still sore at Jake for dropping space solar power from his energy plan.

Doesn't make any difference whether SSP is in the plan or out of it, Jake knew. The plan's not going anyplace.

The Sunday that Tomlinson was to appear on *Sixty Minutes*, Tami happened to be out of town, visiting her family in California. So Jake sat alone in his basement apartment, stretched out on his futon with a bottle of Gatorade—his one concession to the world of athletics—and drowsily watched a football game between the Washington Redskins and the Arizona Cardinals, waiting for *Sixty Minutes* to come on.

The NFL game ground to an end at last, and Jake roused himself from his semi-slumber, uncertain of who won the stupid game.

The interview with Tomlinson took place mostly in his walnut-paneled office in the Hart S.O.B. The senator looked handsome and relaxed as he sat in his shirtsleeves on one of his office's comfortable leather chairs, facing the CBS correspondent Daniel Manley.

Tomlinson was beaming his bright, friendly smile, looking youthful and vigorous, idealistic and energetic. Manley, one of the show's younger interviewers, wore a navy blue blazer over a lighter blue shirt and carefully knotted tie of red and yellow stripes. He looked professionally calm, intelligent, and just a bit skeptical.

"Why does the nation need a federal energy policy, Senator?"

Tomlinson launched into his standard line: use modern technology to make the best out of America's natural resources, create tens of thousands of new jobs, reduce our dependence on foreign oil, make the nation—and the world—cleaner and greener.

"And where does your plan stand right now? Will it be implemented by the government?"

Managing to keep on smiling while looking properly serious at the same time, Tomlinson replied, "The plan is being studied by the Senate energy committee. Under chairman Mario Santino, the committee will hold hearings in which the top energy experts from across the nation will be able to contribute their expertise to the plan."

"So the plan isn't set in concrete."

"Far from it," answered Tomlinson. "We have a long way to go, Dan. But it's a beginning, a place to start the process of producing a rational, comprehensive energy plan for the nation."

Manley nodded, then pursed his lips and said, "One part of the plan involves something called magneto-hydrodynamics. Did I pronounce it correctly?"

Laughing, Tomlinson said, "You did. But call it MHD, it's easier."

"This is an energy system that's being tested in your home state, isn't it?"

"That right, Dan." The screen cut to a view of the MHD rig in Lignite, with Tim Younger and a handful of technicians huddled at one end of it. Jake watched as Tomlinson pointed out the coal hopper, the rocketlike burner chamber, the channel that the hot gases flowed through, and the powerful superconducting magnet wrapped around it.

In a voice-over, Tomlinson explained that an MHD generator was more than twice as efficient as ordinary electric power generators.

"MHD could cut your electric bill in half," the senator declared happily. Then he quickly added, "Eventually."

The camera returned to Manley's slightly dubious face as the interviewer said, "I understand that MHD generators could burn the kind of high-sulfur coal that's plentiful in Montana, without allowing the sulfur to get out and pollute the atmosphere."

"Entirely correct," Tomlinson replied. "That's one of the reasons why MHD is so important."

"Because it can revive your home state's coal industry."

"Because it can allow us to use our country's own natural resources, and use them efficiently, without damaging the environment."

Manley cocked a disbelieving brow at the senator, but he went on to ask, "So what other technological innovations are in your energy plan?"

Tomlinson smiled easily and said, "There's a way to turn the greenhouse gases that electric power plants and factories produce into a clean, efficient fuel for transportation vehicles."

Playing straight man, Manley said, "Oh?"

Leaning forward slightly, his expression serious, the senator said, "It should be possible to take the carbon dioxide that we ordinarily let flow into the atmosphere and, instead of burying it underground, *use* it to produce methanol, a fuel that burns cleaner than gasoline."

"Methanol," Manley echoed. "Isn't that the fuel that race cars use?"

Jake was impressed. Manley's done his homework, he said to himself.

Nodding, Tomlinson said, "You're right again, Dan. Methanol puts out about half the carbon dioxide that ordinary gasoline does."

"But it's corrosive, isn't it? Burns out the engine?"

With a shake of his head, the senator replied, "The engines can be treated with a protective anticorrosion coating. Tests have shown it works fine."

"So you'd have the oil companies switch to producing methanol instead of gasoline."

Jake could see from Tomlinson's face that the senator realized he'd stepped into a trap.

He was silent for a moment, then put on his standard smile and answered, "Gradually, Dan. Gradually. The oil industry could shift part of its infrastructure to producing methanol and mixing it with gasoline. Just the way they now offer gasoline mixed with ethanol. In time, I imagine methanol will become a bigger and bigger part of the mix. But it's not going to happen overnight. No, this will be a process that takes years."

Jake puffed out a breath that he hadn't realized he'd been holding. Good going, Frank, he cheered silently. You got out of that one okay. I think.

With the camera focusing tightly on him, Manley said, "A few days ago we asked Senator Mario Santino, chairman of the Senate energy committee, what his committee is doing with Senator Tomlinson's comprehensive plan."

"Uh oh," Jake said aloud.

The screen showed Santino, in his office, smiling genially at Manley.

"It's an interesting plan," said the Little Saint in his soft voice. "It's the kind of plan that the nation has needed for a long time."

"Then your committee is going to bring it to the floor of the Senate?"

"In time," Santino answered. "In time. Right now we're examining the various segments of the plan. We'll be studying the part that deals with the coal industry first."

"No!" Jake yelled. "It's an integrated plan. You can't take it apart, piece by piece. That'll ruin it."

But there was Santino, patiently explaining how each segment of the plan was going to be carefully studied before his committee would make a recommendation about the full plan to the Senate.

Jake shook his head sorrowfully. "He's killing the plan," he whispered to nobody. "Killing it an inch at a time."

# Monday, Bloody Monday

The morning after Tomlinson's *Sixty Minutes* appearance, Jake was surprised to receive a phone call from the senator.

Jake was in his cubbyhole of an office at WETA, reviewing a new film on space exploration that NASA was urging the station to air. His office was barely big enough to fit a desk and a single visitor's chair, but at least it wasn't a cubicle—it had four real walls, a window that looked out onto the parking lot, and a door Jake could close, even though it gave him a shiver of claustrophobia when he shut himself in.

His desktop screen was showing computer-generated animation of astronauts landing on the frozen crust of Jupiter's moon Europa, with the brightly striped giant planet looming over them, filling half the dark sky.

His cell phone buzzed annoyingly. Jake dug in his trouser pocket for it, thinking that the phone could make a reasonably good sex toy. He saw with some surprise that his caller was Senator B. Franklin Tomlinson.

"Frank?"

"Jake, can you come over for dinner tonight?" Tomlinson's voice sounded tense, worried.

Jake couldn't help answering, "Are you sure you can take the chance of being seen with me?"

"This is serious, Jake. I need your help."

"Dinner. At your house?"

"Yes. Seven thirty."

"Seven thirty. Okay. I'll be there."

He could sense the senator nodding. Then, "Don't park on the street. Come up the driveway."

Jake almost laughed. He remembered that most of the driveway was hidden from the street by elaborate flowering bushes.

He must be in real trouble, Jake thought.

• • •

It was early twilight by seven thirty. The tree-lined street on which Tomlinson's house stood was quiet: no traffic, no cars parked along the curbs, no one walking on the sidewalks. The neighborhood looks like a scene from *The Stepford Wives*, Jake thought.

He drove up the bricked driveway and parked his old Mustang behind a lush azalea bush. As he got out of the car he thought, Maybe I should have taken a taxi; nobody would've spotted my car then.

Almost chuckling at the paranoia, he rang the doorbell and was swiftly ushered into the house by the young, dark-suited butler.

As he followed the butler down the house's central hallway, Jake noted that the pictures on the walls were now Tomlinson family photographs, together with a few original oils, mostly abstracts. Amy's choices, he knew.

Tomlinson and his wife were in the library. The senator was in his shirtsleeves, tieless, gripping a tumbler of what looked like scotch. Amy, wearing a simple knee-length dress patterned in black and white, held a stemmed wineglass in her hand.

Feeling almost shabby in his jeans and rumpled sports coat, Jake said, "Hi."

Tomlinson came to him, hand extended. "Jake, it's good of you to come."

"What would you like to drink, Jake?" Amy asked.

"Same as you," he replied.

As she went to the makeshift bar on the cart by the curtained window, Tomlinson led Jake to the sofa and sat down beside him.

"I think I put my foot in it," he said. His face looked somber.

"You mean on *Sixty Minutes*?" Jake asked. "I thought you came across very well. The papers and blogs were all favorable this morning."

"Senator Perlmutter doesn't think so."

"Perlmutter? Who's he?"

Amy said as she handed Jake his wine, "Chairman of the Senate agriculture committee."

"Agriculture?"

Tomlinson nodded. "He's pissed as hell."

"About your *Sixty Minutes* interview? What's got him so upset?"

"Ethanol."

"Ethanol? What's ethanol got to do with anything?"

Tomlinson took a long swig of his scotch before answering, "The ethanol mandate."

Jake felt his face contracting into a frown. "The ethanol mandate," he echoed.

Tomlinson explained, "For years now, Congress has mandated that gasoline manufacturers have to mix in a certain percentage of ethanol into their gasoline."

"Oh, that," Jake said.

"That," said the senator. "A big percentage of farms are producing crops for making ethanol. Corn and soybeans, mostly. The ethanol goes to the oil companies, who mix it into their gasoline."

The lightbulb clicked on in Jake's mind. "What you said about methanol."

"Right."

Amy interjected, "Frank didn't say anything about replacing ethanol."

"But Perlmutter—or somebody in his office—was

bright enough to figure out that if we move to methanol, his farmers will lose their ethanol money."

"And he's pissed about that."

"That's putting it mildly. Santino was on the phone with me for more than an hour this afternoon. Perlmutter apparently reamed him out over lunch."

"And Santino blames you."

"Who else?"

"So now you've got the farm lobby set against the energy plan," Jake said.

"What the hell are we going to do?" Tomlinson's tone was almost pleading.

Jake took a gulp of the wine, desperately trying to think of something.

"O'Donnell thinks we should just shelve the plan," Tomlinson said. "Scrap it. Too many vested interests are lined up against it."

Looking into the senator's unsmiling face, Jake asked, "What do you want to do?"

"I don't know, Jake. I came to Washington to create a sensible energy plan for the nation. But everywhere I turn, the big guys are against me."

Jake mused, "You can get the MHD part of the plan through, can't you?"

With a slight nod, Tomlinson said, "I think so. I'm not really sure, though. Not after this."

Amy said, "We need your help, Jake."

"Me? I'm the pariah here, don't you remember?"

"You're my idea man, Jake," the senator said, with some fervor. "You're the brightest person I know, and I need you to come up with a way to salvage the energy plan—or at least, the appearance of salvaging it. I'd be satisfied to let Santino bury it for the time being. But I don't want it dropped altogether. Not because some shit-kicking farmers are worried their profits might drop."

Amy corrected, "It's not shit-kicking farmers, Frank. It's the big agribusiness corporations that own the farms."

Jake sank back on the sofa, thinking, Frank's got O'Donnell and a whole staff of Washington professionals working for him, and he's asking me to pull his bacon out of the fire. After he's fired me. After he's admitted that he's willing to let my plan be buried by Santino.

I should just get up and walk away, he told himself. This isn't my fight. Not anymore. I helped Frank get elected to the Senate, and he kicks me off his staff to make Santino happy. What does he expect me to do, thank him for that? Help him, now that he's in real trouble?

Then he looked at Amy, who was staring back at him. And you, too, Mrs. B. Franklin Tomlinson. You jerked me around just as much as he has.

Slowly, Jake rose from the sofa. Turning slightly to put the wineglass on the end table, he straightened up and said softly, "Let me think about this, Frank. Maybe there's something you can do, something we haven't thought of as yet."

He winced inwardly at his use of the word *we*.

# Space Politics

Jake dreaded going to work the next morning. He was supposed to sit in on a meeting that would decide whether the station would air the space exploration film that NASA was pushing. Isaiah Knowles would be at the meeting, Jake knew, and he wasn't looking forward to the NASA man's smoldering resentment.

He had spent the night, and the following morning, trying to think of some way to assuage the wrath of Senator Perlmutter and the farm lobby. A brief computer search showed him that Perlmutter chaired the Senate Committee on Agriculture, Nutrition, and Forestry. The man's biography was standard DC hagiography: another saint of a senator. Born and raised in Nebraska. Son of a small-town banker. After two terms in the House of Representatives he won a seat in the Senate, and he had been there ever since. Jake found nothing useful there.

He wished Tami were in town, so he could talk about the problem with her. It was always helpful to bounce ideas off her; Tami was bright, intelligent, and knew more about inside Washington politics than Jake did. Well, he thought as he parked his Mustang in the WETA parking lot, she'll be coming back this evening. I'll go to the airport and surprise her.

Jake got into the office a little early; hardly anyone was there yet. He powered up the coffee machine and poured himself a mug when it dinged, then went to his desk and scanned through the day's agenda on his computer screen. There it was: ten a.m., NASA film.

Like a little boy trudging reluctantly to school, just before ten a.m. Jake went down the corridor to the conference room. Nobody else was there yet, except Knowles, sitting halfway down the table, looking as unhappy as Jake felt.

"Hello, Ike," said Jake.

"Dr. Ross," replied the former astronaut.

Sitting across the table from him, Jake said, "For what it's worth, the energy plan is as good as dead. So your SSP wouldn't have gone anywhere even if we'd kept it in the plan."

Knowles closed his eyes, like a man who'd seen too much pain and suffering in this world. At last he said, "Sorry your plan got dumped."

"Yeah. Me too."

One by one, the conference table filled up. Five men, including the station manager. Five women. PBS believed in women's equality. With wry amusement, Jake realized that there were five black people at the table, counting Knowles. PBS believed in affirmative action, too. How many Hispanics? he asked himself. No one of Asian descent, clearly.

The station manager—male, white, graying—asked if everyone had viewed the film. Nods and raised hands.

"Well?" he demanded.

The woman sitting next to Jake said, "It's sort of the same old, same old. We've aired at least four films over the past couple of years about space exploration."

Jake saw Knowles's jaw clench, but the former astronaut said nothing.

Around the table the opinions were pretty much the same: the film wasn't all that exciting.

Finally Knowles burst, "Exploring the moons of Jupiter? Finding alien life under the ice? That's not exciting?"

"It's not real," said the young man sitting next to him. "It's all animation, instead of the real stuff."

Before Knowles could reply, the station manager asked him, "Does NASA have a program to send people to Jupiter's moons—a program that exists right now?"

Knowles said, "We've done studies."

"But there's no actual program to send humans to Jupiter."

"Not yet. That's why this film is important. It can help build up popular support for having scientists explore the Jupiter system."

"So you want us to shill for you," said a middle-aged man sitting at the end of the table, smiling as he spoke the words.

Knowles did not smile back. "I want you to help us. We've got to get public support for our programs. You people have a direct line to the public."

In a slightly rueful tone, the station manager said, "Only a small part of the public, I'm afraid. Joe Six-Pack doesn't watch PBS."

"But kids do," Jake spoke up. "In the afternoons, after school. Our demographics show a strong audience there."

"You're suggesting we show this film to the kids?" asked the station manager.

Jake nodded vigorously. "Kids are interested in space. If the show does well, we can run it again in prime time for their parents."

"And grandparents," said one of the older women.

The discussion went on for another half hour, but at last the station manager said, "Okay, we schedule the film for the after-school audience in the late afternoon."

One of the programmers objected, "We have a full schedule of kids' shows every afternoon."

"We can shoehorn the film into our regular schedule. Make it a special. Give it plenty of publicity the week before we air it."

Most of the people around the table were reluctant, but they went along with the station manager's decision with no real opposition. As the meeting broke up and everyone started to leave the conference room, the station manager patted Jake's shoulder. "Good idea, man," he said as he headed for the door.

Jake stood at the table, Knowles stood opposite him.

"Thanks," said Knowles, unsmiling.

"I'm sorry I couldn't do more," Jake said.

"It's better than nothing."

As they both walked the length of the conference table, toward the door, Jake asked, "Why don't you do a film about space solar power?"

Knowles grimaced. "Tried to. Got shot down. The administrator's not interested in SSP."

"He should be."

"You're telling me?"

They reached the end of the table, a few steps from the door.

"You know," Jake said, "the trouble with NASA is that you guys come across as elitists."

"Huh?"

"The average guy sees NASA as a bunch of scientists and astronauts. What you do in space doesn't have any impact on Main Street."

Knowles stared at Jake, his expression halfway between resentment and disbelief.

"I mean," Jake went on, "if NASA could deliver electrical power from space the way you claim you can do, that's something that the average taxpayer could get excited about."

"Yeah?"

"Sure," Jake said, convincing himself. "NASA could make an impact on Main Street with cheap, clean electricity from space."

"It won't be cheap," Knowles objected.

"Okay. But it would be safe, and clean. You could place the receiving stations in the southwestern desert, to begin with. Get support from Arizona, Nevada, Utah—"

Knowles broke into a grin. "Get the Mormons behind us."

"Why not? And California, too. You could get a pretty powerful coalition of senators from those states."

"You're starting to sound like a politician."

Jake shrugged. "If you want to get anywhere in this town, you've got to start thinking like a politician instead of an astronaut."

Rubbing his dark chin thoughtfully, Knowles said, "Let me try this out on a few of the people in my office."

Raising a cautioning finger, Jake said, "Don't try to sell this as a space program. Sell it is an energy program. Bring space technology to the average taxpayer. Make NASA relevant to the general public, instead of just the space cadets and academic scientists."

"Make space technology useful," Knowles said.

"Bring space technology down to Earth," Jake enthused.

"Might work," Knowles agreed. "It just might work." Then he sobered. "If I can sell the idea to the administrator and his flunkies."

"I could ask Senator Tomlinson to get onto that bandwagon."

"But didn't the senator, uh . . . fire you?"

Jake forced a grin. "Sort of. But we're still friends."

"Oh. I see . . . I guess. Thanks, Jake," said Knowles, sticking his hand out. "Thanks a lot."

Jake walked the former astronaut to the station's front door, then headed back to his own cubbyhole, thinking, At least I made him smile. Maybe the idea won't go anywhere, but at least I put a smile on his face.

Then he remembered that he was going out to Reagan National to meet Tami. That put a smile on Jake's face. A big one.

# Reagan National Airport

Jake was always surprised at how small Reagan National really was. Dulles International dwarfed it, as did the BWI out in Maryland. But Reagan National was tucked along the riverfront, a scant few minutes' drive from downtown Washington. It was convenient, especially for DC's politicians and federal employees, and therefore always busy.

When he'd worked for Senator Tomlinson, Jake could park at the special lot reserved for government VIPs. Nowadays he parked much farther away, with the ordinary citizens.

As he made his way through the parking lot and across the road that fronted the terminal building, Jake thought again about Tomlinson's problem with the farm lobby and Senator Perlmutter. Ethanol. He shook his head—as if that would help to generate a useful idea.

But he found himself whistling cheerily as he entered the airport terminal. Tami's flight was fifteen minutes late, so he had plenty of time to get to the area where arriving passengers came in. He mentally kicked himself for forgetting to pick up a bouquet of flowers. Tami would've liked that, he thought.

And there she was, tiny and slim and altogether lovely, striding up the passageway, pulling a rollaway suitcase with one hand, a tote bag slung over her other shoulder. She was wearing dark slacks and a pink sweater over her blouse.

Tami's eyes widened with surprise when she saw Jake among the others waiting to greet arrivals. She hurried up to him and flung both arms around his neck. Jake kissed her as if they'd been apart for months.

"I didn't expect you here," she said, once they had disengaged.

"Thought I'd save you the taxi fare," he answered, grinning boyishly.

As they started toward the door, with Jake towing the rollaway, Tami rummaged in her tote bag and pulled out her cell phone.

"Better call my roommate," she said as she thumbed the flash dial key, "and tell her I won't be home tonight."

Jake's grin widened.

• • •

Over dinner at the sushi bar nearest Jake's apartment, he explained the problem with Senator Perlmutter.

"Ethanol?" Tami asked as she deftly picked up a chunk of rainbow roll.

"Farms grow corn and other crops to sell to the oil companies. They make ethanol out of it and mix it with the gasoline they produce."

Tami's expression turned thoughtful. "I remember doing a story a couple years back about how ethanol was a factor in the Arab Spring uprisings."

"How do you figure that?"

As she dipped her piece of sushi in the tiny bowl of soy sauce, Tami explained, "When farms started selling part of their crops to make ethanol, the price of food went up."

"Not that much," Jake said.

"Not here in the States, maybe, but the price increase was significant overseas. In countries like Libya and Egypt food prices almost doubled in a few months."

Using his chopsticks, Jake picked up a piece of his

unagi roll and managed to get it into his mouth without dropping it.

"People in those countries depended on government subsidies for food," Tami went on. "So when the prices jumped so high, they started demonstrating in the streets."

"Which led to rioting," Jake said, his mouth still full of sushi.

"The governments called out the army to put down the rioters, but the protests just got bigger and bigger."

"Governments were toppled."

"Arab Spring," said Tami.

"Not much came of it," Jake said. "They still have oppressive governments. They just changed hats, that's all."

"Turbans," Tami joked.

"So ethanol production toppled governments in the Middle East."

"It helped."

Reaching for his cup of sake, Jake mused, "So if methanol replaces ethanol, farmers go back to selling their crops for food."

"And food prices go down," Tami concluded. "That's good for everybody—except the farmers."

"Which is why Senator Perlmutter and the farm lobby are pissed with Frank."

"What can you do about it?" she asked.

Almost wistfully, Jake replied, "I wish I knew."

• • •

As they walked through the soft shadows of early evening back toward his apartment, Jake muttered, "Think like a politician."

"What?" asked Tami.

"It's what I told a NASA guy today: he's got to stop thinking like an ex-astronaut and start thinking like a politician."

She looked up at him, puzzled.

"Why is Santino so worked up about Perlmutter? They're both in the same party. They both have strong power bases in the Senate."

"But your energy plan cuts into Perlmutter's turf," Tami said.

"Okay, but what can Perlmutter do about it?"

"Get the farm bloc to vote against the plan when it comes up on the floor of the Senate."

"But it's not going to come up," Jake pointed out. "Santino's burying it."

"Oh. Yes, I forgot."

Thinking out loud, Jake mused, "Presidential election coming up next year. Santino's been approached about running for vice president."

"Who's going to be the party's candidate for president?"

"I don't know," Jake admitted. "But I think I'd better find out."

# Library of Congress

The next morning Jake phoned Kevin O'Donnell from his office at WETA. Senator Tomlinson's chief of staff was stiffly polite, but Jake detected a note of wariness in the tone of his voice.

"I need to pick your brain about a couple of things," Jake told him. "When's a good time for me to drop in on you?"

"Come over to the office?" O'Donnell sounded almost alarmed. "I have a pretty full schedule, Jake. I don't know when I could fit you in."

Jake grimaced inwardly. *I'm still the pariah as far as he's concerned. I bet he doesn't even know that Frank asked for my help.*

Aloud, he said, "It doesn't have to be at the office. I could meet you for drinks, lunch—you name it."

"What's this all about, Jake?"

"I need to understand how the Senate works. Not the rules written on paper: how it really works."

"Does this have anything to do with Perlmutter and Santino?"

"Yes, it does." Jake hesitated a split second, then added, "Ask Frank if it's okay. I'm sure he won't object."

A longer silence. Then, "All right, let me talk with the senator. I'll call you back."

Jake hung up, thinking that the chances were excellent that he wouldn't hear back from O'Donnell.

He was happily surprised, though, when the staff

chief called him late that afternoon. "Tomorrow, in the Library of Congress. Two o'clock."

"Library of Congress. Two o'clock," Jake echoed.

"Meet me in the lobby."

• • •

Jake took a taxi from the WETA building to the Library of Congress, noting as he rode that there were thunderheads building up in the summer sky, dark and threatening. I should have brought an umbrella, he thought. Then he remembered that his umbrella was resting behind the driver's seat of his Mustang, safe and dry.

The library building was another of Washington's marble palaces, vaguely reminiscent of an ancient Greek temple with its columns and stairs fronting the main entrance. In the muggy afternoon heat, Jake was perspiring by the time he reached the top of the stairs and pushed through the door into the welcome cool of the air-conditioned interior.

It was a few minutes before two, and O'Donnell was nowhere in sight among the people passing through the spacious lobby. Jake stood to one side, waiting unhappily. As he looked up from his wristwatch for the third time, he saw O'Donnell coming up the steps, lean and flinty, his suit jacket unbuttoned and flapping in the scant breeze.

He came through the glass door and, hardly nodding to Jake as he strode past, muttered, "Upstairs," and kept on walking, as if he didn't want anyone to see the two of them together.

Thinking that Potomac fever ran a distant second to DC paranoia, Jake followed the rake-thin chief of staff to a bank of elevators and rode with him—and a half-dozen other people—to the second floor.

The elevator doors opened onto the spacious, high-ceilinged reading room with its rows and rows of tables.

Fewer than a third of the chairs were filled, Jake saw: men in their usual DC dark suits, women of all ages and sizes, several poorly clad men who might have been homeless. All of them poring over open books; many of them with hefty piles of books at their elbows. The younger folks sat in front of computer screens.

O'Donnell led him to a side room, not much larger than a booth. But it had a door, and he closed it firmly.

"Private room for VIPs to study books or documents," he explained as he clicked the door lock. Gesturing to the tiny table and its two wooden chairs, O'Donnell asked, "Now what's this all about, Jake?"

Jake sat and studied the older man's pinched face for a moment. He's not happy to be with me, Jake understood. Frank must have told him to meet me, but he's being as discreet about this as he can.

"I need to understand why Senator Perlmutter is so angry about the energy plan," Jake said.

O'Donnell snorted derisively. "Are you really that naïve?"

"I guess I am."

Running a hand across his silly combover, O'Donnell said, "Your plan calls for a major move in methanol production. That means methanol could replace ethanol, which means that farmers who now sell ethanol crops to the oil industry will lose that market. It's not rocket science, kid."

"But they can still sell their crops for food," Jake said.

"The oil companies pay more."

"Anyway, the plan isn't going anywhere, so there's no danger of the farmers losing their ethanol market, is there?" Jake retorted. "Perlmutter must know that."

O'Donnell said, "That's not the point. Perlmutter's main support is from the farm lobby. Any hint of a threat to the farm lobby's interests, he's got to come down on it. Hard."

"So it's a turf war?"

"Sort of," O'Donnell said, reluctantly.

"There's more involved than that, isn't there?" Jake probed.

"There's always more involved."

"Politics."

With a nod, O'Donnell agreed, "Politics."

"Okay," Jake said, leaning in closer to the older man. "Could you explain the politics of this situation to me?"

"Why?"

"Because Frank's asked me to help him get off Santino's shit list, that's why."

O'Donnell fell silent for several heartbeats, his hard dark eyes boring into Jake, his hands fidgeting nervously on the lapels of his jacket.

Finally, "I told the senator to keep you out of this. If Santino finds out that Franklin's asking you for help, the Little Saint'll fry the senator's balls over a slow fire."

"The *senator*," Jake replied, stressing the word, "has asked for my help. And I'm asking you for some background information. I assume Frank's okayed your talking to me."

"Against my advice. I told him to lay low, get the MHD part of the program passed so he can bring it home to his constituents, and let it go at that."

Jake nodded. "I understand. I even agree with you, partially. But I'm in the dark here! I need to know what's going on behind the scenes."

O'Donnell shook his head, muttering, "Amateurs."

Jake said nothing, waiting, while O'Donnell drummed his fingertips on the tabletop.

At last O'Donnell said, almost in a whisper, "Senator McGrath is dying of cancer."

"McGrath? The Senate Majority Leader?"

"It's not public knowledge yet. McGrath wants to keep it quiet for the time being."

"How long—"

"Six months, maybe a little more, maybe a little less. He's going to retire from the Senate at the end of the current session."

"Then he'll be gone by next year's elections."

"That's right." O'Donnell looked almost wistful. "He's been the party's top man in the Senate for the past twelve years: Majority Leader when we were on top, Minority Leader when we weren't. Never heard a word against him, from either side of the aisle. Everybody liked him. Mr. Straight Arrow. Never said an unkind word to anybody. They don't make that kind anymore."

"And Santino's the Majority Whip," Jake said, then added, "I'm not totally ignorant, Kevin."

With an exaggerated sigh of patience, O'Donnell said, "Santino expected to become the Senate's next Majority Leader. He expected McGrath's support to line up the votes for him."

"And McGrath's gone back on Santino? He's not going to support him?"

His thin lips pressed into a tight bloodless line, O'Donnell said, "He's spread the word through the party caucus that he wants the election for the next Majority Leader to be open and fair."

"Does the whole Senate know he's dying?"

With a single shake of his head O'Donnell replied, "Only the top committee chairmen. McGrath has sworn them all to secrecy."

"Then how did you find out?"

O'Donnell made a thin smile and uttered a single word, "Experience."

"So Perlmutter must know."

"Perlmutter knows. And he wants to be the next Majority Leader."

"And that's why he's attacking Santino."

"That's why he's attacking Santino," O'Donnell

echoed. "There's going to be a bloody battle in the party caucus, Santino against Perlmutter. With McGrath sitting it out on the sidelines."

"The farm lobby against the energy lobby," Jake said.

"Not the lobbies, Jake. The Senate blocs. The lobbyists aren't involved in this fight. This is strictly party business."

Jake corrected himself, "The farm bloc against the energy bloc."

"There's more involved than that," O'Donnell said, "but basically, yeah, that's it. Perlmutter against Santino. There's going to be blood on the floor before this fight is over."

"And the energy plan—"

"Is in the middle of it. Perlmutter's taking the position that Santino's invading his turf. Your energy plan will hurt farmers. Perlmutter's defending the poor little farmers against the big, bad fossil fuel industries."

"Bullshit," Jake snapped. "He's defending the agribusiness corporations that own the farms."

O'Donnell really smiled. "At least you understand that much."

"You know that the energy plan will actually help farmers by bringing down the costs of electricity and fuel—even the cost of fertilizer and feedstock will go down once we improve the efficiency of producing energy and cut down on our imports of foreign oil. Lord, we spend seven trillion dollars a year to import oil! Think of how much we'll save—"

O'Donnell cut Jake off with an upraised hand. "Spare me the rhetoric. I know it by heart. I don't believe it, not all of it, but I know the song and dance."

It's not a song and dance, Jake objected silently. It can all come true. If we could only get the plan implemented.

"So now you know the background," O'Donnell said. "Now you know that your little plan has become a combat zone in the battle for the Majority Leader's position."

With a nod, Jake asked, "What do you plan to do?"

"Do?" O'Donnell looked almost surprised. "There's nothing for us to do. Franklin's got to keep his head down and stay out of the battle. If he's lucky, he'll get a bill to back building the MHD demonstration plant back in Montana. That's the only part of your plan that's going to see the light of day."

"But that's only one part of the comprehensive plan."

"Nobody wants your goddamned comprehensive plan!" O'Donnell snapped. "Get that through your thick skull. You think Santino's going to buck the lobbies that fund his election campaigns? You think the Little Saint's going to allow himself to be painted as anti farmers? Get real!"

Jake leaned back in the wooden chair. It creaked in complaint.

O'Donnell pointed a finger at him. "I know that Franklin thinks the world of you. But this is politics, Jake, and it's important to Franklin's survival in the Senate. Stay clear of him. Don't stick your nose into this business; it's beyond your capabilities."

Jake murmured, "Maybe you're right."

O'Donnell said a cheerless good-bye, after ordering Jake to wait ten minutes before he left the booth. Jake nodded obediently and waited, as told.

He's just as paranoid as Brogan was, Jake told himself. Then he remembered that Brogan had been exiled to Ohio because Brogan had tried to help him.

With a labored sigh, Jake checked his watch, pushed himself up from the wooden chair, and headed downstairs toward the lobby.

It was pouring rain outside. Jake stood at the top of the Library of Congress's steps amid a dozen or so other people, all of them waving frantically at passing taxicabs.

It was nearly five o'clock before he got back to the WETA office, soaked from running down the library steps in the drenching rain.

In his mind he heard O'Donnell's warning: *Don't stick your nose into this business; it's beyond your capabilities.*

The hell it is, Jake told himself.

Jake worked late to make up for the time he'd lost at the Library of Congress. When he finally got up from his desk and started toward the building's back door, he remembered that his umbrella was still in his car.

He stuck his head out the door and saw that the rain had stopped. Clouds were scudding across the fat crescent moon, and the parking lot was dotted with puddles, but at least it was no longer raining.

There were only half a dozen cars in the station's parking lot. Only the night-shift technicians were on duty; the regular daytime staff had left long ago.

Noticing how the parking lot's lights made rainbow refraction patterns in the oily puddles, Jake reached into his pants pocket for his car keys as he approached his Mustang.

And felt a terrific blow to the base of his neck. For an instant Jake was flying, weightless, but then he hit the pavement face-first. No pain, but he heard something crunch. My nose! he thought. He started to push himself up, groggily noticing blood dripping onto the rain-wet concrete, when another blow crashed into his ribs. Now the pain was coming, like a tidal wave overwhelming him.

Somebody turned him over. Two men in hoodies bent over him, their faces obscured in shadow. Silently they frisked him, tore the wallet out of his back pocket, then kicked him again.

Jake lay on his back as the pair of muggers sprinted

away. It started to rain again, just a light drizzle, but it felt good, cooling, on his battered face.

He managed to get to his feet and stagger back to the station's rear door. It was locked, of course, and when Jake fished for his keys he fumbled them onto the ground. The rain was coming down more heavily, and Jake didn't have the strength or the inclination to bend over and search for the damned keys.

His vision was blurred, but he found the security buzzer and leaned on it until one of the technicians finally came and opened the door.

"Who the hell—" The kid's eyes went wide once he looked at Jake's face. "What happened to you?"

• • •

Paramedics. Police. To the hospital for X-rays. No broken bones, although Jake's nose was blue and swollen and his right eyebrow was split open. Six stitches.

The cops asked him questions he couldn't answer, including several about how a pair of muggers could have gotten into the fenced-in parking lot.

"They went to a lot of trouble to nail you," said one of the police officers, a middle-aged sergeant with a belly bulged by too many tacos and tamales. "Doesn't make sense for them to climb the fuckin' fence just in the hopes of finding a victim that time of night."

Tami showed up at the hospital, looking terribly frightened. Jake didn't remember calling her.

"Are you all right?" she asked, her face tense with concern.

Bandaged, sore, hungry, Jake managed to mumble, "You ought to see the other guy."

A smile broke out. "At least you still have your sense of humor."

• • •

Tami drove him home, opened a can of chicken noodle soup, and shared it with him. She went to the pharmacy a few blocks away to pick up the pain medications the emergency room physician had prescribed, then stayed the night, making certain that Jake took his pills.

The next morning Tami phoned her own office and told them she wouldn't be in until tomorrow. Then Jake called WETA and started to explain what had happened to him. They already knew.

"Take the rest of the week off, Jake," said his supervisor, a steely woman who had never shown an ounce of human feeling before.

The rest of the week, Jake thought. Today's Friday. No, he realized. It's Thursday. Tomorrow's Good Friday: half the staff will take the day off, and Easter Monday, to boot.

He spent most of the day dozing while Tami phoned banks and credit card companies to tell them of the theft and get new cards for Jake. She used the phone's speaker so Jake could answer the security questions. Most of the time he heard background music and the occasional, "Your call is important to us . . ."

Through it all Jake wondered how and why a pair of muggers would invade the station's parking lot after most of the employees had gone home. Same question the police sergeant raised, he realized.

Were they there to attack me? Specifically? Jake shook his head and winced with pain. Why would they come after me? Who would have sent them? No, that's too paranoid.

Still, he wondered.

Santino? O'Donnell? That's crazy.

That evening, as he carefully brushed his teeth, Jake took a good look at himself. Bandage over his right eyebrow. Nose looking as swollen and blue as a good-sized eggplant.

Tami came to the bathroom door. "Are you okay, Jake?"

He nodded cautiously. "It only hurts when I breathe."

She frowned at him. "Don't play macho man. How do you feel? Honestly."

"Pain's almost gone. The nose only hurts if I touch it."

"The doctor said you might have a concussion."

"I don't think so."

She made a smile for him. "Okay. Come on to bed."

They made love carefully, tenderly, with Tami climbing on top of him. Then she piled pillows around his head so he wouldn't turn over and hurt himself.

The next morning Jake woke up feeling much better. Tami was already dressed.

"I ought to get to work," she said. "Will you be all right?"

"Sure."

"I'll be back around six. Okay?"

He smiled at her. "I'll take you out to dinner."

"Are you sure you want to be seen in public like that?"

His smile widened. "I'll tell everybody that you slugged me."

But once Tami had left, Jake said to himself, Today is Friday. I've got a three-day weekend to think of how we can salvage the energy plan. No, a four-day weekend. I'll call in sick on Easter Monday.

Then he thought, If those muggers were sent by somebody to scare me off, they picked on the wrong guy. I'm going to get the energy plan through, even if it kills me.

He hoped, though, that things wouldn't go that far.

# Easter Sunday

Neither Jake nor Tami was particularly religious, but they attended Easter services at the National Cathedral together. Tami looked splendid in a soft-pink sleeveless dress, topped with a pert little chapeau. Jake pulled his trusty blue suit from the back of his closet. Almost matches the color of my nose, he thought.

After the ceremony they had a big brunch in Georgetown. The weather was warm and clear, although the forecast warned of afternoon showers. They decided to take a chance and walk back to Tami's Dupont Circle neighborhood.

"Are you sure you feel good enough to walk all the way?" Tami asked, eyeing his bandaged brow.

"Sure. I've done enough loafing around."

As they walked through the bright early afternoon, Jake explained what he'd learned from O'Donnell.

"That's all strictly off the record," he told her. "Deep background. Not for publication."

She smiled at him. "You're starting to sound like a politician, Jake. Let me in on the secret, but forbid me from using it on the news."

"I just want you to know what's happening. But if it leaks out, my butt will be in a sling, for sure."

"Like it's not now? What more can they do to you?"

"Get me fired from WETA."

"They can't do that! They wouldn't!"

Jake smiled grimly. "They can and they would. What

did they do to you? We're talking about the big boys here. The power elite."

Tami went silent for half a block. Then, "Well, anyway, what you've told me will help me understand what's going on in the Senate."

"But you can't tell anybody about it," Jake repeated. "Especially the part about Senator McGrath's cancer."

"Is it cancer?"

"Has to be."

"So what happens now?" Tami asked.

"Santino's got to get a majority of the party caucus to vote for him when the Congress reconvenes after its summer recess."

"But McGrath will still be Majority Leader in September, won't he?"

"From what O'Donnell told me, McGrath is going to announce his retirement just before the summer recess."

She giggled softly. "That ought to make for an interesting summer."

"It's not a laughing matter," Jake said. "There's going to be an earthquake once McGrath announces his retirement."

"Santino against Perlmutter. The clash of the titans."

With a sardonic grin, Jake said, "You're right: that'll give the news media plenty of action over the summer."

Plaintively, Tami said, "I wish I was still in the news business."

"Maybe you can be."

"I don't see how. Santino's made me *persona non grata* with every news office in town."

"Maybe so, but you could become what they call 'a reliable source.'"

"You mean you'd feed me inside information?"

"If I can wheedle it out of Frank . . . or Kevin."

"A reliable source. That could be fun."

"Could be dangerous, too."

But Tami grinned at him and said, "I could become the new Deep Throat."

Jake resisted the impulse to remind her that it was a porno movie that inspired that phrase.

• • •

Amy had called to invite Jake to Easter dinner more than a week earlier. "Just a small affair, family only," she had told him over the phone.

"And it won't cause any trouble if I'm seen in the same city block with Frank?"

He could sense Amy smiling. "This is a family dinner, Jake. Frank's father is coming."

Jake felt flattered that the Tomlinsons considered him family. But he realized that the main reason he was being invited was so that the senator could question him about what progress—if any—Jake had made on shaking the energy plan loose from Santino's smothering grip.

His thoughts were interrupted by Amy adding, "So is Connie Zeeman; she's flying in from California."

Uh oh! Miss Hit-and-Run is coming back to town, Jake thought. Almost by reflex he asked, "Is it okay if I bring a date?"

Amy hesitated, then said slowly, "Why yes, of course. That'll be fine, Jake."

"Thanks." As he hung up, he was wondering how much he should tell Tami about his brief affair with Connie. She'll understand, he told himself. After all, that all happened before I met Tami. She'll understand.

Tami did indeed understand. Once Jake explained the situation to her, she laughed mischievously. "You want me to be your bodyguard!"

Jake nodded ruefully at her. "Yes," he admitted. "That's about it."

• • •

Easter Sunday evening Jake drove Tami to the Tomlinson residence.

"Impressive," she said as he parked the Mustang behind the same azalea bushes as before. No other cars were on the driveway.

"The Tomlinsons are old money," he said as he helped Tami out of the car. "Elegant without being opulent."

It was supposed to be a quiet little dinner party, but as soon as the butler ushered Jake and Tami into the library, everyone gaped at Jake's battered face.

"What on earth happened to you?" Tomlinson senior demanded.

"I got mugged. On the WETA parking lot."

"Mugged?" Senator Tomlinson asked, looking startled. "Any broken bones?"

"No. I'm okay. Just bruised." Pointing to his brow, he added, "And a gash. Six stitches."

"Did they get anything?" asked Amy, staring at his bandaged eyebrow and swollen nose.

"My wallet. That's it."

"They didn't want your car?" Connie Zeeman asked.

"My old Mustang? No way. The police said it was kind of strange, though, muggers lurking in the station's parking lot at that time of night."

The elder Tomlinson sniffed, "They weren't criminal masterminds, apparently."

Jake introduced Tami to Connie, who flashed a hearty smile at the diminutive Japanese American woman and said warmly, "You've got a peach, Tami. Don't let him get away from you."

For the first time since Jake had known her, Tami blushed.

Tomlinson senior was his usual stern *paterfamilias*, offering definitive opinions on every subject that came up during the cocktail hour conversation preceding dinner. As the elder Tomlinson held forth on the "totally unproven" predictions of global warming, Jake managed to pull Tomlinson slightly to one side of the group.

"We need to talk."

Senator Tomlinson nodded, without taking his eyes off his imperious father or diminishing his smile by a millimeter.

"I think I've figured out how you can get into Santino's good graces," Jake said.

Looking surprised, Tomlinson turned to Jake. "That would take a miracle."

"I just might have one for you," said Jake, hoping he was right.

# Easter Monday

I f this wasn't so ridiculous it would be tiresome, Jake told himself as he craned his neck to look through his living room window. Set up near his ceiling, the basement window showed a splendid view of the hubcaps of the cars parked along the curb outside. The view hadn't changed in the five times Jake had peeked out there.

Frank's late, Jake said to himself. He should've been here fifteen minutes ago. Maybe he decided not to come, after all. Maybe O'Donnell's talked him out of it. But he would've called; somebody from the office would've phoned me.

Jake had phoned the station to tell his supervisor that he needed another day of recuperation. She wasn't in.

"Hardly anybody's here," said the phone receptionist, sounding cynical. "Easter Monday. Funny how many good Christians we have when they can get a day off out of it."

At last he heard a car squeaking to a stop outside and, standing on tiptoes, saw an unmarked black sedan past the row of parked cars, stopped in the middle of the street.

O'Donnell got out first, followed by Senator Tomlinson. Jake almost laughed at the sight of them: O'Donnell skinny and flinty, his eyes narrowed and suspicious;

Frank tall and elegant, smiling as though he expected passersby to ask for his autograph.

Then a third person came slowly out of the cab: Alexander Tomlinson, the senator's father, tall and lean, stern and imperious.

Jake stepped through his apartment's entrance door and climbed the four steps to the ground level, then hurried along the bricked path to the front of the house. I told Frank to come around the side. Don't want them going up on the porch and knocking on the front door, disturbing the landlord.

"Frank," he called as he strode past the porch. "Hello."

Tomlinson's smile broadened as he said, "Hi, Jake."

O'Donnell nodded curtly while Tomlinson senior fixed Jake with his usual austere gaze.

Jake led them back to the entrance to his basement apartment.

Once they were all in his living room, Senator Tomlinson said, "So this is where you live."

"It's not that far from your house," Jake said. "Almost walking distance."

O'Donnell said nothing. The elder Tomlinson looked around, glanced at the low ceiling, then muttered, "Reminds me of Hitler's bunker."

Jake bit back an angry reply as he gestured to the futon sofa, which he had covered with a colorful shawl Tami had loaned him. Tomlinson *père et fils* sat on the futon, while O'Donnell took the reclinable armchair beside it.

As they sat themselves down, Jake asked, "Can I get you something to drink?"

The senator shook his head. "We don't have all that much time. I've got to be in the Senate for a vote on the immigration bill by four o'clock."

O'Donnell asked, "Do you have any beer?"

Jake nodded while the elder Tomlinson gave his son's staff chief a haughty look, then asked for ice water.

"So what's this all about, Jake?" the senator asked.

From his minuscule kitchen, Jake replied, "Saving the energy plan." He pulled a bottle of Killian's Red from his minifridge, then yanked its one tray of ice cubes out.

"You've got a one-track mind," O'Donnell said, practically growling.

"And," Jake added, "getting Santino the Majority Leader's post."

The three of them sat up straighter.

"If you can do that . . ." The senator's father let the thought dangle.

Jake placed the beer and the ice water on the coffee table, then wheeled his desk chair to the coffee table and sat down. He noticed that O'Donnell hadn't cranked the recliner back from its upright position.

"How's the energy plan going to help Santino?" O'Donnell asked. Almost pugnaciously.

Jake took in a breath, then plunged, "Instead of burying the plan and kowtowing to Perlmutter and the farm lobby, we show how the plan can help farmers to feed the world's poor people."

O'Donnell's bony face twisted into a sour frown. Senator Tomlinson said, "Santino doesn't want to hear a peep about the energy plan. You might as well try to talk him into nuking South Dakota."

Jake shook his head. "Frank, you've got to convince Santino that the energy plan is the only way for him to flatten Perlmutter."

"Have you ever seen the senator from South Dakota?" O'Donnell asked. "It would take the whole defensive line of the Chicago Bears to flatten that overweight bastard."

The senator chuckled, but his father demanded, "What

makes you crazy enough to think the energy plan can help Santino?"

Jake said, "First of all, Santino has got to bring out the point that growing crops to make ethanol pushes up food prices around the world. Perlmutter is starving poor people in Asia, Africa, the Middle East."

Tomlinson senior reached for his ice water as he asked, "Starving children?"

Nodding, Jake added, "And babies."

"I don't know if that's true, Jake," said the senator.

"It's true. I've checked it out."

O'Donnell took a swig of his beer. "So how's your plan going to feed starving babies in Afghanistan?"

Hunching closer to the coffee table, Jake replied, "We produce methanol for the oil companies. Farmers go back to selling their crops for food."

"But that means the farmers lose their ethanol money."

Jake went on, "Yes, but methanol will lower the prices for the fuels that farmers need to power their combines and reapers and other equipment. They come out ahead, economically." Before any of them could re-act to that, Jake went on, "And as new energy technologies like MHD kick in, the price of electricity comes down as well."

"The power companies don't want that," Tomlinson senior pointed out.

"But by selling the carbon dioxide their power plants emit to the methanol producers, instead of footing the costs of burying their $CO_2$ in the ground, they'll be way ahead economically."

The senator mused, "And farms can convert to solar energy and wind power. That'll save them money, too."

"You're cutting into the power companies' profits again," his father warned.

"Not if they get involved in solar and wind systems

themselves," Jake countered. "They can make profits from that, too. And show that they're really interested in protecting the environment."

"Pie in the sky," O'Donnell groused.

"No," Jake snapped. "It's a fundamental shift in our energy priorities. If we carry it off properly, everybody can gain."

Tomlinson senior murmured, "Obamacare."

"No, no, no," Jake insisted. "The plan doesn't call for federal control of the energy industries. It offers tax subsidies for developing new energy technology. Coal-fired power plants can keep on burning coal, and sell their carbon dioxide emissions to the methanol industry. Oil companies' costs will come down, especially as we stop importing so much foreign oil."

The senator rubbed his chin thoughtfully. "I don't think Santino will see things your way, Jake."

"He will if you convince him that the energy plan will win him the Majority Leader job," Jake insisted. Ticking points off on his fingers, "It'll help people in poor nations and even lower the price of food here in the States. It'll cut back on the seven trillion dollars we send overseas every year for foreign oil. Do you realize that two-thirds of our balance of trade deficit comes from importing foreign oil?"

O'Donnell's eyes widened slightly. "Two-thirds?"

"Right. And the plan will help the fossil fuel industries to grow without damaging the environment. It's got something for everybody!"

Tomlinson senior asked, "Including the solar power people and all the other greenies?"

"Including the renewables, yes," said Jake.

Turning to O'Donnell, the senator asked, "What do you think, Kevin?"

Looking sourer than usual, the staff chief said, "It all

sounds lovely. But our bright boy here has overlooked the fundamental problem: the fossil fuel industries don't want a new energy plan. They like things as they are."

"Including the environmental regulations that're coming down the pike?" Jake challenged. "With my plan they can make money selling their carbon dioxide emissions to produce methanol."

"That's a point, Kevin," Senator Tomlinson said, softly.

Rolling his chair slightly toward the recliner O'Donnell was sitting in, Jake asked, "Couldn't you get a few of the key fossil fuel lobbyists together with Frank and Santino to discuss the matter? See if they'll go for it?"

The elder Tomlinson mused, "If you can convince Santino that this will help him become Majority Leader . . ."

"It's a long shot," O'Donnell said.

"But it might be worth trying," said the senator.

"It could get you into Santino's good graces," his father muttered.

"Is this the miracle we need?" asked his son.

"It could be," Jake said. "This plan will do it. If you can convince Santino to use it properly."

Senator Tomlinson made a long, exaggerated sigh. Then, turning to his chief of staff, he asked, "Kevin, can you put such a meeting together?"

O'Donnell shrugged his narrow shoulders. "I can get the lobbyists. Even somebody from Santino's office. But the Little Saint?" He shook his head. "You'll have to talk to him yourself, Franklin."

"I suppose you're right," Tomlinson said, without enthusiasm.

Tomlinson senior got to his feet, slowly, and extended his hand to Jake. "If this piece of political jujitsu actually works, my boy, you'll be worth your weight in gold."

Surprised, Jake took the old man's proffered hand in his own and heard himself blurt, "All I want is my old job back."

O'Donnell snorted dismissively.

Jake smiled wryly and said, "It's a lot safer parking in the Hart S.O.B. than at WETA."

# Getting the Ball Rolling

Jake thought that Margarita Viera gave the lie to the cliché that all Hispanic women are warm, emotional, and overweight. WETA-TV's chief of programming was lean to the point of anorexia, as dispassionate as a blank wall, and as cold as a hired assassin.

When Jake arrived in his office at the station on Tuesday and booted up his desktop computer, the first item on his agenda for the day was a note from Viera: *See me. 9:30.*

Jake almost smiled. He had arrived early, as usual; his desk clock read 8:49 a.m. Still have some time to grab a mug of coffee and check out the rest of the day's schedule.

Promptly at nine thirty he rapped once on Viera's office door, then pushed it open. She was at her desk, on the phone. With her free hand she waved him to the chair in front of the desk.

"Yes, I'll tell him," she said into the phone in her sharp adenoidal tone. "I'll have him call you back."

As she hung up the phone and Jake sat down, Viera focused on Jake's bandaged brow. "That's from the mugging?"

Jake nodded. "Six stitches."

Nudging her sharp chin in the telephone's direction, she said, "That call was from the police. They're looking for you. They say they've found your wallet."

"Great!"

Looking almost pleased, she added, "No cash in it. And the credit cards are all gone."

With a groaning sigh, Jake said, "I had expected that."

"Sergeant Quintero. He says he gave you his card."

Jake nodded again, although he couldn't remember where he'd put the police sergeant's card.

Viera shifted to station business. "This NASA guy, Knowles, he says he's got an idea for a special he wants us to produce."

"He does?"

"He says you gave him the idea for it."

"Oh," Jake said. "The space solar power thing."

"Would you be kind enough to tell *me* what you're cooking up?"

Jake tried to ignore her sarcasm. "I think it's something that can get NASA the kind of public backing the agency hasn't had since the old Apollo days."

"I was just a child then," Viera said. "My brothers were real interested in it. Stayed up to watch the TV broadcasts from the Moon."

"It was an exciting time," Jake said.

Viera's lean face was totally indifferent. "The first landing was exciting, I guess. The rest of them were just the same old thing."

Jake resisted the impulse to shake his head in disappointment.

"So what's the bright idea that's got Knowles so worked up?"

"Space solar power," said Jake. "Using satellites to generate electricity from sunlight in space and then beaming the power down to the ground. Clean electricity. No power plants on the ground burning coal or oil."

"Or natural gas," Viera added.

"Right. The power plant is the sun, ninety-three million miles away."

Looking thoughtful, Viera asked, "Could this replace nuclear power, too?"

"It could."

"Power plants in space."

"NASA could lead the way on this, and show the taxpayers that space technology can help them, the man on the street."

"May I remind you that you work for WETA-TV, not NASA?"

"I know. But if we do this show right—and promote it properly—it could be a big winner for the station, get us lots of viewers."

Viera eyed Jake for a silent moment, then said, "So you think we should produce a special on the subject."

"I think it could be a good idea."

"Of course you do, since it was your idea in the first place."

"It would make a great show," Jake urged.

"It would be a damned expensive show."

Shaking his head, Jake countered, "NASA could provide most of the footage. NASA and some of the industry contractors that've done studies on the idea. All we'd have to do is shoot interviews with key players."

"And man-in-the-street interviews," Viera added. "They're cheap enough."

"I think it would make a really great show."

"Maybe," Viera said, with just the trace of a smile on her thin lips. "Let me get some cost figures run up. Knowles says he can put us in contact with the industry people."

"Good. I think we could win an Emmy with this."

Viera's expression turned scornful. "Don't get carried

away with yourself, Jake. Don't start writing your acceptance speech."

He grinned at her. "You'd be the one accepting the Emmy, not me."

"Maybe. We'll see. You get Knowles to give you the contacts for getting footage. And I mean *good* footage. Hardware. Animation. CGI. Not talking heads."

Jake got to his feet. "I'll call him right away."

He got as far as the door before Viera told him, "And phone that police sergeant."

"Right," said Jake, hoping he could remember where he'd left the cop's card.

As he headed back toward his own little office he wondered if this special about space solar power could be used in the campaign to make his energy plan a weapon in Senator Santino's struggle against Senator Perlmutter. Probably not, he thought. By the time the station produces the show and gets it on the air, the battle over the next Senate Majority Leader will be already decided.

And yet there was something in that kernel of an idea, something that nagged at the edge of his consciousness. If I can get Tami to tell some of her friends in the news media about how the energy plan can help to feed poor people around the world . . . maybe that could start the ball rolling.

Then he remembered that Senator Tomlinson was scheduled to deliver a commencement speech in a few weeks at some university in Pennsylvania. Get him to talk about how energy policy influences the price for food around the world. Get major news coverage, splash it over the blogosphere. That'd get the ball rolling!

Suddenly he remembered where he'd left Sergeant Quintero's card: it was right there in his back pocket, inside a folded-over envelope that he'd used as a makeshift wallet, until he could get to a store and buy a new one.

But now I won't need a new one, Jake thought happily, if Quintero's found my old one.

• • •

Jake had expected the Metro Police station to be a seedy, run-down affair. Instead, it was bright, modern-looking, clean, and well lit. A young woman in police uniform sat at a desk just inside the front door and pointed him toward Quintero's office.

"You're lucky," she said as she put down her phone. "In another five minutes he'd be on his way to lunch."

Jake hurried down the corridor the receptionist indicated and stepped into a large room filled with rows of desks, most of them unoccupied. Quintero was standing off by the windows with a pair of other cops, deep in conversation. But he noticed Jake threading his way through the desks and walked over to meet him.

"Mr. Ross," he said. Jake saw details he had missed on the night of the mugging. Quintero was well over six feet tall, his hair a grizzled, short-cropped salt-and-pepper, his mustache all gray. He had wide shoulders, but his gut hung over his belt noticeably.

"Sergeant Quintero," said Jake.

Leading Jake back toward his desk, Quintero said, "We found your wallet. Money and credit cards weren't in it, though."

"How did you find it?" Jake asked.

Waggling one hand, the sergeant said, "Routine search of the neighborhood. It was in a trash can. Most police work boils down to pounding the pavement."

He opened his top desk drawer and pulled out a plastic baggie with Jake's wallet inside.

"Can you identify it?" Quintero asked.

Frowning in thought for a moment, Jake said, "It's got a picture of my late wife in it, if they didn't take that, too."

"No, the picture's still there," Quintero said, holding the baggie with his fingertips. "What's she wearing?"

Jake squeezed his eyes shut, remembering. "A dress with a flower pattern. She's blond . . . that is, she was blond."

Taking the wallet out of its protective plastic, Quintero handed it to Jake. "She was very pretty. I'm sorry for your loss."

Jake nodded, surprised that just the thought of Louise's photograph could cause him so much pain.

As he accepted the wallet, Jake asked, "I don't suppose you found any fingerprints or anything else you could use to track down the muggers."

"Nah, they wiped it down before they tossed it." Before Jake could reply, the sergeant went on, "But they got a little careless with the credit cards. Used your gasoline card on I-95 in Maryland and again in Rhode Island."

"Rhode Island?"

"Guess they didn't realize we could track the card so fast."

Rhode Island, Jake thought. Christ Almighty, those goons were sent by Jacobi!

# The Lehigh Speech

**A**s O'Donnell had expected, Senator Santino avoided meeting with Tomlinson. "The Little Saint considers our man *persona non grata*," the staff chief told Jake.

They were having lunch together at a busy delicatessen halfway between the WETA office and Capitol Hill. Jake found the corned beef sandwich delicious, especially with the tangy mustard. Lean though he was, O'Donnell ordered pastrami and wolfed it down greedily, much to Jake's surprise. Kevin must have a high metabolism, he thought.

"How about getting together with some of Santino's people and a couple of the lobbyists?" Jake asked.

"He's stalling on that, too," O'Donnell replied. He wiped his chin with his napkin, then said, "It's like I told you, Jake: the Little Saint doesn't want to have anything to do with Franklin or your energy plan."

Jake nodded, but he said to himself, Then we're just going to have to change the Little Saint's mind.

Pulling a thumb-sized USB drive from his shirt pocket, Jake said, "I put together some ideas that Frank can use in that graduation speech he's giving."

Accepting the drive, O'Donnell said dourly, "Lehigh University. Not the big leagues."

"I know," Jake said, thinking, But we can make the big leagues take notice. If we play our cards right. After all, Westminster College in Fulton, Missouri, wasn't the big leagues, either. But Churchill's "Iron Curtain" speech got plenty of attention, anyway.

• • •

"Lehigh University?" Tami asked. "That's in Pennsylvania, isn't it? Up in the hills."

Jake nodded. "In Bethlehem, about halfway between Philadelphia and New York."

Nearly three weeks had passed since his lunch with O'Donnell. They were sitting in Jake's living room, picking at Chinese takeout set in cardboard cartons on the coffee table. Jake had opened a bottle of Chianti, reasoning that Chianti went with just about any food, even moo goo gai pan.

Also on the coffee table was another USB drive, this one holding the entire finished speech that Senator Tomlinson was going to give at Lehigh the next week.

"I've worked with Frank on this speech," Jake explained. "It spells out the relationship between energy policy and world food prices."

"So that's what you've been doing this past month," Tami said, arching a brow at him. "You've been so busy, I was starting to worry you might have found another girlfriend."

Jake felt truly surprised. "Another . . . ?" Then he realized she was teasing him. "I told you I was working with Frank on his speech."

"You mentioned it. That doesn't mean I necessarily believed you." But she was grinning as she said it.

Jake grinned back at her. "The only other woman I've been involved with in the past month is the senator's public relations director, and she weighs close to two hundred pounds."

"I'll bet she had big boobs."

"Like dirigibles," Jake said. "But I prefer slimmer, sleeker women. Like you."

He leaned toward her and they kissed. Then she disengaged and asked, "So the speech is finished?"

"Yes. And it's good, Tami. It's dynamite."

"Says the author."

"I'm not the only one involved in this. Frank contributed a lot himself. So did O'Donnell, and a couple of the speech writers on Frank's staff."

"They must have loved having you involved."

"I'm not involved, not officially. I didn't write one line of this speech. I just provided the information and the ideas that the speech is based on."

"That's what's been taking up your nights," she said.

As he reached for another helping of noodles, Jake said, "It hasn't been easy, working with the senator without being seen in his office or in public with him."

He managed to get most of the noodles into his mouth, but some slipped from his chopsticks to the carpeted floor.

"Damn!" Jake snapped.

Tami grabbed a paper napkin from the coffee table and picked up the noodles. "You're getting better with chopsticks, Jake."

"Better at decorating the floor, you mean."

"No, really better. Those noodles are pretty slippery."

"You haven't dropped any."

"I've been using chopsticks since I was a baby." Pointing to the USB drive with the pair in her hand, she said, "So you want me to hand this out to the bloggers I know?"

"Yes. If we could get it on *Power Talk*, that would be terrific."

Frowning slightly, Tami said, "Everybody wants to get on *Power Talk*."

"Can you do it?"

Tami hesitated. Then, "A former boyfriend of mine had an in with Lady Cecilia. He should be able to help us."

"Former boyfriend?" Jake growled.

"That's all over with."

"Forget it. I don't want you giving him any ideas."

Now Tami looked surprised. "You're jealous?"

"Just being protective," said Jake, reaching for more noodles.

"I can take of myself," she said. "Besides, we went our separate ways more than six months ago."

"Six months ago?"

"Last fall. When I met you."

• • •

Jake couldn't travel to Pennsylvania for Tomlinson's speech, and there was no radio or television coverage of it, so he waited nervously that afternoon and into the evening for some mention of it among the bloggers.

Just before he left his apartment to have dinner with Tami, one of the political blogs popped up a couple of lines:

Senator Tomlinson (R, MT) connects energy policy to the cost of food. In a speech at Lehigh University today the senator said growing crops to produce ethanol fuel has raised food prices around the world.

Not much, Jake thought. He started to close his laptop, but—after a glance at his wristwatch—tried one more blog:

Ethanol starves Third World babies, says US Senator.

Then another:

US Senator claims growing crops for ethanol is an environmental disaster.

Feeling excitement growing inside him, Jake tried the *Washington Post*'s blog:

Senator B. Franklin Tomlinson (R, MT) links ethanol production to soaring food prices in Middle East and elsewhere.

"Is it fair, is it right, for us to literally take the food out of poor people's mouths, when we can move to better energy technologies that will make America the world's leader not only in energy production, but in helping the developing nations to feed their people?" the senator asked.

Proposing a sweeping new energy policy for the US, Senator Tomlinson said, "We have the brains and the skills to change the world. Do we have the heart?"

Jake was halfway through the *Post*'s rather lengthy piece when his cell phone buzzed. Yanking it from his pocket, he saw that the caller was Tami.

"Tami, I'm sorry. I got caught up—"

"I figured as much," she said, her voice sounding cheerful, despite a lot of background noise. "I'm at the restaurant with an old friend. We'll be at the bar when you decide to show up."

"I'm on my way."

Jake snapped his phone shut, turned off his laptop, and sprinted out of his apartment.

# The Blue Lagoon

The Blue Lagoon was a popular seafood restaurant in Georgetown. It took Jake less time to drive there than it did to find a parking place. Finally he gave in and left his Mustang at one of the exorbitantly priced parking lots.

Stepping into the restaurant, Jake was hit by a wall of noise. The place was jammed, and everyone seemed to be talking at once; the music pounding through the ceiling speakers was unrecognizable through the clamor of conversations, except for a thumping bass beat.

People were crowded four deep at the bar, and it took Jake several minutes to find Tami sitting at the far end, deep in conversation with a young, good-looking blond fellow.

As he elbowed his way through the crowd, Tami looked up and spotted him. "Jake!" she called, waving. "Over here!"

She and her friend were at the very end of the bar. Jake worked his way back there and found a sliver of empty space to stand in.

"Sorry I'm late," he said, after pecking at Tami's lips.

She gestured to her companion and said, "Jake, this is Bill Fairweather. Bill, Jake Ross."

Fairweather looked youthfully handsome: pale blond hair combed straight back from his forehead, Nordic blue eyes. He looked solidly built, but Jake noted with some satisfaction that he was at least two inches shorter than himself.

"Bill's with Norton and Ingels, the public relations consultants," Tami explained, almost shouting to be heard over the din of the crowd. "We used to see quite a lot of each other back when I worked for Reuters."

Fairweather grinned at Jake and said, "I'm just one of Tami's fair-weather friends."

Jake smiled weakly at the pun as he shook Fairweather's hand.

Leaning closer to Jake's ear, Fairweather said, "I read your senator's speech. Good job."

"I didn't write it," Jake quickly replied. "I'm not on the senator's staff anymore."

"So Tami told me."

A waiter brushed past Jake, frowning, and Jake realized he was standing in the space that led back to the kitchen.

"Can we find a table?"

"Are you kidding?" Fairweather replied, with a patronizing smile. "We'll be lucky if we can get another stool here at the bar for you."

Tami said, "Bill knows Lady Cecilia."

"Really?"

The harried bartender came up and asked Jake, "Whattaya want?"

I want to get out of here, Jake thought. Aloud he said, "White wine."

"Chard? Pinot gris? What?"

"Sauvignon blanc?"

"You got it." And the bartender hustled away, down the bar.

Fairweather said, "I've known Ceci since she started her blog, back during the Bush administration. Bush Dubya."

Tami asked, "Can you get us to meet her?"

Before Fairweather could answer, the bartender came back and placed a wineglass on a coaster. "You wanna set up a tab?"

Jake wanted more than anything else to get away from this noisy, crowded bedlam. But he glanced at Tami and nodded. "Yeah."

"And bring us some dinner menus," added Fairweather.

"Only bar menus here," said the bartender.

"That's fine."

Tami touched Fairweather's arm and repeated, "Can you get us to meet Lady Cecilia, Bill?"

"I don't see why not."

Jake knew he should be happy about that. But he didn't like the idea of being grateful to Fairweather for the favor. He especially didn't like the idea of Tami being grateful to him.

• • •

Despite a thundering headache by the time the three of them left the Blue Lagoon, Jake Googled Lady Cecilia as soon as he got back to his apartment, after dropping Tami off at her Dupont Circle place.

Cecilia Goodlette was a lady by virtue of her third husband, some Englishman with a title. Born in upstate New York, Cecilia had gone through four husbands altogether, divorcing two and burying two, including the Englishman. She grew wealthier each time one of her marriages ended, through either a divorce settlement or an inheritance.

She had started her blog, *Power Talk*, as a sort of gossip column about Beltway society, a prurient peek at the antics of DC's rich and powerful. Although she signed her write-ups "Lady C.," everyone in the District immediately realized who was dishing up the dirt.

Instead of shunning her, the politicians and power

brokers made her a celebrity and fed her choice tidbits about who was doing what to whom inside the Beltway. With fame came power, and everyone who was anyone strove to be mentioned on *Power Talk* as often as possible.

• • •

True to his word, Fairweather wangled an invitation for Jake and Tami to Lady Cecilia's latest bash, a quiet little cocktail party at her home near Capitol Hill.

Wearing his trusty tuxedo, Jake drove to Tami's apartment. Before he could get out of the Mustang she came hurrying down the steps, looking magnificent in a glittering silvery mid-thigh cocktail dress.

Tami offered her cheek as she ducked into the convertible. "Don't smudge my lipstick."

He gave her a peck and they drove off toward Capitol Hill.

"You're awfully quiet," she said as they inched through the early-evening traffic.

"It's my shirt studs," he said. "Sometimes they come loose."

Tami looked at him for a silent moment, then said, "It's not the shirt studs, Jake. What's bothering you?"

In the shadows of the car's interior, she looked so beautiful, so serious.

"Fairweather," he admitted.

"Bill?" Tami said, surprised.

"What's he want in exchange for getting us into this party?"

Tami's face grew serious. "You're thinking like a politician again, Jake."

"Nobody in this town does something for nothing," he muttered.

"That's true, I suppose."

"So what does he want?"

"Can't you guess?"

Looking straight ahead, both hands gripping the steering wheel, he answered, "You."

Her eyes went wide, then she giggled. "Me? Don't be silly."

Jake felt surprise, relief, curiosity all at once.

"Then what?" he asked.

"He wants Senator Tomlinson."

"Tomlinson?"

"Of course," Tami answered, matter-of-factly. "He wants you to use your influence to get the senator to meet with him, so he can pitch taking on Norton and Ingels as his public relations representatives."

Jake felt slightly stunned. "But Frank's already got a PR rep."

"A small-timer, according to Bill. He thinks your senator is going places, and Norton and Ingels can help him."

"That's it?"

Tami answered smilingly, "That's the way things get done in this town: I'll introduce you to this one if you'll introduce me to that one."

Jake let out a relieved sigh. "I'll be damned."

Tami patted his knee. "Nobody's interested in me except you. Now let's meet Lady Cecilia."

# Lady Cecilia

From the outside, Cecilia Goodlette's home didn't seem to be all that special: a row house on a side street within the shadow of the Capitol's dome. But the houses looked wider and in much better condition than the row houses Jake had known as a child. The sidewalks were clean, and each house on the block had a tiny square of grass in front of it. Compared to his old neighborhood, this was posh.

Once he and Tami were inside, the "quiet little" cocktail party turned out to be forty or fifty people, the cream of Washington's power elite. Most of the men were in tuxedos, the women in sweeping gowns aglitter with jewels. Jake recognized several senators and members of the president's cabinet, all sipping champagne or harder booze and chatting with each other amiably.

Jake marveled at the intricacies of Washington society. Politicians who were at each other's throats in public were talking together here like long-lost friends.

Tami and Jake stood just inside the house's front door, in the small entryway. A young woman in a cocktail waitress's black short-skirted dress carried a tray of champagne flutes to them. Through the archway that led into the living room they could see that the party was already in full swing.

"That's Senator Perlmutter," Tami pointed out, "over by the fireplace with the secretary of agriculture."

Perlmutter was obese, almost totally bald, his face

florid and his hands gesticulating madly as he yammered into the agriculture secretary's ear.

Bill Fairweather materialized out of the crowd, smiling pleasantly, a highball glass in one hand.

"Welcome to the zoo," he said.

Tami lifted her champagne flute and smiled back at him.

Jake asked, "Where's Lady Cecilia?"

"Kind of abrupt, isn't he?" Fairweather said to Tami.

Still smiling, Tami replied, "Don't play games, Bill. You said you'd introduce us."

"I will. I will. Just hold your horses."

Looking past Fairweather, Jake recognized Senator Santino in the crowd. And standing beside him, looking thoroughly uncomfortable in an ill-fitting tuxedo, was Jacobi.

Jake turned to Tami. "Come on. I want to talk to that guy."

He tugged her through the crowd, leaving Fairweather standing in the entryway, looking nonplussed.

Santino was talking earnestly with a handsome elderly woman while Jacobi stood frowning uneasily with an untouched champagne flute in one meaty hand.

"Good evening, Senator," Jake said, loudly enough to make the Little Saint turn away from the woman.

"Oh!" Santino seemed startled, but quickly recovered. "Dr. Ross. Imagine meeting you here. And Ms. Umetzu, isn't it? Delighted to see you again." Turning back to the elderly woman, he introduced, "This is Mrs. Larabee, one of the directors of the Smithsonian. Edna, this is Dr. Jacob Ross, formerly with Senator Tomlinson's staff, and Tamiko Umetzu, formerly with the Reuters news agency."

Both *formerlies* were your doing, you sneaky son of a bitch, Jake grumbled inwardly.

Barely holding on to his temper, Jake said, "Tami, meet Bert Jacobi, from Providence, Rhode Island."

Jacobi forced an uncertain smile.

Santino resumed chatting with Mrs. Larabee, while Jake maneuvered himself next to Jacobi.

"You know," he said, fingering the scar on his brow, "I got mugged a few weeks ago."

"Yeah?"

"A couple of thugs from Rhode Island."

"No kiddin'."

"Did you send them?"

Jacobi grinned knowingly. "Me? Why would I do somethin' like that?"

"You tell me."

Jabbing a stubby finger at Jake's chest, Jacobi said, "Lissen, kid. If you got mugged, you was probably in a place you shouldn'ta been. You stay where you belong, you won't get hurt."

"I'll decide where I belong," Jake said tightly.

With a shrug, Jacobi said, "Then you'll prob'ly get mugged again. Or worse."

Senator Santino stepped between them. "Mr. Jacobi is right, you know," he said to Jake in his soft, unpretentious tone. "You should be more careful, Dr. Ross."

Jake realized that his free hand had clenched into a fist. Jacobi looked totally unconcerned, Santino almost amused.

Tami clutched at Jake's arm. "Come on, Jake. Bill's waving at us."

Jake let her drag him away, wondering what he would have said next if she hadn't.

Fairweather, looking pleased with himself, said, "You wanted to meet Lady Cecilia. There she is."

Jake followed Fairweather's eyes and saw, standing by the bar with a couple of other middle-aged women, a short, thickset woman with a painfully plain, thick-lipped frog's face and a pageboy hairdo that seemed an obvious wig. This is the dynamo behind *Power Talk*? he wondered. Cecilia Goodlette was wearing some sort of Asian outfit, a knee-length tunic of brilliant red with black trim, over snug-fitting black trousers. No jewelry, except for a diamond ring that looked almost too big for her to lift.

She was dumpy and squat, her face far from attractive, but her eyes sparkled with intelligence and good humor. Four husbands, Jake thought as Fairweather led him and Tami toward Lady Cecilia. She certainly didn't get them with her sex appeal.

She was showing off her stupendous diamond to the two other women.

"It's like the Hope diamond," she was saying. "It came with a curse. My second husband!"

The women guffawed and, as if on cue, Lady Cecilia Goodlette turned toward Fairweather just as he got within arm's reach. She extended both her chubby little hands to him.

"Bill," she gushed. "So glad you could come."

Fairweather bussed her on the cheek, then turned and introduced Tami and Jake.

Barely as tall as Jake's shoulder, Lady Cecilia took his extended hand in both of hers and said, "How come you haven't brought your handsome boss tonight?"

Taken aback, Jake stuttered, "I . . . I don't work for Senator Tomlinson anymore."

"You don't?" The little woman seemed shocked by the news. "What happened?"

Before Jake had time to think of an answer he heard Tami say, "Jake ran afoul of Senator Santino."

"Really!"

"That's not for publication," Jake said quickly. "It's strictly off the record."

"Oh Jake," Cecilia said, "you know that nothing's off

the record with *Power Talk*. But don't worry, I won't attribute you as my source. Now you've got to tell me what happened!"

Without a word to the women she'd been talking with, Cecilia led Jake, Tami, and Fairweather away from the bar and through a door into a quiet room that was almost bare except for the desk and flat-screen computer monitor atop it. The room was lit by a single lamp on the table beside the only other piece of furniture: a long, angled couch.

"I'd heard that there's some sort of trouble between Senator Tomlinson and Santino," she said, sitting herself on one side of the couch and gesturing for her guests to sit on the other side, facing her.

"It's actually a conflict between Santino and Senator Perlmutter," Jake said.

"Ahh," said Lady Cecilia, with a knowing smile. "The Little Saint and the blimp from Nebraska."

Tami giggled and Fairweather grinned. But Jake asked, quite seriously, "Did you read the speech that Senator Tomlinson gave at Lehigh University last week?"

"Read? A speech?" Cecilia looked aghast.

"It lays out the relationship between our current energy situation and the worldwide price of food."

"Why don't you tell me about it."

Jake glanced at Tami, who nodded.

Lady Cecilia purred, "Don't worry, Jake, your name won't be mentioned in any way."

Fairweather urged, "It's okay, Jake. She'll keep your name out of it."

Jake said, "It'd be better if you heard this from the senator himself."

"I'd love to!" Cecilia said. "I'd *adore* doing an interview with him. He's very sexy. But until now I didn't think he'd have anything interesting to say."

Fairweather said, "You know, Jake, your senator comes across as a dumb blond."

You're the blond, Jake retorted silently. Frank's got dark hair.

"He has a lot to say," Jake told Lady Cecilia, "but until now he's been sort of muzzled by Santino."

"He needs a good PR rep," Fairweather said.

"Maybe," said Jake.

Sitting primly on the couch, Lady Cecilia coaxed, "Why don't you explain the business to me, so I won't appear a total ignoramus when I meet your senator."

Mission accomplished! Jake thought. She wants to interview Frank. The ultimate DC blog is going to be Frank's megaphone.

So he began explaining the energy plan, its relationship to food prices, and the struggle between Santino and Perlmutter.

# Tomlinson Residence

Jake was only mildly surprised when Kevin O'Donnell phoned him at WETA the following morning.

"He wants to see you," said the senator's chief of staff.

"Okay," Jake said guardedly.

"His house, this evening. Can you do that?"

"Can I bring a date?"

O'Donnell's voice snarled, "This isn't a party, Jake. It's business."

Thinking that he'd have to break his dinner date with Tami, Jake asked, "Will he at least feed me?"

He could hear O'Donnell huffing angrily. "Oh, so you get Lady Cecilia to call him and you think you're a big cheese, huh?"

"Not me," said Jake. "I'm just an expendable nobody."

"Will you be there tonight or not?"

Surprised at how resentful he felt, Jake said, "I'll be there. Seven o'clock okay?"

"Seven will be fine."

No sooner had Jake replaced his desk phone in its cradle than it rang again. This time it was Earl Reynolds.

"Hello, Earl," he said pleasantly.

Reynolds's tone was not pleasant. "The senator got a call this morning from some dude at Norton and Ingels."

"Bill Fairweather," said Jake.

"Right. So now you're a PR consultant?"

Jake puffed out a breath. "No, I'm just returning a favor."

"And you've got the senator onto *Power Talk*, too."

"I guess I did."

"I could have gotten him onto *Power Talk*, you know. We didn't think he was ready for that, not yet. We were staying low, out of Santino's way, and now you bust in and make a mess of everything."

Holding on to his rising temper, Jake replied evenly, "Sorry if I trod on your toes, Earl. I thought I was helping, not hurting."

"If Frank wanted your help, he wouldn't have fired you."

As mollifyingly as he could manage, Jake said, "Yeah, I suppose so."

"Just stay out of my turf," Reynolds said. Jake got the mental impression that he was trying to sound like one of the teenaged toughs in *West Side Story*.

"I'm only trying to help Frank."

"Yeah. And we don't need any damned Norton and Ingels, either!" Reynolds hung up with a bang.

Jake held the phone for a moment, then shook his head. No matter what I do, it's wrong, he thought. At least, that's what *they* think.

•  •  •

Late that afternoon, as Jake was tidying up his desk before leaving for home, one of the news producers popped his head through his doorway.

"Got a minute?" she asked.

Jake tried to remember her name. Gloria something, he thought. Tall and lank, with stringy dark hair falling past her shoulders.

"A minute," he said.

Stepping into his office, she said excitedly, "There's a tropical storm gathering strength in the Gulf of Mexico.

The Weather Service's named it Belinda. They say it could become a hurricane and—"

"Isn't it kind of early for a hurricane?"

She shrugged. "Season began June first, but, yeah, they don't usually spool up so soon."

Before Jake could ask why she was talking to him about the storm, she explained, "Looks like Belinda's heading for the offshore oil rigs off the Louisiana coast. By the time it hits them it'll be a full-fledged hurricane. Maybe category three."

"Like Katrina," Jake breathed.

Nodding, the producer said, "So what happens to those oil rigs if the storm hits 'em?"

Jake said, "They're built to withstand a pounding."

"Yeah, but they shut down, don't they?"

"For a day or so."

"Maybe more?"

"Could be. Depends on how much damage the storm does."

"So what does that do to gasoline prices?"

He saw at last what she was driving at. "Gas prices go up, naturally. For a few days. Maybe a week."

"More than a week?" she asked eagerly.

"Depends on how much damage the storm does to the rigs, how quickly they can get back on line after it blows over."

"Gas prices spike for a week or longer," she said, looking pleased.

Jake nodded minimally. "Could be."

"Okay. Great. Thanks." And she left his office.

Jake shook his head. News people. The more it's burning or bleeding, the more they like it. Or drowning.

• • •

As he drove toward Tomlinson's house, Jake realized why O'Donnell was ticked off. I'm showing him up!

Frank ditched me, but I still got Lady Cecilia to call him for an interview on *Power Talk*. O'Donnell didn't do it, I did.

And Reynolds, too. He's afraid I'm invading his turf. Almost, Jake smiled to himself. Behold the lowly turtle, he thought. He can't make progress unless he sticks his neck out. O'Donnell and Reynolds don't want to stick their necks out; they're afraid of getting their heads chopped off.

Maybe I ought to be afraid of getting my head chopped, Jake told himself as he parked his Mustang behind the azaleas. But what the hell more can they do to me? I've got nothing to lose.

The senator opened the front door himself, looking serious, almost somber, his shirtsleeves rolled up to the elbows, his tie pulled loose, and his collar unbuttoned.

"Hello, Jake," he said, gesturing Jake into the foyer. With an almost apologetic grin, he explained, "Butler's night off."

Jake followed him down the hallway to the library. O'Donnell was already there, sitting in one of the armchairs with a tumbler of whiskey in his hand.

"Amy's out, too," Tomlinson said, heading for the bar set up on the rolling cart. "She's at some charity dinner in Alexandria."

"Just us guys," Jake said, following the senator to the bar.

"Help yourself," said Tomlinson, as he splashed scotch into a lowball glass. Jake poured himself a glass of water, thinking, Better keep a clear head.

Tomlinson sat on the sofa, Jake took the chair by the coffee table, opposite O'Donnell.

"I've agreed to do an interview on *Power Talk*," the senator said.

Jake nodded.

"Santino's not going to like it," said O'Donnell. "I

think we shouldn't do it unless we clear it with the Little Saint first."

"But suppose we ask him about it and he says no?" Tomlinson asked. "What then?"

"He won't say no," said Jake. "Not if you make him understand that you'll be cutting Perlmutter's legs out from under him."

"Cutting Perlmutter . . . ?" O'Donnell looked disgusted. "Get real, Jake! You can't hurt Perlmutter."

"I can't," Jake shot back, "but Frank can."

"By attacking the ethanol mandate?"

"That's right. Frank can come across as the senator who cares about how ethanol production causes hunger in the poor areas of the world. How it raises the price of bread in your neighborhood supermarket. And the price of beef."

"So you want Franklin to take on the farm lobby?"

Leaning forward, toward O'Donnell, Jake said, "I want Frank to show how his energy plan can help farmers—and everybody else."

Before O'Donnell could react to that, Jake turned to the senator and said, "You've got to make Santino see that your energy plan can get him elected Majority Leader in September."

Tomlinson clasped his drink in both hands. "So I'll have to tell Santino that the energy plan can hurt Perlmutter."

"No!" Jake snapped. "Show the Little Saint how it will help *him*. He'll understand that anything that helps him hurts Perlmutter."

O'Donnell muttered, "I don't like this one little bit. Franklin, you should be keeping your head low and staying out of the spotlight. Hell, I could've gotten you onto *Power Play*, but we agreed you didn't want to get Santino pissed at you."

Grimly, Tomlinson said, "He couldn't be more pissed

with me than he is now. Maybe Jake's right, maybe it's time to fight back."

"It's a mistake," O'Donnell insisted. "A big mistake."

Tomlinson broke into a grin. "Maybe. But it's better than doing nothing. Set up a meeting with Santino for me, Kevin, would you please?"

"You'll be committing political suicide."

"Maybe. But that's better than being buried alive, like I am now."

Jake said, "Why don't you bring me along when you meet with Santino? You can blame the whole situation on me."

Tomlinson glanced at O'Donnell, then said, "Not a bad idea, Jake."

The expression on O'Donnell's face could have etched steel.

# Senator Santino's Office

**S**antino blinked three times as Tomlinson and Jake stepped into his office.

"Dr. Ross," he said, without getting up from behind his desk. "You seem to be everywhere these days."

The office was so big it took Jake and Tomlinson almost a dozen strides to reach Santino's desk. As they approached, Tomlinson said, "Jake's an old friend. He's much more than a staffer to me."

"So I see," said Santino. "So I see. Well, sit down. Tell me what I can do for you."

Jake realized Santino had decided to see them alone, without any of his staff present. Is that a good thing or a bad one? he wondered. Is he recording what we say?

As Senator Tomlinson settled into one of the chocolate brown leather chairs in front of Santino's desk, he said, "I've been asked to appear on *Power Talk*."

"Appear?"

"Lady Cecilia wants to interview me, on camera, for her blog."

Glancing at Jake, Santino said darkly, "About your energy plan, I presume."

"About how the energy plan can get you elected Majority Leader," Jake blurted.

Santino leaned back in his desk chair and smiled, like a snake. "And just how will your plan accomplish that, may I ask?"

Tomlinson said, "The ethanol mandate has raised food prices around the world."

"I know that. Regrettable—unless you're in the agribusiness industry."

"The energy plan will encourage farmers to resume producing food," Tomlinson went on, "and at the same time lower their costs with cheaper fuel and cheaper electricity."

"In ten years or so," Santino countered.

"Less than that," Jake said. "In three years the cost of gasoline will be ten percent lower than it is today. Maybe more than ten percent."

"And you think that will balance the income farmers will lose if the ethanol mandate is eliminated?"

"You don't have to eliminate the mandate," Jake said. "Just subsidize methanol production for five years. Let the farmers and everybody else buy gasoline that's mixed with methanol. Let the free market do its work."

Pointing a lean finger at Jake, Santino said, "With government subsidies for methanol? That's hardly a free market."

"The subsidies will be temporary. Five years."

"Young man, there's no such thing as a temporary subsidy. Once a subsidy is in place, it's practically impossible to get rid of it."

Jake countered, "The ethanol mandate has been reduced several times over the past few years by the EPA, hasn't it?"

Santino pursed his lips before answering. "That's true. Support for the mandate is weakening. That's why Perlmutter is defending it so fiercely. He knows he's vulnerable there."

Tomlinson broke in. "So by backing the energy plan you can show the world that you're acting to lower global food prices. It wouldn't take much to show that most of the farmers in the United States actually work for agribusiness corporations. You could expose Senator Perlmutter as a tool of the agribusiness industry, a man who doesn't care how much a loaf of bread or a slice of meat costs the American taxpayer. To say nothing of the hungry people in the poorer nations of the world."

Steepling his fingers as he leaned back in his desk chair, Santino asked mildly, "That's the line you intend to take on *Power Talk?*"

"I don't intend to attack Perlmutter," said Tomlinson. "But I think the viewers will be able to put two and two together."

Santino lifted his eyes to the ceiling and said, so low that Jake could barely hear him, "But will the members of the Senate get that message?"

"Their staff aides will," said Jake. "And they'll realize that you're the man they want as the next Majority Leader."

"Really." Santino's tone was halfway between skepticism and ambition.

Tomlinson said, "Of course, I'm only a very junior senator. But I think that this energy plan could help you a lot, sir."

"Really?" Santino repeated.

Silence fell over the room for several agonizingly long moments.

"I think my appearance on *Power Talk* could be the first step in your campaign against Perlmutter," Tomlinson said. "Of course, I wouldn't mention the senator by name, but—"

Raising a hand, Santino said, "I understand. I see the picture. You'd better not mention my name, either."

Tomlinson nodded. "But I should mention that the energy committee is reviewing the plan."

"Yes. Of course. And mention that the committee is very much aware of the relationship between energy prices and food prices. Tell them that our plan will help the farmer *and* the consumer."

Barely able to contain his delight, Jake added, "And poor people around the world!"

Santino closed his eyes briefly. "Yes, that too."

# Power Talk

It was pouring rain as Jake drove to Lady Cecilia's house. Belinda had hit the Gulf Coast hard, and this storm was a spinoff from the hurricane as it made its way inland from the Louisiana coast. *It's supposed to get weaker as it moves inland,* Jake thought. *If it can generate this much rain here in Washington, it can't be all that weak.*

There was no place to park; the curbs were bumper to bumper with cars. As he drove slowly along the puddled street, windshield wipers swishing, Jake searched for an open spot. He spotted a space, but it turned out to be a driveway. He didn't see Tomlinson's black sedan anywhere along the block. *Of course,* he thought, *Frank didn't have to park. He had his driver let him off; when he's finished he'll call for the driver to pick him up again.*

At last he found an open space, two blocks from the house. Jake backed into it carefully, then reached behind his seat to pull his foldable umbrella out from the seatback pocket.

Umbrella or not, by the time he reached Lady Cecilia's house Jake was wet and miserable. A servant in a dark suit opened the door for him, then jumped back as Jake shook the dripping umbrella over the doorstep.

With a disdainful look, the servant took the umbrella from him, deposited it in a half-filled stand, then hissed, "This way, sir."

Jake was led through the living room, his shoes squishing on the carpeting, to the sparsely furnished room that Cecilia used as an office. This morning it had been turned into a TV studio. A chunky bearded fellow was sitting on a rickety-looking swivel chair with laptop computer open on his knees, staring intently at its screen. Senator Tomlinson and Lady Cecilia were chatting amiably, facing each other on the angled couch. Kevin O'Donnell was standing by the door, arms folded across his chest, like a grim-faced security guard.

Tomlinson looked up as Jake entered the room, feeling as irritated as a drenched hen. O'Donnell nodded dourly by way of a greeting.

"Here's Jake now," the senator said.

Lady Cecilia made a smile that looked forced. "We were just about to start without you."

"I had trouble finding a parking space," Jake said, standing at the doorway.

Cecilia looked surprised. "You could have gone up the alley at the end of the block and parked behind the house."

Jake made an apologetic grin, thinking, Now you tell me.

"All right," Cecilia said, suddenly all business, "let's get to work."

The bearded technician lumbered to his feet, carrying the smallest video camera Jake had ever seen between his thumb and forefinger. Without any preliminaries, Cecilia beamed a wide smile from her froggish face and said, "Hello everybody. I'm talking with Senator Frank Tomlinson, who has a plan to make America the world's leader in energy."

Tomlinson put on his "aw, shucks" smile.

Turning to the senator, she began with, "With Hurricane Belinda knocking out the oil rigs in the Gulf of Mexico, how high will gasoline prices rise?"

Obviously taken aback by the question, Tomlinson replied, "Could be a big spike in prices at the pump, Cecilia. Maybe a thirty to fifty percent rise over the next week or two."

"And how would your energy plan help to avoid this kind of price jump in the future?"

Tomlinson visibly relaxed. Smiling, he said, "Well, we're not going to stop hurricanes. But once the energy plan is working, the cost of gasoline and other fuels will come down noticeably."

"Won't that hurt the oil industry?"

"No, it won't, because their costs are going to go down, as well. Most people don't realize it, but the United States is the biggest oil producer in the world nowadays, what with shale oil and fracking and other new techniques. But with the new technology that my plan supports, the oil companies' costs will go down. They'll be producing more oil at lower prices, and making more profits from it than they do now. The same applies to the coal industry as well."

"Doesn't that sound like pie in the sky?"

"So did electricity, once upon a time. So did airplanes." Breaking into a grin, Tomlinson added, "Why, when railroads were first being built, somebody in Congress declared that if you tried to go faster than twenty-five miles an hour you wouldn't be able to breathe!"

She laughed politely, then asked, "Why do we need an energy plan?"

Looking directly into the camera, Tomlinson put on his serious face and said, "We live in an interconnected world. Agribusiness corporations encourage farmers to plant corn and soybeans to produce ethanol fuel. That cuts into food production and raises food prices around the world—and here at home, too. Fossil fuels produce most of the electricity and all of the transportation fuels we use, but they also produce deadly greenhouse gases that warm the world's climate."

Lady Cecilia said, "Yes, but how will your plan improve the situation?"

Easing into a smile again, Tomlinson replied, "We have new technologies that will allow us to burn fossil fuels without damaging the environment. In fact, we can take the carbon dioxide that fossil fuels emit and turn it into clean, highly efficient methanol fuel. We have sunlight, which pours a thousand times more energy onto the ground than we use today. We have electric cars. Wind power."

"Nuclear energy?"

"That too, if it can be made safe enough. It's time that we coordinated all these technologies and used them to make energy cleaner, more abundant, and cheaper for the American people—and for people all around the world. The United States could become an exporter of new energy technologies. We can help the world's poorest people, cut our imports of foreign oil, and make the world cleaner and greener."

"With your plan."

Nodding, Tomlinson said, "It's time to look at the whole picture, energy-wise. Time to use the brains and the skills that we have to make a coordinated energy policy."

"Could that really be done?"

"The Senate energy committee is studying the plan." Looking into the camera again, Tomlinson said earnestly, "I want to make one point perfectly clear. This is not an either/or proposition. It's not *either* we continue to burn fossil fuels *or* we switch to solar and wind power. It's not *either* we grow corn for ethanol *or* we eliminate the ethanol mandate altogether. There's room for all the energy technologies we have, and then some! It's time that we put all our capabilities together into a sensible, rational plan that will lower energy costs while raising profits for the industries that produce energy for us."

Lady Cecilia seemed taken aback a bit by Tomlinson's fervor. But she quickly recovered enough to ask, "So where does your plan stand at this moment in time?"

"As I said, Cecilia, the Senate energy committee is studying the plan. The next step will be to bring it out onto the floor of the Senate for debate, and then a vote."

"And the House of Representatives?"

"They'll want to debate it and vote on it, too, of course. Then it goes to the president for her signature."

"Suppose the Senate passes your plan, but the House rejects it? Or the president vetoes it?"

Tomlinson's face turned grave. "Then we'll continue to flounder around as we have been for far too long. Energy prices will continue to rise. The United States will continue to send seven trillion dollars a year—and more—overseas to buy foreign oil. We'll get more power shortages, blackouts. And food prices will continue to go up, as more and more farmland is turned over to ethanol production."

"Not a pleasant prospect," said Lady Cecilia.

"No, it's not." Tomlinson shook his head once, then said to her, "Look, a minute ago I said this isn't an either/or situation. Well, in the final analysis, it really is. Either the United States comes up with a rational, comprehensive policy for energy, or we continue to flounder around and get poorer every year."

Cecilia jumped to her feet and shouted to the cameraman, "That's it!" Extending both her hands to Tomlinson, she said, "Well done! That ought to start people buzzing!"

Jake saw that Tomlinson looked surprised, then pleased as he allowed Lady Cecilia to pump both his hands eagerly.

# Unemployed

The rain was down to a spattering drizzle as the dark-suited servant opened Lady Cecilia's front door for Jake, O'Donnell, and the senator. Wordlessly, he took Jake's still-dripping umbrella from the stand just inside the door and handed it to him as if it were a rotting fish.

Stepping outside, Jake saw a patch of blue sky among the scudding gray clouds. Might be a good omen, he thought.

Tomlinson was grinning happily while O'Donnell used his cell phone to call for their chauffeur.

"I thought it went well," the senator said.

"It did," said Jake.

"Kind of quick, though. Hardly a couple of minutes."

With a shrug, Jake said, "It's for the blog. Short attention spans."

Tomlinson nodded, but he still looked concerned.

Jamming his phone into his jacket pocket, O'Donnell groused, "We'll see what the Little Saint thinks of it."

The black sedan pulled up.

"Can we drop you someplace?" Tomlinson asked Jake.

"I'm parked a couple of blocks down the street," Jake said, pointing.

"Hop in, then."

The three of them crammed into the sedan's backseat.

As the car took off, Tomlinson said, "Jake, I want to thank you. You made this happen."

Jake thought, Should I ask for my job back? Is this the right time?

O'Donnell pricked that balloon. "Don't start the victory celebration just yet. Wait 'til we get Santino's reaction."

Tomlinson nodded soberly. "We ought to get a reaction from him before the day's out. Cecilia said the interview will be posted on her blog before lunchtime."

And Jake thought, Better keep my mouth shut. For now.

• • •

As he passed the WETA newsroom on the way to his office, Jake saw that several of the TV monitors were showing satellite images of a hurricane. He stopped and stared through the newsroom window, wondering what was going on. Belinda was supposed to be breaking up over Arkansas and western Tennessee, he knew. Yet this looked like a full-blown hurricane, its eye easily discernible amidst its swirling white clouds.

Then he saw a caption at the bottom of the screens. Hurricane Carlos. Jake sighed. Another one. And it's not even the Fourth of July yet.

• • •

Just after lunch Jake got a phone call from O'Donnell.

"Santino called Franklin," said the chief of staff.

Eagerly, Jake asked, "And?"

"And the Little Saint intends to start hearings on the energy plan next week."

"Hearings?"

"He'll be calling in energy experts from all over the map," O'Donnell said, sounding excited in spite of himself. "The hearings will generate a lot of publicity."

"That's good!" Jake exulted. "Great!"

"He wants Franklin to speak to the full committee first. Give 'em an overview of the plan. There'll be coverage by C-SPAN and all the major news outlets."

"Terrific!"

"Franklin's meeting with Santino tomorrow morning, to plan what he's going to say."

"That's wonderful."

His voice lowering a notch, O'Donnell went on, "Jake, I owe you one. I was wrong about this and you were right."

"The important thing is that the plan is going to see the light of day."

"And Franklin's going to get into the public eye. With Santino backing him."

Jake nodded, then realized that O'Donnell couldn't see him. He asked, "Is there anything I can do to help?"

"You've already done it. Getting Franklin on *Power Talk* was a coup, Jake. I didn't think it would work, but it certainly did. Thanks. I mean that. Thanks a lot, Jake."

Jake was grinning widely as he hung up. But then he realized that O'Donnell didn't say a word about taking Jake back onto Tomlinson's staff.

• • •

Late that afternoon, almost at quitting time, Jake got another phone call. From Margarita Viera, his boss. "Come to my office before you go home," she said. Then hung up.

Still feeling elated about the reaction to Tomlinson's *Power Talk* interview, Jake rapped on Viera's door a half-hour later.

"You want to see me?" he asked, from the doorway.

She looked up from her cluttered desk. "Yes. Come on in and sit down."

Jake did as he was told.

Viera scribbled on a legal-sized tablet, then put her pen down and gave him a hard stare.

"I saw your ex-boss on *Power Talk* this afternoon. The interview's gone viral—inside the Beltway."

Jake nodded, thinking that hardly anybody outside the Beltway had even heard of *Power Talk*. But here in DC the blog was as primal an addiction as morning coffee.

"So when are you leaving us?" Viera asked.

"Leaving?" Jake blinked with surprise.

Making a sour face, Viera said, "Don't be coy, Jake. I hired you because Alexander Tomlinson said you needed a job. He's been a big contributor to PBS over the years, and he said you were a topflight science guy. Not that we needed one, but we made room for you."

"I appreciate that," said Jake.

"I asked around and found why Senator Tomlinson had to let you go. But from what I've seen today, he'll be happy to have you back working for him."

With a sardonic grin, Jake replied, "He hasn't told me that."

Viera's brows rose. "Really? Well, maybe it's too soon."

"Maybe."

"At any rate," Viera said, "we've got several really good prospects among our summer interns, and I want to hire one of them, full-time."

Jake saw it coming. Oh no, he said to himself.

Viera continued, "But all our slots are full. We don't have room for a new hire—unless I let somebody go."

"And I'm somebody."

Waving one hand in the air, Viera said, "You're not a news person, Jake. I mean, you've done okay for a novice, but your heart really isn't in our business, is it?"

"I guess not," he admitted.

"This kid I want to hire is really good. But you don't

have to go right away, Jake. The end of the week will be time enough. Okay?"

No, it's not okay, Jake thought. But he nodded and got up from his chair. I'm going to join the ranks of the unemployed, he realized.

# Fourth of July

D oesn't Congress take its summer recess around now?" Tami asked.

"They're taking off the rest of the week. Summer recess doesn't start until the end of the month," Jake said morosely.

They were sitting in the living room of Jake's basement apartment. The TV was showing a baseball game: Washington Nationals against the Philadelphia Phillies. Jake paid no attention to it. He had muted the audio.

"Don't you want to go to the picnic?" Tami asked. "It'll be fun."

"If it doesn't rain."

Tami looked at him. "Boy, you really are down."

He puffed out a sigh. "As of tomorrow I'm going to be unemployed. Maybe unemployable. I've got the mark of Santino on my forehead."

Tami looked alarmed. "You're not going back to Montana, are you?"

"I might have to," he said. Then, "But even if I do, I don't have a job waiting for me there."

"Don't you have tenure at the university?"

"An assistant professor doesn't get tenure."

"Well, that stinks."

Despite himself, Jake laughed. Weakly. "I'm glad I've got one fan, at least."

Shaking him by the shoulder, Tami said, "Come on,

let's go to the picnic. It'll be fun. You'll enjoy meeting my coworkers."

Jake pictured himself sitting on the grass with a bunch of strangers while ants nibbled at his lunch and mosquitoes stung him. With any luck I'll pick up Lyme disease, he thought. He reached for the TV remote and clicked on the Weather Channel.

"Let's see if it's going to rain."

"Party pooper."

Still muted, the TV screen showed a tropical city drenched in a torrential downpour, wind blowing roofs off houses, rain so thick he could hardly see the other side of the street. Then it cut to a palm-fringed beach where mammoth waves surged across the sand and the trees were bending over almost double. A rickety wooden pier was near to collapsing, and several beachfront homes were already flooded.

"Hurricane Carlos," Tami breathed, staring at the devastation.

Jake shook his head. "They say that God must love the poor, because he made so many of them. But every time there's a disaster the poor get hit the hardest."

The view cut to a map that showed the hurricane squarely over the Bahamas. It was so big that its western side covered the Florida coast all the way up to Lake Okeechobee. And the cone that showed where it might be heading over the next two days had Washington, DC, directly in its middle.

"We're going to be in for it," Jake murmured.

"Maybe it'll turn away," said Tami.

He got to his feet. "Come on, let's make hay while the sun's shining."

She jumped to her feet, smiling broadly.

"And get a tankful of gas for the car," Jake added.

• • •

"You're not the only one who watched the news," Tami said as she sat beside Jake in his Mustang. The gas station was crowded with lines of cars waiting to fill up.

"Belinda knocked out the oil rigs on the Gulf Coast," Jake said, as much to himself as to her, "and now everybody wants to fill his tank before Carlos hits."

Bright sunshine smiled down from a clear blue sky. Hardly a cloud in sight. Yet Jake had the ominous feeling that a monster was lurking nearby, shambling toward them.

"Five dollars and thirty cents!" Tami gasped, pointing to the prices listed on the gas station's sign. "That's highway robbery!"

Ordinarily Jake would have chuckled at her inadvertent pun. Instead, he simply nodded. "Supply and demand, Tami. Supply's down because the Gulf oil rigs are out. Demand is up because people want to get out of town before Carlos hits."

"Maybe we should go out of town, too," Tami suggested.

Inching another car length closer to the pump, Jake countered, "And go where?"

"Pennsylvania. West Virginia. Anyplace north and west of here."

He shook his head. "We don't know where the storm's going to strike, or when. We could be running right into it instead of escaping from it."

Frowning unhappily, Tami said, "I have an aunt living in Harrisburg. Haven't seen her in more than five years, though."

Jake thought briefly of Steve Brogan, in Ohio. How would he react if we suddenly showed up on his doorstep, refugees looking for shelter?

The car behind him bleated its horn as the car in front of him drove away from the gas pump. Jake suppressed an urge to yell at the jerk. Instead he pulled up at the pump and popped the cover on his gas tank.

He got out of the Mustang and slid his credit card into the slot on the pump. Nothing happened. Puzzled, he slid it again. Again nothing. The guy behind him honked again and yelled out his window, "Come on, asshole."

Before Jake could react, a harried-looking man in grimy slacks and baggy shirt came hurrying to the pump, slim and dark-skinned, his thinning hair disheveled.

"So sorry, sir, this pump is now empty."

"Empty?"

"All the petrol is gone. My apologies, sir."

Jake looked at the five other pumps. Each of them had at least half a dozen cars lined up.

The station attendant made apologetic motions with his hands. "I am afraid, sir, that by the time you get into line at one of the other pumps and actually reach the pump, it will be empty also. My regrets."

Jake huffed, shot the driver behind him an angry glare, then ducked back into the Mustang.

"They ran out of gas?" Tami asked.

Putting the car in gear, Jake said, "Might as well go to the picnic. I don't have enough gas to get out of town."

"Me neither," Tami said. "I intended to fill up tomorrow, on my way to work."

"We're going to be here when the storm hits."

"Maybe it won't be so bad."

"Maybe," said Jake. Without any conviction whatsoever.

# Hurricane Carlos

All through the picnic Jake sensed an unease among the people from Tami's office. The sun was still shining brightly out of a blue sky flecked with chubby white clouds, yet there was a tension in the air. Hamburgers, hot dogs, beer, and anxiety. Well before three o'clock people started drifting away, heading home—or maybe out of the area altogether.

Jake drove Tami back to his place. Knowing it was probably an exercise in futility, he opened his laptop and looked for a couple of open seats on any airline heading out of Washington. Nothing. All flights were full.

"Looks like we're staying here," he said to Tami.

She made a smile for him. "Might be fun, living through a major hurricane. In Florida they have hurricane parties, don't they?"

"Until the electricity cuts off," Jake said. The moroseness in his tone made Tami's smile wink out.

Getting up from the sofa, she said, "I'd better get back to my place. At least it's on the third floor."

Looking around at his basement apartment, Jake said, "Better than here."

"Why don't you come with me?" Tami blurted. "Pack a bag and stay at my place until the storm's over."

"What about the women you share the apartment with?"

"To hell with them. I don't care what they think."

Jake shook his head. "Tami, I don't want to upset your relationship with your apartment-mates." He remembered her telling him, months ago, that the four women lived cheek-by-jowl in the cramped apartment and shared a single bathroom.

"You'll be all right here?" she asked.

"I'll be all right. After the storm blows by we'll go out to dinner at the Maison Blanche."

Looking relieved and anxious at the same time, Tami said, "All right. I'd better go, then."

He walked her out to her car, parked at curbside. It was a lovely summer night. Jake could see the summer triangle of Deneb, Vega, and Altair twinkling high above.

The calm before the storm, he thought.

•  •  •

It was his last day at WETA. As he cleaned out his desk, Jake kept glancing out the window. The sky was clouding up, turning gray and menacing. He thought he saw a flash of lightning, but that might have been merely his coiled-up nerves.

He went to say good-bye to Viera, only to find she had already left. The offices were deserted as a ghost town; just about everybody had gone home, or out of the city. Jake went into the newsroom, where almost every TV monitor showed Hurricane Carlos: satellite imagery, views of the Carolina coast being battered by huge angry waves, shots of the highways leading out of DC, clogged with cars.

Jake pictured himself in that mammoth traffic snarl, running out of gas on the highway while the storm tore the roof off his convertible. I'm better off hunkering down in the apartment, he told himself.

By the time he got home the sky was gray and ominous and it had begun to rain. It was easy to find a parking space; half of the tree-lined street was empty.

As he hurried through the pelting rain from his car to his apartment, he saw his landlord, draped in a flapping raincoat, pushing a wheelbarrow from the shed at the far end of the garden toward his door.

Before Jake could ask when the man was doing, he said, "Sandbags. Heavy rain comes down your steps, could wet your living room."

Sandbags! Jake thought, picturing levees along a flooding river. He helped the landlord place them around the edge of the well leading down to his door as the rain intensified and thunder boomed.

"Better take a couple for inside the door," the landlord said.

Getting soaked, Jake took a sandbag in his arms. It was heavy and gritty. He nearly tripped and fell as he started down the four steps, but he managed to right himself and unlock the door, after putting the sandbag down at his feet. The bottom of the stairs was already puddled.

Jake got inside, out of the rain, and dragged the soggy sandbag in after him. Stripping off his wet jacket, he headed straight for the TV and turned on a local channel.

"The Emergency Management Agency has declared a hurricane emergency," said a pert young blond woman, smiling as if she were announcing a wedding. "Make certain you have plenty of batteries for flashlights and emergency lamps, and fill your bathtub with water for drinking, in case water service is temporarily suspended."

"I don't have a goddamned bathtub," Jake snarled at the screen. "Just a shower." His one flashlight was solar-powered, a gift from Wilmer Nevins. He wondered how long it would last without sunlight to run it.

But he went to his kitchenette and started pulling jars and bottles out of the shelves, to fill with drinking water.

The TV switched to the station's weather forecaster,

wearing a navy blue blazer and a grim expression. He swept an arm across a map of the area, swathed in red.

"As you can see," the forecaster was saying, "the storm will pass to the east of the metropolitan District area. Looks like Annapolis is going to get a direct hit. We'll have plenty of rain here in DC, and extremely high winds, with gusts up to ninety miles per hour or more."

A sudden hard thump against his front door made Jake drop the bottle he was holding; it clattered into the sink but didn't break.

What the hell was that? he asked himself.

Hurrying to the door, Jake yanked it open and found another sandbag at his feet. The landlord must've tossed it down here, Jake realized. It was raining harder and the wind had picked up considerably.

Just then his phone rang. Jake dragged the wet and gritty sandbag inside, slammed the door and went to the phone by his desk.

"Hello."

"I gave you another sandbag," came his landlord's laconic voice. "You'll probably need it."

The man hung up, leaving Jake nodding to himself and thinking, It's going to be a helluva night.

# Blackout

So far so good, Jake told himself, shakily.

The wind was screeching outside and he could hear the rain drumming against the windows that looked out onto the street. It was dark as midnight out there, even though the clock said only seven thirty.

Jake had pushed the two sandbags against his door, like a soldier trying to protect himself from an attacking enemy. He had filled every bottle and jar he could find with water and tried the solar flashlight, which lit up brightly. He quickly turned it off, not wanting to drain its battery needlessly, and put it down on the coffee table.

Standing in the middle of his living room, Jake turned slowly, nervously, surveying his battlefield. So far so good, he repeated to himself.

Then he saw that water was trickling down the wall from the bottom of his windows.

Jesus! He ran to the bathroom, yanked an armful of towels from the linen closet and dumped them on the sofa. Puffing with exertion, he pulled the sofa away from the wall, banging it against the coffee table, and spread the towels on the floor. Hope they'll soak up the water, he thought. It's only a trickle. Not that bad. But he knew it would get worse.

He had to urinate. Fear fills the bladder, he thought as he dashed to the bathroom.

When he came back to the living room the TV showed

that Carlos was approaching Annapolis. The announcer's voice explained, "It's a fast-moving storm, and the metropolitan DC area should be out from under it in a few hours."

A few hours. Jake got a mental image of an old movie about a submarine crew drowning as water poured in and filled their cramped compartments.

His cell phone buzzed. He yanked it out of his pocket. Tami, he saw.

"Hi, Tami."

Her voice asked, "How're you making out, Jake?"

"Okay, so far. How about you?"

"It's awfully noisy, but we're in good shape. We thawed out a pizza and we're drinking beer with it."

He almost smiled. "Good for you. Any leaks?"

"On the third floor? We're not getting flooded, Jake."

"I meant your windows. I'm getting some leakage."

"Is it serious?"

"No, but my landlord's going to have to repaint my living room once this is—"

The lights flickered.

"Uh oh. Our lights just flickered," Tami said.

"Mine, too."

He heard a crash outside, and the apartment went totally dark. The TV screen winked out and the surge protector on his computer started beeping.

"You still there?" he yelled into the phone.

"Yes." But for the first time Tami's voice sounded frightened.

"Sounds like a tree got knocked over out on the street," Jake said. "Or maybe it was just a limb. Must have clipped the power line."

"Jake! Our lights went out!"

Blackout, Jake thought. "Stay calm," he said, feeling his own innards quaking.

Tami said, "If the cell tower goes down—"

Her voice cut off. The cell phone's screen read NO SIGNAL.

Tower's gone, Jake realized. The wind outside was howling like a furious monster. The apartment was totally dark. Jake slowly edged to where he thought the coffee table was, trying to see through the darkness. There was no light at all; even the streetlamps outside had gone out.

His shin bumped the coffee table's edge. Bending down, groping, Jake's fingers found the flashlight. He turned it on, never so grateful in his whole life for a bit of light.

Jake made his way to his desk, picked up the telephone there, and tapped out Tami's apartment's number, hoping that the land line was still working. It was, but all he got was a busy signal.

Four women, he groused. Her phone's going to be busy as long as the line still works.

He hung up the phone and it immediately rang. Snatching it, he heard his landlord's somber voice. "You okay down there?"

"Got some water leaking from the windows," Jake said. "Otherwise things look okay."

"Good." The landlord hung up.

Jake went to the sofa and sat down, tense and strained. He turned the flashlight off and leaned back. Close your eyes, he commanded himself, and get some sleep. But he couldn't sleep. He heard the wind yowling and the rain hammering and now and then bumps and crashes that made his insides jump. It seemed endless. Rain and wind, wind and rain. Stop it! he screamed silently. Just go away and leave me alone!

He looked at the luminous numbers on his wristwatch. In ten minutes I'll turn on the flashlight, he told himself, see how everything's doing.

He went to the bathroom again, wishing he were someplace else, anyplace else. Back in Montana, even a blizzard wasn't as bad as this. He pictured himself on a tropical beach or, better yet, trudging across the barren dunes of a sandy desert baking under a blazing hot sun. Or maybe on the Moon, in a spacesuit like Knowles must have worn. No hurricanes on the Moon. It's quiet and peaceful up there.

He returned to the living room, guided by the flashlight's beam. Water was streaming down from the windows, but the towels seemed to be absorbing it. So far. Swinging the beam toward his door, he saw water seeping under the sandbags, creeping across the floor toward him.

What a mess, he moaned to himself. What a god-damned stupid mess. And there's nothing I can do about it. Not a mother-loving goddamned thing.

Try to sleep, he thought. Yeah, sure. Sleep through a hurricane. Joe Cool.

Still, he got up from the sofa, flicked on his flashlight again, and went to his bedroom. He shut its door, and the manic roar of the storm was tamped down a little. No windows in here, Jake told himself. No way for the water to get in. He sat on the bed and turned off the flashlight. Total darkness. Nothing but me and the storm. Carlos and me.

Without taking off his clothes or even his shoes he stretched out on the bed and squeezed his eyes shut. Try to sleep. It'll be over soon. Tomorrow the sun will come out and Carlos will be far away.

Yeah, but it's not tomorrow yet. Still got a long way to go.

Even with his bedroom door tightly shut, he could hear the wind howling out there and knew the water was leaking into his living room. He tried to think if there was anything in the apartment resting on the floor. Any books or magazines on a bottom shelf?

He sat up and reached for the blanket folded at the foot of the bed. Pulling it over himself, shoes and all, Jake curled into a fetal position and tried to force himself to sleep.

# Aftermath

Somebody was talking to him. Jake opened his eyes. They felt gummy. And somebody in the living room was talking.

He slowly pulled himself to a sitting position, feeling weary, grungy in his wrinkled, sweaty clothes. He realized he had fallen asleep after all.

The bedside lamp was on! And the voice he heard from the living room was the TV.

The power's back on! And the wind had died away. His bedside clock was blinking 12:00, but his wristwatch showed it was 6:23 a.m.

Jake threw off his tangled blanket and got to his feet. He went to the bathroom and saw through its narrow slit of a window that the sun was shining brightly outside.

It's over, he realized, feeling a huge wave of relief wash over him. It's over.

He urinated into the toilet, then washed his hands and splashed cold water over his face.

He went into the living room and saw that an inch-deep puddle of water covered half the room, from the door almost to the coffee table. The wall below the windows was water stained. But the sun was shining out there, and the electricity was on. Every lamp in the room was alight, and the TV screen showed the same weather forecaster, looking just as tired as Jake felt, explaining that Hurricane Carlos was now weakening as it moved northward, into New Jersey.

His cell phone still read NO SIGNAL, but Jake went to the phone on his desk and called Tami.

A stranger's voice answered.

"Is Tami there?" he asked.

"Yes. Who's this—Jake?"

"Right," he answered, realizing that Tami must have told them a lot about him.

Tami came on. "Jake! How are you? How's—"

"I'm fine. My living room's wet, but otherwise everything's okay. You?"

"No worries," she said. "Dry and safe, but our electricity's still out."

"We're okay here. You'll probably get your power back in a little while."

He could sense her smiling. But she said, "Jake, I've got to get off the line. Nora's expecting a call from her mother in Tennessee."

"Okay. Remember, we have a dinner date."

"Maison Blanche."

"I'll pick you up at seven, okay?"

"Wonderful. See you then."

She hung up. Jake put the phone down, then went back to the bedroom to shower, shave, and dress. When he returned to the living room he stepped through the puddle and slid the soaked sandbags away from his front door. When he opened it, more water sloshed in. But he ignored it and climbed up the steps, into the garden.

It looked like a battle zone out there. The line of bottlebrush trees along the side of the property was bent and sagging; one of the trees had fallen against the shed in the rear of the garden. The oaks back there looked okay, although Jake saw plenty of tree limbs and leaves scattered across the grass. The ground was wet, puddles here and there. Jake's shoes were getting soaked even more as he walked across the garden.

The house on the other side of the property was dark and still. They must have left town, he thought. But then he realized that the streetlights were still dark. Well, it's daytime now, he told himself. Walking to the front of the house, he saw that several trees had come down along the street—one of them squarely on a house's roof—but none of the houses showed a single light.

The whole neighborhood's still dark, but we've got electric power. Jake wondered how that could be.

His landlord stepped out onto the porch.

"Good morning!" Jake called to him.

"Morning."

The man's wife came out beside him, plump and smiling. "How are you?" she asked.

"I'm okay," Jake replied, "but I'm afraid the floor of the apartment is soaked. And the windows leaked pretty bad."

"I've already called a cleanup service," said the landlord. "They're pretty busy. It'll take a few days before they get here."

Jake nodded. "I'll mop up the water in the living room."

"Could get some mold," the landlord said, as dispassionate as a robot. "You ought to find someplace to stay until the cleanup people take care of it."

Before Jake could respond to that, the landlord's wife said, "Come inside and have some coffee with us."

Jake thanked her, but as he started up the porch steps he asked, "How come you've got electricity? Nobody else seems to—"

The landlord stabbed a lean finger upward. "Solar panels on the roof. Didn't you ever notice them?"

"Solar . . . ?" Jake broke into laughter. "Well, I'll be damned!"

"Oh, don't say that," the wife cautioned. "God might hear you and take you at your word."

Jake clicked his teeth shut and followed the introverted landlord and his warmly gracious wife into the kitchen.

• • •

Solar panels on the roof, Jake said to himself as he sat at the kitchen table and munched on whole wheat toast with butter and jam. He never mentioned them to me, and I never noticed them. But as soon as the sun came out, he got electrical power.

Jake made a mental note to contact Nevins and ask him about marketing household solar panel arrays as a protection against power failures.

"Do you have someone you can stay with for a few days?" the landlord's wife asked.

With a shake of his head, Jake said, "I'm afraid not. I'll have to get a hotel room."

"They'll be jammed," said his landlord.

"Maybe."

"They'll charge double, most likely."

Before Jake could reply to that, his cell phone buzzed. They must have repaired the tower, he thought as he pulled it from his pocket.

B. F. Tomlinson, read the phone's screen.

Somewhat surprised, he asked, "Frank?"

Tomlinson's voice replied, "Jake, are you okay? How'd you make it through the storm?"

"I'm okay, but my apartment got kind of flooded."

"I was worried about that, you being in the basement. Amy thought we ought to ask you to spend the night with us, but by then the cell phones were out and I don't have your apartment's phone number here at the house."

Glancing at his landlord, who was resolutely keeping his eyes on his own plate of bacon and eggs, Jake said, "That's awfully good of you, Frank. Thank Amy for me."

"Will you be okay now? How badly is your place flooded?"

"We'll need a professional cleanup crew. I'll have to find a hotel room for a few days."

"Nonsense. You come here."

"Your house?"

"We have plenty of room, and as long as the auxiliary generator works, we've got electricity. Come on over."

"Frank, that's awfully good of you."

"And once you get here, we can talk about your rejoining the staff."

"Really?" Jake's voice squeaked. Inwardly he frowned at how eager and grateful he sounded.

Well, I am eager and grateful, he told himself as he thanked his landlord and wife, then went downstairs to his apartment and packed a travel bag for a few days' stay at *chez* Tomlinson.

He wasn't even disturbed when he saw that his Mustang's roof had leaked badly and the seats were all wet. Instead, as he went back to his apartment for a roll of paper towels, Jake felt happy that the car's roof hadn't blown off altogether.

# Preparations

C ommittee hearing starts Monday," Tomlinson said, looking eager with anticipation.

"Unless they're postponed by the storm," Amy said.

"I doubt that," said Jake.

The three of them were sitting in Tomlinson's living room after a late-morning brunch served by the cook. The big TV screen on the wall showed cleanup efforts under way around the city. Electrical power was still off for most of the metropolitan area, except for places that had standby emergency generators, as the Tomlinson residence did.

Savoring the coffee that Amy had poured for him, Jake said, "You know, the house I'm in has solar panels on the roof. We got electricity as soon as the sun came up."

"The panels weren't damaged by the storm?" Amy asked.

"No. And I guess the wind blew off any debris that might have landed on them. They worked just fine. All they needed was some sunshine."

Tomlinson saw what Jake was driving at. "Solar panel emergency kits. The city ought to look into that."

"And hospitals should put them on their roofs," said Jake. "Stores, shopping malls."

"Gas stations," Amy added.

With a grin, Jake said, "I know just the guy you

should talk to, Frank." But then he wondered if Wilmer Nevins would want to talk to a US senator.

• • •

Jake rode with the senator that afternoon to his office in the Hart Building, where they worked on the opening statement that Tomlinson was to make at the energy committee's hearing on Monday.

When they arrived, five staff members were already in the office, including Kevin O'Donnell. None of them seemed surprised to see Jake with the senator. O'Donnell stuck his hand out and said, "Welcome back, Jake." And that was that. The rest of the afternoon they worked together as if Jake had never been fired, huddled around the circular table in the conference room.

Toward six o'clock, O'Donnell asked the senator if he wanted to keep on going or adjourn for the day and finish the prep work the next morning, Sunday.

Tomlinson grinned at his chief of staff. "I have a dinner date this evening. With Senator Santino."

O'Donnell's eyes went wide. "When did *that* happen?"

"Last night. He phoned me at home in the middle of the storm and said he wanted to go over what I intended to say on Monday. I'm sorry I forgot to tell you about it, Kevin. What with the storm and all . . ."

O'Donnell looked upset, almost pained. "You've got to keep me informed about these things, Frank."

"You're right. I'm sorry." But Jake thought that Tomlinson didn't look sorry. He seemed almost amused.

The phone on the row of cabinets along the wall rang. O'Donnell waved everybody off and picked it up. "Senator Tomlinson's office."

He listened for several minutes, then said, "I'll ask him. Hold on."

Looking over at the senator, across the circular table,

he said, "It's Earl Reynolds. WETA is asking if you can squeeze in a half hour for their local news show tomorrow morning. They want you to tell them how your energy plan would help the city cope with natural disasters like this hurricane."

Tomlinson hiked his brows questioningly. O'Donnell nodded. The senator said, "Okay. Tell him I'll do it."

Jake wondered if he should try to take credit for WE TA's interest. But then he had a better idea.

• • •

"Solar Solutions?" Tomlinson asked. "I don't think I've ever heard of them."

Jake and the senator were riding to WETA for the Sunday morning news show. Jake had already phoned Wilmer Nevins and asked him to meet them there before the broadcast.

"I think this is an opportunity for you to mention how solar panels could be used to provide emergency electrical power during a blackout."

"Once the sun comes up," Tomlinson said.

"They can charge batteries during the daytime and let you run on them during the night."

"Really?"

"Frank, they've been setting up systems like that for years in poor villages in Africa and Asia. The same kind of setup could work as emergency generators during a blackout."

The senator still looked uncertain.

"Just talk to Nevins for a few minutes before the show," Jake urged. "He's been doing this sort of thing for years."

"If Reynolds doesn't object."

Jake urged, "Frank, Earl's a great PR guy, but he doesn't know much about energy systems."

"Okay," Tomlinson said. Reluctantly.

Nevins was deep in conversation with Reynolds when Jake and Tomlinson arrived at the station's green room.

Jake introduced Nevins to the senator.

"You put up solar panels," Tomlinson said as he shook Nevins's hand.

With an almost boyish grin, Nevins said, "It turns out that my people put up the system on the house Jake lives in."

Jake saw that Nevins was almost a head shorter than the senator, but thicker in the torso and limbs. His tightly curled hair was silver-gray, his face weathered and tan. In contrast, Tomlinson looked like a tall, elegant patrician. Which he is, Jake realized.

After a few minute of intense talk, the senator turned to Jake. "Maybe we should put this idea of emergency solar systems into the energy plan."

"No!" Nevins snapped, alarmed. "Keep the government out of it!"

Puzzled, Tomlinson asked, "You don't want government support?"

"We don't need it. We've got more work than we can handle, as it is."

With a grin, the senator asked, "But you don't mind if I mention the idea on today's interview?"

Nevins looked clearly torn. "You can say what you want to. It's still a free country."

One of the station's assistant producers stuck her cornrowed head through the green room door. "You'll be on in five minutes, Senator. I'll bring you onto the set and mike you up."

Reynolds pulled Tomlinson away from Nevins. "Don't spend the whole interview talking about solar. Stay above any single technology. Explain the plan as a whole."

Tomlinson nodded, but he looked toward Nevins as he did so.

As the assistant producer guided them down the hallway and onto the set, Jake asked, "How did your dinner with Santino go?"

"Peaches and cream," Tomlinson replied. "Mario is already seeing the energy plan helping him to win votes for the Majority Leader's spot."

Jake felt pleased. But as they stepped around a fake wall and onto the brightly lit set, he wondered if the plan would be enough to win the election for Santino. And what would happen if it didn't.

Without a word to anyone, Reynolds made his way to the control booth, above the set, leaving Jake and Nevins standing behind the cameras as the senator settled himself onto a high plush swivel chair beside the news show's female anchor. Her colleague, a bright-faced young man in a loud tie, was seated at her other side. In a surprisingly deep, authoritative voice he read from the teleprompter:

"In the aftermath of Hurricane Carlos's impact on the region, we have Senator Franklin Tomlinson with us this morning, to discuss how the energy plan he's developed could help the city cope with natural disasters and power blackouts."

The female anchor, a hard-eyed blonde, smiled professionally into the camera, then turned to Tomlinson.

"Senator, can future energy developments allow us to get through a storm like Carlos without blackouts?"

Tomlinson turned on his smile, too, and answered, "Yes, definitely. In several ways."

"Such as?"

"Well, for one thing, we could use solar energy. I have a friend who lives in a house that has solar panels on its roof. As soon as the sun came up, the house had electricity."

Out of the corner of his eye, Jake saw Nevins's cheek tic.

"But what about during the night," the anchorwoman asked, "when the sun isn't shining?"

"Solar panels can charge a battery pack during daylight, and the batteries can provide electrical power until the sun comes out again."

Nevins folded his arms across his chest, then quickly unfolded them again. He's coiled tight as a drum, Jake realized.

"So your energy plan includes government support for solar energy?"

Tomlinson said, "Encouragement, not support."

"Encouragement?"

His expression turning serious, Tomlinson said, "From what I've learned about the solar energy industry, they don't need a massive government program. They're already building solar energy systems for private homes, shopping malls, factories, and other facilities all across the country."

Before the anchorwoman could ask another question, Tomlinson went on, "My plan will include significant tax credits for private individuals and small companies who buy solar panel systems. That way, we encourage the use of solar energy without spending a penny of taxpayers' money."

The anchorwoman blinked once, then asked, "No government funding for solar?"

"It's not needed. Not for this kind of solar energy." Leaning closer to the woman, Tomlinson said, "You see, what we're talking about here is private homeowners and small businesses making their own decisions to go solar. We don't need a massive government program for that. We can encourage them with tax incentives, all right, but we shouldn't try to inject government bureaucracies into a business that is already doing okay on its own."

Nevins visibly relaxed.

But the anchorwoman persisted, "So you think that solar energy could help prevent blackouts?"

Breaking into a wide grin, Tomlinson replied, "As long as we have trees near power lines, there'll be blackouts when a big storm hits. What I'm saying, Sylvia, is that homes that have solar panels will be able to provide their own electricity for themselves when a blackout occurs."

"And what about when there's no storm? When the weather is bright and clear?"

"They can get their electricity from sunshine, naturally," Tomlinson answered. "Several states have passed laws that allow homeowners to sell solar-derived electricity to their local utility companies when their panels produce more electricity than they need."

"Sell electric power back to the power company?"

"That's right. That helps homeowners to recoup the money they invested to put up their solar panels."

"How do the power companies feel about that?"

Tomlinson cocked his head to one side, thinking before he spoke. Then, "In general, the idea has worked out pretty well. Solar panels on private homes produce the most electricity when the sun is shining the brightest. In states like Texas, for example, when the weather is at its hottest, the utility companies *need* the extra electric power that the solar homes produce, to feed all the air conditioners that are running at top power."

Nevins was nodding happily. He only had a few minutes to talk with Frank, Jake thought, but he must have made quite an impression.

"And another thing," Tomlinson went on. "You could manufacture portable solar electric systems as emergency power generators. Hook 'em up to houses during a blackout, so they have power until the electricity grid comes back on line. That could develop into a whole new product line for hardware stores."

"Portable emergency solar power systems," the anchorwoman echoed.

"But the energy plan is much broader than any one technology," Tomlinson said, earnestly. "The plan encompasses all our energy technologies and all our energy resources in an organized, comprehensive way."

"It sounds wonderful," said the anchorwoman. "I wish we had the time to go into it in detail." Before the senator could say anything, she turned to the camera and said, "We'll be back after a word from our supporters."

"We're out," shouted the floor director. The same assistant producer stepped up to Tomlinson and unclipped his lapel mike.

Tomlinson shook hands with the anchorwoman and the assistant producer, then walked over to where Jake and Nevins were standing.

"That's it, apparently," he said.

Reynolds showed up, his handsome face set in a dark scowl. "You spent the whole interview shilling for solar panels," he grumbled.

Tomlinson made a disarming smile. "I thought they'd give me more time." Turning to Nevins, he went on, "Anyway, I ought to get a decent discount when I get Wilmer here to put panels on my roof."

Nevins grinned and Jake thought that he'd made a convert of the senator. But had he made the best use of the TV time? Clearly Reynolds didn't think so.

# Senate Hearing Chamber

Jake watched the opening session of the energy committee's hearing from a seat in the last row of the ornately decorated hearing room. O'Donnell and Reynolds were sitting up front, just behind the little desk where the witnesses would testify.

Santino, sitting in the center of the row of committee members, gaveled the hearing to order. The rows of benches for the audience were only half-filled, mostly with witnesses who expected to be called on. Not much media attention, Jake saw. C-SPAN and a couple of local TV stations. He didn't see any network news cameras in the chamber. There ought to be more, he thought. Reynolds hasn't come through for Frank.

Santino was at his self-effacing, passive-aggressive best as he introduced, "Senator B. Franklin Tomlinson, of Montana, who has proposed a sweeping energy plan for this committee to consider."

Tomlinson was at his best, too, as he left his seat among his fellow committee members and went to the witness desk: smiling, handsome, self-assured. He took the chair and looked up directly at Santino as one of the committee's staff members unfolded an easel and stood it beside the desk.

After thanking Santino and the committee for the opportunity to present his plan, Tomlinson began, "Energy is the key to everything we do, and everything we hope to do. From growing food crops to exploring outer space, energy is central to all our needs, all our hopes, all our dreams."

Jake knew the words by heart.

"The comprehensive plan I'm proposing is aimed at three interlocking objectives," the senator went on. "Strengthening America's economy, strengthening our national security, and protecting the environment.

"If we use our strengths and our skills wisely," he urged, "we can not only lead the world in energy production, we can also create thousands of new jobs, lower the cost of energy around the world, lower the cost of food around the world, and make the world safer, wealthier, and healthier."

From his seat in the back row, Jake studied the committee members sitting on either side of Santino. They didn't seem terribly enthused. Or even much interested. A couple of them were whispering to aides who crouched behind them. One was staring off into space, half-asleep. Santino himself, though, smiled and nodded at Tomlinson like an old teacher pleased with a bright new student.

O'Donnell got up and unfolded a chart, which he placed gingerly on the easel standing beside the witness desk. Jake saw the complex diagram they had created over the weekend. It detailed how the energy plan included fossil fuel resources, the carbon dioxide capture technology that produced methanol fuel, and nuclear, solar, wind, and hydroelectric power.

As Tomlinson carefully explained the chart, stressing that it was revenue neutral, the senator from Ohio asked to be recognized. Santino didn't seem surprised.

"Senator," the Ohioan said to Tomlinson, "d'you mean you'd *force* utility companies and factories to buy equipment that will capture the carbon dioxide their plants emit?"

Still smiling, Tomlinson replied, "The recapture equipment isn't that expensive, Senator, and the companies can then sell the carbon dioxide to companies that will use it to produce methanol fuel. Not only is that less expensive than burying the $CO_2$ underground, it will pay for the expense of buying the recapture systems."

The senator from Ohio did not look convinced. He was an imposingly large, stocky, gray-haired man. Jake thought he might have played football for Ohio State when he was younger.

"And all this carbon dioxide will be used to produce methanol fuel?" he asked.

"That's right, Senator. Methanol is a relatively clean, high-energy fuel. Oil companies can mix it with their gasoline, making it cleaner and less expensive—in the long run."

"And what happens to the farmers who're growing crops that're used to make ethanol?" the Ohioan demanded.

He's a stalking horse for Perlmutter, Jake realized. Santino didn't look alarmed, though. He must have expected this.

Unrattled, Tomlinson replied, "The agribusiness corporations can sell their crops for food, the way they did before the ethanol mandate was enacted. Global food prices will go down, poor people around the world will pay less for their food." Before the senator could respond, Tomlinson added, "And food prices here in the US will go down as well. Even in Ohio."

A few people in the audience chuckled, but the senator from Ohio was clearly unhappy. "While American farmers get poorer," he growled.

Breaking into his most dazzling smile, Tomlinson countered, "No, Senator, they won't get poorer, because the prices they pay for fuel for their farm vehicles and electricity for their homes will be coming down, too. The farmers will be better off, and the big agribusiness corporations will make higher profits."

Santino tapped his gavel. "Let's move on, shall we?"

"One more point, if you please," the senator from Ohio said.

Santino dipped his chin accommodatingly.

Turning back to Tomlinson, his chunky face grim, the Ohioan pointed a finger as he accused, "Isn't this grandiose plan of yours nothing more than an attempt to get federal funding for the MHD power generation scheme, back in your home state of Montana?"

Tomlinson looked startled, but he quickly masked his surprise. Quite seriously, he replied, "I'm glad you brought that up, Senator. Yes, MHD power generation is a part of the comprehensive plan, but only a part of the whole. Using MHD will allow the coal-fired power plants in your state of Ohio, Senator, to generate electricity more efficiently, and much more cleanly."

"So you claim."

Smiling again, Tomlinson said, "I invite you to Montana, sir, to see for yourself our MHD generator and how it performs. Once you're convinced about MHD, perhaps you can help the electric utilities in your state—and the coal companies—to take an interest in this marvelous new technology."

The senator from Ohio did not look pleased.

# Debriefing

thought it went very well," said Tomlinson, leaning back in his desk chair with a glass of scotch in one hand. It was the end of a long day spent at the energy committee hearing.

Sitting in front of the desk, Jake saw that O'Donnell and Reynolds, sitting there with him, both looked pleased. The normally dour staff chief was even smiling.

Reynolds said, "I've already got four requests for TV interviews for you. And several blogs want you to talk to them, including *Power Talk*."

"Lady Cecilia?" Tomlinson asked, grinning. "Again?"

"It went just about as well as could be expected," O'Donnell said. He, too, had a drink in hand. "Better, even."

"That's because you always expect the worst, Kevin," the senator joked.

Jake's hands were empty. He had a dinner date with Tami coming up, and the wine they'd share would be enough of a celebration for him.

"Santino seemed pleased," Tomlinson said. "Did you see him smiling at me?"

Jake remembered Steve Brogan's words about the Little Saint: *He's the kind of guy who can smile at you while he's knifing you in the back.*

"All the other witnesses were favorable," Reynolds said.

With some of his normal cynicism, O'Donnell replied,

"That's because they were all hand-picked by Santino's staff. No dissenters allowed."

Jake mentally ran through the people who had testified: coal industry, oil industry, electric utilities, automobile industry, nuclear power, solar, windmills, and a woman from the environmental lobby—Santino's people had covered the waterfront.

"We should have brought Bob Rogers in from back home," Tomlinson said, almost wistfully. "He could have explained the MHD technology to the committee."

"No!" O'Donnell snapped. "No special privileges for MHD. That'd look too much like you're loading the dice."

Tomlinson looked almost hurt, Jake thought. But he nodded at his chief of staff, then took a long swig of his scotch.

"So where do we go from here?" Reynolds asked O'Donnell. "I can fill up the senator's dance card with media appearances, if you like."

O'Donnell shook his head. "Pick the top media outlets only. National news shows. Blogs that have plenty of followers. No penny-ante stuff."

"I ought to attend every one of the committee's sessions," Tomlinson said.

"Right. You should be seen as interested first and foremost in the committee's business, not as a prima donna who's put his plan before the committee but who's too busy doing media interviews to attend to the committee's work."

Jake silently agreed. Makes sense, he thought. Frank should come across as serious, hardworking, and determined to get his plan accepted by the committee.

• • •

That evening Jake picked up Tami at her EarthGuard LLC office in a sturdy old stone building off Farragut Square, not far from the White House.

"How'd it go?" she asked as she ducked into his Mustang.

Disappointed, Jake complained, "You didn't watch the hearing?"

Tami grinned at him. "Some people have to work for a living. We don't have time to watch C-SPAN all day."

"It went pretty damned well," Jake said as he pulled the car into the traffic streaming along K Street.

"Santino was okay?"

"Like Santa Claus, almost," Jake said.

Her expression grew serious. "That's when you have to be on your guard, Jake. He was all smiles while he was getting me fired."

"Not this time," Jake countered. "Frank's energy plan is going to sail through the committee and be ready for a floor vote by the time the Senate reconvenes after its summer recess."

"If Santino gets the Majority Leader's post," said Tami.

Jake realized she was right. If Perlmutter becomes Majority Leader, the energy plan is sunk.

• • •

They had dinner at Ruth's Chris Steakhouse, where they'd had their first date. Tami was strangely quiet all through the meal. Jake had to make the conversation, which made him feel uncomfortable, awkward. He was accustomed to letting her chatter pleasantly about her day, her plans and problems.

As they walked back toward his car, Jake asked, "Why so quiet, Tami?"

She looked up at him. "Have I been quiet?"

"Pretty much. Something on your mind?"

"Santino," she said. "I worry that he's leading you into a dead end."

"Dead end?"

"You don't know him, Jake," she said, suddenly fervent. "You don't know him the way I do. He's despicable."

The intensity in her voice took Jake by surprise. "You're still sore at him?"

"No, not angry. I'm afraid of him. Jake, I'm frightened. Frightened for you. You don't understand what he's capable of."

They had reached the Mustang, parked at curbside on a side street.

"He got me fired from the senator's staff," Jake recalled. "But he doesn't seem upset that I'm back with Tomlinson."

"He got you mugged," Tami reminded.

Reflexively touching his nose, Jake muttered, "That was Jacobi."

"It was Santino. Jacobi doesn't do anything without getting Santino's clearance first."

"You think?" Jake asked.

"I know," said Tami.

# Politics

Tomlinson's energy plan was pushed out of the head-lines by Senator McGrath's announcement that he was retiring from the Senate because of ill health. Washington buzzed with speculation about who the next Majority Leader would be.

"It's going to be Santino," Kevin O'Donnell predicted confidently. "Perlmutter's seen as being too pushy."

"Since when does pushy disqualify a man for a job in this town?" Jake asked.

The two of them were having lunch together in the Senate dining room, after a morning spent at the energy committee hearing. Across the quietly ornate room, Tomlinson was lunching at Santino's table, together with two other members of the committee.

With that slightly annoyed look on his face when-ever he dispensed wisdom to a junior staffer, O'Donnell explained, "You don't understand, Jake. In the Sen-ate you're supposed to make your way through the chairs."

"Through the chairs?"

Nodding, "You work your way up, a step at a time. Perlmutter's trying to jump over Santino and grab the Majority Leader's job. But it's not his turn. He's making a lot of the older, more experienced senators upset with him."

"What about the younger senators?"

"They're watching what happens. If Perlmutter can

break the usual routine, the Senate won't be the same place anymore."

Jake remembered some old joker's description of the United States Senate: "That grand old retirement home for the feebleminded and the criminally insane." It was good for a laugh, he thought, but not *entirely* accurate.

Inwardly, he wondered. The Senate's farm bloc was large and powerful, and there were whispers all around the Capitol about how Perlmutter was calling in every favor he had ever handed out since arriving in the Senate, more than a decade earlier. If there was resentment that he was pushing himself too fast, Jake hadn't seen it.

But O'Donnell's been around a lot longer than I have, he told himself. A lot longer than Frank has, too.

Tomlinson spent most of his days dutifully attending the energy committee hearings, which were digging into the details of the energy plan. Santino faithfully chaired every meeting. Jake wondered when the Little Saint found time to campaign for the Majority Leader's position.

"He needs McGrath's blessing," O'Donnell pointed out, during one of Tomlinson's bull sessions at the end of the working day.

The senator's office was practically empty. Tomlinson was leaning back in his comfortable desk chair, his customary scotch in one hand, as his chief of staff reviewed the day's events. Jake sat beside O'Donnell, listening, learning.

"It's going to be a close vote," O'Donnell was saying. "Damned close. If Santino can get McGrath's nod, though, that'll clinch the deal."

Frowning slightly, Tomlinson said, "Santino's the Majority Whip, he's logically the next in line for the Majority Leader's post, isn't he?"

"He was, until Perlmutter started pushing for it."

Jake remembered O'Donnell's earlier wisdom about coming up "through the chairs." Apparently he didn't think that was so important now. He asked, "Why hasn't McGrath come out for Santino?"

"He's playing politics," O'Donnell said, his voice dripping contempt. "Waiting to see which of them offers the most for the job."

"Offers the most what?" Jake asked.

"Favors. Party allegiance. Promises to back the policies McGrath has backed."

"And jockeying for the party's ticket next year," said Tomlinson. "Perlmutter wouldn't mind being the pick for vice president."

O'Donnell almost smiled. "That'd be a good way to get him out of the Senate."

"If he wins," Tomlinson pointed out.

"Is there some bad blood between Santino and Mc-Grath?" Jake asked.

"Not that I know of," said O'Donnell. "Or anybody else I've talked to."

Tomlinson said, "Maybe I should ask Santino himself about it."

"No!" O'Donnell actually winced. "That's an awfully sensitive subject, Franklin. You should steer clear of it."

Smiling, the senator said, "Oh, Mario and I have become pretty friendly over the past few weeks. I think he might confide in me." He paused for a heartbeat, then added, "Especially if I can bring a couple of extra votes onto his bandwagon."

"Extra votes?"

Tomlinson said, "Gutierrez and Ellison."

"New Mexico and North Dakota?" O'Donnell asked, incredulous.

Nodding slowly, the senator said, "Gutierrez would love to have New Mexico go solar in a big way. We could put up major solar facilities out in the desert, use some big tracts of the old White Sands Missile Range. Plenty of acreage there to put up solar panels."

"You've talked to him about this?"

His smile widening, Tomlinson replied, "I met him a couple of weeks ago at that charity dinner you talked me into attending, Kevin."

O'Donnell looked surprised and pleased. But then he asked, "And Ellison?"

"Wind farms. Plenty of space in North Dakota, and the wind blows pretty damned hard across the prairie."

Jake wanted to laugh. "So you're selling parts of the energy plan in exchange for votes for Santino."

"That's politics, Jake."

"Does Santino know about this?" O'Donnell asked.

"Not yet. I wanted to run it past you before I nailed down their votes. Once I've done that, I can tell it to Santino."

Nodding so vigorously that his combover slid across his forehead, O'Donnell said, "Sounds good to me. Do it."

Turning to Jake, Tomlinson said, "See, Jake? I'm learning to be a politician."

Jake grinned back at the senator. But he was thinking, By the time this is over he'll have sold every part of the plan. To help Santino become Majority Leader. I hope the Little Saint appreciates it.

# The Little Saint

A late-afternoon thunderstorm was drenching Washington, so Jake and Senator Tomlinson walked along the tunnels that connected the various Senate and House buildings with the Capitol.

"You could get lost in here," Jake said as they strode briskly along the well-lit underground walkway. It was impeccably clean, not a scrap of paper littering its painted concrete floor. The walls looked as if they had been scrubbed down only a few hours ago. My tax dollars at work, Jake thought.

As they made their way through the crowd of people avoiding the downpour up on the streets, the senator said, "I've heard that New York City—Manhattan, at least—has whole shopping arcades underground. You can go for miles without ever going up on the street."

Jake nodded, then suddenly jumped aside as a teenager on roller blades zoomed past them.

"They shouldn't allow that down here!" he complained.

"Messenger," said Tomlinson. "Just doing his job."

Jake huffed. "Maybe the Postal Service should try that."

"Try getting their union to accept the idea," Tomlinson said, chuckling.

They reached the Russell Building and rode a crowded elevator up to Santino's floor, then hurried through the marble hallway to the senator's suite of offices. The place looked somber. Jake knew that Tomlinson's staff was busily preparing for the summer recess that would start with the weekend. But Santino's people looked hushed, downcast, gathered in little knots of two or three, whispering.

As an aide led them to Senator Santino's private office, Jake asked, "What's going on? Why all the long faces?"

The aide—pudgy, round-faced—looked at Jake with disdain. "Haven't you heard? Senator McGrath was rushed to the hospital this afternoon. They don't expect him to last the night."

Oh my god, Jake thought. No wonder the place looks like a funeral parlor. McGrath is dying, and he hasn't anointed Santino to be his successor.

Santino's inner office was just as funereal. The Little Saint sat behind his desk, hunched over slightly, his hands clasped prayerfully on the desktop. Four of his top aides were sitting in front of the desk, equally downcast.

Without rising from his chair, Santino asked Tomlinson, "You've heard?"

Nodding as he approached the desk, Tomlinson said, "McGrath is terminal."

"Without giving me his blessing," Santino whispered, barely loud enough to be audible.

One of the aides got up and offered Tomlinson his chair. Jake found an empty place on the sofa, along the side wall.

"He *promised* me," Santino said, almost whining. "Less than a year ago, he promised me that he'd back me once he stepped down."

Tomlinson said, "Maybe he'll make a deathbed declaration."

Santino waved both his hands angrily. "No, he'll go to his grave in silence. He's turned his back on me."

One of the aides said, "At least he hasn't come out for Perlmutter."

The expression on Santino's face could have etched solid granite.

Keeping his face serious, Tomlinson said, "Well, I have some good news for you, Mario: Gutierrez and Ellison will vote for you."

Santino blinked slowly, once, twice. "Both of them?"

"Solar and wind power," said Tomlinson.

One of Santino's aides broke into a smile. "That could give you a majority!"

"If we can hold Bellamy and his bunch in line," Santino said. But his bleak expression had eased somewhat, Jake saw.

"We'll hold them," the aide said grimly. "They *owe* us—er, you, that is."

Jake leaned back on the sofa as Santino's aides counted votes. It looked as if it would be a close squeeze, but they assured themselves that they had enough votes to win the party caucus in September.

By the time the meeting broke up, even Santino was smiling. Guardedly.

• • •

"It's going to be an interesting summer," Tomlinson said as he and Jake walked back to the Hart Building.

A cutthroat competition, Jake realized. And it'll all take place beyond the notice of the news media. Perlmutter and Santino twisting arms for votes, trying to win other senators, moving mountains to hold on to the votes they already had. Fifty-one senators, each one of them asking, "What's in this for me? For my state? For my backers?"

"What I don't understand is why McGrath didn't come out with his backing for Santino," Jake said. "According to the Little Saint, McGrath promised his support. Why hasn't he made good on his promise?"

"He's at death's door, for god's sake," Tomlinson replied. "He's got other things on his mind."

As they turned into the tunnel that led to the Hart Building, Jake shook his head. "From what I've heard about McGrath, he doesn't break promises. He's known as a man of his word."

They reached the elevator lobby, and Tomlinson pressed the call button. Looking down at Jake, the senator said, "You know, it could be that what McGrath told Santino and what Mario heard are two different things."

Stepping into the elevator and leaning on the 2 button, Jake said, "Santino's no fool. If he heard McGrath promise his support, that's what McGrath did. And now he's withdrawn it. Why?"

"Might be because he's out of it," Tomlinson said, grimly. "He's dying. No time for politics."

Jake stayed silent, but he couldn't believe that a man of Senator McGrath's long political career wouldn't have left some record of his support for Santino. No, he withdrew his support and left the Little Saint out in the cold, to sink or swim on his own.

Why?

# Declaration

Senator McGrath died the next day. According to the news release from his office, the Senate Majority Leader "slipped away peacefully in his sleep."

Tami told Jake, "That's the public relations people's way of saying he was doped up to his eyebrows when he died."

They were having dinner at a sushi bar near Dupont Circle. Jake had become fairly adept at using chopsticks, although he still spent a couple of moments at the beginning of the meal perfecting his grip.

"He died without giving his support to Santino," Jake muttered.

"So?"

He looked up from the unagi eel roll he was enjoying. Tami didn't seem at all concerned about the struggle for the Senate's majority leadership. Gazing across the table at her smiling, perfectly lovely face, Jake asked himself why he was so wrapped up in it.

And the answer came to him immediately. If Santino doesn't win, the energy plan goes down the toilet. The only reason the Little Saint is backing the plan is because we convinced him it can help him beat Perlmutter. If Perlmutter wins, Frank becomes numero uno on Santino's shit list.

Win or go home, he thought.

But I don't want to go home, he told himself. I want to stay here. With Tami.

"You're awfully quiet," she said, her smile diminishing slightly.

"I love you, Tami." Jake was surprised to hear himself say it, to admit it, to declare it. But he realized it was true. I love this woman. I really love her.

The truth of it almost stunned him. After Louise was killed in the car wreck, Jake knew he'd lost the one woman he wanted to spend all eternity with. In time, he engaged in brief flings here and there, but that was physical need, not love. And now here was Tami, sharing his life, sharing his bed, and he loved her. It wasn't that he'd stopped loving Louise; he would never stop loving her. He never could.

But, as he sat in the dimly lit restaurant, looking into Tami's almond eyes, Jake realized that love wasn't divisible. It was not a finite quantity. His love for Tami didn't diminish the love he still felt for Louise. Love could expand, grow, increase, and strengthen and bring new joy to life.

Tami's face grew serious. "That's a big word, Jake," she whispered. "Love."

"I love you," he repeated.

She lowered her eyes briefly, then looked up at him again. "I love you, too, Jake."

He dropped his chopsticks, half rose, and leaned across the table to kiss her. Tami's lips felt warm and soft and inviting.

She giggled. "Your tie is in your soy sauce."

He plopped down on his chair again. "Who cares?" And he swished the end of his tie in the little bowl of sauce.

• • •

That weekend Tami moved into Jake's apartment. He saw that her belongings were modest: a couple of suitcases of clothes, a bulging briefcase of papers, a laptop computer.

"No furniture?" he asked as he helped her tote the bags from her car.

"It was all secondhand junk. I left it with my roomies."

Jake introduced his fiancée to his landlord and wife. She was warmly gracious, he stiffly formal.

"We'll have to find a parking space for you along the street somewhere," the landlord said.

His wife threw a mock frown at him. "Come on, now. You can park your car in the garage and let her have your space at the curb."

The landlord looked less than pleased. "I'll have to clean out the garage."

"About time," said his wife.

• • •

That evening, as they sat on the futon in Jake's living room watching a slow-paced BBC television drama, Jake muttered, "I still can't figure out why McGrath went to his grave without making good on his promise to back Santino."

Her head resting against his shoulder, Tami replied, "Are you certain that McGrath made a promise?"

"Santino is. He even said that McGrath has turned his back on him."

"Some conflict between them?" Tami asked.

"Something," said Jake. "I wish I knew what it was."

Tami stretched and yawned. "Let's turn in. I've got an early morning tomorrow."

With a grin, Jake said, "A motion to go to bed is always in order."

"Robert's Rules of Order?"

"Ross's rules of romance."

# Summer of Indecision

ongress adjourned for the summer. Senators and representatives left DC, ostensibly to spend the summer months among their constituents, mending fences, doing favors, making promises, and taking in campaign contributions.

Of course, many members of Congress had to take trips here and there, to investigate this or that. Various European and Middle Eastern capitals were popular destinations. Senators and representatives showed up in Beijing, Sydney, and Tokyo as well. With their families. At taxpayers' expense.

In Washington, despite the muggy, almost stifling weather, the city seethed with speculation. Although the big conventions that would pick their party nominees for president were still a year away, rumors, guesses, predictions were on everyone's lips.

The Democrats would renominate the president, that much was sure. But would she stick with her first-term vice president or opt for a fresh face? Six candidates were running to be the Republican nominee, four of them governors of various states, the other two hugely successful business tycoons. Again, who would be the nominee for vice president? Perlmutter was a leading guess, among several other senators and a former secretary of defense.

And beneath all that highly publicized hoopla was the question of who the Republicans would pick to be the next Majority Leader of the Senate. Both Santino and Perlmutter had left Washington for their home states. But they each were waging a deadly serious campaign, with hardly a word in the news media about it.

Jake tried to keep his mind on his work, refining the details of the energy plan. He lunched with Wilmer Nevins a few times and, with some trepidation, showed him the section on solar energy.

Nevins scanned the report as he gobbled his lunch, in an Italian restaurant near the White House. Jake worried that he would spatter the pages with tomato sauce.

At last he handed the report back to Jake, with a tight smile.

"I think it's pretty good, Jake. You've finally got the picture right: solar electric goes from the bottom up, individual installations, not a big, grandiose government system."

"Bottom up," Jake echoed, then quickly added, "With tax incentives."

Nevins's smile widened. "Tax breaks are always helpful."

"And the bit about using portable solar arrays for emergency electrical power in a blackout?" Jake asked.

"It's a reasonably good idea," Nevins said. "In fact, the Federal Emergency Management Agency has put out a purchase request for ten thousand emergency rigs."

"FEMA? No kidding!"

His smile turning just the slightest bit cynical, Nevins admitted, "Some government programs aren't so bad, after all."

• • •

Senator Tomlinson was back in Montana, but he kept in touch with his Washington office almost daily through Skype sessions. As the dog days of August overwhelmed

Washington with soggy, debilitating heat and humidity, Tomlinson looked bright and relaxed by the swimming pool at his family's mansion.

"What's the news, Kevin?" he asked cheerfully, sitting in a recliner beach chair at poolside.

Jake was in O'Donnell's office, sitting to one side of the chief of staff's desk, so that Tomlinson could see them both. O'Donnell had been slow to warm to Jake, but now he made certain to invite Jake in to these videophone conversations with the senator.

"The Majority Leader's race is still neck and neck," O'Donnell replied. "By our count, Santino's going to win, but there's a lot of bad blood. The party's divided almost down the middle. That could be bad for next year's presidential campaign."

"Perlmutter's up for reelection next year, isn't he?" Tomlinson asked.

"Right," said O'Donnell. "Santino isn't."

"So Perlmutter's busy back home in Nebraska, campaigning for his reelection."

"What else?"

"And Santino's in Rhode Island."

"Look, Franklin, the whole damned Senate is scattered all over the country," O'Donnell said. "And at least a half dozen of them are overseas on *fact-finding* trips."

Tomlinson laughed at the cynical emphasis O'Donnell put on *fact-finding*.

Reaching for the tall frosted glass on the table beside his recliner, the senator asked, "So who's handling the campaign for Majority Leader?"

"Staff," O'Donnell said. "The working stiffs who stay here in DC."

"And how's it going?"

"Still awfully damned close. Santino's ahead, by our count, but it wouldn't take much to change things."

His expression turning serious, Tomlinson asked, "Is there anything we should be doing?"

O'Donnell started to reply, thought better of it, and hesitated. At last he said, "Nothing. Unless you can bring a couple more votes over to Santino's side."

Jake popped up with, "Did that senator from Ohio ever take you up on your offer to show him the MHD rig?"

O'Donnell said, "Zack Danner. He's due to visit Montana next week."

"That's right," Tomlinson said. "I've got a whole tour mapped out for him. Apparently he's quite a fisherman. My father and I are going to take him up to our lodge on Sandy Creek."

Nodding, Jake said, "See if you can get him committed to Santino while you're at it."

"What do you have to give him in return?" O'Donnell demanded.

"MHD power generation," said Jake. "Most of Ohio's electric utilities burn coal, don't they?"

"A lot of them are switching to natural gas."

"Either way, MHD can produce more kilowatts per pound of fuel. Danner might like that."

With a smile, Tomlinson said, "He might, at that."

• • •

That evening, Jake drove Tami down to the riverfront for dinner at the Cantina Marina. Even with the Mustang's top down, the stubborn heat and humidity made him feel as if they were driving through steaming soup.

Once he'd parked the car, Jake pulled up the convertible's roof. Tami, sitting beside him, pointed to the starry, cloudless sky. "You think it's going to rain?"

"It might," said Jake, as he fastened the roof's edge to the top of the car's windshield frame.

"Weather forecast calls for clear and dry," she said, with a hint of teasing mirth in her voice.

"Uh-huh. But it only takes one little cloudburst to soak the car."

Jake got out and went around the car to lend his hand to Tami. She waited obediently for him to open her door. It had taken Jake several weeks to get her to allow him to be a gentleman.

"Besides," he said, as they started across the parking lot toward the lights of the restaurant, "an open top is an invitation to thieves."

Tami laughed. "Like a ragtop is going to stop anybody."

"It has so far," he said.

The Cantina was barely half full. Jake asked the hostess for the same table they had sat at the first time they'd met.

"You're sentimental," Tami said as they followed the young woman out onto the patio.

"I guess I am," Jake admitted.

"That's fine."

Halfway through dinner, Tami said, "I bumped into an old friend this afternoon. One of Senator McGrath's senior aides."

Jake put down the spoonful of crayfish soup he had just lifted from the bowl in front of him. "Oh?"

Mock-scowling at him, Tami said, "Don't 'Oh' me, Jake. She's an old gray-haired lady. Very dignified. She's been with McGrath for ages."

"Oh," Jake said, in a completely different tone.

"She showed up at the EarthGuard office, out of the blue. I think she's looking for a job, now that McGrath has died."

"She's not looking for another senator?"

"Of course she is. But she's always been interested in environmental issues. She's covering all her bases."

Jake returned his attention to the soup.

Tami said, "I made a date to have lunch with her tomorrow. Maybe I can find out why McGrath dropped his support of Santino."

"You think?"

"If anything significant happened between them, she'd know about it, I'm sure."

"Just watch your step," Jake said. "If anything significant did happen, it could be dynamite."

# The Deal

When Tami came home to the apartment the next evening Jake immediately asked her, "How was your lunch?"

"Puzzling," she said, tossing her handbag onto the coffee table and heading for the kitchen.

Jake followed her. "Puzzling? How so?"

"According to Matilda—Senator McGrath's aide—he and Santino had a meeting in McGrath's private office a few days before McGrath announced he was retiring."

Jake mused, "That must be when McGrath told the Little Saint that he wasn't going to back him for Majority Leader."

As she pulled a half-empty bottle of chardonnay from the refrigerator, Tami said, "Must be. They had a shouting match. The two of them screamed at each other."

"Santino? He raised his voice?"

"McGrath, too," Tami said, as she poured herself a glass of wine. "Matilda said she's never heard him sound so angry."

"What the hell were they arguing about? The Majority Leader vote?"

Shaking her head, Tami replied, "Matilda thinks that was part of it, but only part. There was something else, something that made McGrath withdraw his support for Santino."

"What was it?"

"Matilda doesn't know. Nobody in her office knows—

she asked around and everybody there was just as surprised as she was. I mean, McGrath was always a sweetheart, never a cross word out of him. All of a sudden he and Santino are behind closed doors hollering at each other like a pair of barroom bozos."

"What the hell could have caused that?" Jake wondered.

"Whatever it was, it broke the friendship the two of them had. Twenty years of friendship, shattered in one afternoon."

Jake took the bottle from her hand and poured himself a glass. "What the hell could have caused that?" he repeated.

Tami went back to the living room, slipped off her high-heeled shoes, and dropped onto the futon. "It must have been something personal," she said. "They didn't have any political differences, not before the blowup and not afterward."

"Except that McGrath dropped his support of Santino for Majority Leader."

"He was pretty shaken up afterward," Tami said. "Matilda says his health went downhill pretty steeply after their fight."

"And nobody in McGrath's office knows what it was all about?"

"Nobody."

Jake sat on the futon beside her. "Then the answer must be in Santino's office. Or maybe back in Rhode Island."

• • •

Santino returned to Washington two days before Labor Day. So did Perlmutter.

O'Donnell was almost hyper with anticipation. "They're running neck and neck down to the wire," he told Jake.

"Is Santino still ahead?"

"By a nose," O'Donnell said. Then he amended, "A nostril."

The vote for Majority Leader was scheduled for the party's Senate caucus, the Tuesday morning after Labor Day. Tomlinson returned to Washington that Saturday, with his wife, and invited Jake and Tami to a Labor Day barbecue at his house.

When Jake drove up the driveway, the young butler directed him and Tami around the side of the house, to the backyard. Tomlinson, Amy, Kevin O'Donnell, and several other office staff people were already there, all of them in shorts and casual shirts, as Jake and Tami were wearing.

And in the midst of them all stood Senator Mario Santino.

He looked stiffly out of place, in his usual three-piece gray suit. Doesn't he own any other clothes? Jake wondered.

Despite his outfit, Santino seemed completely at ease as he shook hands with Jake and Tami.

"It's good to see you again," he said, smiling benignly.

"Good to see you, Senator," said Jake, warily.

Dressed in Bermuda shorts and an expensive-looking golf shirt, Tomlinson sauntered up and pointed to the trio of coolers resting on the grass beside the big gas grill. "Help yourselves," he said, grinning. "Beer, Coke, Gatorade, whatever you want."

"Before you do," Santino said, "I can only stay a few minutes, and I have a little announcement to make."

O'Donnell drifted up to them. Like the senator, he was wearing shorts and a sports shirt.

"I had a meeting with Bryan Perlmutter this morning, in the Capitol," said Santino, his expression somewhere between cheerful and sly.

"This morning?" Tomlinson asked.

"Yes. We've come to an agreement."

"You have?" O'Donnell blurted.

"Yes. He will not oppose my election to Majority Leader and I will support his bid to be the party's vice presidential candidate next year."

Jake felt the air gush from his lungs. Just like that, he thought. You give me what I want, and I give you what you want.

"You've saved the party from splitting apart," Tomlinson said, sounding almost awed.

Still smiling, Santino made a stiff little bow. "I suppose I have." But then he went on, "Of course, we're going to have make a minor concession or two to the energy plan."

"Concession?" Jake snapped, suddenly frightened.

"Yes. We reinstate the ethanol mandate for the next five years and put the methanol idea under study, instead of pushing for its immediate implementation."

Jake yelped, "But that tears the heart out of the plan! It wrecks everything!"

"No," Santino said firmly. "It merely delays certain phases of the plan. You'll still get your MHD pilot plant in Montana, your tax breaks for solar installations, and just about everything else you wanted."

"But it won't be revenue neutral anymore," Jake countered. "It'll cost billions."

"That can't be helped. On the other hand, the plan's costs will be spent in Ohio and Montana and plenty of other states that can use the federal money."

"Including Rhode Island," Jake growled.

O'Donnell grabbed at Jake's arm, and Senator Tomlinson said, "I'm sure this will all work out for the best."

"Indeed it will," said Santino. "Indeed it will."

And Jake thought, It'll work for Santino's best. He's

going to be Majority Leader, and Perlmutter's going to run for vice president. But the plan's being picked to pieces.

One look at O'Donnell's grim face, though, was enough to make Jake keep his mouth shut.

# The Morning After

For the first time in his life, Jake got roaring drunk. He left Tomlinson's party shortly after Santino did and drove Tami to a sports bar near their apartment, then proceeded to down several scotches in quick succession.

"So the energy plan gets its balls cut off, so what?" he grumbled as they sat at the bar, where four huge TV screens were showing four different baseball games. "Santino can say his committee has produced a plan we can all be proud of. Big fucking deal."

Tami tried to shush him. "It's a beginning, Jake. It's not the end of the world, it's the beginning of what you want."

He looked at her blearily. "Half a loaf is better than none, huh?"

"Yes, it is," she said firmly.

"Half a loaf isn't worth shit," Jake said. "I didn't come to Washington to do a half-assed job." Raising his voice, he cried, "Give me liberty or give me death!"

Some of the other patrons sitting around the bar threw unhappy glances at Jake. One of them said, "Tone it down, pal." Another, older man just grinned at him.

Tami slid off her barstool. "Come on, Jake, it's time for us to go home."

"Home is where the heart is," Jake said, slurring his words slightly. "Home is where, when you go there, they have to take you in. Did you know that? Robert Frost said that."

Tugging at his arm, Tami led Jake out of the bar and to his Mustang. "I'll drive," she said.

"I'll walk," said Jake, weaving slightly while he stood in place at the curb.

Tami opened the passenger side door and helped Jake fold himself into the car. "You're in no condition to walk," she said.

• • •

Jake slept most of the morning, and when he finally got out of bed, his head throbbed dully.

Tami had already gone to work; she had left a note on the kitchen counter, a lopsided heart with "Luv U" printed inside it. Alone in the apartment, Jake phoned her office.

"Hello, dear." Her voice sounded as pleasant as always. "How do you feel?"

"Like an idiot," he said.

"You were pretty looped last night."

"Yeah. I'm sorry."

"It's okay. You were trying to drown your sorrows."

"Stupid."

"Are you going to your office?"

Jake frowned, contemplating the alternatives. "No, I think I'll phone in sick. I don't feel up to talking with Frank or Kevin. Especially Kevin."

He could sense Tami nodding. "Okay. Try to relax, Jake. And remember, most of the plan is going to get through. It's a good beginning."

"Yeah," he said halfheartedly. "I guess so."

After a shower and shave Jake felt good enough to watch C-SPAN. The party's caucus was strictly off-limits to the TV cameras, but late in the afternoon the announcement came through. Senator Mario Santino was elected the Senate Majority Leader by acclamation, a unanimous voice vote.

Santino and Perlmutter appeared side by side before the cameras, all smiles and handshakes and good fellowship.

"We intend to put up a united front as we move forward toward next year's presidential election campaign," Santino said, with his best saintly smile.

Perlmutter nodded hard enough to make his wattles shake. "Our party is united, and we're ready to show the world what we can accomplish."

Yeah, Jake said to himself. Like using my energy plan for toilet paper.

• • •

Alone in his apartment, Jake opened his laptop and tried to figure out how much was left of the energy plan. Without the central concept of producing methanol from the carbon dioxide that electric utility power plants emitted, the plan was pretty much of a shambles. He tried to pick up the pieces: MHD for Montana, renewables for states like New Mexico and North Dakota, even the nutty tidal energy project for Rhode Island.

And the mandate that required gasoline manufacturers to include a percentage of ethanol in the products they sold. Perlmutter's farm lobby is guaranteed another five years of that.

It's not a plan anymore, Jake realized. It's not a comprehensive program that brings together new energy technologies and the nation's natural resources. It's a pork barrel. Just like so much else of Washington's political wheeling and dealing.

Disgusted, Jake closed the laptop and leaned back on the futon. It had never been a comfortable piece of furniture; now it felt like a medieval torture rack.

McGrath and Santino had a fight. That thought came back to him like an inescapable truth. Those two self-contained old men were screaming at each other like fishwives. Why? What did McGrath find out that made him drop his support for Santino?

Whatever it was, McGrath took it to his grave with him. Jake sat up straighter, fists clenched on his knees. There must be some way I can find out what it was. There's got to be.

But how?

Would Perlmutter know? And if he does, how would I go about getting the secret out of him?

Maybe Jacobi could help me, Jake thought. Santino said he's good at plugging leaks. Maybe if I told him there's something that Perlmutter's holding over Santino's head . . .

Jake shook his head. You're grasping at straws. Besides, the last time you visited Jacobi, you got mugged a few months later.

He got to his feet, went to the kitchen, and made himself a cup of instant coffee. It's lousy, Jake thought as he took a cautious scalding sip, but at least it's coffee.

His cell phone buzzed. Jake hurried to the bedroom and picked it up off his night table. The phone's minuscule screen read: KEVIN O'DONNELL.

"How're you feeling, Jake?" O'Donnell's voice asked.

"Hung over," said Jake.

"One too many, eh?"

"Three or four too many."

O'Donnell chuckled. "You heard the news? Santino's our new Majority Leader. By acclamation."

"Whoopee."

"Franklin wants you in the office bright and early tomorrow. He wants to get the energy plan out on the floor of the Senate as soon as possible."

"What's left of it."

"Don't be a sore loser, Jake. You've still got more than three quarters of what you want."

Jake squeezed his eyes shut and decided not to argue. "Tell Frank I'll be there bright and early tomorrow."

"Good. Now go back to bed and sleep it off."

O'Donnell clicked off. As Jake folded his phone shut, a new thought struck him.

If McGrath knew something that shook Santino down to his shoes, and if I find out what it is, maybe I could use it to get Santino to reinstate the methanol program and make the plan whole again.

# Rework

Jake did indeed arrive at the office bright and early. Hardly anyone else was there. The young receptionist by the suite's front door was putting on some dark red lipstick. The other desks that Jake could see were unoccupied. He didn't even smell coffee perking.

The receptionist put her mirror down and said to Jake, "The senator wants to see you."

Surprised, Jake blurted, "Now?"

"He said you should go to his office as soon as you showed up."

Jake headed directly for Tomlinson's office. A glance at his wristwatch told him it wasn't yet eight a.m.

Sticking his head through the senator's partly opened door, Jake asked, "You wanted to see me?"

Tomlinson nodded and gestured to one of the chairs in front of his desk. "Have a seat, Jake."

Kevin O'Donnell came in before Jake could get himself settled in the leather chair.

"Better close the door, Kevin," said the senator.

O'Donnell shut the door quietly and took the seat beside Jake.

Tomlinson said, "I want to rework the energy plan and get it out on the floor of the Senate as quickly as possible. Now that Santino's the Majority Leader, we need to cash in our chips before he forgets that he owes us."

"If he hasn't already," said O'Donnell, in his usual dour tone.

Ignoring that, the senator focused on Jake. "Most of the plan is intact. You'll have to put the ethanol mandate in and move the methanol idea down to a study status."

Jake objected, "That ruins any chance we had of making the plan revenue neutral."

"Can't be helped."

O'Donnell pointed out, "The fiscal hawks in the House aren't going to like that. They'll say the plan's another goddamned pork barrel."

"That's what it is now, isn't it?" Jake said.

Tomlinson frowned. "Jake, don't make the best the enemy of the good. There are a lot of good things in your plan. Just because we didn't get everything we wanted doesn't mean we abandon your plan."

So it's my plan again, Jake thought.

"How soon can you cobble together a document that covers the ethanol and methanol details?" O'Donnell asked.

"It'll also have to reinstate the whole carbon sequestering business," Jake realized. "The coal lobby will *love* that."

"How soon?" O'Donnell repeated.

Sullenly, Jake said, "Give me a week."

"No more than that, Jake," said Tomlinson. "I want to get this through the committee and out for a floor vote while it's still hot."

"Yeah. Right."

• • •

It took Jake exactly four hours to rewrite the parts of the plan that needed to be changed. Vic Wakefield is going to be disappointed, he thought as he worked. But what the hell, he'll get a fat study contract out of this. Not the full-steam-ahead methanol program I promised him, but he'll have to be satisfied with what I can get for him.

Briefly he thought about Isaiah Knowles at NASA and his dream of building space power satellites. The meeting between Tomlinson and Knowles's NASA brass had never come to fruition. Well, maybe later, Jake said to himself.

By six p.m. Jake had completed the rewrite of the plan. As he sat at his desk reviewing it, page by page, on his computer screen, O'Donnell popped into his office unannounced.

"Sun's over the yardarm, Jake," said the chief of staff. "You in the mood for a drink?"

Jake realized O'Donnell was trying to be nice to him, but he shook his head. "I did enough drinking Monday to last me for a while."

O'Donnell laughed and said, "Okay. See you tomorrow."

Jake stayed at his desk, rereading the butchered plan all over again, but his mind kept returning to the question of Santino and why he and McGrath had had that screaming match.

How can I dig into this? he asked himself time and again. Who would know how to begin?

Reynolds, he told himself. Earl's a PR guy, he knows a lot of people around town. Maybe he'd have a lead for me. Jake got up and headed for Earl Reynolds's office.

Reynolds was closing his door, briefcase in hand and blue blazer buttoned, just about to leave his office as Jake approached him.

"Got a minute, Earl?"

The public relations director glanced at his wristwatch. "For you, Jake, ninety seconds."

They went back into Reynolds's office. He leaned his rump against the edge of his desk without letting go of his briefcase. "It's your nickel, kid."

Jake remained standing. "A couple of weeks before McGrath died, he and Santino had a loud argument. I need to find out what it was about."

Reynolds gave a little snort. "Santino and McGrath? Lotsa luck, friend."

"How do I dig into this?" Jake asked. "Who might know something about it?"

"Damned if I know. Are you sure it actually happened, and it's not some news guy's fishing expedition?"

"It happened."

"The Little Saint and Mr. Straight Arrow." Reynolds shook his head. "You can't touch either one of them."

"But somebody must know something."

"Forget it, Jake. It must have been something personal between the two of them. Let it go at that."

"Come on, Earl. I need to find out. The senator could use the information."

"That kind of information could backfire on Frank. Better to steer clear of it."

Jake suddenly thought, "Lady Cecilia! She knows everything about everybody, doesn't she?"

His handsome face settling into a scowl, Reynolds raised a finger. "One: if she knew, she'd have already put it on her blog." A second finger. "If it hasn't been on *Power Talk*, then either she doesn't know, or . . ."

"Or?"

"Or it's too damned dangerous for public consumption."

"Too dangerous?"

"Some subjects are too hot, even for *Power Talk*."

Jake thought that over for all of three seconds. "I can't imagine Lady Cecilia being afraid of anything."

With a *hmpf*, Reynolds replied, "She's got more brains than you do, kid. If Lady Cecilia knows anything but hasn't made it public, it must be pretty damned scary."

# Snooping

ady Cecilia was fascinated with Jake's story.

"McGrath and Santino were screaming at each other? About what?"

"That's what I'd like to know," said Jake.

They were sitting in Lady Cecilia's living room, he on a plush sofa covered with garish stripes, she on an oversized upholstered armchair that reminded Jake of a royal throne. The chair was much too big for Cecilia's diminutive figure: she looked like a chubby little girl sitting on it, her feet resting on an ornate ottoman.

Her eyes narrowing slightly, Cecilia murmured, "Georgie McGrath was very widely admired in this town. Not an enemy in the world. Now that he's dead, digging into his past would be seen as disrespectful. People would get angry."

"What about Santino?" Jake asked. "How much do you know about his past?"

Cecilia pursed her thick lips, thinking. "Nothing scandalous. He isn't called the Little Saint because he's a hell-raiser."

"Family?"

"Confirmed old bachelor. Never a hint of shame about him."

Jake thought, If she doesn't know anything, then nobody does. On the other hand, if she does know, she's not telling me.

"Look," he said, "I'm not trying to hurt Santino. He's my boss's committee chairman—"

"And Majority Leader of the Senate," Cecilia added.

Nodding, Jake went on, "I want to protect the senator from a potential source of embarrassment."

Cecilia smiled knowingly. "Come on, Jake. You want to get him to reinstate the parts of your energy plan that he wants you to chop out."

"You know about that, eh?"

"Of course I know. Don't you follow my blog? I've done three items on Senator Tomlinson in the past three days."

Jake admitted defeat and left as graciously as he could.

• • •

That evening, Jake poured out his troubles to Tami over a takeout pizza dinner at home.

Tami said, "If Cecilia knew anything juicy it would have been on *Power Talk* already."

"I don't think she knew about the argument between McGrath and Santino," Jake replied as he sprinkled red pepper flakes on his slice of pizza. "That took her by surprise, I'm pretty sure."

"Then maybe she'll start digging into it."

"Maybe."

Tami insisted on washing the dishes, such as they were. Jake had served the pizza on paper plates; there was nothing to wash except the two forks and knives they had used. They hadn't yet finished their bottle of Chianti.

Jake went to his desk and opened his laptop. On an impulse, he called Steve Brogan, at his home in Dayton.

As soon as Brogan's baggy-eyed face appeared on his screen, Jake realized he was probably interrupting the man's dinner.

"If this is a bad time to talk . . ."

Brogan shook his head. "My wife's on an overnight visit to the clinic, and my son's out with his hoodlum pals."

"Clinic?" Jake asked.

"Tests, checkups," said Brogan, with an air of helpless acceptance. "She seems to be holding her own, the Alzheimer's isn't getting any worse. Or maybe I'm not noticing any changes."

"I hope she's okay."

"Yeah. Me too. So, what can I do for you, Jake?"

Jake spent the next quarter hour talking about his frustrations.

"Santino and McGrath?" Brogan looked incredulous. But then he said, "It must have been something big to get those two hollering at each other."

"So big that nobody knows anything about it."

"Or they're not telling you what they know."

"So what do I do?" Jake asked.

"Dig. Snoop around."

"I've tried talking to people. Nobody admits to knowing anything. Most of them are just as surprised about this as you were."

Brogan looked disappointed. "Jake, you've got to learn how to twist arms."

"I can't force people to talk."

"No, but you can dig into Santino's background. And McGrath's."

"What do you mean?"

"They have medical records, don't they? They file income tax returns, don't they? Santino was in the Marine Corps, I think. Look him up!"

"I don't have access to that kind of information."

"You're a legislative aide to a United States senator," Brogan said. "Use that power, for god's sake."

"You think that would work?"

"You won't know until you try it."

• • •

With some misgivings, the next morning Jake began telephoning the Social Security Administration, the Department of Veterans Affairs, even the Internal Revenue Service.

He was impressed with how every bureaucrat he spoke with wanted to cooperate with a US senator's aide. Records were opened to him, files made available, information flowed in.

"Always glad to help the United States Senate," said more than one of the people Jake talked to. He began to understand how the National Security Administration and other federal agencies could acquire so much data on ordinary citizens. It wasn't really difficult to do.

But poring through the avalanche of data was another matter. Jake didn't dare tell Tomlinson or O'Donnell what he was doing. He was getting reams of information, but if there was anything significant or useful in it, he would need a team of analysts to ferret it out.

He had only himself. And Tami.

Night after night they scrolled through years of data about Santino and McGrath.

"My god," Jake exclaimed as he studied Santino's military record. "The Little Saint was a Marine rifleman. He was in the invasion of Grenada in 1983. He got a Good Conduct Medal."

"Of course," she answered dryly.

"And a Purple Heart."

Tami looked up from her laptop screen. "He was wounded?"

"Hurt in a truck accident."

She returned to the records she was scanning.

The Navy also provided medical records. With a little judicious telephoning, Jake found that Santino still availed himself of the VA's medical services. He could find nothing significant, though. The Little Saint's health was fine, for a man his age. A minor heart murmur was the only significant finding.

The hardest nut was the IRS. They refused to release the income tax returns for either man without a court order, although they assured Jake that neither McGrath nor Santino had ever been audited or under suspicion of tax evasion.

"He really is a little saint," Tami concluded, bleary-eyed from searching computer files.

Jake reluctantly admitted defeat. "There's nothing here that could possibly be a reason for their argument."

"There's got to be something," Tami said. She got up from the futon and stretched the stiffness from her back.

"What we need is a real data analyst," she said. "Maybe a team of data analysts."

Jake shook his head. "We can't let anybody know we're digging into their backgrounds. If that leaked out, my name would be three grades below mud."

A week later, Jacobi phoned.

# Warning

It was the first day of autumn on the calendar, but as Jake leaned back in his desk chair and glanced out his office window, it still looked like summer in Washington, DC. The trees were in full green leaf, people were walking along the street in short-sleeved blouses and splashy sports shirts, the sun was shining brightly out of a blue sky marred only by a few fat cumulus clouds.

Jake's phone rang.

"How're you doin', kid?" Bert Jacobi's voice. Unmistakable.

Jake suddenly felt shaky. "I'm okay," he said slowly, trying to keep the tremor out of his voice. "You?"

"I'm in town for a few days. We oughtta talk."

"What about?"

He could sense Jacobi's lopsided face scowling. "I'll tell ya when I see ya. How about after work, six o'clock?"

Jake nodded and said, "That'd be fine."

"Where you wanna meet?"

Someplace very public, Jake thought. Someplace where there would be plenty of witnesses.

"How about the bar at the Hilton Hotel?"

Jacobi was silent for a moment, then he replied, "Nah, too fancy. Make it Murphy's Pub. Nice neighborhood dump. It's a coupla blocks from your apartment."

"I know where it is," Jake said, his insides clenching.

"Six o'clock." Jacobi hung up.

Jake held the phone receiver frozen in his hand. He knows where I live, he realized. The thought frightened him badly.

· · ·

Murphy's was indeed a nice neighborhood spot. Jake and Tami had gone there often for hamburgers or fish and chips. Jake drove home and told Tami about Jacobi.

"Jacobi?" she asked. "He's connected to Santino, isn't he?"

Jake said, "Yeah. The last time I saw him, I got mugged a few nights later."

She nodded knowingly. "Jacobi. The muscle guy."

"I'll make it quick," Jake promised. "We can have dinner afterward."

She caught the obviously worried expression on Jake's face. "Do you want me to come with you?"

"No! I don't want you anywhere near Jacobi."

"All right," she said. "I'll give you 'til seven o'clock, then I'll come after you."

"You stay here. I'll be home by seven, I'm pretty sure. If it looks like I'm running late, I'll phone you."

Tami looked dissatisfied, but she murmured, "Seven o'clock."

· · ·

Jake got to Murphy's a few minutes after six. Jacobi was already sitting in one of the booths that ran the length of the bar, nursing a dark beer. His burly frame seemed to be wedged into the narrow booth; his dark suit jacket looked a size too small for him. The expression on his strangely uneven face seemed darker than both the suit and the beer.

Jake made his way past the crowd at the bar and slid into the booth opposite him.

Jacobi's lips twisted into what might have been a

smile. Or a sneer. "I was startin' to think you was standin' me up."

"It's only five after," Jake said.

"Yeah."

"So what's this all about?"

One of the harried bartenders hustled up to them. Before he could ask, Jake ordered a glass of pinot grigio.

"You like Italian wine?" Jacobi asked.

"Some."

"My uncle useta make wine. Grew the grapes in his backyard."

"Was that legal?"

Jacobi shrugged. "Long as the local cops got a few bottles every Christmas, it was legal."

The bartender plunked a wineglass in front of Jake, then swiftly headed back to the busy bar.

Hunching over the table, Jake said, "You didn't come here to talk about wine, did you?"

"Hell no."

"Then what?"

His scowl returning, Jacobi said, "You been stickin' your nose where it don't belong."

Jake's mouth went dry. "Oh?" he managed to say.

"The VA, the Marines, you been snoopin' into Santino's background."

"Nothing illegal about that."

"Maybe it ain't illegal, but it sure ain't healthy."

"Are you threatening me?"

"Just what the fuck are you lookin' for?" Jacobi demanded.

He knows what I've been doing, Jake said to himself. Of course he knows! You think that out of all those faceless bureaucrats you talked to, not one of them told Santino's people that you were poking into his records?

"Well?" Jacobi insisted.

Trying to put as positive a spin on the matter as he

could, Jake answered, "Senator Santino had a big blowup with Senator McGrath. I was afraid that Perlmutter might use whatever it was that caused the argument against Santino, hold it over his head."

"Santino and Perlmutter buried the hatchet."

"For how long?" Jake asked. "If Perlmutter knows something that could hurt Santino—"

"He don't."

"Are you sure? How can you be certain?"

For the first time, Jacobi seemed slightly taken aback. But he said, "Don't bullshit me, kid. You want to find something about Santino that *you* can hold over his head."

"No," Jake objected. "That's not—"

"Drop it," Jacobi said flatly. "Just drop the whole business. You could get yourself mugged again. Or worse."

"Are you threatening me?" Jake repeated.

"I don't make threats, kid. I make promises."

With a bravado that he really didn't feel, Jake said, "You just proved to me that Santino has something he wants to keep hidden."

Lowering his voice to a guttural growl, Jacobi warned, "Just drop the whole business, kid. It's bad for your health. Yours, and your Jap girlfriend's, too."

"She's got nothing to do with this!"

"The hell she don't. Like I said, drop this business, or both of you'll be sorry."

# Collision Course

H e threatened me?" Tami looked more angry than afraid.

Miserable, Jake nodded.

He had returned home as soon as Jacobi left Murphy's—without paying for his beer—and told Tami what had happened.

Sitting next to him on the futon, Tami said, "Bert Jacobi. He's bad business, Jake. I started looking into his relation to Santino when I was doing that environmental story that got me fired from Reuters."

"He can be pretty scary," Jake admitted.

"So what are you going to do?"

Jake looked into her almond eyes. "I can't risk your getting hurt."

Strangely, Tami smiled. "That's a good out, isn't it? You'll do what he wants because you don't want me to get hurt."

"It's the truth," Jake said.

Taking both his hands in hers, she asked, "Jake, if I weren't involved in this—"

"But you are. I involved you."

"If I weren't involved in this," Tami repeated. "If we had never met and I didn't know you from Adam, if you had to face Jacobi by yourself, what would you do?"

"I'd drop the whole business. One mugging is enough."

"That's not the truth, Jake."

"The hell it isn't."

With a shake of her head, Tami insisted, "If you were in this by yourself, you'd push ahead, wouldn't you? Jacobi's threats wouldn't stop you."

"Don't kid yourself, Tami. I'm no hero."

For a long moment, Tami said nothing. She stared at Jake, as if trying to X-ray him with her eyes.

Finally she repeated, "So what are you going to do?"

"Exactly what Jacobi told me to do: stop snooping into Santino's past."

Tami looked disappointed. But before she could say anything, Jake added, "We've already got reams of information here. We don't have to go out and get more. We've got so much now that we can't digest it all."

"Oh! So we keep sifting through it, looking for something significant."

Jake nodded. "And we start sifting through the information I got about Jacobi, last spring. Maybe what we want is in his files, not Santino's."

"You think?"

"Let's see."

• • •

As far as the world beyond their basement apartment could tell, Jake had stopped prying into Santino's past. The first cold rains of autumn stripped leaves off the trees, and Washingtonians began wearing raincoats over their sweaters.

The Senate's energy committee conducted hearings on Senator Tomlinson's gutted energy plan. Everything chugged along smoothly. Santino chaired the hearings, smiling benignly as representatives of the fossil fuel lobbies gave their somewhat reluctant approvals to what was left of the plan.

Jake and Tami spent their nights scrolling through the data they had acquired about Santino—and Jacobi.

The days grew shorter, the nights frostier. As Halloween approached, Tami was ready to admit defeat.

"There's nothing here, Jake," she said. "Let's give it up and go out for dinner."

"To celebrate our defeat?" he said.

"We've been at it for more than two months, and we haven't found anything useful."

With a reluctant sigh, Jake got up from his desk chair and crossed the living room. He reached out his hand and helped Tami to her feet.

"You're right," he admitted. "Let's treat ourselves to a decent meal."

Dinner was almost pleasant, but as they walked home arm in arm through the chilly shadows, Tami said, "I still think Jacobi's the key to all this."

"Why's that?"

"News reporter's instinct," she said. "It was when I started poking into Jacobi's background that Santino got Reuters to can me."

"Coincidence, most likely."

"Maybe," she said. But she didn't sound convinced.

As soon as they got back to the apartment they immediately went back to searching the data they had accumulated.

An hour or so later Tami muttered, "That's funny."

"What's funny?"

"The Rhode Island records don't have a birth certificate for Jacobi."

"You're searching Rhode Island files?" Jake yelped, alarmed. "I thought we were just going to search the stuff we've already accumulated."

Tami soothed, "Public records, Jake. Everybody's got a right to scan them."

"If Jacobi finds out . . ."

"He won't. Besides, there's no birth certificate for him on record."

"Maybe he wasn't born. Maybe he was built in a laboratory, like Frankenstein's monster."

She made a disparaging face. "I found a birth certificate for Santino without trouble. But nothing for Jacobi."

"Maybe he wasn't born in Rhode Island."

"According to a newspaper article about him, he was. They even gave the date. It was a piece about his twenty-first birthday celebration, when his father took him in as a full partner in Jacobi and Sons."

Jake felt his brows knitting into a frown. He got up from his desk and went to bend over Tami's shoulder.

"Maybe Umberto isn't his original name. Try looking just for Jacobi."

Tami worked her laptop's keyboard for a moment. Then, "Here it is! Baby boy born to Mrs. Caterina Jacobi, the right date."

Jake sat down beside her.

"But look," Tami said, pointing to the image of the birth certificate, "there's no name listed for the father."

"That's kind of weird," Jake said.

"Strange, at least."

Suppressing a yawn, Jake said, "Come on, let's go to bed. I've got to be at the committee hearing tomorrow morning."

Still bent over her laptop, Tami said, "You go brush your teeth. I'll come in after you're finished."

Jake let the yawn come out, then turned and headed for the bedroom. He undressed, brushed his teeth, thought about turning on one of the late shows, decided against it.

As he was getting into bed, he heard Tami exclaim, "Aha!"

He started to come around the bed, but Tami appeared in the doorway, glowing with triumph.

"You found something?" Jake asked.

Smiling hugely, she said, "I used my old newshound muscles."

"Huh?"

"I figured that Jacobi might have been adopted. So I pulled up the Catholic adoption agency's records. They're computerized and, sure enough, there's an adoption file for Umberto Jacobi, the right birthdate."

"But his birth certificate said his mother was Mrs. Jacobi, didn't it?"

"Yes, but his father wasn't Mr. Jacobi. Not until they adopted him."

Jake stared at her. "Wait a minute. His mother . . ."

"She had an affair! She gave birth to an illegitimate boy!"

"And Jacobi senior adopted the boy."

"Right. Because the boy's father was his old friend Mario Santino, just returned home from the invasion of Grenada! With a Purple Heart!"

Sinking onto the bed, Jake asked, "You think?"

"That's what made McGrath turn against Santino. Mr. Straight Arrow couldn't condone a scandal like that!"

"Santino had an affair with Jacobi senior's wife, and the old man adopted the baby?"

"And forgave his wife. He must have been a bigger saint than Santino."

"But it all happened more than thirty-five years ago."

"McGrath couldn't support Santino with that little secret in the Little Saint's past," Tami insisted. "Imagine how much fun the bloggers would have with that juicy tidbit!"

Jake reached for her wrist and pulled her down on the bed beside him. "Tami, this is dynamite."

She bobbed her head up and down. "Isn't it?"

"If you're right . . . if this is true, we're on a collision course with Santino."

"I'd like to see the look on his face when you spring this on him."

"Yeah. And Jacobi's."

# California

I t took Jake another full day to decide on his next step. A full day of attending the ongoing energy committee hearings, then lunching with Senator Tomlinson and spending the afternoon going through the motions of working.

He half-listened politely to a visitor from the National Institutes of Health briefing him on the consequences of cutting NIH's budget for stem cell research. Then a pair of lobbyists in almost identical dark gray three-piece suits spent an hour extolling the benefits of opening several national parks to drilling for natural gas. Finally an earnest young woman in a tight sweater pleaded with him to get Senator Tomlinson to join the movement to outlaw all genetically modified crops.

By the time Jake drove home, he had made up his mind.

"We're going to California," he told Tami the instant she came through the apartment's door.

Surprised, she said, "We are?"

Jake nodded vigorously. "I've got vacation time coming to me. I imagine you do, too."

"Kind of abrupt, though, isn't it?"

"I ought to see Vic Wakefield and break the news to him that his methanol project has been cut down to a study program."

"You've got to go all the way out to San Diego to give him the bad news?"

As he headed for the kitchen and the bottle of Soave in the refrigerator, Jake explained, "It's the decent thing to do. Tell him face-to-face. Winston Churchill said that when you're going to kill a man, it doesn't cost you anything to be polite about it."

She eyed him suspiciously as he began to pour two glasses of wine. "This doesn't have anything to do with Jacobi, does it?"

Jake came around the counter that separated the kitchen from the living room and handed Tami her glass. As casually as he could, he replied, "Well, I thought it might be nice for you to spend a few days visiting your family."

"They're in Fresno, not San Diego."

"Yeah. I'd like to meet your folks. Then I could hop down to San Diego while you're visiting in Fresno."

"You want me out of town."

"I want you safe."

• • •

Tami's parents were warm and friendly, not a trace of the traditional Japanese formality and stiffness that Jake had expected. Then he realized that the Umetzus had been in the States for four generations. They're as American as I am, he told himself.

The Umetzu family wasn't small, despite the fact that Tami was an only child. Her parents each had several siblings living in the Bay area. They all got together—aunts, uncles, and five of Tami's cousins—for a happy, laughter-filled dinner in an Italian restaurant in downtown Fresno.

The next day Tami drove Jake to the Fresno Yosemite International Airport in their rented Toyota Camry.

"I'll be back on the six o'clock flight," Jake said for the eleventh time as they pulled up at the terminal curb.

"I'll be right here, waiting for you."

He gave her a peck on the lips and ducked out of the car, computer bag in hand.

• • •

Vic Wakefield looked more resigned than downcast.

"I thought it was too good to be true," he said, his round face serious, pensive.

Jake was sitting beside him on a worn-out sofa in Vic's office at Wakefield Laboratory, down at the San Diego waterfront. Through the room's only window he could see a row of sleek gray Navy destroyers anchored in the harbor.

"I'm sorry, Vic," Jake apologized. "Politics got in the way."

With a humorless smile, Wakefield said, "Might turn out to be good, in the long run. It was a big jump to go from our lab work to a full-scale production plant. Maybe a study program will be better for us."

Jake heard the bitterness in his voice. Trying to put as good a face on the situation as possible, he said, "Look at it this way, Vic. Your methanol process is now a part of the overall energy plan. Once the plan is put into action, you'll be part of the national energy policy."

Wakefield gave him an odd look. "Will the plan ever be put into action?"

"Yes," Jake snapped, reflexively. "It may not be as big and as comprehensive as we wanted, but it's going to get through the Senate energy committee and out onto the floor for a vote before this session is over."

Before Wakefield could comment, Jake added, "Santino's the Majority Leader now. He controls the Senate's agenda. He'll push the plan through."

"With a study program for our methanol process."

"Damned right."

Wakefield's smile brightened. "I want to thank you, Jake. I know you've gone to bat for us."

"I'm just sorry I couldn't do better for you."

"It's a start. We'll take it a step at a time." Waving one arm, Wakefield said, "We're a lot better off now than we were a year ago, aren't we?"

• • •

Wakefield drove Jake to the San Diego airport. As his car pulled away from the curb, Jake's cell phone buzzed.

It was his landlord. "You had a burglary," he said, with no preamble, his voice gravely dark.

"A burglary?" Jake gasped.

"Last night. After midnight. We heard somebody thumping around downstairs and called the police."

"What did they take?"

A pause. People rushed by, heading into the terminal building or coming out and searching for their ride while Jake stood transfixed at the curb, phone to his ear.

Finally the landlord reported, "We looked through the apartment with the police officers. The place is a mess, but it doesn't seem that anything was taken. Of course, you'll have to go through the apartment yourself and see if anything is missing."

"Did they catch the guy?"

Again the landlord's voice hesitated. It's as if he has to think twice before he opens his mouth, Jake thought, with growing irritation.

"No, by the time the police got here the burglar was gone."

Jake realized he would have to cut his California visit short. "All right," he said into the phone. "I'll catch a plane first thing tomorrow. I'll let you know when I'm arriving."

"Good." The landlord clicked off.

Jake stood there as the crowds swirled by, wondering, What were they after? Good thing I brought my notebook with me; all our files are in it. Then he thought, Tami's laptop! Did they get her files?

Jake hurried into the terminal and raced for his plane. He tried to call Tami as he dashed toward his gate but got only her voice mail. He didn't leave a message. I'll tell her about this when I see her at the airport.

When Jake's plane touched down on schedule at Fresno Jake called her again, but he got only her voice mail again. Feeling annoyed, he hustled out to the curb, trying to remember what their rented car looked like.

But Tami was not there waiting for him.

# Fresno Yosemite International Airport

S tanding at curbside, Jake yanked out his phone again and called Tami's parents.

"She left early, said she wanted to do some shopping," her mother said. "She said she'd pick you up."

"But she's not here!"

Mrs. Umetzu didn't seem upset. "Maybe she got stalled in traffic. Or maybe she's driving around the airport. They won't let you wait at the curb, you know."

"Yes, I know. But she should be at the cell phone lot, at least."

"Have you tried calling her?"

"Twice."

"Then she must be in the car. The rental car doesn't have Bluetooth, I imagine. And she wouldn't pick up her cell phone while she's driving. She'll be along soon, you'll see."

Jake didn't think so. He stood there at curbside, a thousand possibilities racing through his head, all of them bad. Jacobi's snatched her, he thought. He knows that she found out he was adopted and came out here to grab her before she could tell anybody. He knew we were going to California; Santino's people have spies in Tomlinson's office, of course.

What should I do? What can I do?

His phone buzzed.

Jake fumbled it out of his pocket. "Hello." He half expected to hear Jacobi's low, menacing voice.

Instead, it was Tami. "Jake! I'm sorry I'm not there yet. I'm on my way."

"Where are you?"

"At a police station downtown. I'll be at the airport in fifteen minutes or so."

"You're okay?"

"I'm fine. See you in a little bit."

It took Jake three tries to finally click off his cell phone, his hands were shaking so badly. He walked over to an empty bench near the baggage-check counter and sat to wait for Tami.

She's all right, he said to himself. She's all right. Only then did he wonder, What the hell is she doing at a police station?

• • •

It was twilight by the time the rented black Camry pulled up at the curb. Jake ducked into it. Tami seemed perfectly okay, although her usual cheerful smile was replaced by a dead serious expression.

"What happened?" Jake asked. "Why were you at a police station?"

"I was being followed," Tami said, her eyes on the airport traffic.

"Followed?"

"I noticed a gray Ford sedan following me when I left the house this afternoon. All the way downtown, right behind me." Tami's voice was flat, unemotional. "When I parked in a municipal garage, they came in right behind me and parked a few spaces away."

"They?"

"Two men. Big guys. Hard faces. Wearing sports jackets. Big shoulders."

"You're sure they were following you?"

"Every store I went into, they waited outside."

"Did they say anything to you?"

"No, they just followed me. It was spooky."

Tami pulled the car onto the freeway lane heading toward downtown Fresno.

"When I got into the car again to come get you at the airport, they tailed me, in the same gray Ford."

"So what happened?"

A hint of a smile curved her lips slightly. "When I went back to the parking building, I deliberately walked past their car—"

"Jesus!"

"They weren't in it," Tami said. "They were still walking along behind me. Anyway, I saw their license number. When I drove out of the garage and they came out behind me, I used the car's GPS to find the nearest police station and drove straight to it."

Jake felt admiration for her cool levelheadedness. "Smart," he muttered.

"I told a police sergeant what was going on, and that I was frightened. He looked up the license number I gave him."

"And?"

"The car was registered to the local FBI office."

"The FBI!"

"That's what the police sergeant told me."

Jake leaned back in the passenger's seat. "Why would the FBI be following you?"

"I'll bet it was because a certain US senator asked them to keep an eye on us," Tami replied.

"Santino?"

"One of his people, more likely. When a senator asks a federal agency for help, they respond."

Jake recalled how cooperative the various agencies he had called had been. "But the FBI."

"Santino wants to know where we are."

"And why."

They drove through the gathering darkness in silence

for several minutes. At last Jake said, "Santino wants to show us that we can't get away from him. He can find us, wherever we go."

Tami nodded. "He's made his point."

With a bitter chuckle, Jake said, "He can use the FBI to track us, then get Jacobi or some other thugs to grab us."

"Whenever he wants to."

"He's telling us we'd better not try to make any trouble for him."

"That's why Santino got Reuters to ax me," Tami said. "It wasn't the environmental story. He thought I was getting too close to finding out that Jacobi is his son."

Jake remembered, "For what it's worth, our apartment was burglarized last night."

For the first time, Tami looked startled. "Burglarized?"

"My landlord says they didn't seem to take anything, but I'm going to fly back to Washington tomorrow and check out the place."

"We've really got Santino worried," Tami said.

"He's sure as hell's got me worried," Jake said, with some fervor.

Tami nodded. Then, glancing at her rearview mirror, she said, "I may be a little paranoid, but the same pair of headlights have been following us ever since we left the airport."

# The FBI Field Office in Fresno

J ake slept uneasily that night in Tami's parents' home.
In the morning, Tami told her parents what was going on.

Her father got up from the breakfast table and went
to the kitchen wall phone.

"Dad," Tami called after him, "what are you doing?"

Mr. Umetzu's face was calm, but his voice radiated
cold fury. "Calling the local FBI office. They can't ha-
rass law-abiding citizens! It's racism. It's fascism! My
father fought in the US Army in World War II. He was
decorated for valor. And now the FBI is harassing his
granddaughter?"

Jake pushed his chair from the table and went to Mr.
Umetzu's side. "Maybe I should talk to them," he suggested gently.

Umetzu didn't let go of his grip on the phone.

"I'm a United States senator's legislative aide," Jake
explained. "They might pay more attention to me."

Umetzu reluctantly handed the phone receiver to
Jake, muttering, "Racism."

• • •

The head of the Fresno office of the Federal Bureau of
Investigation was a pleasant-looking Hispanic woman
with graying hair and skin the color of lightly done
toast. Slim and smartly dressed in a sky-blue skirted

suit, she smiled politely as Jake told her about the car that had followed Tami.

"And the local police said the car is registered to this office?" she asked, sounding incredulous.

"That's what they told me," Tami said. Pulling a scrap of paper from her purse, she went on, "Here's the license number."

The FBI chief glanced at the paper, then put it on her desk. "I'll check this out," she said.

"We'll wait," said Jake.

Her pleasant smile dimming a little, the woman picked up her phone and asked for the motor pool. She read off the license number that Tami had given her, then nodded once and hung up.

"According to our records," she said to Jake, "that car was in our garage all day yesterday and last night."

"That's impossible," Tami snapped. "I saw it. I wrote down the license number. They followed me all day and well into the night."

Cocking her head to one side, the woman said, "I don't see how that could be, Miss Umetzu. Our records show—"

Jake demanded, "How could Tami write down the license number? She didn't think it up out of the blue. She isn't clairvoyant."

Her brow wrinkling, the chief replied, "I'll have to look into this. Where can I contact you?"

Jake knew they were being dismissed. "I'll be back in my office tomorrow," he said, reaching for his wallet. "Here's my card."

"Legislative aide to Senator B. Franklin Tomlinson," the woman said. "Very impressive."

"Not as impressive as Senator Santino," Tami quipped.

"Senator Santino? Isn't he the new Majority Leader?"

Jake got to his feet and reached for Tami's hand. To

the FBI chief he said, "Thanks for your time. I'd appreciate it if you would look into this and let me know what you find. Tami's father is very upset about this. He thinks it's harassment."

"Hardly that!" said the chief, as she rose from her desk chair.

"And racism," Tami added.

The chief frowned, but said nothing.

Once they had left the FBI office, Tami said, "That was a whole lot of nothing."

"Stonewalling," Jake said. "Santino's got more clout than Tomlinson."

# Home Again

Tami went back to DC with Jake. Part of him wanted her to stay with her parents, but he realized that she wouldn't be truly safe until they had reconciled their problem with Santino. So he relented and let her fly back home with him.

As they waited for their flight in the Fresno airport, Jake phoned Kevin O'Donnell to tell Tomlinson's chief of staff that he would be in the office the next afternoon.

O'Donnell sounded mildly amused. "Cutting your vacation short, eh?"

"It wasn't much of a vacation, Kevin."

"Meeting the in-laws never is," O'Donnell replied, laughing.

Jake said, "I'll tell you all about it tomorrow. In the afternoon, most likely."

"Sure. Take your time. Officially, you're still on vacation."

• • •

It was well past the dinner hour by the time the airport taxi pulled up at the 49th Street house. As he got out of the cab, Jake saw the front door open; his landlord came out onto the porch.

"Everything is just the way it was when the police left," he said, without preamble. "We haven't touched a thing."

Jake pulled his roll-along down the flagstone path

around the side of the house and hefted it down the four steps to his door, with Tami and the landlord behind him. The landlord took Tami's bag down the steps.

Jake unlocked the door and clicked on the lights.

"Oh my," Tami said, her voice hollow.

The living room was a shambles. Coffee table over-turned, futon pulled away from the wall, every drawer of Jake's desk yanked open and its contents spilled on the floor. Kitchen cabinets opened, cans and bottles and jars littering the floor.

"They left the refrigerator door open," the landlord said. "We shut it after the police left."

The bedroom was equally uprooted: mattress pulled off the bed, bedclothes strewn across the floor, medicine chest in the bathroom opened, every shelf emptied, the floor covered with opened bottles and a carpeting of pills.

Jake said grimly, "They made a mess, all right."

"Is anything missing?" the landlord asked.

"Who the hell knows?" Jake snapped. "It'll take a week to straighten everything out."

Tami pointed a trembling finger at the folding table on the side wall. "My laptop's gone," she said, in a hushed voice.

Jake reached out and gripped her arm. "Come on, we're going to a hotel."

• • •

After a fitful night's sleep in a modest hotel near the American University campus, Tami and Jake spent the morning trying to straighten up their apartment.

"Why did they make such a mess? What were they looking for?" Tami asked as she stretched clean sheets on their bed.

"Your laptop," Jake said. He was on his knees, scooping up the aspirin pills that had been thrown onto the bathroom floor.

"But it was right there on the table, out in the open. They didn't have to wreck the place."

"No, they didn't have to. But they did. That's their message to us. They can ruin us, destroy us, any time they choose."

She sank onto a corner of the bed and started to sob. "I feel so . . . so helpless. Like I've been raped."

Jake got to his feet and went into the bedroom to sit down beside her. As he slid a protective arm around Tami's shoulders, he felt a smoldering rage growing inside him. The wiseguys always muscle you to make you do what they want. Ever since he'd been a kid, he'd had to deal with thugs and outright crooks who made pain and humiliation their major tools.

He kissed Tami on the side of her face, then said softly, "I've got to go to the office. Will you be okay here by yourself?"

She nodded.

"I'll be back in time for dinner. Pick a good restaurant, you deserve a treat."

With a cheerless smile, Tami said, "Like a good little doggie?"

"Like my brave little pet," he said.

"I don't feel very brave, Jake."

"I know. Stay upstairs with the landlord and his wife. We don't have to finish cleaning this mess."

"No," she said. "I'd rather have something to do."

"Okay." He stood up. "If anything bothers you, anything at all, you run upstairs and call me."

Nodding, she said, "I will."

"I've got to get to the office," Jake said. "I've got to put an end to this."

• • •

It was nearly three p.m. when Jake got to the Hart S.O.B.

"The senator's on the floor," said the receptionist when he asked where Tomlinson was. "Senate's in session."

"Where's Kevin?"

"In the conference room with Reynolds and some people from Norton and Ingels."

"Let me know when he gets finished."

Jake went to his own office, slid into his desk chair, and grabbed the telephone. "Please get me Senator Santino's office."

The Little Saint was in the Senate chamber, same as Tomlinson. Jake asked the aide who answered the phone to schedule a meeting as soon as possible.

"With Senator Tomlinson?" the aide asked.

Jake lied, "Yes. As soon as possible. This evening, if you can."

A moment's hesitation. Then, "I'll call you back."

As Jake hung up, one of the administrative aides appeared at his doorway. "Mr. O'Donnell is free now."

"Thanks."

Jake made his way to O'Donnell's office and told the staff chief what he'd learned about Santino and Jacobi.

For once, O'Donnell looked impressed. Shocked, in fact.

"He's Jacobi's father?"

Jake nodded tightly.

"You've got evidence for this?"

"My apartment's been burglarized. The fucking FBI tailed us when we were in Fresno."

"That's not evidence," O'Donnell said.

"It's good enough for me. I need to tell Frank about this. We've got to have a face-to-face with Santino."

O'Donnell shook his head. "Not so fast. Let me think about this. There are a lot of angles to this."

"I'm not going to wait until they kidnap Tami! I'm going to see Santino and get this settled. The sooner the better."

"Wait 'til Franklin comes back to the office."

"The Senate might be in session all night."

"Then Santino will be on the floor, too, won't he?"

Jake started to reply, then realized that O'Donnell was right. As long as the Senate stays in session, Santino would most likely be right there in the Senate chamber.

But not Jacobi.

# Maneuvering

Jake stewed restlessly in his office until six o'clock. O'Donnell stuck his head through the doorway and said, "Senate's still in session. Big debate about the immigration bill."

Jake nodded unhappily.

"I'm going home," O'Donnell said. "You might as well go, too."

"In a few minutes," Jake said.

His face stern, O'Donnell said, "Don't do anything foolish, Jake. Wait 'til you can talk to Franklin. Tomorrow morning."

"Yeah, sure."

"I mean it," O'Donnell said.

Nodding again, Jake replied, "Okay. I'll wait for Frank. Tomorrow morning. Bright and early."

"That's the ticket."

But once O'Donnell left, Jake looked up Jacobi's cell phone number from his office phone's records.

And got a pleasant recorded male voice informing him that Mr. Jacobi was unavailable, please leave a message at the tone.

"It's Jake Ross," he said into the phone. "We have to talk. As soon as possible." Then he left his cell phone number.

Jake got up from his desk and put on his leather car coat. The office was almost empty; most of the desks were dark. As he headed for the door, he pulled his cell phone from his pants pocket and called Tami.

She did not answer.

Suddenly worried, Jake raced down to the basement garage, jumped into his Mustang, and drove home. Tami wasn't in the apartment. He saw that she had straightened up the place. But she wasn't there.

He ran around the house, up onto the porch, and pounded on the front door. The landlord's wife opened it, looking startled.

"Have you seen Tami?" Jake asked before she could open her mouth.

"Not since this afternoon," she replied. "She left in a hurry."

"Where'd she go?"

"I don't know. She didn't say. A taxi pulled up, and she ran out to it."

"When was that?"

The woman blinked, trying to remember. "Oh, it must have been about four thirty, maybe a little later. She took a taxi."

Jake stood there, puzzled, frantic, frightened. She would have called me to let me know where she was going, he said to himself. Or left a note, at least.

"Is something wrong?" the landlord's wife asked.

Jake said, "I don't know. I—"

His cell phone buzzed. Jake yanked it from his pocket. "Tami?"

Jacobi's voice answered, "It's Bert Jacobi. You said you wanted to see me."

"Where's Tami?"

"Your Jap girlfriend?"

"Where is she?"

"How should I know? I'm in Providence, not DC."

"You're lying!"

Jacobi chuckled. "Get your nerves under control, kid. I don't know where your girlfriend is, and I don't care. You called me and said you want to see me. What about?"

Jake walked away from his landlord's wife, leaving her standing at the house's front door, and went down the porch steps.

"We've got to talk, face-to-face."

Jacobi grunted. "Yeah, I guess we do. I can fly down to DC tomorrow morning."

"Okay. Call me when you get to Santino's office. I'll see you both there."

"Good."

Before Jacobi could hang up, Jake said, "If anything's happened to Tami, I'll kill you."

"Tough talk, kid."

"Anything at all. I want her safe. I want her with me. Tonight. Now. Otherwise I tell the whole story to the news media."

Jacobi said nothing.

"And then I'll kill you," Jake repeated. "That's a promise."

The phone clicked dead.

Jake stood there in the nighttime darkness with the phone in his hand. He realized it was chilly; a cold wind was making the trees sigh.

What to do? he asked himself as he headed down the path to his apartment's door. What can I do?

He went back into the apartment and sank onto his desk chair. What can I do? he repeated. Where is she? What's happened to her?

His phone buzzed again. He put it to his ear.

"Jake?"

"Tami!"

"Are you all right?"

"Are *you* all right?"

"Yes." But her voice sounded weak, unsure.

"Where are you?"

"I'm in the Capitol building, in the Majority Leader's office."

"What? How'd you get there? What's going on?"

"They want you to come here. Right away."

"They? Who's they?"

"Security police. They said you were hurt!"

"I'm not hurt. I'm fine."

"Thank goodness."

"Are you okay?"

"Yes, but the security officers said Senator Santino wants to talk to the two of us."

"I'll be down there in fifteen minutes," Jake said.

"Drive carefully," said Tami.

Jake almost giggled at that. "I will," he promised.

• • •

It took more than fifteen minutes. Jake parked in the Hart Building, then sprinted down the tunnel that connected to the Capitol. The Senate was still in session, but there were no tourists wandering through the building at this time of night; the tunnels were practically deserted.

Once he got to the Capitol, Jake had to ask for directions to the Majority Leader's office; he had never been there before. At last he found it, and he saw that a uniformed Capitol security officer was standing in the hallway, in front of the door, his arms folded across his chest. The man was well over six feet tall and carried a heavy-looking pistol in a holster at his hip.

Jake went up to him. "I'm Jacob Ross. Senator Santino wants—"

"Dr. Ross," the guard said. "Go right in." And he opened the door.

Jake stepped into a smallish anteroom, paneled in

dark wood. Two more uniformed security officers—one of them a woman—jumped up from the wooden chairs they'd been sitting in, by the door.

"You're Jacob Ross?"

Jake showed them his ID card.

"Right through there, sir."

Jake went through the open door into a bigger room, and there was Tami, sitting in a leather chair in front of a heavy mahogany desk, looking small and vulnerable and worried, but not at all frightened.

She jumped up and flung herself into Jake's arms.

"They told me you'd been hurt!" she blurted. "An automobile accident."

Jake kissed her. Then, "I'm fine. Are you okay?"

"Yes, yes."

Holding her hand, Jake turned back to the door to the anteroom, where the two security officers were still standing.

"What's going on here?" he demanded.

"Senator Santino wants to see you," said the male officer. "Both of you."

Jake glanced at Tami, then said, "Good. I want to see him."

# Confrontation

The two security officers went back into the anteroom and closed the door behind them, leaving Jake and Tami alone together. They sat side by side in the dark brown leather chairs in front of the Majority Leader's desk. Jake glanced at his wristwatch: it was almost midnight.

The witching hour, he thought.

"What happens now?" Tami asked.

"Now we wait."

"Can't we go home?"

Jake pursed his lips, thinking. "I don't believe those cops outside would actually stop us if we insisted on leaving. But I want to have this out with Santino, the sooner the better."

She nodded glumly.

Jake looked around the office. Not much to see. The massive dark desk, a couple of wooden chairs along the far wall. No windows. Framed photos on the walls of earlier Majority Leaders such as Lyndon Johnson, Howard Baker, Harry Reid: men who had used this office to meet with senators, to persuade, cajole, or intimidate men and women over issues great and small.

Turning back to Tami, he asked, "Somebody told you I'd been injured in an automobile accident?"

"They said you were in the infirmary here in the Capitol building. But when I got here they told me that was a mistake, and I should wait here for Senator Santino.

Later on they said I should phone you and tell you to come here."

"So now he's got us both here, waiting for him."

"I don't like this," Tami said. "We should leave."

Jake didn't argue. Instead, he went to the TV remote on the desk and clicked on the flat-screen set on the opposite wall. As he expected, it was tuned to C-SPAN.

And it showed the Senate floor emptying. The senators were filing out of the chamber.

"Session's over," Jake said. "He ought to be here any minute."

Tami seemed to sit up straighter, square her shoulders, as if bracing herself to face the enemy.

Mario Santino opened the door and entered the office. He looked tired, bent, almost frail. Jake got to his feet automatically as Santino headed to the desk.

"Good evening," he said softly, slipping into the high-backed swivel chair behind the desk. "I'm glad you could both come."

"We didn't have much choice," Jake said, sitting down again.

Santino made a little smile. "Love makes people do strange things." Pointing at Tami, he said, "You came here because you thought he"—he nodded toward Jake—"was injured. And you, Dr. Ross, came because she was here."

"I came because I want to talk to you about your son."

Santino's pale face flushed slightly. "Yes, I suppose you do."

"Bert Jacobi is your son, isn't he?" Jake said.

"Do you have any evidence of that?"

"We know he was born to Mrs. Caterina Jacobi and then adopted by her husband," Tami said.

"That's not evidence that I was his father."

"It was enough to get Senator McGrath to drop his support of you," Jake said.

Santino's ice-cold gray eyes flared. He took a deep breath and placed both hands flat on the desktop. "The late Senator McGrath was a fool."

"But he could have told the news media about your affair with your best friend's wife," Tami said.

"That would have been . . . troublesome."

Tami said, "You could scotch this whole rumor with a simple DNA test."

Santino shook his head. "No, I can't do that."

"Then the story's true!" Jake said.

Santino started to say something, but checked himself. His eyes shifted away from the two of them, as if he was looking at something that wasn't really there, something from deep in the past.

"You think you know all about it, but you don't," Santino said, with quiet intensity. "What do you know about pain, about love and shame and guilt hanging over you like a dark cloud? All these years. All these years."

The Little Saint glared at them, but then his anger seemed to dissolve. He sagged in his chair and said in a near whisper, "I loved her. Do you know what it's like to love someone so deeply that you don't care what happens, just so long as you can be with her?"

Tami stared at him.

"Salvatore Jacobi was a monster, a brute," Santino went on, his voice low but trembling with ancient emotions. "He was twice Catherine's age. His family and Catherine's family arranged their marriage. She loved me, not him! But I had nothing, I was just a poor man working his way through college. He was going to inherit his father's company, his family was well off. They forced her to marry him."

Jake saw that Santino's hands had clenched into fists.

"So I dropped out of college and joined the Marines. To get away from her. I fought for my country. And when I came back home . . . when I saw Catherine again . . ." His voice broke and he lowered his head.

"So Jacobi really is your son," Jake said, his voice equally low.

"He killed her," Santino muttered. "She died within a year, and he brutalized little Bert. If I'd had the courage . . . the strength . . . but I didn't. There was nothing I could do. Nothing."

"You went into politics."

Still staring into the past, Santino said, "Yes. That was the road to strength, to power. The old man died at last, and Bert inherited the coal company. He's always supported me, like a good son."

"I can see why you want to keep this a secret," Tami said. "It would ruin your image, wouldn't it?"

"It all happened nearly forty years ago." Santino's voice sounded almost like a guilty little boy's whine.

Jake said, "But it would damage you now, wouldn't it? The Little Saint, an adulterer, with his friend's wife."

Santino seemed to stir himself, pull his focus back to the here and now.

Raising a finger to point at Jake, he said, "You. You and your kind. Holier than thou, the lot of you. You come into Washington all full of righteous zeal. You want to change everything. Things that have taken years to build, you want to tear down overnight. You'd destroy everything I've worked to accomplish, wouldn't you? You'd destroy me!"

Jake countered, "I don't want to destroy anything. I want to build a strong and sustainable energy policy—"

"Nobody wants your damnable energy policy!" Santino snapped.

"You mean the fossil fuel lobby doesn't want it."

"And the farm lobby," Santino said. "America is doing fine on energy. We'll keep on doing fine."

"For how long? Five years? Ten? While we keep on

damaging the global climate and sucking every drop of oil and gas out of the ground? What happens then?"

"We have enough coal for another century or more."

"It's time we start to move to a sustainable energy policy that doesn't ruin the environment, that builds new industries, that creates new jobs."

"Pipe dreams! You're talking nonsense."

"No, I'm talking about a future where America leads the world in energy technology and our economy is stronger than ever."

"Spare me the platitudes. I've heard them all before."

"It's going to happen," Jake said. "We're going to move to an energy policy that's more than just the fossil fuel industries."

"Over my ruined career! My ruined life!"

"Nothing needs to be ruined," Jake said, as reasonably as he could manage.

"You and your pretty-boy senator," Santino went on, almost snarling now. "You want to change everything, climb over my dead body."

"No, that's not what we want."

Santino started to reply, but caught himself and said nothing. He took a deep breath, visibly struggling to suppress his burning anger.

Almost as calmly as when he first came into the office, Santino asked Jake, "So what do you propose?"

"I want the energy plan approved by the committee and then the full Senate."

"And what else?"

"That's all. That's what I came to Washington for. That's what I've been trying to accomplish for Senator Tomlinson."

"That's all?"

"That's all."

Santino almost smiled. "That's all for now. But what about tomorrow? What about the next time you want something from me? You'll hold this threat over my head again, won't you?"

"No, we won't," Jake said. "I promise you. And Senator Tomlinson will give you his word, too, I'm sure."

"Will he?"

"I'm sure of it."

Santino seemed to think it over for a few moments, then he said, "I suppose I'll have to take your word at face value. I have no choice, do I?"

"You can count on our word," Jake said.

"Yes, I'm sure I can. But Bert, he's another issue altogether. He's very loyal to me, you know. And he can get, well . . . emotional."

# The Tunnels

Jake led Tami out of the Majority Leader's office and down into the tunnels that connected the Capitol to the various congressional office buildings.

Although the corridors were brightly lit even after midnight, Jake couldn't avoid the feeling that they were fleeing down some dank, dark passageway in an ancient castle, trying to escape a lumbering monster that was pursuing them. Hardly anyone else was in the tunnels, but Jake stared at each passerby as if he might be a murdering thug.

"What he said about Jacobi," Tami said, puffing a little as she scampered to keep up with Jake's longer strides, "you don't think the man would try anything violent, do you?"

"I do," Jake snapped, glancing over his shoulder to see if anyone was following them.

"You do?"

"Who do you think got me mugged?"

"Oh!"

He took a wrong turn, got slightly lost, and had to retrace their steps. Finally he found the passageway that led to the Hart S.O.B. Instead of going to the underground garage, though, he pulled Tami to the elevator bank.

"Aren't we going home?" she asked.

"Not yet."

They went up to the second floor and to Senator Tomlinson's suite of offices. Jake fumbled with the electronic key, but the front door popped open at last.

"What are you going to do?" Tami asked.

"Call Frank," he said as he headed for his own office.

"At this time of night?"

"I told O'Donnell about all this, but Kevin's a DC guy. If he thinks it smarter to keep quiet about it, he'll keep quiet. He'll check all the angles and then let Santino's people know that they can count on him to keep everything hushed up."

Tami plopped down onto one of the chairs in front of Jake's desk. "But you told Santino that you'd keep quiet about it."

Tapping on his computer keyboard to pull up his telephone file, Jake nodded and said, "Santino doesn't believe me. Even if he does, he wants to make sure we don't talk."

"Make sure?"

"As in murder. Jacobi's already on his way here."

"You really think we're in that kind of danger?"

"I really do."

Senator Tomlinson's private, emergency phone number came up on the screen. Jake clicked on the digital recorder as the phone put through his call.

His desktop screen showed a smiling portrait of Tomlinson while the senator's voice said, "Hello. This is Senator Franklin Tom—"

The screen suddenly showed Tomlinson, in his shirtsleeves, collar unbuttoned. He appeared to be in his bedroom.

"Jake, what's wrong?"

"Sorry to disturb you at this time of night, Frank."

"We were just having a nightcap. What's wrong?"

"Santino's after us."

"What?"

Jake bawled out the whole story; Santino, Jacobi, the not-so-veiled threat. "I want Tami to be safe," he said. "None of this is her fault, but I've got her into this without realizing how much danger I've put her in."

Tomlinson glanced away. He must be looking at Amy, Jake thought.

"All right. The two of you come over here and stay a few days until we can get this straightened out."

Jake felt a surge of gratitude rush through him. "Thanks, Frank."

"Tonight," Tomlinson said, firmly. "We'll wait up for you."

Nodding, Jake said, "We'll go home and pack a couple of bags. We'll be at your place in about an hour. Okay?"

"Fine," said Tomlinson.

Before the senator could hang up, Jake added, "I've been recording our call. All the info we have on Santino and Jacobi. It's on the recorder in my desk."

"Good thinking," said Tomlinson. "See the two of you in an hour or so."

Jake killed the phone connection and looked up at Tami. "We've got a hideout," he said, with a weak grin.

Getting up from her chair, Tami said, "Well, let's get to it."

They went down to the garage. Jake felt a little spooky, as if Jacobi or one of his hoods would pop up from behind a parked car, but they made it to his Mustang without a problem.

When they arrived at 49th Street Northwest, though, their house was in flames.

"Oh my god!" Tami said.

Fire engines blocked the street, and firefighters were

pouring water onto the blazing roof. Jake saw his land-lord and the man's wife standing in bathrobes by a Fire Department sedan, amid the hoses snaking across the street.

Without a word, Jake made a U-turn and sped off for Tomlinson's house.

# Aftermath

They stayed the night with the Tomlinsons. Once Jake told them about the fire, the senator grimly called the DC police.

"Your landlord and his wife are all right," Tomlinson said, looking up from the phone. "Looks like the house is pretty badly damaged, though."

"We had just moved back in after the burglary," Tami murmured. "Just yesterday."

Jake simmered with anger. "Find Jacobi. He did this. If not him personally, he got somebody to torch our apartment."

The senator's wife looked unconvinced. "Why would he do that? What would he gain?"

"It's a warning," Jake said. "He's coming after us."

Tomlinson, still in his shirtsleeves, went to the phone again. "I'm going to get some protection for you."

Trying to smile, Amy said, "I'm going to get us drinks. What would you like?"

• • •

The next day was a numbing succession of meetings with the police, the insurance people, and the private detective agency that Tomlinson had contacted.

Sitting in the insurance company's bright, spacious office, Jake listened to the claims adjuster tell them, "Apparently the painters who redid your living room left some cans of paint in your utility room. That's where the fire started."

"The painters were there months ago, after Hurricane Carlos," Jake objected. "And they didn't leave any cans of paint in the utility room."

The claims adjuster, a slim, dapper man in a smart tweed jacket, shook his head. "The cans were there."

"Whoever set the fire must have brought them in."

The adjuster's brows rose. "You think this was deliberate arson?"

Jake asked, "Were there any signs of a forced entrance?"

"The front door of your apartment wasn't forced. The door to the utility room was too charred for us to tell."

"It was arson," Jake said flatly.

Obviously uncertain, the adjuster said, "Well, we'll certainly have to look into that angle."

• • •

The private investigator's office was much smaller than the insurance adjuster's. The head of the firm looked serious and fatherly: bald, heavyset, with piercing blue eyes.

"Senator Tomlinson has requested twenty-four seven protection for the two of you."

Jake nodded numbly. It was all starting to seem like a bad dream, an endless nightmare. Tami looked equally frozen, exhausted by the events that were overwhelming them.

"You won't have to look around for our team," the investigator assured them. "They'll be near enough to protect you."

"For how long?" Jake asked bleakly.

The older man smiled. "For as long as it takes, son."

Jake forced a smile, thinking, He means, for as long as Frank foots the bill.

The man pulled open a drawer of his desk and took out two small plastic buttons encased in plastic baggies.

"Carry these with you wherever you go," he said, handing them to Jake and Tami. "Miniaturized radio beacons. They'll allow my people to track you minute by minute."

• • •

Once they'd left the investigator's office, Tami and Jake passed a restaurant on the corner of the street. The day had turned chilly; flat gray clouds were covering the sky, matching Jake's mood almost perfectly.

"Lunch?" Tami asked. "I'm starving."

"Oh," Jake said, surprised that she could think of food. "Sure."

The restaurant had some tables on the sidewalk, but Jake thought they'd be more comfortable indoors.

"Outside," Tami urged. "We won't have too many days left when we can eat out on the sidewalk."

Jake wanted to argue, but decided not to. She's right, he thought. We may not have too many days left, period.

Once they sat at one of the tables, Jake called his landlord's cell phone number. Before he could ask how the man and his wife were, the landlord said curtly, "I suppose you know that you've broken your lease."

And he hung up.

With a sigh that was almost a snort, Jake started to tuck the phone back inside his jacket, then thought better of it.

"Who're you calling?" Tami asked.

"Jacobi."

Her mouth formed a tiny little "Oh."

Jacobi answered on the second ring. "I had a feeling I'd be hearing from you."

Jake said, "We still have to talk."

"Yeah?"

"Yeah. You burned us out but you didn't kill us."

"Hey, I didn't do anything. You had a fire, that's tough luck. But don't hang it on me."

"And pigs can fly."

"What the hell's that supposed to mean?"

"When can we talk? Face-to-face."

"I'm still in Providence."

"How soon can you get down here?"

"Why should I?"

"Because if you don't, the whole world's going to find out that Mario Santino is your father."

Silence, for several heartbeats. Then Jacobi said, "You don't learn real quick, do you?"

"What's it going to be?"

Grudgingly, Jacobi said, "I'll fly down this afternoon. I'll phone you when I get there."

"Good," said Jake.

Tami was staring at him from across the table. "Is he coming here?"

"This afternoon."

"And you really think he's responsible for the fire?"

"Who else?"

A young, pink-faced waiter took their lunch orders and went back inside the restaurant. Jake thought the kid was smart; stay indoors where it's warm as long as you can.

Focusing on Tami, he asked, "Do you have a recording device? Something small enough to keep in a pocket?"

She shook her head. "I did. But it was in the apartment."

"Yeah. I should have realized that. Well, after lunch we'll go buy one."

"And some clothes," Tami said.

"And an overcoat," Jake added.

# Jacobi

After lunch, Jake and Tami returned to the Tomlinson residence. The senator was at his office, but his wife played hostess to them.

"It's an awkward time of day," Amy said as she led them to the library. "Too late for lunch, too early for cocktails."

"I ought to be at the office, too," Jake said.

Amy shook her head. "Frank said you should chill out here. He's got an appointment to talk with Santino this afternoon."

"I should be there," Jake said.

"Frank wants you to wait here," said Amy, gesturing to the sofa. "He said he'll call you after he's talked with Santino."

Jake plopped down onto the sofa. Tami sat beside him. "I'm still officially on vacation," she told Amy. "Until next week."

"By then, all this should be settled," Amy said.

"I hope so."

The three of them sat there in the library making small talk while Jake waited with increasing impatience for Jacobi to phone. He said he was taking an afternoon flight, Jake thought. How many flights are there from Providence to Reagan National? Maybe he's coming on a private jet.

Amy and Tami were chatting quite naturally about

clothes and all the other things that had been lost in the fire.

"I can go shopping with you, if you like," Amy volunteered.

"That would be fun," said Tami.

Why isn't Jacobi calling? Jake asked himself. What's he doing, *walking* here from Rhode Island?

"The weather's getting cold, isn't it?" Amy said. "I'd like to get Frank to go back home for some skiing as soon as the snow gets deep enough."

"Where do you go?" Tami asked.

Jake's cell phone buzzed. He yanked it from his pocket so swiftly he thought he might have torn his trousers.

"I just landed," Jacobi's voice said, in a low growl. "I'll take the Metro to the Capitol stop. You can meet me there."

Jake said, "Right. Capitol stop." He turned the phone off and got to his feet.

Tami stood up beside him.

"You stay here with Amy," Jake told her. "I'll see Jacobi by myself."

"But—"

"No buts," Jake said. "I want you safe here."

• • •

By the time Jake drove his Mustang to the Hart Building garage and then made his way along the chilly streets to the Metro station two blocks south of the Capitol building, the sun was setting. The going-home rush was in full swing: streets clogged with cars, buses, taxis inching along; sidewalks crowded with people. The Metro station was jammed wall-to-wall with office workers eager to get home.

Searching through the crowd, waiting on the station platform for Jacobi's short, stocky form, Jake wondered if he'd find the man. On the other hand, he thought, crowds are good. Too many witnesses for him to try any rough stuff.

He tried to see if the private investigators who were supposed to be protecting him were in the crowd. How would I know who they are? Jake asked himself. The head of the PI firm told us not to worry, they'd be nearby even if we couldn't see—

"Hello, kid."

Jake nearly jumped out of his skin. Jacobi was standing beside him, wearing a black leather coat, his balding head hatless.

"I . . . I was looking for you," Jake stammered.

"Well, here I am."

Jake started to push through the crowd, heading toward an exit. "We have to talk."

"Yeah."

"My office is only a few blocks from here."

"Nah, not your office."

"Then where?"

"Why not right here?"

His lopsided face grinning, Jacobi grasped Jake's arm hard enough to be painful.

As Jacobi led him through the crowd on the station platform, Jake's mind was spinning. At least he's not going to try to shove me under a train. But where's he going? Can the PIs track me underground? Will the beacon's signal get through all the concrete around us? Where the hell are they, anyway?

Jake saw that Jacobi was dragging him toward the men's toilet. He wants to have a private conversation in the men's room?

But then Jacobi went to the separate room reserved for handicapped persons. He pushed the door open and dragged Jake inside. Then, turning, he locked the door.

"There's never nobody in these crip rooms," he said. "Now we can talk without anybody interruptin' us."

As surreptitiously as he could, Jake slipped a hand into his jacket pocket and turned on the digital recorder he and Tami had bought a few hours earlier.

"All right," Jake said, "I met with Senator Santino and worked everything out. He's satisfied that neither Senator Tomlinson nor I will tell anybody about him being your actual father."

Jacobi's misshaped face settled into a scowl. "He's satisfied. I ain't."

"Look, if you think—"

"You think you can keep my real father under your thumb? The hell you can. I'll kill you first. And then that Jap girlfriend of yours."

Jacobi reached into his jacket pocket and pulled out a heavy-looking metal object. Brass knuckles! Jake realized. Jesus Christ, he's putting brass knuckles on his hand!

"Now, wait," Jake said, backing away from the man.

"I got these from the son of a bitch who pretended to be my old man. He used them on me now and then. Rearranged my face. They really hurt."

Jake looked past Jacobi to the locked door. Jacobi was barring his way.

"You're gonna get beat to death," Jacobi said, almost smiling. "You brought some fairy kook here inta the bathroom with ya, and he robbed ya and beat ya to death."

Jake backed away until he felt the sink against the backs of his legs. He couldn't retreat any farther. "You can't do this. I've got security people guarding me."

"Yeah? Where are they?"

And Jacobi launched an overhand punch at Jake's head. Jake tried to block it, but the punch landed on his cheek with an explosion of pain. He crumpled, but Jacobi grabbed his lapels and hauled him up.

"Not yet," he growled.

Another punch, to Jake's abdomen. The air gushed out of him and his eyes glazed over. He's going to kill me! Jake told himself. He's going to kill me!

"Your fairy boyfriend's gonna bash your head against the sink, kiddo," Jacobi said, puffing slightly as he reached for Jake's head. "Until your brains are mashed. Until you're dead."

# Death Duel

Jake slumped to the tiled floor, but before Jacobi could hit him again, he wrapped his arms around Jacobi's knees. The man tottered and fell on his back with a loud *thwack*.

Burning with pain, Jake crawled up Jacobi's body, grabbed at the man's ears, and started to pound his head against the floor. Jacobi rammed both his fists into Jake's ribs, then rolled over until he was on top of Jake.

Grinning fiercely, he said, "Not bad, kid. But not good enough."

Jake reached for Jacobi's throat, Jacobi's eyes—fingers searching for anything that would get this monster off him. Jacobi grabbed at Jake's left hand and bent the fingers back until bones snapped. Jake yowled with pain.

Jacobi struggled to his knees, then his feet, while Jake tried to scuttle away from him. He heard a pounding, thumping noise and wondered what it was. Probably your heart working overtime, he thought.

"You got no place to go, kid. No place but hell."

Still on the floor, Jake tried to kick the trash can into Jacobi's legs, but the man brushed it aside, laughing.

He stepped toward Jake, who struggled groggily to his knees and leaned an elbow on the sink, trying to get up.

Jacobi advanced toward him, adjusting the brass knuckles on his right hand.

Desperately, Jake lunged at the man, wrapped his

arms around his middle, and drove with his legs with what was left of his strength. Jacobi tottered backward until his back reached the wall.

With his left hand Jacobi grabbed Jake by the hair and pulled his head back. Then Jacobi raised his right fist. Jake saw those brass knuckles, already sheened with his blood. He twisted sideways and pulled Jacobi down onto the floor again, then planted his knee in the man's groin. Jacobi squealed with pain, and Jake staggered to his feet.

A weapon, he thought as Jacobi started to get up. I need a weapon.

The door splintered open, and two men rushed in and grabbed Jacobi. Both of them were big, solid bruisers. Like a wild man Jacobi shrugged them off, then swung his brass-knuckled fist at one of them. Jake heard the crunch of broken bone, but the second man smashed a vicious backhand chop at the base of Jacobi's neck. He dropped to the floor, gasping.

Jake stood there, shaking with pain and fear, as the two young private investigators looked from him to Jacobi's prostrate body and back to him again.

"Hard to track you once you went down into the Metro," the nearer of the two PIs said.

His partner, holding a blood-soaked handkerchief to his cheek, kicked Jacobi in the ribs. "Son of a bitch," he snarled.

"But we found you," the first investigator said. "That's the important thing."

Jake looked down at Jacobi's semiconscious form. "Better late than never," he said, with some fervor. Then he sank to his knees and passed out.

# Hospital

Jake awoke to see Tami sitting on a padded chair, her chin on her chest, half asleep. He realized he was in bed, in a hospital room, neat and clean, pastel walls and smelling faintly of antiseptic. One window. It was bright morning outside.

He blinked his eyes, trying to focus better. Everything looked slightly fuzzy, and his head felt as if it was swaddled in bandages. Reaching up with his right hand, he realized that he *was* bandaged. And two fingers of his left hand were immobilized by a double splint and more bandages.

Tami's eyes popped open. "You're awake!"

She jumped up from the chair and went to the bed; bending over Jake, she kissed him firmly on the lips.

"Ouch!"

Tami looked horrified. "Oh, I'm sorry, Jake. I forgot that—"

He tried to smile and found that his whole face seemed frozen. He reached out his good hand and wrapped his arm around Tami's slim form.

"Easy now," he said. She kissed him again, lightly.

"The detectives found you," Tami said.

"Good thing they did. Jacobi was going to kill me."

The door opened and a chubby Hispanic-looking nurse came smiling in. "Good morning! And how do we feel this lovely morning?"

Jake winced inwardly at her good cheer. "Kind of numb," he answered.

"That's the anesthetic they pumped into you. It'll wear off in a couple hours."

While the nurse took his wrist, Tami pulled her cell phone from her purse. Before Jake could ask she said, "Senator Tomlinson said to call him as soon as you woke up."

Remembering, Jake asked, "The recorder in my pocket. Did you find it?"

Nodding, she said, "And listened to it. Mostly scuffling and grunts."

"There ought be enough on it to send Jacobi to jail."

"Plenty," Tami said.

Considering that he was in bed the whole time, the morning was quite busy. The nurse took Jake's blood pressure, then a doctor came in and listened to his heart. A police sergeant showed up, looking rather bored, and got Jake to sign a formal complaint. Then the head of the detective agency showed up, looking concerned and fatherly, with more forms for Jake to sign.

"You had my people worried when you went down into the Metro," the man said. "Hard to track you down there."

"But they found me," Jake said, feeling grateful.

"That's what they're paid to do."

"Jacobi?"

"He's in custody. My people turned him over to the transit police, who handed him to the Metro PD. He's gone totally silent. Lawyered up. They want a psychiatrist to examine him."

Jake nodded, thinking, Jacobi won't say anything that would hurt his father. He won't mention Santino's name at all.

Tami hovered over him all morning and shared a

hospital lunch with Jake. He started to feel a dull thrumming ache that seemed to pervade his entire head and body. Another nurse came in and gave him two pills that looked suspiciously like aspirin.

Shortly after an orderly removed Jake's lunch tray, Senator Tomlinson strode into the room, smiling brightly. Kevin O'Donnell, right behind him, looked gloomy, as usual.

"You're okay?" Tomlinson asked.

Jake tried to nod, but it hurt. "I'm okay," he said.

O'Donnell offered, "The doc says you must have a really hard head. No broken bones."

Jake held up his splinted left hand.

"I meant your head," O'Donnell said.

There was only the one chair in the room, so the senator, O'Donnell, and Tami all stood clustered around Jake's bed.

"What about Santino?" Jake asked.

Tomlinson's smile faded, but not by much. "The Little Saint is much embarrassed by the whole episode."

"Embarrassed? He sent Jacobi after me."

"No," O'Donnell countered. "He said Jacobi acted entirely on his own."

"And pigs can fly," Jake muttered.

"It doesn't matter," said Tomlinson. "Jacobi's going to be in jail for a long time, and Santino's not going to have anything to do with him."

"And the story about Jacobi being his son?"

"That stays among us. No further."

Tami said, "You'll have that over him."

With an almost rueful nod, Tomlinson said, "Yes, true. In a strange sort of way, it's made us allies. Santino's become very friendly to us, and he's promised that the energy bill will go to the Senate floor before the month is out."

Jake heard himself say, "The original plan, with the methanol development."

"Don't push your luck," O'Donnell groused. "Your methanol guy gets a study program. That's enough."

"No, it's not," Jake said, surprised at his own insistence. "We ought to get the original plan, in its entirety."

"Santino won't go for that."

"Why not? He doesn't have to worry about Perlmutter anymore. He's the Majority Leader now."

With a sardonic grin, Senator Tomlinson said, "Jake's right, Kevin." Turning to Jake, he said, "How about a pilot plant, instead of the full-ahead development program? That would make your methanol guy happy, wouldn't it?"

Jake started to nod, but a twinge of pain stopped him. "Pilot plant," he agreed. "That's a good start."

O'Donnell frowned but gave in. "Okay, we'll write that into the plan and get it out onto the floor of the Senate."

"How soon?" Jake asked.

"Before Thanksgiving," Tomlinson said. O'Donnell nodded, warily.

"Good," said Jake.

His smile returning to its full wattage, Tomlinson said, "Think of it as an early Christmas present, Jake."

I paid for it, Jake said to himself. I've earned it.

"You did a good job, Jake," O'Donnell finally admitted, only slightly grudgingly. "We're going to get the energy plan passed by the Senate. Franklin's already being besieged by the news media."

"And lobbyists," Tomlinson added.

Jake said, "Tami was a big help. A very big help."

"So why don't you marry the lady?" Tomlinson suggested. "We can have the ceremony in the National Cathedral, if you like."

Jake felt like grinning, even though his face was still somewhat numb. Tami was beaming, though, he saw.

"We have a lot to talk about," he said to her.

"Yes, we do."

# Thanksgiving

I t was the day before the Senate recessed for the Thanksgiving weekend.

Jake and Tami sat in the Senate's half-empty visitor's gallery, watching the vote on the energy bill lumber through the yeas and nays. Jake's head was no longer bandaged, although he still had the splint on his left hand.

The clerk called out, "Senator Gutierrez, New Mexico?"

"Yea."

"That's twenty-two," Tami whispered, excitedly.

"Nine against," Jake whispered back.

New York voted nay; North Carolina, yea.

"Twenty-three."

"Senator Ellison, North Dakota?"

"Yea."

"Senator Danner, Ohio?"

Jake held his breath. Danner had gone out to Montana to see the MHD rig but had promised nothing.

"Yea."

Jake grabbed Tami and hugged her. "We're going to make it!"

The security guard standing at the door, two rows behind them, hissed a shushing sound.

The final vote was fifty-six in favor, thirty-eight opposed, and six abstentions.

•  •  •

It wasn't a victory dinner, officially, but the Tomlinson home was jammed with senators, aides, news reporters, and—of course—Lady Cecilia.

"We still have a long way to go," Senator Tomlinson was saying to Cecilia. "The House has to vote on the bill, and then it goes to the president."

Cecilia's frog face was all smiles. "She's indicated that she'll sign it."

Tomlinson nodded. "That would remove it from being a campaign issue next year."

Standing a few feet away from them, Jake also nodded. We've passed the biggest hurdle. We're on our way.

Senator Santino was not present. Jake wondered how the Little Saint would deal with Jacobi. He can't afford to get close to him, Jake thought. Jacobi's on his own.

Jake had been subpoenaed to testify at Jacobi's trial. Assault and battery with a deadly weapon. Could be worse for Jacobi, Jake thought. They could have charged him with attempted murder. He's claiming temporary insanity; got a gaggle of psychiatrists examining him. Almost, Jake felt sorry for the man.

Almost.

Tami came up beside him, a champagne flute in her hand.

"You're not celebrating?" she asked, seeing that Jake was empty-handed.

"I'll celebrate at our wedding," he said, with a grin.

She put on a disapproving frown. "Christmas Eve. I still think you're pretty cheap, you know."

Jake countered, "No, I'm thrifty. One present for both Christmas and our anniversary. You ought to be proud that you're marrying such a frugal guy."

With a sad little sigh, Tami said, "I'm marrying a politician."

"Who's a politician?" Senator Tomlinson broke into their bantering. "Jake? No, Jake's a purist. He's the one who kept us on the mark, always pushing for the energy plan, no matter what came up against us."

*Us*, Jake thought. Success has a thousand fathers.

Tomlinson senior came up beside his son. "Congratulations, Jake, on your impending nuptials."

The senator said, "Not on getting our energy plan passed by the Senate?"

"Oh, that too," the older man said. "But getting your plan passed isn't the end of the game, you know."

Senator Tomlinson agreed. "Yes, we have to get it through the House and get the president to sign it into law."

Tomlinson's father shook his head sternly. "Oh, the president's going to sign it, she's smart enough to get on the bandwagon. That's not what I meant."

"What, then?"

Focusing on Jake, the elder Tomlinson pointed out, "Once your plan becomes law, then you have to make it work."

"That's right," Senator Tomlinson agreed. "We've got the White House to think about."

"That's eight years from now," his father said.

With a cocky grin, Tomlinson said, "Maybe four."

His father tried to frown.

Jake stared at the senator. He's thinking about the White House. He's not satisfied with the Senate.

And what am I thinking about? he asked himself. Making the energy plan work. Keeping all the special interests from whittling it to pieces. Maybe helping Isaiah Knowles to get a space solar power program started at NASA.

Then he turned to Tami and realized that whatever happened, she was his future.

He reached for her free hand as he said, "We're only just beginning, aren't we?"

# TOR

Voted

## #1 Science Fiction Publisher
## More Than 25 Years in a Row

by the *Locus* Readers' Poll

---•---

Please join us at the website below
for more information about this
author and other science fiction,
fantasy, and horror selections, and to
sign up for our monthly newsletter!

www.tor-forge.com